I0586597

Accounts of Furlasia:
Days of Trepidation
Written by
M.P. VanderLoon

Print on demand provided by Createspace and
Ingram Spark
ISBN-13: 978-0-9975194-6-4
ISBN-10: 0-9975194-6-0

For Autumn

(Love you, sis)

Acknowledgements

Well its finally arrived. The ending to my trilogy. It was a long road but the finish line finally emerged. Getting to this point has been an amazing journey of self discovery. I learned a lot about myself during this project, but as always, no journey worth taking comes without help.

For starters, the obvious biggest influence in my life is my husband, Derek. He may not be a reader but he is quite supportive and reads all the little snippets I send him. Not only that, but he listens to me go on and on about story details. Having him listen to me really helps keep me motivated. Not to mention, he's been really chill about all the costs I put into these books. That's a nice bonus to an already great situation. Love you babe!

Another big support has been my coworkers at the bus garage I work at. Most of them have been really excited by my progress and quite encouraging. They treat me like the local celebrity which really makes me feel like I'm more important than I actually am. Its much appreciated.

I'd rather not go on and on about all the things that led to this book. I'd much rather have you jump in and enjoy the finale. So flip past this page and get to the good stuff!

Peridian Sea

Terria

Hills of Edmere

Morlay

Cristol

Cristol Lake

Rangmar

Roo

Ecglides

Arlen Bog

Berloth Forest

Neveraus

Solorian

Grottos of Bane

Frond

Jandoon

Twentieth Forest

Hora Mountains

Furlasia

$\mathcal{P}$rologue

Warm air filled the gentle breeze, bringing with it a wonderful sense of euphoria. The day was early, but already it looked like a storm was lingering on the horizon. That didn't stop her though. Sitting in the middle of a tall field of dry grass was Idrix Jouls. She was a portly girl, which meant she was no stranger to second helpings. Her large messy curls hung down in front of her face, covering much of her eyes. She liked it this way. It made her seem ominous, which was exactly how she wanted to be viewed. Too much of her life was in the spotlight. Her mother saw to that. The princess of Solarian had to be regularly seen at her father's side. She hated the attention. But what was she to do?

As she took a deep breath, she carefully laid herself down onto her back, looking up towards the sky with a beaming smile. The clouds danced just for her. The sun repeatedly tried to evade them but was without luck. Today, the clouds proved the toughest. Idrix didn't mind. She took just as much joy from a cloudy day as she did a sunny one.

An hour faded away much faster than it ought to. Soon she heard the familiar sound of her mother calling her name. Her words carried like a powerful song in the wind. She quickly sat up, looking around in a daze. She had fallen asleep. It was dark now. The sky offered no light this evening. Not even the moon was strong enough to beat the clouds. Such thick, stubborn clouds they were.

Walking into the rear entrance of Abissal Keep, she was greeted by the usual servants. Everyone looked to be in a chipper mood. It was pretty normal. Dinner time in the castle was always something special. Her mother — the queen — frequently opted to prepare the feast herself. Sure, they had cooks that could do the work. But she didn't want that, not all the time anyways.

"Idrix, you're late," King Dador remarked. He gave her a warm glance. Dador— unlike his daughter and wife— was fair skinned. Pale even. The marriage had at first been met with great criticism but before long, Idrix was born, and the naysayers shut up. The princess was undoubtedly special, there was no denying it.

"I fell asleep," she replied as she rubbed her shoulders. "It's chilly out there."

 King Dador looked at her with a disapproving smirk.

"Your mother will not like you being outside so long without something to cover yourself with."

"Well then don't tell her," Idrix replied. Dador laughed, looking toward a nearby servant with a wink.

"But how do I explain to her what happened if you get sick?" He asked.

"I won't," Idrix confidently replied. "I don't get sick."

The dinner bell rang in the distance, carrying its demanding cry to their ears with a tune that was impossible to ignore.

"We better get going," Dador noted.

They raced through the various halls, with Idrix remaining a constant few steps ahead, until they reached the dining hall. The table was set, and the atmosphere was vibrant. Servants and maids carried in plates and platters, and as they stepped inside, they simultaneously drew a deep breath.

"Dinner is served," Queen Allisa smiled with a curtsy.

***

Elsewhere, in a place very different than Furlasia, a conflict was ensuing. Lines were being drawn in the sand, and emotions were at an all-time high. This place beyond time, beyond laws, was called *Zoralos*. However, in Furlasia it was simply referred to as the *God Realm*. It was a place of beauty, but not in the sense that most thought of. Time was tangible. Love was something that could literally be held in the palm of your hand. Here, in this fable dimension, the gods and goddesses kept watch over the galaxies. Each of them had an important job, but none of them was quite as important as Undr. The High Father's most prized son, his eldest, the one he entrusted with keeping the others in line. It was a duty he took very seriously.

Most of the deities in this place remained harmonious, obedient and pure, but there was one, who sought more. As Gravi looked down at the Milky Way galaxy, she could feel a hatred boiling within her. Her mind was twisted with thoughts of rebellion. She hated following orders, worse, she didn't understand why she had to.

"Sister," Alom called out. She turned, frustration filling her every core.

"What is it?" Gravi asked with a hint of aggravation; she was in no mood for his tiresome conversations today.

"He found out what you did. He wants to speak to you."

She looked around, taking in the sights of the large room. *Zoralos,* for all intents and purposes, was what many would think of as the *universe*. It housed many galaxies, all of them separated into their different quarters.

"How did he find out?" Gravi asked, with a hint of disappointment in her voice.

"You were betrayed. Parix. The idea didn't sit right with him," Alom replied.

Gravi turned around, floating toward Alom with contempt.

"That fool. Such a disappointment."

"Let's go," Alom replied. "He's waiting for you."

He turned and started making his way down the hall. Together they floated to their destination. Two formless beings of energy. Yes, in Zoralos there was no traditional appearance to anyone. All were made of energy. Formless beings without legs, arms, or heads. They were clouds of electrons, with each of them featuring a color unique to their mood. Gravi for instance, was a mixture of gold and blue at this moment. Alom, on the other hand, was a shade quite similar to teal. As they continued through the universe, they passed by the various galaxies, each of them contained behind a thick layer of crystal. They appeared to all be vacant, which for Gravi didn't feel like a good sign. They were likely all waiting in the *Atiaum*, Undr often enjoyed making public displays of his punishments. Gravi's concern deepened at the thought. Perhaps, she had finally gone too far.

They entered the Atiaum, and just as she had expected, everyone was there. All her siblings had gathered to witness the conversation. As the others took notice of her arrival, the whispers stopped, and all attention suddenly turned to Undr, who currently hovered at the upper level. His form was filled with sparks and flashes of light, a clear indication of his present mood. *Anger.*

"Gravi," Undr called out. "You have been summoned here to answer for your latest act of defiance."

Alom quickly left Gravi's side and joined the others on the far side of the room. Now alone, and the center of attention, she could feel the sting of betrayal. She turned towards Parix. As she did, a few flashes of light emerged from within her, and her color changed to black.

"You need not direct your anger towards Parix. He was simply doing his duty. It was right of him to tell," Undr explained. An arm suddenly appeared from his side, holding in its hand a small black stone.

"Why did you steal this?" Undr questioned.

In his hand, he held *fear*.

Her color suddenly turned grey, the energy within her, coming to an abrupt standstill.

"I have no defense. I wanted it. I wanted to use it," she explained.

"You know father has forbidden us from using fear. It's too dangerous. So tell me. Why would you disobey our father?"

She glanced towards Parix once more, which provoked another spark within her cloud.

"Why do we listen to someone who doesn't even have the decency to be here with his children? Who gives us mindless tasks while he does nothing," she rebutted.

From the side of the room, gasps could be heard. Her siblings, all apparently feeling the same emotion, changed to a dark shade of yellow.

"It's true. He makes us watch over the galaxies, while he does nothing but make more of them. Spreading us even thinner than we already are. Working us nonstop, without any sign of an end. I'm tired of it. I'm ready to be free of this."

Undr quickly teleported to floor level, bringing himself mere inches from his insubordinate sister.

"Our purpose is greater than that of ourselves. The galaxies depend on us. They need us to maintain order. Without the galaxies, the universe would crumble. Our home would be destroyed."

"Oh yes. The threat he has made time and time again," Gravi moaned.

"Falsehoods."

Undr surveyed the room. He had to be firm; he couldn't be weak, not now, not with his siblings watching. Betrayal could not be taken lightly. Disobedience had to be squashed.

"Why fear? Why did you steal fear?" He questioned.

"It's the most powerful tool he created. It's capable of toppling empires and ruining the galaxies. It would free us from this burden."

Undr moved closer, dropping the stone to the floor.

"Sister, I have told you over and over again, if you do not wish to do your job, you don't have to. You can be freed. Father can decommission you. But no, you refuse that option. Time and time again you refuse his offer," he roared.

"You offer me slavery or destruction, and you wonder why I am defiant?" Gravi thunderously bellowed.

Undr sighed, looking at his sister with profound disappointment, his inner energy swirling blue.

"Which galaxies did you infect?" He questioned.

Her energy suddenly radiated white. *Excitement.*

"The Milky Way and Egsiar," she replied with a chuckle.

Suddenly, Undr grew immensely in size, his anger boiling over in a spectacular fashion. He was tall now, almost as tall as the very room they occupied. His energy glowed red, inside were bright flashes, like a thunderstorm was taking place within him. Beams of energy erupted from within, striking Gravi in multiple places, prompting her to moan as the pain crept through her.

"Egsiar is my galaxy!" He roared. "How dare you!"

The two of them quickly began bouncing around the room, crashing into various beams, leaving many of them cracked. The fight was on. The animosity had boiled over. Egsiar was the oldest galaxy in Zorlos. It was the first one the High Father created. It was with great trust that Undr was put in charge of it. Now this, this betrayal, this attempt at sabotage, could've ruined it all.

"You follow him so blindly, and yet you don't even know why!" Gravi yelled as they crashed into each other with a flash. The energy from the impact sent a shockwave into the air, adding to the existing cracks in the beams.

"You're going to bring the whole place down," Alom cried out in panic. He received no response, no acknowledgement. Gravi and Undr continued their fight, pummeling each other with beams of twisted energy.

As the madness continued, the others quickly vacated, each of them dashing to their assigned galaxies in hopes of keeping them safe.

"You will threaten his reign no more!" Undr called out. At that moment, a large beam of energy erupted from within him, grabbing Gravi and pulling her toward him. She crashed into him yet again, sending out a shockwave.

Undr quickly looked up, taking notice of the damage that had occurred. The others were right; this fight would ruin their home. He had to take it elsewhere. With his grip on Gravi firmly secured, he pulled her out of the Atiaum and into the halls. She protested and screamed all the way, but his grip remained firm.

"This ends now," he roared.

He led them into his quarters and peered at Egsiar. Without a moment's thought, he dived into it, pulling Gravi with him.

******

Idrix sat in the field of grass, yet again looking up at the skies. It was a habit she couldn't fully explain. Always, she felt an interest in what was in the space surrounding their planet. *Such a wonderful place it must be*, she had frequently said.

It was midafternoon. The day was looking to be sublime. There were some clouds in the sky, but they didn't interfere with the sun like they had the day before. Today, the whole sky seemed to get along. A harmonious display of majestic art. She sighed deeply as she watched a cloud that looked like a dog chase after another cloud that closely resembled a bone. *How neat*, she thought.

"Rusty," she called into the air. The display had apparently reminded her of her dog, provoking a sudden interest in his company.

"Stupid dog," she whispered after hearing no response.

Suddenly, as if he heard the insult, the familiar sound of cheerful barking was heading towards her. He approached with his ears back and an eager tail. Quickly, she dropped to her knees, opening her arms as wide as they would go. With little regard for her safety, Rusty jumped into her, causing them to both fall over. Together they rolled in the grass, and she laughed while Rusty barked. It was perfect. A perfect moment. But like all moments, they came to an end. This moment came to an end in a rather unique way. In the skies above, there was the sound of screams. She quickly pushed Rusty off, looking up. Two colors were traveling towards the surface, sparking all the way down.

"What is that?" She questioned.

The two balls of color suddenly crashed to the ground, creating a massive dust cloud that filled the air.

Like all dogs worth their weight and time, Rusty suddenly took off, heading toward the unknown with little regard for safety.

"Rusty, wait up!" Idrix called out.

She tried her best to keep up, but as she neared the crash site, she began to feel a pulse. Fear was climbing into her. There were grunts of pain and anger coming from ahead. She decided to use caution. After all, it wasn't often that anything fell from the sky. As she dropped to the ground, she slowly crawled, trying her best to remain unseen. Her heart raced faster than she could ever recall as she neared the confrontation. It was indeed a battleground, and what a strange one it was. The two balls of light that she had seen crash were bumping into each other at an alarming rate. It continued for a few more moments, and with each crash, the shapeless balls of color began to form into something. Eventually, two people stood before her. A man and a woman, both of whom looked winded and angry.

"It's over Gravi," Undr called out as he kicked her to the ground and sent a beam of energy to secure her.

"You have poisoned my galaxy. Ruined it. Now you get to live with the consequences."

She lay on the ground, continuing to struggle as she watched her brother with spiteful anger.

"You're gonna stay here for the rest of your life. And until your energy expires, you will remain here." He turned around and drew a shape on the ground with his finger. A door suddenly appeared in the ground, and a bright light shone from within its opening.

"Wait," Gravi called out. "Don't leave me here. I'm sorry. I've learned my lesson."

Undr looked at her and shook his head.

"No sister," he paused. "You haven't. But you will."

Suddenly he jumped into the opening and vanished from sight. Gravi screamed as loud as she could as she struggled with her restraints. Alas, she had gotten free, but the opening was gone.

"No!" She yelled as she looked up to the sky.
Suddenly she lifted from the ground, flying towards the sky at a fantastic speed.

Idrix continued to remain crouched, her hand covering her mouth as she watched the strange woman flying into the air. As she reached the skyline, she bumped into something. An invisible force of some kind. The strange woman tried multiple spots, all with the same results. Eventually she gave up, falling back to the ground with a heavy heart. Quickly, Idrix laid down, holding her breath as best she could.

"I'm trapped," Gravi whispered to herself. Grief-stricken, she glanced around, taking in the sights while a furious rage built up within her. As it did, her hands began to glow, a powerful energy filling them.

With a terrible cry of anger, she thrust her hands to the ground, sending a dreadful wave of energy across the land. Ice and snow began to spread all around her, slowly making a journey across the land.

As Idrix noticed what was happening, she jumped to her feet and started running back towards the palace.

"Rusty!"Idrix called out, trying her best to outrun the stampede of icy winds. In the distance, she could just make out the distressed dogs bark. She paused, turning around, hoping he was ok. He was. In fact, he suddenly jumped into her, knocking her back. As she lost her balance, she tripped and fell into a small pond that had once been her favorite swimming spot.

Panic took over her. The water was cold. Her swimming was weak even in times of relaxation, and now, faced with fear, it was rather poor. Slowly she began to sink, but not Rusty, he promptly swam toward the edge. She sadly watched as he climbed out of the water, seemingly abandoning her. He didn't make it far, however, because as soon as he was clear of the water he came to a standstill, frozen in place by the icy winds.

Her vision continued to cloud as the icy crystals moved closer to her, eventually holding her still. She was frozen now, trapped in an icy prison. Each moment, she could feel herself getting more light headed. The last thing she managed to see was the faint outline of a shadow as the surface of the pond turned solid.

Gravi looked around at the ice-covered land: her eyes were black, hatred had become all she knew. In the palace ahead, she could hear the screams of people quickly fleeing. There were dozens of them, all of them running away from the palace without any thought of looking back. She peered at them with hatred as she contemplated killing them. She lifted her hand, preparing to fire a beam of energy toward the crowd when suddenly something caught her eyes. There was a single pair of people who weren't running. They stood still, looking troubled and scared. She saw something at that moment. *Love.* They paused out of love. They faced terror, looked it straight in the eyes and didn't run. Was it possible that love was stronger than fear?

"You're gonna stay here. For the rest of your life, until your energy expires, you will remain here."

His words rang in her ears, filling her mind with panic and anger. She continued to watch the strange pair as they stood still, eventually turning solid. As the warmth left their body she grinned, a hateful grin indeed.

"We shall see.

Chapter 1

Lord Fae watched with dread as the energy beams crashed into the protective vortex that encompassed Cristol. As expected, it held up. For now. She drew a deep sigh of relief, one that only lasted a moment.

"Attack!" Agavordis called out. From around him, hundreds of Akordans emerged, swords drawn and ready to fight. It had begun. The war of the dead.

She gulped as she hopelessly watched.

"Where are you?" She whispered to herself.

***

Apothiciss charged wildly toward the battlefield, her brothers and sisters following her lead. As they neared the mayhem, they drew their weapons, letting out fierce growls. They crashed into a battalion of Akordans and began swinging their swords with ferocity. It was tragic. It felt wrong. Once actually put into the situation, the scenario felt wrong. Each swing of the sword towards her fellow species felt like a massive betrayal. She felt remorse. Ashamed even. She brought up her sword, blocking the attack of a giant brutish Akordan.

"The traitor!" He bellowed as he glared at her with hate-filled eyes. She clenched her jaw, holding her form as he tried with all his might to bring his weapon down on her.

"She's over here!" The Akordan yelled out. But to who? He quickly brought his foot up and kicked Apothiciss in the chest, sending her falling to the ground.

"You are not mine to kill," he sneered. With that, he turned, thrusting his sword towards another.

She lay on the ground, catching her breath for a moment, around her, the battle was in full force. Already, she could detect the scent of death in the air. Already, the air reeked of blood and guts. She continued watching with dismay as all around her swords clashed into swords. Sneers of hate and growls of anger filled her ears like a depressing opera. Suddenly, she was lifted up and brought to her feet.

"Are you ok?" An Akordan soldier asked. She stood silent. As she opened her mouth, preparing to reply, a sword emerged through the skull of the soldier. His eyes rolled back, and his mouth fell open. Dead. In the flash of an instant, he was no more.

"Sister," Krytus scorned, freeing his sword from the creature's skull.

***

Quarlin observed the battlefield; it was hectic, to say the least. All around him, lights and sparks flew. The Arnouts did their very best to show their true strength. It was impressive, to say the least. The Akordan soldiers were tough, but magic was a different kind of fight. He watched with pride as one of his fellow kin lifted an Akordan into the air, using only his mind, and then broke all the creature's limbs. It howled and cried, before being dropped to the ground in a twisted mess.

"Good job," Quarlin congratulated. His pride was cut short by a sudden beam of ice being hurtled towards him. He lifted his hand, quickly deflecting the attack. Looking ahead, he could see that the undead soldiers were charging into the field. Each of them had been gifted with a bit of power, just as it had been in the first war.

"Now the real fight begins," he whispered. He jumped into the air, spinning in a circle, before crashing into a pile of the undead. He quickly drove his sword into a couple of the ones he had managed to knock down. They screeched as the light left their eyes. With wide-open jaws, they spat out some kind of black tar, covering Quarlin's armor in their sticky substance.

"That's new," he noted. He continued thrusting his sword into the foes until they had all been taken care of. Looking around, there were still plenty of fights to be had, though. A large blast of green energy darted above, heading once again for the city walls. Agavordis, his attacks would not cease so easily. The necromancer was still quite far away, keeping his distance. *Coward*, Quarlin thought to himself.

***

Agavordis sighed in disappointment as his attack hit the invisible vortex, causing nothing other than a fascinating light display. He turned, looking at Vigil with glowing eyes, then shrugged.

"She's hiding in there," he sneered. He turned his attention back to the city ahead.

"She's not gonna make it easy." He smiled as he realized his sudden appreciation for her resilience.

As he looked at the battlefield, he let out a grin. To his left sat Herratia, atop an Uborox looking mostly unamused about the situation taking place. Her eyes darted back and forth, taking in the various feuds that were taking place. There were so many happening, but only one actually piqued her interest. Krytus and Nevo had both charged in with the first wave. She tried to scan the field, hoping to spot either of them, but alas, it was too crowded.

"Herratia," Agavordis called out. "It's time to earn your place at this table."

She slowly turned her head towards him as he looked at her with excitement.

"Show me what you can do," he ordered.

She looked ahead once more at the battlefield, then quickly disappeared from the back of the Uborox. Agavordis looked towards Vigil with a satisfied beam before returning his focus to the field ahead. In the distance, he could hear a familiar shriek, it filled the air like a toxin, bringing with it a fantastic blast of energy. Suddenly, the field was filled with the screams of a dozen Arnouts, all of them being torn to shreds in attacks that were so quick, it was hard to tell where they were coming from.

"She's good," Vigil noted.

Agavordis silently nodded his head in agreement and quickly jumped off his beast.

"You're going into that?" Vigil questioned.

He looked at her and nodded.

"You're the general of this army. You need to stay here. You have to command it," she lectured.

He peered at her, looking around in disappointment.

"Get back here," Vigil sternly commanded. She turned around, looking toward the idle giants that stood by, awaiting a command.

"Get to work," she ordered. The giants groaned in acceptance and began to march toward the battlefield, their mouths hung droopy, and their arms swung wildly. Agavordis watched with excitement as the two behemoths began to reach for a couple Arnouts that were flying in the air. The Arnouts were quick, however. They flew in circles around them, casting bits of energy as fast as they could. Feeling the sting of disappointment, Agavordis jumped into the air, flying toward the Arnouts with haste.

"Septus!" Vigil called into the air.

As he neared the giants, he crashed into one of the attacking Arnouts. Quickly, he placed his hands on both sides of the Arnouts skull, and as he did, his hands began to heat up with energy. Before long the skull was entirely engulfed in flames. With smug satisfaction, Agavordis released his grip, letting the body fall to the ground.

**

"So, you traveled all this way to die?" Krytus sneered. He looked at Apothiciss with a bloodthirsty smile. Around him, the battle continued. Soldiers killing soldiers. Akordans killing Akordans.

"I came here to stop you. And that boy you bow down to," Apothiciss replied.

"Then you've wasted a trip."

Krytus quickly swung his sword toward her. Their blades met in the middle with a loud clang, the force of the impact so great that sparks erupted from the contact point. They took turns, aggressively trying their best to kill each other. It was a fight long in the making. She was good. Her skill with a blade was unmistakable. Krytus quickly ducked, narrowly missing a decapitation. Without warning, he was suddenly grabbed from behind by a passing Arnout soldier. He was tossed to the ground with a telekinetic push, where he was nearly trampled by numerous sets of feet.

A mystical blade, made entirely of energy, made its way quickly towards his skull. The attack was clever; this phantom sword was a skill he had never seen an Arnout use before. He rolled to the left, just missing the blade. As quickly as he could, he jumped to his feet, scanning the field just in time to see Apothiciss charging at him. Promptly, he readied himself, his anger filling him with intense adrenaline. He had just taken a step forward when something suddenly froze him in his tracks. His anger-filled growl was massively deep. He struggled to free himself, but the magic holding him was too strong.

"So long brother!" Apothiciss shouted as she neared with her blade held at shoulder level.

Krytus gulped as he watched his doom incoming. He had just thought himself defeated when suddenly the force that had been holding him was released. Behind him, he heard a thud and a chuckle. He didn't have time to look to see what had happened. He crouched, lifting his hand in a quick swipe and grabbed Apothiciss by the throat.

***

Quarlin floated in the air, looking over the battlefield with concern. The number of enemies didn't seem to be shrinking much. In fact, if anything, it seemed he had more soldiers than before. He continued to observe the battlefield, taking sudden notice of an Arnout soldier dispatching an Akordan. His satisfactory smile soon faded as he watched the downed Akordan slowly rise and start navigating the field. Its eyes glowed red like the other Akordan ghouls.

"Oh no," he whispered to himself.

With fear finally entering his heart, he turned and looked towards the palace, scared for the first time that the city could be breached. In the sky ahead of him, he could hear the incessant laughter of Agavordis who hovered in the air, firing beams of energy towards the Arnout army. With his jaw clenched so tightly that he could've surely lost some teeth, he soared towards him, sending his own energy towards the young necromancer.

***

Agavordis beamed as he took notice of the Arnout general heading towards him. Quickly, he fired two beams of energy his way, only the beams didn't stay single; they combined and formed a grid. The attack was unexpected, to say the least. Quarlin attempted to stop, but his speed was too great.

"Ahh!" He yelled, before crashing into the grid of searing hot energy. Moments later, chunks of flesh and blood rained down atop the battlefield, bringing with them a sense of doom. Agavordis laughed maniacally, before sending a couple more beams to the crowd.

Chapter 2

Emlin stood silently next to Thadeus, as Stephenson examined the injured general's knees. He had been relying heavily on a cane ever since the ambush attack from Killigan, his disgruntled cousin. Stephenson carefully ran his hands over the various bumps and grooves of the kneecap, pushing in certain places as he checked for reflexes and pain. Thadeus sat with his eyes looking toward the ceiling. He was aggravated. He hated being the center of attention.

"Just give me a damn tonic," Thadeus finally blurted out.

Stephenson looked up with a startle; he carefully sat up and looked towards Emlin, who nodded in agreement.

"A tonic can fix the pain but not the damage. I'm not sure if you're truly ready to get back into the field," Stephenson advised.

"But he'll be able to?" Emlin questioned.

Stephenson paused, looking toward Thadeus with skepticism.

"I mean technically yes."

"I'll take it!" Thadeus called out. Stephenson jumped in surprise, then slowly stood up and wandered over to his suitcase. He rummaged around for a moment or two, then finally turned around, holding in his hands a large needle.

"This should numb the pain," Stephenson advised. Thadeus gulped as the High Leech approached carrying the largest needle he had ever seen. Wasting no time at all, Stephenson inserted the needle just on the backside of the knee, pushing in all the liquid contained in the vial. Thadeus winced at its strange feeling.

"It's cold," he commented.

"Yes, that's perfectly normal," Stephenson replied. He turned around, headed back to his case and began rummaging about once again. Slowly, he turned to face Thadeus once again, this time carrying a small vial with a yellow liquid. He carefully brought the vial to Thadeus and handed it to him.

"Drink this," he commanded. Thadeus turned to Emlin with confusion. What was this?

"Do it," Emlin added.

In a quick motion, Thadeus dumped the contents down his throat. Spicy, almost like he had just ingested pepper juice.

"That should help bind the bones," Stephenson explained. He turned to Emlin and nodded.

"Will that be all?"

Emlin nodded, as she did, Stephenson turned around, grabbing his bag and exiting the room. Now alone, Emlin looked towards Thadeus, whose face looked flushed.

"Do you think you'll be ready to travel by tomorrow?" She asked. He ignored her for a bit, the stars in his eyes were mesmerizing and just a tad bit distracting.

"General," Emlin abruptly yelled.

"Tomorrow?" Thadeus questioned. "We're leaving today."

***

An hour later, Emlin found herself sitting atop Becca, a sword on her hip and a bow tossed across her chest. Next to her, on a horse of his own, was Thadeus. He too was armed, although not nearly as well. Gertrud and Fiona, his two daggers, that was all he would carry. Behind them was the Vanguard army, what remained of them anyways. They would take most of the remainder, leaving only a dozen in Terria as enforcement. The war in Cristol took precedence.

"Are you ready?" Thadues asked, looking at Emlin with doubt.

"As I'll ever be," she replied. Thadues nodded and turned his horse to face the men.

"Ok boys. We're getting a tad bit of a late start. Our brothers are already out there, fighting for the freedom of Furlasia. Let's not waste any time."

With that, he gave his horse a firm kick and away they went. This battalion of men was smaller than the first wave they had sent. As such, each of these men was able to be on horseback. It would make for a much faster journey. With any luck, they might catch up to Sabasio before they reached Cristol. But who knew? As they continued their journey through the woods of Tordenth, Thadeus found himself continually impressed by the Queen's bravery and determination. When he first met her, he thought she was nothing more than a spoiled brat who liked to play tough. He was wrong. There was more to her than that. She was a warrior. More of a fighter than he could've ever imagined.

Tree after tree, shrub after shrub, they continued their journey with haste. The men were silent, all that could be heard was the gallop of the horses and their occasional neighs of complaint. Every once in a while, a horse would get distracted by the prospect of a tasty treat, but with a firm pull of the reins, it was easily put back on course. Still, it wouldn't be too long before a water break was in order. Horses didn't care about schedules or appointments, if thirst or exhaustion kicked in, there was little that could be done to motivate them. Thadues considered this, however, the path he had taken would pass right by a stream. A stream which would serve as a good stopping point.

An hour later, they neared Jordoon, a large lake that sat between Cristol and Terria. He slowly pulled on the reins, signaling his horse to come to a stop. The others all followed his lead. Slowly, each horse approached the water line, each taking a turn at quenching their thirst.

"How are you holding up?" Emlin asked, looking to Thadues with a slight hint of concern.

Quickly he jumped from his horse, landing in the moistened sand at the edge of the lake. His landing was wobbly, but he promptly caught his balance.

"Seems fine," he noted. Emlin looked at him with admiration. He was a tough man indeed. She found herself wondering what kind of ideals truly drove this man. Who was he really? Stiletto? Or someone else?

"I'm proud of you Thadues," Emlin noted. He looked up at her with surprise.

"I am. I know how hard it must have been to keep such a terrible secret buried. I'm sorry you had to go through that."

He looked at her with seriousness, before finally mustering a smile.

"I'm happy to hear you say that your highness," he replied. *Wow*, he thought to himself, *I've never called her that.*

Quietly, he climbed back atop his horse and looked at the men. Most of the horses had finished drinking, some of the men had snuck off to take a leak, but soon, they would be ready to resume their journey. They waited for an additional ten minutes before taking off again. Past the lake they went, eventually coming to the edge of the Tordenth forest. Finally, they could hear the screams and sounds of metal. They were close. Cristol was only a few hours away. As the sounds of battle rang in their ears, Emlin and Thadues shared a glance and a gulp. He turned his attention forward and gave his horse a firm kick.

"Ha!"

Chapter 3

It had all been a dream. The past twenty years. The war had never ended. The time in-between was just a vivid dream, a hallucination brought on by dark magic. At least, that's how it was starting to feel for Kunklestick. As he rode on the back of Leddi, he found himself filled with déjà vu. How could he not? Darkness threatened the land once more, just as it had all those years ago. If that wasn't like déjà vu, he didn't know what was.

He rode steadfast and determined; there was no time for cowardliness, no time for weakness or hesitation. Cristol was under attack. If it fell, the surrounding cities would likely surrender. He knew this, and he feared this. Cristol had always been the heart of Furlasia. The Arnouts were the shining example of power and divinity. If they fell, if they lost, a feeling of hopelessness would resonate over the land. And that was why Agavordis picked it as his first attack. Eliminate the strongest city first. It was a smart tactic.

On a horse next to him rode Zanna and his dear brother Didorumpus. Together the three of them rode in silence with the Tin Men just at their backs. No one was eager, and no one was excited.

"We're getting close now," Didorumpus said, ending what had been nearly two hours of silence.

Zanna gulped as she kept her hands firmly attached to the reins.

"Stay by me and all will be fine," he added.

She remained silent, offering no response. Her focus remained on the task at hand.

"She's gone mute," Didorumpus called out to his brother.

Kunklestick turned, looking at his brother and then shooting Zanna a glance.

"She's scared," he noted. "She's not ready for this."

Didorumpus closed his eyes, thinking back to their training sessions. Zanna had been quite impressive in her ability to pick up the spells they had taught her. Not to mention, she hatched her Grimwort faster than any wizard he had seen before.

"I think she'll surprise you," Didorumpus replied. In the distance, the sounds of mayhem were starting to creep into the air. The battle sounded like a distant thunderstorm. Cristol was near. He closed his eyes once more, this time concentrating on the sounds around him. There was the whine and hiss of the steam carts that were directly behind them, the chatter of the animals in the trees, and distant whispers. He quickly opened his eyes, looking around the forest and trying to locate the source.

"Do you hear that brother?" He asked aloud.

Kunklestick turned toward him, shooting him a glance of confusion.

"What?" He asked.

"I thought I heard whispers," Didorumpus replied. He continued to look around, the forest was a blur, Wildfire's speed was too great to actually see anything clearly. That didn't stop him from trying though. He closed his eyes once more. The whispers seemed closer, more pronounced and there seemed to be many of them. He looked around again and then shrugged it off.

The journey continued for a couple more hours until finally, they emerged in the plains of Cristol. Kunklestick quickly pulled on Leddi's reins, signaling her to stop. Zanna mimicked the action, and behind them, the steam carts did as well. There it was. Directly in front of them was the battlefield. There were thousands scattered around. Kunklestick winced as he took notice of the two giants that stood in the middle of it all; they kicked their legs about and swung in the air at the pesky Arnouts that had taken flight. As she observed the chaos, Zanna could feel tears forming in the corners of her eyes.

"Such senseless madness," she whispered.

Kunklestick looked at her, his expression growing serious.

"Zanna," he started. "Stay by us. Don't try to do anything heroic. The best thing you can do is offer backup."

He returned his attention forward and sighed.

"We have fewer wizards than the last war. Our best hope is that Septus hasn't really learned his powers."

In the distance, a large beam of green energy dashed toward the sky, before coming down in multiple smaller beams and wiping out close to twenty soldiers.

"You had to say that didn't you," Didorumpus winced. Behind him, the soldiers gasped, fear finally finding its way to them.

Kunklestick carefully pulled on his set of reins, signaling Leddi to face the soldiers. She eagerly did as told, likely thinking they were going to head back. Much to her disappointment, that didn't happen.

"Listen up," Kunklestick preached. "Agavordis is just a man—nay—a boy, and like all boys, he's arrogant. Do not step onto that field with fear in your heart. I want you to step out there with anger. Anger over having your lives threatened. Anger over watching hate spread across this land in such spectacular fashion. Anger over his blatant betrayal and misunderstanding about what makes Furlasia so superb. It's not about our technology. It's not about our wealth. It's not even about the beauty of the landscapes. It's about the people. The people populating this great land. It's all of you that makes this place what it is. He's threatening your very way of life. He's threatening who you are and what you hope to become. So march out there with anger. March out there for Furlasia!"

He paused, looking to Zanna with a smile.

"And whatever you do. Don't let that son of a bitch hit you with a spell."

All at once the Tin Men began to cheer. He had given them hope. He had given them a reason. A reason to fight until their last breath. And fight they would. Kunklestick quickly turned Leddi around and looked towards Zanna.

"Stay with Dido," he reminded.

"Do you think Nikalas is going to come help?" Zanna asked.

"He will do whatever he needs to do," he replied. The battlefield was feverish, different magical attacks traveled through the air like confetti. There was an unexpected variety to the spells. It was as though Agavordis wasn't the only one on the battlefield with magic. *A troubling notion indeed*, Kunklestick thought to himself.

"Are you ready brother?" Kunklestick questioned.

"Aye. Let's end this," Didorumpus replied. Without further ado, Kunklestick gave Leddi a kick and away they charged, soaring far ahead of the Tin Men. The steam carts, after all, could only go so fast. Zanna tightened her grip as Wildfire dashed towards doom with so much speed she had to give her a gentle tug, she certainly wasn't interested in beating her mentor to the fight. Up and down they bounced, the impact surely would leave some bruises, but that didn't matter. *If all I get is a bruise today I'll be happy*, she thought.

The closer they got to the battle, the more pronounced the footsteps of the behemoths became. They continued using their size to their advantage, stepping on soldiers left and right.

"By Undr," Zanna whispered.

As they reached the edge of the Akordan forces, Kunklestick tugged on Leddi's reins. Quickly, his loyal steed came to a halt. Wildfire did the same. They wasted no time as they quickly dismounted from their horses. The battle was already well underway, and time was not a luxury they had any more. Zanna looked around, taking in the sights and listening to the howls and growls of the Akordans. Behind them, the loud hiss and squeal of the steam carts coming to a stop seemed as good a sign as any. The Tin Men had arrived.

Kunklestick reached into his robe, pulling out his wand, and quickly expanding it into a staff. Zanna and Didorumpus rapidly did the same. Together, the three of them stood, facing terror in its greatest form.

"Shall we go?" General Sinclair questioned as he slowly approached in his cumbersome suit.

"Have your men clear a path," Kunklestick ordered. "We need to get in there and find Agavordis and whatever else is responsible for all those energy beams we're seeing."

"Understood," Sinclair replied. He hastily turned to his men and withdrew his obnoxiously wide blade. The others followed suit, looking at him with eagerness.

"We need to clear a path for the wizards!" He yelled out. "Are we ready?"

The men raised their swords in the air and let out a massive roar. Without wasting any further time, the soldiers began to charge into the field, pushing by the rebel Akordans. Slowly a path was being made. It wasn't long before the Tin Men were fully engulfed in the action, their large swords finally finding some targets.

The three wizards stood idly by, waiting for their moment to push through. Zanna didn't mind, however, as she felt no urgent need to enter the chaos. Next to her stood Kunklestick, he was silent, his hands firmly gripping his staff and his eyes glued forward. His solemn hush was almost alarming. What was he feeling? Fear? Anger? Regret? Zanna silently pondered. Suddenly, he stepped forward.

"It's time," he calmly said. The Tin Men had cleared a perfect path. There was an opening down the middle of them. It almost felt majestic, like a royal entrance. Together, they made their way down the path, each of them feeling something different. Around them, conflict ensued. Akordans fighting Akordans. Tin Men fighting corpses of Akordans. Arnouts fighting corpses of Arnouts. It was a tremendous sight indeed. Slowly, they made their way towards the middle of the conflict. The point at which the three armies met. That's where he would be. That's where their fight would take place.

Zanna gulped as a Tin Man quickly collapsed into their path, missing Kunklestick by mere inches. They had hardly reeled from the shock, when an Akordan burst through the gap, licking his lips as though he were at a buffet.

"Osscious," Kunklestick quickly proclaimed as he aimed his staff forward. The creature abruptly fell to the ground, its limbs going limp like rubber, shock filling its eyes. Kunklestick gently laid his staff onto the ground and loomed over the downed soldier. Quickly—with an impressive amount of strength—he lifted him up.

"On your feet son," he ordered as he shoved him back into the action.

Didorumpus neared the rubbery Akordan with a coy grin. Holding his staff above the creature's head, a sharp edge suddenly formed. With a quick motion, he brought it straight down into the beast's skull, ending its growls of anger.

"You have to destroy the cerebral functions," he explained to Zanna. She grimaced as Didorumpus withdrew his staff. The blood-covered bottom suddenly returned to its normal rounded shape.

He turned around in time to see his brother had resumed his journey towards the center. With a hastened step, he caught up and returned to a casual march. The three of them continued forward, ignoring the battle going on all around them as best as they could. The march seemed forever, the center field seemed light years away, but at long last, it had arrived. Kunklestick took a deep breath and observed the battlefield. There was no more time to waste.

"Inginimo!" He suddenly called out, sending a solid white streak of energy soaring into a few hastily approaching Akordan ghouls.

"Inginimo," Didorumpus and Zanna mimicked. Their spells found similarly approaching ghouls.

They were in the thick of it now, Akordans both living and dead started charging towards them.

Chapter 4

Emlin rode atop Becca, who was galloping at full breakneck speed. It took all her strength to not get thrown off, it wasn't easy, but falling certainly didn't sound appealing. Ahead of her was Thadeus, who also rode with an urgent purpose. In fact, all the horses were running at full speed. They were close, the sounds of war echoed in the air like a distant bell. The louder the sounds of destruction and pain became, the faster she could feel her heart beating. She wanted him dead, and she wanted to be the one to do it. He had it coming. She didn't fear him. No, her greatest fear was seeing Broli, Inca or her father. She dreaded seeing them as mindless drones working for Septus. The notion made her skin crawl something awful.

As they exited Tordenth, the darkness of the day could be seen. Cristol covered in overcast, dark clouds smothered out all chance of hope or joy. Onwards they pressed, the battle getting louder and louder. Ahead of them, they could just make out the first wave of Vanguards, many of whom had been forced to make the trip on foot.

"We made good time," Emlin called out. Her words went unheard. Thadeus continued forward, pulling on his reins as they neared the battalion. As his horse approached, the men stepped aside, making room for him to make his way to the front.

"Thadeus?" Sabasio called out in surprise as he turned his horse toward them. He nodded toward Emlin as she approached just behind Thadeus.

"Either we made good time, or you've been moving slow," Thadeus noted, skipping past any pleasantries.

"I'd say a bit of both," Sabasio admitted. "We didn't have the benefit of having everyone on a horse."

A loud crash in the distance stole their attention, sending a tremble beneath their feet.

"What was that?" Emlin asked.

"Who knows," Thadeus replied. "We need to get in there."

He gave his horse a firm kick, and Emlin bravely followed his lead. Headlong they pressed, leaving Sabasio alone with his thoughts. Emlin turned her head back, taking notice of the fact that the men had begun to run.

"Ay Nu Hoya!" They called into the air as they struggled to keep up. It was a chant, a battle cry. It meant *For the Queen*. As she heard the words, it brought her discomfort. The notion that all these men were going to war in her name didn't sit right. She didn't want people fighting for her. No, she preferred to do her own fighting. As she continued to gallop toward doom, she ran her hand carefully along the curved form of her bow, memories of her first time using it coming to mind.

***

"Now pull it back," Septus instructed to Emlin, who had her fingers wrapped tightly around the drawstring of her new bow. She nodded, using all the strength she could muster to pull the string back. It took more force than she had expected but eventually she got it. Her arm began to tremble as she held the string in place, aiming at a distant target.

"Close your left eye. Focus only on that target. Take in the environment around you. Is it windy? Which side of the target is the arrowhead facing?"

She did as instructed.

"It looks like it's a little to the right of it," she replied.

"Ok, so you need to aim to the left a hair, account for that slight variance," he instructed.

She nodded as she shifted her aim.

"Ok. Let it go."

She did. Into the air the arrow soared, cutting through the wind like butter as it headed towards its destination.

Suddenly her smile faded as she witnessed the arrow's direction curve downwards. It landed firmly in the dirt just in front of the tree she had aimed for.

"Fuit," she whispered.

"Don't beat yourself up. It takes lots of practice to get good. Almost no one hits the target their first try," he explained with a cheerful smile.

She sighed, shrugging her shoulders as she lowered the bow in disappointment.

"Try again," Septus prompted.

Emlin shot him a fierce look. An angry look. She was hardly in the mood. But something in his eyes suggested he wasn't going to take no for an answer. Reaching into the quiver, she pulled out another arrow and lined the end up into the nock. Shooting him one last glance of aggravation, she pulled the string back, quickly lining up her shot. She sluggishly closed her eyes, taking in the feel of the situation. A calm breeze gently blew against her neck, it was subtle, almost unnoticeable, but it was there. There were whispers in the trees above, conversations between the animals. The slight flutter of wings from various birds. Slowly, she opened her eyes, looking at the tree with intensity.

"You can do it Em," Septus encouraged.

With a quick motion, she released the arrow, watching it soar into the distance like an angry child running from his parent. It continued forward with startling speed until it finally found its mark. With a firm thud, it landed dead center in the target.

"Did it hit?" Emlin asked hesitantly. Septus turned his gaze and smiled a broad beaming smile. Promptly, he turned toward her and threw his arms open.

"I did it?" Emlin questioned. He nodded silently.

"Oh thank Undr," she exclaimed as she ran into his arms. Together they stood embraced in each other's arms. He held her firm, taking a deep breath as he took in her scent. Berries, she always managed to smell like berries. It was uncanny, a tonic no doubt from one of the local apothecaries.

He wouldn't complain. The scent was his muse, kept him up at night with a smile.

"Thank you," Emlin whispered. Septus pulled back, giving her a coy grin.

"Hey, you're the one that did it. I just coached you through it."

He leaned in, grabbing her head on each side and planted a kiss firmly on her soft lips. She did the same, grabbing the back of his head and savoring the moment.

***

"Let's do this," Thadeus exclaimed as he jumped from his horse. In a startlingly quick motion, he withdrew Fiona from her holster. In no time, she had found a new residence. Yes, the dead center of an Akordan skull seemed like as friendly a place as any. As the creature fell to the ground lifeless, Thadeus found himself smiling with pleasure. How he had missed this, the thrill of combat. Sitting in the general office had provided more bore than he had preferred. He had at one point tried to deny it, but he couldn't any longer, he was thrilled when Hervott approached him with a task. Stilletto. That's who he truly was. Here, in the face of extinction, he was finally ready to admit it. He would be Thadeus no more.

"Whoa," Emlin called to Becca as she neared the action. She quickly dismounted as promptly as she could, withdrawing her sword, and joining the general.

"Ha!" She called out, bringing her sword quickly across the chest of a nearing Akordan ghoul. There was no blood — no — this creature's blood dried up long ago. Its menacing face twisted and contorted as it glared at her with malice and hate. As its mouth opened up, small snowflakes could be seen, floating around, hovering in between the many teeth like a car dodging cones. Suddenly, the flakes began to glow, and seconds later a beam of ice was emerging from within its violent yawn.

"Fuit!" Emlin called out as she quickly raised her sword. The beam of ice came hurtling towards her like a raging blizzard with a grudge. Her mind hit a standstill. She panicked. Doom seemed inevitable when suddenly, Thadeus grabbed her, pulling her aside so firmly that she nearly fell to the ground.

"Watch yourself," he lectured. Shaking his head in disappointment, he grabbed another ghoul, lifting it off the ground and snapping its neck. Emlin winced at the sight. She appreciated his savagery; it had saved her life more than a couple times. Nevertheless, it was never a pleasure to see.

She shrugged off her disgust and quickly continued swinging her sword, taking out a new foe every few seconds. There were many of them, they were clearly outnumbered, but so far, they weren't that hard to kill.

"Grab him," Emlin called out as she shoved a Terrian ghoul towards Thadeus with a firm push. He turned around just in time to plant Gertrude straight into the creature's skull.

"What gives?" He questioned. She had nearly replied when suddenly they took notice of the fact that the ghouls had surrounded them on all sides. Each of them had opened their jaws to a surprising width, and within each mouth was a ball of ice, just waiting to be expelled.

"Emlin," Thadeus whispered. "Duck."

All at once, the ghouls expelled their frigid beams of ice, which traveled towards them in an almost beautiful display. They dropped to the ground just in time to avoid the frosty attack. In the dirt they lay, hands covering their heads, with chilly snowflakes falling upon them. Emlin looked towards Thadeus as they lay patiently waiting. As she looked at him, she found herself trying to fathom what thoughts ran through his head. She knew so little about him, a notion that she was beginning to regret. She closed her eyes, tuning out the harsh sound of the icy blasts. Suddenly the ghouls began to drop. One at a time they fell to the ground in a slump, holes burned into each of their heads. The Vanguards had made it at last.

"Watch out for the Queen," Sabasio commanded as he stood with his eyes squinted and his finger firmly gripping the trigger of his Beacon. They made an opening. The surrounding ghouls all dropped dead. There were plenty more to be had, but for now, it seemed the threat of immediate danger had passed.

"All clear," Sabasio called out. Slowly, Thadeus and Emlin climbed to their feet, taking in the grim sights. At that moment, Thadeus found himself feeling an odd appreciation of the Beacons. It was the second time in recent memory that they had saved his life.

He turned around, surveying the surrounding ghouls that were continuing towards them. As he looked at Emlin, he could see in her eyes what she was thinking. He quietly nodded.

"Sabasio," Thadeus called out. "The queen and I are going to push through. We need to get to the center of it all. That's where Septus will be."

Sabasio nodded. Behind him, a soldier began to fire upon the nearing ghouls.

"Hathin, Morti, go with them," he instructed without turning his head. Two soldiers emerged from behind him, proud looks decorating their faces. They lifted their Beacons, firing at some of the ghouls as they moved their way toward Emlin and Thadeus.

"We'll handle this wave," Sabasio commented. Thadeus nodded and turned around, daggers drawn and ready to fight. He pushed forward, stabbing at the various ghouls, next to him, Emlin did the same. In the distance behind them, they could make out the familiar hiss of the Beacons as the Vanguards began to attack.

"Ay Nu Hoya!" The soldiers called out as they continued their fight.

Silently, Emlin, Thadeus, and the two soldiers continued to fight their way through. The further into the crowd they got, the more terrifying the creatures became. There were Delopars, Akordans, Terrians, and men. All of them at various stages of decay, all of them mindlessly trying to kill them. Quickly, Emlin swung her blade, slicing the throat of a ghoul that was about to expell an ice attack.

"Not today," she whispered. Behind her, she could hear screams of panic as the soldiers began to get overrun. The fluttering of wings above caught her focus. Looking up, she noticed a dozen Arnouts flying high in the sky. Something was off about them though, their eyes glowed red. They were servants. The Arnout ghouls hovered in the air, casting powerful telekinetic waves towards the Vanguard soldiers. Into the air they flew, many of them falling with such force they weren't likely to get back up.

"Ahh!" Emlin screamed as a pair of claws found their way across her chest. She had gotten distracted. Returning to her focus, a Delopar ghoul stood in front of her, red-eyed and mindless. She froze in place, horror surging through her like a virus. It was Inca. Or at least, her shell. Emlin watched her as though she was stuck in fog, frozen in place. The ghoul took another swipe at her, this time scratching her clear across the face.

"Your Highness!" Thadeus called out. He brought his blade into the gut of a ghoul and quickly turned around.

Emlin stood frozen still. Her face and chest oozing blood from her various wounds. *That's not her*, she told herself. Suddenly, she lifted her blade, shoving it into Inca's gut with a forceful push. The two of them fell to the ground, around them, other ghouls sought to join the confrontation. The Inca ghoul growled and hissed as Emlin knelt above her, looking her in the eyes, trying to find a soul. There was none. She was empty. With tears in her eyes, Emlin reached to the side of her, grabbing the severed arm of an Akordan ghoul, and brought it down into Inca's face. Over and over again, she continued the attack, until alas, there was nothing left but a bloody stump.

"My queen," Morti exclaimed as he approached her from behind. He quickly slammed the butt of his weapon into the face of a ghoul, prompting its face to cave in.

"My queen," he repeated, grabbing her arm and lifting her to her feet.

"Emlin," Thadeus called out, he paused, looking to the ground at the bloody remains of a Delopar. His heart beat rapidly as he contemplated the possibility. As he looked towards Emlin, he saw the blank look of shock that had masked her face the first time she had seen the dead begin to walk.

"Is it her?" He asked. Emlin silently nodded. Without warning, a firm set of hands approached him from behind, finding their way on each side of his head. *Fuit.* One firm twist, and he fell to the ground, dead. Emlin looked up from the mess and gasped in horror. It was Broli.

Chapter 5

Articus knelt silently on the ground, observing the old tower that had long been deserted. Next to him knelt Sillimon. Penny had stayed behind to keep an eye on Methalda. The streets were mostly vacant. The dead had seen to that. He watched the entrance with turbulence, biting his lip all the while.

"I don't like this," he whispered to Sillimon, who was drawing pictures in a patch of dirt. Sillimon quickly looked up from his drawing and looked towards the entrance.

"What do you think?" Articus questioned. Sillimon looked the building over with curiosity.

"I think it's risky," he replied. "Maybe we should just call the whole thing off."

Articus paused in thought, then turned his attention back to the tower.

"I don't like this," he repeated. He quietly stood, entering the streets and moving towards the tower entrance.

"Articus," Sillimon called out. No response. Letting out a protracted sigh, he jumped to his feet and headed into the streets.

"I thought you said you didn't like this," Sillimon complained.

"Josiah is dead," Articus replied as he paused in front of the door. "I want to find out why." He grabbed the door's handle and gave it a quick turn to the left. The door was old; it hadn't been used for some time. It squeaked as it slowly drifted open.

He stood silent as the entryway came into sight. It was empty apart from an old, worn out table. On the table sat a piece of paper. He groaned as he slowly neared the desk. On the paper was the same logo that had been on the note from before. A circle with a reflective glare in the top corner.

"What in the name of Undr?" Sillimon whispered as he neared the desk and looked it over.

"He's toying with us," Articus sighed. "It's just a game. Josiah's death was fun to him."

"Why do you assume that?" A voice said from behind them. Standing in the doorway, dressed in long dark robes was a Delopar.

"Who are you?" Articus demanded as he turned around. "Where is the Dark Thief?"

The Delopar chuckled.

"Come with me. I'll show you," the Delopar replied. He turned and headed back into the streets.

"I don't think we should," Sillimon cautioned.

Articus turned, looking his comrade over with skepticism and a bit of a smirk.

"You're afraid of a Delopar?" He quickly dashed across the tower entry and through the door.

"You're not?" Sillimon called out as he followed.

Into the streets they went, following the mysterious Delopar through various twists and turns. As their path progressed, it became increasingly apparent that they were headed for the shoreline. Articus followed with curiosity as they approached the shore, he couldn't help but wonder where the creature was leading them. There was nothing to be seen apart from the water.

Finally, at the water's edge, they came to a stop.

"What are you gonna try to do? Drown us?" Articus called from a distance. He had hesitantly decided to hang a few feet back. A decision Sillimon seemed more than fine following.

"You are a paranoid bunch aren't you?" The Delopar asked as he continued to look towards the water.

A distant sound began to make its way to his ears. Articus angled his head as he looked into the vastness of the Peridian Sea. There was nothing to be seen apart from water, and yet, he felt fairly certain a ship was approaching.

"Do you hear that?" Sillimon whispered. Articus remained silent, keeping his eyes firmly trained on the water ahead. All of a sudden, his jaw dropped open. Appearing before them, out of thin air, was a large ship. Dark smoke rose gently into the sky from its various pipes, disappearing into the darkness of the clouds.

"What in the name of Undr?" Sillimon exclaimed with shock.

Articus silently approached, keeping a safe distance from their Delopar guide. A door on the side of the ship suddenly popped open, and a long bridge made of some seemingly flexible wood extended to the shore. Articus gawked at the display. The bridge had been quite long, a good thirty feet at least. It hovered over to the shoreline with ease and came to a gentle rest on the rocky shore. Without uttering a word, the Delopar slowly made his way across, feeling fairly confident his guests would soon join him.

"Keep close," Articus instructed as he nervously approached the bridge. Together, the two of them cautiously crossed, marveling all the way at the strangeness. What technology was this?

Once they had stepped inside the ship, they were greeted with the familiar sight of the Delopar. He stood silent, grinning smugly from ear to ear. "Pretty neat huh?" He asked as they came to a stop in front of him.

"What are we doing here?" Articus asked, deciding to skip past the discussion. He felt on edge, and his teeth clenched tighter each minute he lingered in this stranger's company.

"Follow me," the Delopar advised. He turned, pushed open a door and stepped into a rather cramped hallway. It was lined all the way down with doors and was rather narrow. No more than one person could travel these halls at a time, that much was clear.

Down the hall, they followed, coming to a stop at a door on the left side that was three doors from the end. The guide quickly pushed the door open and stepped aside, gesturing for his guests to enter.

Articus looked him over with suspicion as he turned and stepped into the gloomy room. Inside sat a figure who was shrouded in darkness, sitting silently in a chair looking out towards Morlay.

"Thank you for coming to see me," the figure said. The voice was strange, wispy, like a wind was blowing with each word.

"Who are you?" Articus firmly demanded. Behind them, the Delopar closed the door and stepped inside. A large glass box to the left of the chair suddenly caught his eye. The *Arc Blade*.

"You're him," Articus exclaimed. Slowly the figure turned, revealing a woman with dark skin and tattoos that glowed decorating her face.

"My name is Jinn, but most know me as the Dark Thief," she replied. Slowly, she rose from the chair, revealing her feet that didn't touch the ground. She hovered like a shadow. Her bottom half seemed to be made entirely of mist.

"What are you?" Articus questioned, looking her over with concern.

"I am a Kajj. One of the few remaining members of a species that existed before most. We were the first to walk this land. Great Undr's first blessing to the land," she explained.

"I've heard of them," Sillimon happily announced. "They are supposed to be long gone."

Jinn hovered toward them, smiling inquisitively.

"That's what we want you to think," she grinned.

"Why did you use us?" Articus abruptly asked.

Jinn turned, slowly bending down and picking up the glass encasement. With little effort at all, she pushed her hand inside, pulling the blade free as though it were a bubble rather than glass.

"Umm," Sillimon commented.

Jinn approached them, holding the blade out in front of Articus.

"Do you know what this weapon does?" She asked.

Articus shook his head, a frustrated look masking his face.

"The Arc Blade is an ancient weapon. Left here by the High Father Undr. The protector of Daulest. It was left here as a fail-safe. A way for us to rise against the gods if the need should ever arise," she explained as she set the weapon into Articus' hand.

"It was the Kajj that placed it into the encasement. Made sure it was kept safe for all these years, hoping there would be no need to use it," she paused.

"Many years ago I met someone. Someone who told me something most interesting."

Articus looked the blade over; it was surprisingly light, like holding a phoenix feather. Its handle was wrapped in leather, and its blade was marked on both sides with strange writing, symbols almost.

"What did this person tell you?" Articus asked, finally returning his gaze to Jinn.

"I could tell you," she paused. "But I think *she* should tell you herself."

Without offering any further explanation, she carefully brushed past them, her shoulder just barely grazing Articus. The Delopar escort quickly opened the door, stepping aside once again and offering a gesture of approval to the two guests. Articus and Sillimon glanced at each other, then shadowed Jinn out into the narrow hall.

She swiftly approached the door at the end and nudged it open. This room, like the other, was poorly lit and had a monotonous feel to it. That didn't matter, however, what piqued Articus' interest was the elderly woman who sat quietly in front of a small fireplace, stitching what looked like socks. As they stepped inside, Jinn approached the fireplace and perched herself mutely next to it.

"Come into the light so I can see you," the elderly woman requested, her voice was raspy, weakened by the years.

Articus nodded, edging his way to the light and stopping as soon as his face had become illuminated.

"I don't bite," she added as she set her project down onto her lap. Sillimon sauntered behind Articus and came to a pause.

"Why did you send for us?" Articus questioned.

The elderly woman shook her head and smiled. Her skin was dark, her hair — grey and tattered, her lips were quite chapped, and her teeth were quite stained.

"Don't you want to know who I am?" She asked, with a delicate grin.

"Sure," Articus replied.

"My name is Idrix," she nodded. "Thank you for assisting with the capture of the Arc Blade. I do feel quite sorry for your loss. I didn't know your friend, but his reputation was rather famous."

"Josiah was a good man," Sillimon said, speaking up for the first time since setting foot onto the boat.

Idrix slowly rose from her chair, her steps were shaky, but she slowly approached Articus and paused in front of him.

"You know what the Arc Blade is I take it. Jinn no doubt filled you in," she said.

Articus nodded.

"Good. That's good," she replied. "Long ago, when I was a little girl, I lived in a great palace called Abissal Keep. My parents were royalty. I was their only daughter and the princess."

She slowly turned towards the fireplace and approached, holding her brittle hands out to recover some of its lavish warmth.

"This was many many years ago. Back before the Great Freeze," she elaborated.

"Anyways, to get to the point. One day, I was out in the fields playing like I so often did, when I saw something strange fall from the sky. Two shapes of color. They crashed to the ground in front of me and turned into a man and woman."

She closed her eyes as she relived the infamous day. It had been nearly one hundred years, and still, she remembered it like it was yesterday.

"They were gods. One of them was Undr, and the other was Gravi. Even back then, we knew that Undr was the guardian of the land. But what I learned that day, was that Gravi had done something very wrong. Bad enough to get her exiled from the heavens and left to live out her days here. Undr shamed her, told her that this was her punishment, that she was not allowed to return. After that, he left, leaving her alone in the middle of Solarian."

The events continued to unfold in her mind, a violently surreal dream.

"That's when it happened. The Great Freeze. She cursed Solarian, damning it to ice and killing my parents. I myself was trapped in a lake of ice. I don't know how I survived, but I did. I got out. When I saw the horrors that had occurred, I knew Undr had made a mistake leaving her here. She was dangerous and spiteful. She would need to be stopped."

She turned around, looking towards Jinn and then returning her gaze to Articus.

"Years later, I formed a secret society called the *Decoyers*. Our mission — to find and kill Gravi. A mission I will see completed before my dying day. That's why we needed the Arc Blade. It's the only weapon that can do it. But the Arc Blade is incomplete. A gemstone is missing from its hilt. This stone is what powers the blade. Without it, the blade won't work."

Articus looked towards Sillimon and huffed.

"You still haven't explained why you used us. Why you led us into a trap," he bellowed.

"Jinn is good," Idrix started. "She's one of the best, but even she can't get into the palace without a distraction. You were that distraction. We hadn't planned on it ending the way it did, but please understand, the death of your friend pales in comparison to what is coming."

"What's coming?" Sillimon questioned.

"The end of all things," Idrix replied. Sillimon gulped as he looked towards Articus with a fearful gaze.

"What do you mean?" Articus replied.

Chapter 6

Apothiciss swung her sword towards Krytus, her blade clashing against his armor with a rattle. He sneered, grabbing her, and pulling her towards him.

"Your breath is as terrible as your swordsmanship," she taunted, as she drove her knee into his groin. He coughed, releasing his grip and stumbled back. She had just thought to grin when Nevo came up from behind, grabbing her and squeezing her tight in his arms.

"You shouldn't have come here sister," Nevo roared into her ears. His grip was strong, and it threatened to crush her. As she looked towards the sky, it began to blur, erasing as unconsciousness set in.

"Ahh!" Nevo cried out as a sword cut into his tail. Reeling in pain, he dropped Apothiciss and quickly turned around. Staring back at him was one of the Akordan soldiers, rebel Akordans to him.

He roared, as he charged at the soldier. They clashed together, and soon fists were flying back and forth.

As he returned to a standing position, Krytus eyed his sister with anger and disappointment. He hated her. She had betrayed him, betrayed their mother, betrayed their ideals. She and all her followers deserved nothing more than a gruesome death, and yet, as they locked eyes, time seemed to halt. In the silence of the moment, his mind wandered back to the beginning, to the times where she had been there for both he and Nevo. Protected them, fed them, taught them, and even loved them.

"Raaah!" He roared as he brought his sword crashing towards her. Apothiciss quickly dodged the maneuver, letting his weapon land firmly into the dirt. She looked towards him, finally realizing that she was unarmed and began to look around, studying the dead and looking for a suitable weapon.

As she located one, she scooped it up, using not her hands, but her tail. She quickly gripped the blade, sending her tail back and brought it up just in time to block another incoming attack from Krytus.

The swings came much faster this time, there was more anger lodged inside each swipe. Death would come for one of them, that much was clear. Apothiciss was skilled and rather tenacious, each time her sword met his, it nearly knocked it clear from his hands. Krytus tried his best to counter her moves, but the further along the battle continued, the harder it was becoming. Her resolve was unwavering.

He grinned as a Delopar ghoul approached, firing a beam of ice in her direction.

"Fuit," Apothiciss called out as the beam struck her in the back, pushing her forward and nearly causing her to lose her balance. Krytus was inches from her now. He pulled his arms back, preparing to drive his blade into her gut. However, Apothiciss lunged forward suddenly, digging her jaw into his neck.

He roared in pain as her teeth quickly sunk deeper into his neck and blood began to ooze slowly into her mouth. With a quick motion, she pulled back, tearing a decent chunk of flesh from his throat.

"Brother!" Nevo cried out from behind. In a quick thrust, he plunged his blade into a small opening in Apothiciss' armor.

"Ugh," she moaned as she looked down. Protruding through the front of her torso was the tip of a blade. It stung, its penetration felt hot against her usually cold skin. Slowly, she dropped to the ground. In front of her, Krytus did the same. His throat had been ripped open, a deadly wound indeed but despite his pain, he kept his eyes fixed on her. A sinister grin painted its way across his face as she drew her last breath. At long last, he had seen her betrayal punished. With her soul now departed, she toppled over, landing rightfully in a pool of her own blood. Krytus winced, as his wound began to feel chilled, and before long, he also surrendered to death.

"Brother!" Nevo called out as he rushed to Krytus' side. It was too late. Into his arms, Krytus fell, asleep, the last sleep he would ever know. With a heart full of rage, Nevo looked at Apothiciss, who still struggled to hold onto life. He looked around, seeing Krytus' blade. In one quick motion, he lopped off her head, sending it falling to the ground in a roll.

"Brother," Nevo sobbed as he held Krytus in his arms. There was no response; he was gone, forever trapped in darkness. For the first time in many years, tears came to his eyes. He looked upon his brother's vacant shell with distorted eyes.

"Who do these feuds benefit?" he whispered to his brother's still body. They were the very same words he had uttered all those years ago when Krytus and Apothiciss had nearly slain each other at first. Now here he was, years later, faced with the results as though he had never stopped the fight in the first place.

He sat still, trapped in his grief as the battle raged on around him.

***

Agavordis continued his persistent attacks on the Arnouts. They were tough, but he was tougher than them. In the far distance, he could hear the ever-obstinate shrieks of Herratia, and he smiled as he imagined the mangled remains of her fury. Next to him stood his princess, his goddess, Vigil. She too fought with determination. Dozens of frozen souls stood around her, stuck in a moment, unable to move. The Tin Men were no match for her, try as they might, her chilly powers quickly seized up the moving parts of their mechanical monstrosities.

Suddenly a sword flung towards him, it was large, rather hefty. Quickly, he lifted his hands and formed a shield. The blade shattered into a million tiny pieces, littering the ground with sharp shards of metal. He turned, looking at the tin soldier who had launched the attack. With a smug smirk, he swooped his hands upwards, summoning a creature made entirely out of rocks from beneath the ground.

"What the…?" The soldier called out as two hands grabbed his feet. He looked down, noticing the vacant eyes in the stone creature, its mouth hung wide as it exerted its sturdy grip. Agavordis promptly seized the moment and neared the soldier.

"A life of honor ends with a forgettable death that no one will ever know about," Agavordis threatened. His right hand began to glow a vibrant green and swiftly, without warning, he plunged it into the man's gut. The heat from his flames easily burned through the armor, searing the man from the inside out. As he withdrew his hand, the soldier began to choke, spitting up blood and making it very obvious that he was in misery. With a content grin, Agavordis looked to the sky, his red eyes piercing the heavens, and then, using his powers, he sent the man flying upwards. As the man's form began to shrink, he quickly moved his arms, mimicking the motions of opening a package. At that moment, the soldier's body was torn in half, raining blood upon the field like snow on a wintry day.

"See," Agavordis whispered as the man's torso fell to the battlefield with a thump.

"You're more powerful than I could've imagined," Vigil noted from behind him. He turned with a smile and approached her.

"To be honest," he leaned in to kiss her. "I didn't know I could do that." He lifted his hand, firing a beam of energy towards a tin soldier that approached from the right. Vigil did the same, hurling a pillar of ice towards an Arnout. Her attack, however, was not as successful. The Arnout blocked the icy beam with a quick upwards swoop, then gave Vigil a firm telekinetic push.

"Septus!" Vigil called out as she soared through the air. Agavordis angrily turned towards the Arnout and fired two beams of energy his way. Without any warning, however, an orb of white energy appeared, holding him hostage and restricting his movement.

"That's enough Septus," a voice called out from behind him. His spherical prison was lifted off the ground, slowly turning and revealing an angry Kunklestick. In his hands, he held his staff firmly, and from the top of the staff, a white light was protruding, leading to the orb that was holding him.

"This ends now son," Kunklestick firmly demanded.

"For you maybe," Agavordis replied. His red eyes began to glow brighter, and his palms began to glow green. As he summoned his powers, the orb of light holding him began to fade, and before long, Kunklestick had lost his control over the energized prison.

Agavordis landed on the ground with a light thump.

"For me, however," he whispered. "It's just getting started."

At that moment, a bright flash appeared, bringing with it colorful stars that hindered their sight. With the light finally fading, Kunklestick rubbed his eyes, startled by the sudden addition of Herratia.

"Herratia dear," Kunklestick nodded.

She looked at him with adoration and bowed her head.

"You need not show this old fool respect," Agavordis noted.

"Kunklestick is a legend," Herratia replied. "An important figure in Furlasia's history. No one deserves our respect more."

"Very well," Agavordis replied. He turned towards Kunklestick and offered a bow.

"Thank you for your service to our great land." Rapidly, he fired a beam of energy, sending it towards Kunklestick with alarming haste.

"But your service is no longer required."

"No!" Zanna called out, swiping her wand towards Agavordis and sending a yellow beam of light crashing into his beam. The energies met with a firm clash, bits of unchecked power splashed about like a rapid waterfall. Agavordis squinted as he held his focus. Between the two spells, an orb appeared, and for the briefest of moments, it glowed yellow.

Herratia roared into the air as she waved her arms about. In an instant, she appeared inches from Kunklestick and gave him a firm push, knocking him to the ground.

"Oh no you don't!" Didorumpus yelled, as he quickly thrust the top of his staff into her.

"Embarga."

A hot ball of blue light formed at the top and began to burn the witches flesh. Suddenly, however, she disappeared.

"Where are you, witch?" Didorumpus whispered.

"Here," she whispered into his ear. He quickly whipped around and was greeted by the snarling teeth of Herratia. She snapped at him, nearly taking off his nose, but something stopped her. A beam of energy wrapped around her and gave her a strong pull. Kunklestick. He had risen to his feet.

The orb between the two spells continued to edge towards Zanna, slow at first, but then suddenly quite fast. As she eyed the green orb hurtling towards her, she knew it to be a bad sign. She dropped her spell, falling into the dirt as fast as she could. The maneuver, it seemed, worked. She had just missed getting hit by the harsh orb of energy. With her face in the dirt, she aimed her wand forward, towards Agavordis' feet. She focused. She didn't know the proper spell, only what she wanted done. Slowly but surely, a beam began to creep towards his feet. Zanna had just cracked a hint of a smile when suddenly a pair of hands grabbed her feet and gave her a pull.

"Now!" Vigil called out to Agavordis. He quickly approached and looked down.

"I remember you," he whispered. "You're that whore from the tavern. The one I burned to the ground. What was it called? Mother Margary's?"

Zanna's eyes filled with fury at the mention of her late mother's name. With a firm kick, she freed herself from Vigil's grip and rolled to the left, nearly getting stepped on by Kunklestick. The elder mentor promptly reached down, offering her a hand and pulling her to her feet. In the distance, a siren scream filled the air, followed by a bright light.

Zanna nodded in appreciation and then quickly turned around. Standing in a line were Vigil, Herratia, and Agavordis.

"The odds seem fair," Agavordis called out. "But can your team really match mine?" He motioned toward Vigil, who became completely engulfed in ice. Then to Herratia, who began to wag her tail and lick her lips. With a wide grin and glowing red eyes, he looked upon the three wizards.

"Boastfulness is a tactic used by the weak," Kunklestick replied. Agavordis took a step forward and lifted his hands towards them.

"Prove it."

Chapter 7

Nikalas rode silently on the back of a carriage pulled by a Grimwort. Here in Cap Ti Mor, it seemed the creatures were regarded mostly as horses. He had found it strange at first, but had gotten used to it. In fact, he wasn't even sure if they could fly in this strange place. Next to him sat a lovely young woman with tan skin, blue eyes, and brown hair that hung to her mid back. Her name was Kell Si, and she was his official mentor, appointed by Roros himself. Together they strolled over fields of grass that were populated with rolling hills and not much else. The sky, while still blank, was bright as ever.

He still didn't have access to the full extent of Cap Ti Mor, but he had unlocked at least one privilege. The obscure effect of clay had finally been lifted. Now he saw the world the way it mostly should be, albeit, some places were still blank and the sky was still empty. He was relieved however to be rid of the clay effect. It was just too strange to take seriously.

They continued over a few more rolling hills until the Grimwort came to a slow stop. Kell Si quietly stepped from the cart and onto the grass. Like all the other gnomes in this place, she was freakishly tall, close to seven feet he thought. Her outfit, like the others, was comprised of a motion portrait. Hers was a snowstorm, although he couldn't guess why.

"We're here," she softly explained. He looked around, taking in the sight. To his eyes, it looked the same as all the rest of the plains he had been shown.

"There's nothing here," he replied. Kell Si shook her head as she motioned for him to step out of the cart. He shrugged, letting out a deep sigh, then did as told.

His feet hit the plush green grass and all of a sudden, the environment began to change. The rolling hills slowly faded, making way for an elegant landscape of crystal blue water and small islands.

"Wow," he whispered.

"It's beautiful, isn't it?" Kell Si remarked. She turned, walking down a slight incline towards the edge of the water.

"How is it possible for me to miss so much?" Nikalas questioned.

"People tend to miss a lot of things that are right in front of them," she replied. Coming to a stop at the water's edge, she turned and grinned at Nikalas before stepping into the water. Just a few feet ahead was one of the many small islands. With little effort, and the speed of a shark, she swam to the island, and as she climbed ashore, she turned, giving him a wave.

"The next piece of the puzzle is here," she yelled. "But be aware. This water is not what it seems. This is the lake of purity. Through these waters, no impure soul can pass."

He looked around, gave his usual confident smirk, and quickly approached the shore. Coming to a pause, he placed the tip of his finger into the lake. It was surprisingly warm, almost like a bath.

"This won't be so bad," he whispered. Wasting no further time, he jumped into the water. However, the water turned to tar almost instantly, holding him in place and threatening to drown him.

"What the hell?!" He called out. "This is disgusting."

Kell Si, smiled as she sat on the ground, folding her legs pretzel-style.

"It seems you're not pure enough yet, Nikalas," she called out.

"Get me outta here!" He called out.

"I cannot. This test is yours. One you must pass," she replied. He continued to struggle as the sticky mess gripped his body, the more he moved, the further down he sank.

"How?" He called out, continuing to struggle against the syrupy mass. Down he continued to sink.

"I told you this is the lake of purity. No impure soul can cross it. You need to unburden yourself. Let go of your demons. Leave the foolish man behind. Only then will you be able to cross."

"How the hell do I do that when I'm drowning?" Nikalas bellowed. With each passing moment of struggle, he continued to creep deeper and deeper into the recesses of the tar.

"Close your eyes," Kell Si instructed. "I shall join our minds. Teach you how to purify your thoughts. Only then, will you be free."

Nikalas sighed, taking as deep a breath as he could and closed his eyes. His mind tried its hardest to remain clear. He tried to ignore the doom facing him by thinking only of her. *This is stupid*, he thought. He quickly opened his eyes, and to his dismay, found himself in the center of a crowded street.

"Whoa," he whispered. A hand quickly tapped his side. It was Kell Si; she was dressed in modest clothes, a blue dress and a pair of heels. Her appearance somehow looked human, but he knew it was her.

"Come on," she whispered. "He's getting away."

"Who?" He replied with an equally muffled tone.

She lifted her arm, pointing a single finger to a young man on the far side of the street.

"You," she explained.

Without further explanation, she dashed across the street, almost bumping into several different people. No one paid her any mind. In fact, no one paid either of them any mind. And even though the city was crowded, it felt like they were the only ones there. Nikalas eyed the citizens with curiosity as he struggled to keep up. Each face was different, each person unique in their own way. Ahead of them, his doppelganger continued to allude to them, almost as though he knew he was being followed.

"What is going on?" Nikalas panted, as he bumped shoulders with an unsuspecting well-dressed man. To his surprise, the man stopped, looked at him dead in the eyes with a silent stare, and then froze. Locked in a moment of anger, his fretful gaze continued until alas, Nikalas decided to resume his pursuit. As he turned around, the man returned to his business, joining the masses of strange people. Kell Si remained silent, keeping her attention on the doppelganger.

They slowly turned into an alley and paused. Ahead of them, the doppelganger stood hunched in the shadows, talking to a strange man in low tones. Their words faded with each passing step between them. Curiosity finally took the better of him, and cautiously, Nikalas approached, trying his best to remain silent.

"Don't make me come down here again," the doppelganger said to the faceless man.

"I'm sorry sir. It won't happen again, I promise," the man pleaded.

"It better not. You heard about Matthis, right? He had an unexpected fall from the top of his apartment building. I'd hate for you to have such an accident. It's so slippery out there after it rains."

Slowly, Nikalas crept closer, continuing to remain mute as a mouse.

"Next week I want double. I can't let this kind of shit slide. You need to pay up."

Suddenly, Kell Si coughed, abruptly grabbing the attention of the doppelganger Nikalas.

"Who the hell are you?" The doppelganger demanded as he turned and saw his clone.

Nikalas froze in his tracks, staring like a deer caught in headlights.

"I said, who the hell are you?!"

The doppelganger quickly approached, grabbing Nikalas by his shirt and lifting him into the air. With one firm motion, he brought the back of his hand up and suddenly, there was nothing but darkness.

Time passed, and darkness continued to hold him, feeding him bits and pieces of dreams, appetizers of escape. Alas, he awoke secured to a chair and the feeling of ice-cold water being poured mercilessly all over him. It jolted him awake like a pacemaker did to someone with a bad ticker.

"Ahh!" He blurted out as he realized he was staring at a man who looked exactly like him.

"They sent you to try to wipe me out huh?" The doppelganger asked.

Nikalas paused, looking around the room, taking notice of Kell Si. She stood silently in the corner, seemingly going unnoticed by the doppelganger.

"Uh, no," he slowly replied.

The doppelganger laughed and approached wearing brass knuckles, flashing them in a threatening gesture.

"Come on," Nikalas grinned. "You're not gonna use those on me."

Wham! Across the face. The impact was so severe, he felt certain his jaw would crack. By some miracle, however, it didn't. But alas, he finally knew what it felt like to be on the receiving end of brass knuckles. The sensation was quite terrible. He imagined his jaw as a concrete wall and the knuckles as the wrecking ball tasked with tearing it all down. Ghastly.

"What was the plan? Kill me and then plant you in my place? You kinda look like me. People might fall for it," the doppelganger questioned.

From a door to the left, a man silently strolled in, holding with him a stack of documents. He was an odd-looking man, long red hair, pasty skin and ocean blue eyes. Not unlike Septus, actually. The man mutely sauntered over to the doppelganger and handed him the papers, shooting Nikalas a glance and then quickly looking away, almost as if scared.

"What is this?" The doppelganger demanded. He slowly flipped through the pages, then looked up and peered at Nikalas.

"Those damn Akordans will never learn will they?" The doppelganger roared as he kicked over a chair.

"What?" Nikalas asked, dismayed by the familiar term being used in a place that so closely resembled Earth.

"You're with them. I know it," the duplicate accused. Nikalas shook his head, feeling rather frustrated with Kell Si's lack of assistance. What was she waiting for? Why wasn't she helping him get out of this? That's when it dawned on him. The Lake of Purity. He couldn't be free until he purified himself. This doppelganger, he was the problem, he was the cause of the tar and he would need to be dealt with.

"You're right. They did send me. You see, they think you don't have a spine," Nikalas taunted. "They think you've gone soft."

The doppelganger angrily approached and withdrew a knife from a side holster. In a quick motion, he brought the blade to Nikalas' throat and grinned.

"Soft, huh?" He taunted.

"Yea, soft. You know. A pansy. Someone who can't get it done," Nikalas replied. He quickly lifted his hand and decked the clone in the face. The doppelganger stumbled back, grabbing his jaw and looking at Nikalas with dismay.

"How the hell did you?"

"It's easy. You're me. And I can't tie a knot for shit," Nikalas replied. He quickly grabbed his clone by the shirt and held him up. He grinned as he realized his awesome strength, no doubt a side effect of this place not actually being real.

"Look kid. Join me. We can wipe out the Akordans and run this city by ourselves. You don't need them."

Nikalas silently looked towards Kell Si, hoping for a gesture of instruction. She remained still, mute and unnoticed by the doppelganger.

"I don't know what you're talking about," Nikalas started. "But you're done running amuck in here. You're doing nothing but bringing this place down."

Suddenly, from behind him, a gun fired, sending a bullet careening towards him and striking him right in the gut. He fell, dropping the doppelganger and tumbled to the floor.

The doppelganger quickly gave him several firm kicks, each kick adding to the already excruciating pain from the bullet wound.

"Kell Si!" Nikalas cried out. She remained silent, offering no help. Kick after kick, he continued to be pummeled by his clone, unsure how much more he could take. *Get up*, he thought to himself. In a quick motion, he rolled to the left, dodging the kicks and promptly pulling himself up.

The two Nikalas stared at each other, hatred filling each of their eyes. Behind him, the sound of a gun cocking raced to his ears, preaching danger to him. Quickly, he leapt forward, grabbing his clone and pulling him in front of himself. The bullet tore through the both of them, but whereas Nikalas survived, the doppelganger exploded into a pile of black sand.

Suddenly the room began to shake, like a violent earthquake was taking place beneath their feet. Kell Si slowly emerged from the shadows, looking towards Nikalas with concern.

"What is that?" Nikalas questioned.

"Your anger," she replied. "It's collapsing."

All of a sudden, the walls began to crack, items fell from their shelves and glass windows began to explode inwards, peppering glass all over them.

"We have to get out of here," Kell Si advised. She promptly headed towards the exit and pushed it open. The effect of the earthquake was everywhere. It shook the entire city. Around them, buildings had begun to shake and sway, the unnatural motion prompting a monsoon of glass to fill the air.

"What do we do?" Nikalas asked, looking around in a panic.

"This is your mind," Kell Si replied. "You tell me."

Nikalas scanned the city streets, taking in the sights of the crumbling buildings. Something in the distance caught his eye. It was a door, one that looked oddly familiar.

"That way," he pointed. Together, the two of them ran through the hectic streets. All around them, the citizens screamed, running themselves mindlessly into walls and crumbling to the ground in piles of sand. Onwards they moved, getting closer and closer to the door. It was red, with faded paint that was chipping at the edges. As they got close, the building began to crumble, raining bricks and sand all over.

Almost there, Nikalas thought. He dodged a falling brick and then hurriedly grabbed the handle, turning it with utter determination.

Darkness filled his mind, and his thoughts went blank. Slowly, in the middle of a place vacant of all thoughts and sound, small specs of color began to appear. Before long the colors joined together, forming a landscape.

"Nikalas!" Kell Si yelled from the shore bed. He looked around and realized he was surrounded by fresh blue water on all sides. Ahead of him, just a few feet, was Kell Si. She smirked, clapping with excitement as he began to swim towards her.

"You completed your first test," she remarked as she pulled him from the water. Exhausted, he lay onto the grass, looking up towards the sky, watching the clouds prance around the sun with an energy similar to the one currently lurking within him.

"Hey!" He exclaimed. "The sky. I can see it."

He beamed as he continued to observe the serene landscape that surrounded them. In the skies above, a flock of phoenixes flew, their crimson feathers hung wildly from their elongated tails, demonstrating once again, the extreme beauty this place had to offer. In the waters around them, fish jumped about, snapping at curious neon green bugs that flew in peculiar swirl patterns. It was as though he had suddenly been whisked away into a painting, an expensive painting filled with many colors. He was finally seeing Cap Ti Mor, the real Cap Ti Mor. It was worth the wait. He had never seen a more beautiful place. *I wonder how Zanna's doing,* he thought to himself with a smile.

Chapter 8

Kit sat silently across from the strange man whom she had only met a few days prior. They rode together, in the back of a carriage being pulled by a couple fierce-looking horses. Across from them, the High Mother sat, silently reading a book. She remained silent, poring over the pages as the carriage continued to lead them towards uncertainty.

"You know," she finally said. "Your species always had a creative spark to them. Rather remarkable I must say."

Kit looked towards her captor and shrugged.

"You don't talk much do you?" High Mother asked.

Kit stared at her with intense eyes. If looks could kill, hers would be like a ninja, holding a sword while riding atop a t-rex.

"Don't worry. You don't have to talk to me. I don't need you to talk. I just need you to serve."

"I'll never serve you!" Kit exclaimed.

High Mother set the book down, a look of dismay crossing her face.

"I beg your pardon?" She paused. "You'll do exactly as I force you to. I thought you would've learned that by now."

She chuckled and reached into a handbag, pulling out a small bottle and taking a quick sip of its mysterious contents.

"What's that?" Kit questioned.

"Don't talk to her," her fellow captive snapped, spitting towards High Mother's feet.

"Why you ungrateful ingrate," High Mother roared, bringing the back of her hand across his face in a quick motion.

The harshness of the strike caused his glasses to fall off his face and into his lap. Slowly, Kit reached for them, picked them up, and placed them back on the man's face.

"How sweet of you," High Mother mocked. "Perhaps you really do care for him. I always assumed you were just using him."

Kit turned towards her with confusion.

"It's a fair thought," High Mother explained. The carriage came to an abrupt stop, and from above, footsteps could be heard as their driver dismounted. There was a soft knock on the door, as though the driver himself was nervous to be heard.

"We've arrived," the man said timidly from the other side of the metallic door.

"Well, let us out then," High Mother scoffed.

The door slowly pulled open, and as it did, the smell of ash and fire traveled inside, bringing with it a faint smoke.

"Get out," High Mother demanded. Both of them quickly did as commanded, taking a small step before arriving on the metallic ground. Kit looked down bewildered by the harshness of the ground beneath their feet. It wasn't like anything she had ever seen, not in Furlasia nor anywhere else. Surrounding them on all sides were sharp rocks and in the distance, there were fires burning that looked eternal and without cause. High Mother stepped out from the carriage, taking a deep breath and cracking a smile.

"Home sweet home," she sighed. Kit continued to look around until she saw a large castle. It loomed in the sky like a monolith, begging for attention. From the top of its tower, a large blue light shone, piercing the sky with its glorious light.

The entrance to the castle slowly opened, its squeak loud enough to be heard from quite a distance away. Emerging through the entrance, were two women, dressed in nothing, naked as the day they were born with ruby red skin. Kit's eyes widened with embarrassment as she observed the perverse nudity. Slaves. There was something different about them though, their bodies didn't have the traditional anatomy. There were no nipples on the tip of the breast. No reproductive organs at their front. It seemed almost as though they weren't real people at all. Symbols of the snake devouring the skull were tattooed all over their bodies. They approached slowly, with steps that were in sync.

"Welcome home Lord Gravi," they greeted, also in sync.

"Thank you, dears. Would you show our guests inside? Help them get comfortable. They will be staying with us for a while," High Mother explained.

"Where are we?" Kit questioned.

High Mother smiled as she looked around.

"It's not a place many know about. In fact, it's not even in Furlasia. Just on the outside of it actually. Sanlorus it's called," High Mother replied.

"Take them inside," she restated to her slaves.

The red-skinned women sauntered over to Kit and her fellow captive, taking them by the shoulder and guiding them slowly towards the castle entrance. High Mother followed, her posture and steps seeming decidedly more relaxed, each sway of her arms felt intentional, and with each step, the smugness painting her face grew more noticeable. This was her oasis, her secret; no one knew about this place, not even Septus. This was her world. Her place to rule, her place to be the goddess she once was. As they stepped inside, the two slaves continued to lead her prisoners away.

"It's good to be back, Jacob," High Mother smiled, looking back at her driver.

"May I take your coat?" the nervous servant asked. She silently nodded and began to shrug it off. Once he had relieved her of the bothersome furs, she strolled into the center of the room and laughed.

"Oh how I missed this place," she heckled. From her hands, emerged red clouds of dust. Looking up, to the top of the tower, she slowly rose, the dust carrying her high into the air. Taking one floor at a time, she floated, heading towards the very top, to a small opening.

As she neared the opening, the scent of fire and smoke crept into her senses. She had designed this on purpose. She wanted that connection to the land. She wanted the open window. She couldn't stand feeling confined, it reminded her too much of Zoralos. Made her feel like she was still under her father's thumb.

Through the opening she passed, coming to a gentle rest next to the large beam of light that soared high into the air. She paused next to it, placing her hand into its scorching hot energy. Quickly her skin began to cook off, floating up towards the sky in specks of dust. Once the flesh had dissolved, it was time for the bones. She continued to hold her hand firmly, letting the bones vanish, leaving nothing. With a cold, blank stare, she pulled her arm back. At the end of her arm, where a hand would normally be, was a ball of energy, it glowed and shimmered.

"Soon I will return. Soon I will get my revenge," she whispered. Her head tilted up, looking towards the sky, towards the darkness of the space above. The beam had so far proved useless. She had at one point hoped she could pierce the layer that kept her contained on Daulest. If she could break free of this wretched planet, perhaps she could find her way through Egsiar, and get clear of all this. That hadn't worked. Now it served as nothing more than a constant reminder of her goal. Only now, her eyes weren't looking towards the sky. They were aimed at the ground. That's where his door was. That's how Undr had exited the day he cast her out.

"And when I get back there. I'm going to burn that whole place to the ground."

She closed her eyes as she envisioned her brother, recalled the feud that had led her here. It seemed like yesterday, the fact that it had been almost a hundred years, was a hard pill to swallow indeed. Her eyes continued to focus on the ground at the foot of the tower. She didn't have a heart, not literally, but nevertheless, it was filled with hate. Hate that had been slowly adding up for decades. Suddenly she felt a tremor beneath her feet, subtle at first and then it began to increase its intensity. She grinned, watching as the tremors shook the ground.

"I hear you brother," she whispered.

The next morning, she found herself sitting in the middle of a chamber. Heavy, white gas surrounded her, engulfing her in its light grasp. As she continued to sit amongst it, she kept her focus on the task at hand. The war had started. Septus had so far been very useful, but he couldn't be in all places at once, and there was something she needed to see done very soon. The Arc Blade. It had been stolen from Ramir Keep. This was troublesome to ponder. For many years now, she had known of its placement inside the decadent palace, but had never bothered to concern herself with it due to its containment. But something about the theft caught her attention. Rumors of the uncannily silent thief had begun to circulate around the city. Who was this reticent bandit?

Behind her, there was a light knock on the door. It was subtle, most would've missed it, but her hearing was sharper than most.

"Come in," she called out, turning her chair to face the door. Slowly it pulled open, squeaking all the way, bringing with it dim light from the outer halls. From the river of light, emerged Jacob, he coughed as he stepped within, covering his mouth to shield it from the smoke. Slowly, he approached. With each passing minute, it became easier to see her.

"What is it, Jacob?" She questioned as smoke continued to surround her.

"My Lord," he paused. "Something strange is going on with our guests."

She rolled her eyes as she slowly rose from her seat. She was naked, nothing but her serpent bracelet decorated her body. As she neared, Jacob shook, the awkwardness of her appearance weighing on him like a ton of bricks.

"It's nudity Jacob," she explained. "Do not shy away from the natural form of your species. Now tell me, what is going on?"

He straightened up, trying his best to avert his eyes from the terrible sight.

"They appear to be talking to each other," he replied.

"Jacob my dear," she paused. "Tell me you didn't interrupt my process to tell me they are talking to each other. Of course, they are talking. They are sharing a cell."

"No My Lord. They aren't using words," he explained.

"Then how do you know they are talking?"

"I sensed it," he retorted.

She turned around, headed towards her chair and grabbed a robe. She slipped it on quickly and approached him once again.

"Let's go," she ordered.

They silently wandered the halls of the castle, making their way past many locked rooms, each of them containing slaves. All of them kneeling as they chanted silent whispers into the air. Hopeless souls with nothing to do but serve. All of them had been stripped of their clothing and turned into red skinned, sexless beings. As she passed their doors, each of them jumped to their feet, pressing their faces against the small glass windows they had been allowed.

"Praise Gravi," they cried out, in unison.

She continued her journey, ignoring the little bit of fame she had acquired until she reached her destination. Without lifting so much as a finger, she shoved the door to the cell open and stepped inside in a dramatic display of power.

"Jacob tells me you two like to talk," High Mother accused.

Kit rose to her feet, pulling the strange man up with her.

"Where is our son?" Kit demanded. High Mother beamed, approaching them with a newfound respect.

"Impressive," she whispered. "How have you managed to free yourself?" She turned towards Jacob and shot him a glance of question.

"How?" She investigated.

"I do not know My Lord," Jacob replied. "Perhaps it is their proximity to each other."

"Where is Nikalas?" Kit demanded. High Mother grinned, approaching Kit and placing a firm hand on her chin.

"Your tone," she whispered, squeezing the chin with a firm grip.

"Will not do." She turned towards Jacob. "It's time."

He bowed in understanding then quietly wandered toward the two captives. As he neared Kit, he glanced at her with hesitation, fear perhaps.

"Jacob," High Mother pestered. He shrugged his paranoia and then grabbed Kit by the arm. In a quick fury of emotions, the would be captive, kicked him in the knee, sending a resonating shatter through the room.

"Ahh!" He roared as he fell to the ground.

"Now now," High Mother proclaimed as she sent a funnel of red dust hurtling towards Kit. It grabbed her, restraining her arms and legs. Keeping her still and contained.

"That was not very nice."

As High Mother neared, Kit spat in her face with red, anger filled eyes.

"I remember everything now," Kit roared. "You kidnapped us. Forced us into your servitude. Stole us from our son."

High Mother carefully wiped the spit from her face and rolled her eyes.

"Oh please. Don't try to pretend you were parents of the year. You're the ones who were sneaking off to Furlasia at night, using the Tobin you stole from Hervott," She retorted.

She turned around, sending a funnel of red dust gently towards Jacob. It formed a padding around his knee and healed his wound almost instantly. He slowly rose, nodding his head in appreciation.

"What were you even doing? Why were you coming back here? You had a life and a son."

Tears came to Kit's eyes as she remembered her name. Trisna. She was once known as Trisna. Long before the war.

Long before she fled the land. She was Trisna. Memories of
their final night on Earth came rushing back like an angry
rapids hell bent on drowning her.

"Why come to such a dangerous place and risk all you
had with your son?"

Chapter 9

The night air was chilly, especially traveling at over twenty knots, which was certainly far more impressive than the little chugger of a boat Articus was used to. He stared at the vast dark canvass of water, as the air blew wildly through his hair. Next to him stood Sillimon, together they rode towards an uncertain destiny. So much had happened in the past few hours. They had met Jinn and Idrix and had learned of the long-standing mission of the Decoyers, a secret society dedicated to hunting rogue gods and demigods. They had killed many demigods in their days, but gods were different. They were harder to kill. And the big prize — Gravi — would be their most difficult mission yet.

They were heading towards a place they had never ventured nor had planned to. A place that would be full of dangers and perils. Adrasia. It lay just across The Peridian Sea. It was here that the rumored missing piece of the Arc Blade was hidden. It was here that Furlasia's last hope waited. But it wouldn't be easy, there would be many obstacles, and it would be well guarded by people who know a thing or two about conflict. That's why the Decoyers needed them. It was the ultimate heist, one that would need a large crew.

The journey across the Peridian Sea would normally take close to a week. But for them, with this mechanical monstrosity, it would only take a couple days. Which was good, it would be plenty of time for Methalda to heal and be ready to help. Jinn watched over her, keeping her company and offering little amounts of her power to help her get to full health. The Kajj didn't have magic or the gift of flight like the Arnouts did, but they did seem quite quick to heal, a trait they could gift to others when needed. This *gifting*, however, came at a cost, during the transfer, the host Kajj would be weakened and left vulnerable to damage. Luckily for Methalda, the middle of the sea seemed to be a safe place.

"I've never been on open water like this before," Sillimon remarked as he looked over the side of the deck and into the murky, chilled waters.

"Really?" Articus replied. "That's surprising."

"Why?" Sillimon questioned.

Articus shook his head as he looked towards the quaint man that was Sillimon. He hadn't known him long, barely a couple years, but it was long enough to learn what truly pushed this odd, nerdy man. Penny. She was his reason for doing all he did. The life of crime he had picked up was acquired so that he could give her a better life. *You're not doing this alone*, Penny had said. She herself, was no stranger to danger and was anything but soft-hearted. She had agreed to let him join the Society, but only if she went with him everywhere. They were a true pair. A perfect example of love.

"It just seems like you would've taken Penny out for some traveling. There's so much more to see in the world than just Furlasia," Articus replied.

He looked out towards the dark horizon.

"When this is over you should take her somewhere. There are boats that can be hired that cross the seas. They have private rooms and food and even dancing. She would love it."

Sillimon smiled as he pictured the two of them off on some romantic boat ride. He had thought about it before but had never really been sure he could afford it. It wasn't cheap crossing the seas. In fact, it was more reserved for the upper-class citizens. But perhaps after this, he would be able to afford it. Idrix, after all, had promised them a small fortune for their assistance. Whether or not she would deliver was up in the air, but Sillimon seemed keen to think so. He was always looking for the best in people. Always believing the world was inherently good.

"Excuse me," a voice said from behind. They quickly turned around to be greeted by one of the members of the Decoyers. Her name was Sam. She was younger—in her twenties, with short red hair and plenty of freckles. She was thin framed and looked as though a gust of wind could blow her away.

"Dinner is ready down below. Please join us. Idrix wants you to meet the rest of the team," she explained.

Articus nodded and looked towards Sillimon, who seemed rather excited by the idea of a hot meal. It had been awhile since they'd had one. All Silva had been able to offer them was bread, she had run out of supplies and didn't want to risk leaving them in her home unattended, and who could really blame her?

They followed the petite woman past the various lifeboats and anchors until they reached the entrance to the basement. The steps were narrow. On each side, were two very skinny handlebars and above the stairway hung a light. As the boat rocked against the many waves of the sea, they found themselves swaying back and forth, bumping into each side wall many times before reaching the bottom. She quietly led them down the narrow hall and upon reaching the center door on the right, she stopped and pushed it open. Instantly, the aroma of freshly prepared food filled their sense. It smelled like fish.

"Welcome," Idrix said in her normal raspy voice. She sat at the head of the table and next to her sat some kind of gas tank with a hose and a mask coming off the end of it.

"Have a seat."

Articus looked towards Methalda and smiled, she looked a lot better already. There was a color to her cheeks again, and her face looked less exhausted. He nodded towards Idrix, then quickly took a seat next to Methalda. The dining room was small. It contained a single table that had been secured to the floor and sat only about six. Behind each chair, only a few inches, in fact, was the wall. The room was dimly lit and stunk of coal, but it seemed like a luxury regardless. Yes, it was as good of a dining spot as one could hope for on a medium-sized boat.

In the center of the table sat a couple courses and sides. A large copper pot contained a stew of some kind. Next to that, a smaller platter held slices of uncooked meat. There were rolls and enough oranges for each person to have one. In no particular order, people began to reach in and grab food. The ladies seemed to receive preferential treatment, being served by a couple of the guys. Methalda smiled with appreciation as Articus handed her a full plate. Penny, on the other hand, had to elbow Sillimon, and give him a glare of dissatisfaction before he forked over his plate. Quietly, he began making a new one.

"Well, since we are all gathered," Idrix paused. "I think now would be a good time to introduce everyone."

Most ignored her as they forked food into their mouth.

"Stop eating for a moment and introduce yourselves. We will start in order of seating. Say your name, where you're from and what brought you here today." Still, everyone continued eating.

"NOW!" Idrix roared, her voice filled the air like a thundercloud. Promptly causing unanimous fork drops.

"We will start with you," she pointed to her left, to a man with eyes that were as wide as they were tall, his skin was hairy and his cheeks sunk in. A Delopar, the very one that had first introduced them to this new strangeness.

"My name is Dorrin. I am from the outskirts of Morlay and I came here to seek vengeance for my mother, who was raped by a demigod."

Idrix nodded and pointed to the next. A woman with tan skin, green eyes, and curly, eighties style hair.

"I'm Kadeen. I am from a small village outside Cristol. My son was taken by the High Mother and forced into her service. I will see her dead."

Next, she pointed to a slender man, who stood in the corner, holding his plate as he ate. His skin was blotchy, riddled with eczema and his head was crudely shaved.

"Adam, I came from the very place we are heading to now. Adrasia. When I was a boy, I migrated to Furlasia with my family. I met Idrix at a Penecoth gathering and have been her friend since."

"My name is Dajreem," a young man with dark skin, short hair and cheerful brown eyes said.

"I came from Newlarian. A small city, hidden in stone, just outside Solarian. I am here to get revenge for the slaughter and ruin of the once great city of Solarian."

"Jinn. I am from a place that's far from here. Penute. It's a small village where the last of my people dwell. It's on a small island just off the Norh Sea."

Next, came the young woman who had shown them to the dining room.

"My name is Sam," she informed. "I don't do much here. I mostly just make sure everyone is on task and that food is provided."

"She's being modest," Dorrin inserted. "None of this would be possible if it weren't for her contributions. A team is only as good as its help."

He looked at her with a smile.

Idrix paused, looking at the newcomers and pointed to Articus.

"And you," she said. "Why are you here?"

He set his fork down and looked towards Methalda, a heaviness filling his heart as thoughts of Josiah rushed to his mind.

"For years now, I considered myself part of something bigger than myself. A conduit of hope. Helping to look out for the smaller man that was so often ignored by the kingdom. But soon I realized, there is no hope. Hope is a luxury that has been stolen by the dark forces that live in the shadows, poisoning Furlasia." He stopped and looked towards Penny and Sillimon.

"I'm here for the cure."

Methalda looked around the room as she realized her time had finally arrived.

"Josiah was my best friend. I loved him. He sacrificed himself for the greater good without even realizing it. I'm angry. Angry at your deception of us," she looked at Jinn, and her eyes narrowed.

"Angry that I am here and Josiah is not. I am here to avenge him."

Idrix cocked her head with concern as she looked towards Articus. Her response brought more questions than answers.

"And what of you two?" She asked, pointing towards Penny and Sillimon.

"We are here because the Society is a team. We don't leave each other hanging in times of need. We will travel to the ends of the world if it means staying together," Penny replied.

Idrix nodded in satisfaction.

"That's an excellent answer and a very key mentality to the Decoyers. We are each a finger on a hand. Separate, we are weak and breakable. Together, we are a fist. It takes a fist to fight injustice," Idrix explained. She looked around the room, glancing at Jinn and the two nodded at each other.

"We would like you to join our team. We want you to become part of the solution. We grieve for your loss, we really do. Jinn said that Josiah was always very kind to her. If we are to best avenge him, we must work as a team. Join us. Bind with us. Together, we can destroy Gravi. Together, we can save Daulest from the evil that threatens to destroy it."

Articus looked around at his fellow Society members and nodded.

"We are with you," he stated.

"Good. That's very promising. I see this as an important step in the right direction. The devil has been walking amongst us. Preaching lessons of love while secretly believing in hate. We here in this room will stop her," Idrix paused and looked towards Methalda.

"Welcome to the Decoyers."

Chapter 10

Emlin stood frozen, dread in her eyes, as she watched Thadeus fall to the ground in a lifeless slump. Behind the former general stood, Broli. Her former friend who had been plunged back into the world as an undead abomination in order to fight for her former lover, Septus Crane. If that wasn't a mouthful, she didn't know what was.

"Broli," Emlin cautiously raised a hand. "You don't want to do this. This isn't you."

The leviathan of a man walked towards her, paying little heed to her pleads of reason.

"Your Highness!" Morti called out. He quickly raised his Beacon and began to fire a steady and focused beam of energy. Quickly, Broli reached down, grabbed the remains of Thadeus and launched them towards the Vanguard soldier in a surprisingly fast bit of movement. The slain corpse crashed into him, promptly causing the beam from the Beacon to angle up, shooting blindly into the sky. He fell. The weight of Thadeus' lifeless body kept him pinned.

Emlin lurched forward in a panic and quickly dove to the ground between Broli's legs. In one quick motion, she scooped up Thadeus' discarded daggers. With one in each hand, she sliced at Broli's legs, then gave herself a firm push with her feet and scooted back. Broli paid little mind to the mild scratches he had incurred. Instead, he turned around, just in time to catch Emlin off guard as she climbed to her feet. His fist soared toward her with breakneck speed, crashing into her chest and sending her flying back a few feet.

"Ugh," she bellowed as she hit the ground with a firm thud, kicking up a bit of dirt as she landed. On the ground she lay, intense pain radiating in her chest. Slowly, she tried to sit up, but the pain was too intense. It held her still.

In the distance, Morti continued to struggle to free himself from the weight of Thadeus' still corpse, and he needed to. Broli approached. Death neared with a blank stare and two big fists.

"Ahh!" He roared out as he gave Thadeus a firm push, the body lazily rolled off and came to a stop. Wasting no further time, Morti began to run back towards the rest of the Vanguard army, paying Emlin no further mind. What was he supposed to do against a beast of this size? As he continued his retreat, he found himself pushing through ghouls, knocking them down like a bowling ball to a collection of pins. It seemed to be going well. His men were just ahead, and there he would reach safety. Without warning, however, a strong arm gripped him. His retreat came to an abrupt stop as a mostly decayed Akordan held him tight in its grasp. His fist found its head promptly, over and over he pummeled the creature, to no end. His attempts at escape came to a quick end as the beast opened its mouth, sending a beam of ice straight towards him. From the face down, he became a frozen block. A remnant of a once honorable man.

"Keep moving forward!" Sabasio called out as he continued to take aim at various foes. His aim was near perfect. Headshots, all of them. None of the ghouls was a match for him. The Vanguards continued to push forward, wiping out many of the dead foes with headshots. Those that weren't headshots however, quickly rejoined the attack force. As they continued to push towards the center, towards the entrance of Cristol, Sabasio found himself pausing in shock. In front of him stood the frozen remains of Morti. His heart began to race as he began to fear the worst. The Queen. Was she safe?

He gave his men zero warning as he took off, running down the field in search of his number one priority. Morti had failed. Could that mean Emlin had perished as well? His fears were further amplified as he noticed the remains of his former general. He blasted a clearing, wiping out a dozen ghouls and then quietly knelt to Thadeus' side.

"My friend," he whispered as he placed his hand gently atop the general's vacant eyes.

"This time I couldn't save you." He quickly stood up and fired a precise shot at Broli who was silently approaching. The shot pierced the skull quite perfectly. The once deadly ghoul fell to the ground in an instant, tripping another ghoul in the process.

"Emlin!" Sabasio called out to the air.

On the cold, blood-stained ground, Emlin continued to lie, the pain radiating throughout her chest with intensity. She could hear Colonel Sabasio in the distance calling her persistently. She had wanted to respond, but each time she opened her mouth, she could find no words. Finally giving up, she forced herself to roll over. In a bit of luck, she was able to reacquire the daggers Thadeus had dropped. As she finally found her feet, she began swinging the blades about madly, slicing ghouls here and there, while not actually killing any of them. The daggers were light. She had seen him use them once before and his aim had been impressive. With those daggers in his hands, Thadeus was as skilled as any marksman with a Beacon.

She looked forward, taking a step back for leverage and then launched one of the daggers at a Terrian ghoul that was hastily making an approach. Fiona soared through the air, leaving in its trail a slight whisper and then came to a sudden stop in the creature's skull, just between the eyes in fact. Emlin gawked in dismay as the creature collapsed to the ground.

"Wow," she whispered.

She turned, looking towards another and then launched Gertrude. Again, the blade found its home in a skull, a human ghoul this time.

In shock, she looked at her hands, trying to figure out what had just happened.

"Whoa," she whispered under her breath. Like an Amazonian warrior, she let out a mighty roar, then charged towards a couple ghouls. With ninja-like reflexes, she brought her foot up, swinging it with a round motion, and knocked a couple ghouls down. She had bought herself a little space, not much, but enough to retrieve the two daggers. Re-armed, she turned, looked back at Cristol and started fighting through the mass.

Adrenaline coursed through her veins like a toxic poison, fueling her, giving her a surge of energy like she had never known. It was hatred that was fanning the flames of war. Her hatred of Septus, and all he had caused. Cristol wasn't far now, she could hear the mechanical hiss of the Tin Men in the distance, she was close, her chance to end this was almost in hand.

***

Laying in the cool and slightly damp grass was as comforting as it could ever be. Most women would've scoffed at the idea of getting filthy and damp, but not Emlin. She cared not about appearance. She continued to take deep breaths as Septus caressed her chin with his soft hands. He moved over her smooth skin with delicate precision, smiling all the while. When he reached her neck, he leaned his head in and gave it a gentle kiss.

"That tickles," she blushed. Septus quickly pulled back, his cheeks turning red with embarrassment.

"Oh," he paused. "I'm sorry."

"Maybe if you go a little lower," she replied with a grin. He blushed for a moment, then swiftly brought his lips to her neck, a bit lower this time. Slowly, he pulled down on her dress, revealing just the top of her cleavage and gave it a couple gentle kisses.

"I'm ready," she whispered.

He shot up, taken back by the remark.

"Are you sure?" He replied. "We don't have to."

"Do you want to or not?" Emlin sternly rebutted.

"Of course I do," he replied.

"Well then don't act so bashful," she smirked. Wasting no further time with debate, he motioned for her to sit up, once she had, he swiftly unzipped the rear zipper on her elegant, yet simple red gown. He smiled as her back came into view; her skin looked so clear, free of any blemishes apart from a small birthmark on the left side of her spine. She carefully began to slide the top down until nothing but her pure form was revealed. With heavy breaths, she turned towards him. He shot his eyes down, abashed at the sight of her breasts.

"Hey," she whispered, bringing her index finger under his chin. "It would be easier if you looked at me." She calmly reached down and lifted his shirt, hesitating for a moment as she brought it over his head. His chest was peppered with small amounts of ginger hair, it was sporadically placed. Freckles decorated his skin, everywhere except around his nipples. She smiled as he looked down once again.

"You're perfect," she smiled. He looked down at his bare chest and grinned as he rubbed his stomach.

"No," he paused. "You're perfect."

She smirked as she leaned closer, then, as if trying to be sneaky, she planted a kiss on his lips.

"I love you," she whispered, with her lips still pressed against his.

***

Her eyes were filled with persistence as she continued to push past the large masses of undead foes. She killed where she had to, but for the most part, she tried to navigate past them. Even with the unusually useful daggers, she knew it was best to try to not take on any more conflict than she needed.

After what seemed like eternity, she finally caught up to the Tin Men. Their mechanical blades came down against their foes with a force so great it threatened to crack the very ground beneath them. There were hundreds of them, all of them seemed unstoppable, but to her dismay, dozens of slain soldiers littered the ground. Her eyes scanned the area as she continued to seek Septus, he had to be close, she was sure of it. Beneath her feet, the ground trembled, she had never seen war, only heard of it, but this seemed more tumultuous than she had expected. In the skies above, Arnouts could be seen, some of them living, many of them dead. They flew towards one another, firing energy towards each other with violent speed.

A thunderous rumble in the far distance seized her attention. Turning her head, she looked towards Cristol in time to see a massive explosion of energy.

"Septus," she whispered.

Her eyes widened as she turned her focus to the path ahead, she needed to get through, but the battlefield was far thicker here than it had been before. There were at least two ghouls to each Tin Man, and the numbers seemed to be getting worse. Each ghoul that didn't receive a killing blow to the head, quickly got back up, occasionally taking out a soldier or two before being officially dealt with.

She lifted the daggers and inhaled a deep, protracted breath. Each moment she spent immersed in the conflict, the worse she could feel the sting of anxiety. It poked at her like a branch, a branch covered in thorns, each thorn cutting just a little bit deeper. The sensation was inescapable. There was only one cure for this pain, only one way to quell the nagging angst that threatened to break her. She had to move forward. Her safety be damned. This war was bigger than any one person.

Gertrude and Fiona continued to aid her passage, taking out ghouls with considerable ease. But the deeper she got, the more dire the situation became. Behind her lingered a couple Tin Men, no doubt they recognized her and decided to provide some security. She had no complaints. With the help of the pair of soldiers, they continued making their way past the ghouls, avoiding a fair many of them.

To her left, a loud growl filled the air, traveling to her ears and bringing with it a chill. An icy blast frantically hit her legs, locking her in place. It burned, the temperature of the ice was far below that of normal ice, frostbite would take mere minutes, total loss of the limbs would follow. Quickly she began stabbing at the ice with the daggers, it was difficult, but slowly it began to chip away.

A loud thump echoed behind her. Turning nothing but her head, she caught a horrifying glimpse of a skeletal giant. It inched closer to her, knocking down Tin Men and ghouls alike.

"Oh no," a soldier cried out as the giant's large foot came crashing down upon him. His blood and guts quickly littered the ground, oozing from underneath the giant's foot like a splattered jelly sandwich.

"Fuit," Emlin whispered to herself as she continued to chisel away at the icy constraints. A few Tin Men quickly approached the giant, swinging their swords with forceful precision. As their blades struck, tiny pieces of bone fragments flew into the air. It was an honest effort but unfortunately served very little good. With a furious swipe of its mighty arms, the giant knocked over a few of the soldiers before grabbing one and lifting it into the air.

"Take it down!" The soldier cried out as he found himself face to face with the beastly doomsday servant. Once again, the Tin Men continued to chop at the giant's feet, but it was too late. Like a pitcher on the mound, the giant rolled its arm back and gave the soldier a firm toss, sending him crashing into the distance.

"Come on," Emlin whispered as she fidgeted with the ice. She continued jabbing a few more times until at last enough had been chiseled away to free her. She was free, but the cold had done its damage. At her first step, she fell, face first, into the dirt.

As she lay, contemplating the seriousness of the situation, that's when she felt it. A firm grip, it grabbed her, wrapping all around her like a harness and lifted her into the air.

Chapter 11

The night sky did its best to display what little light it had to offer. The moon was hidden this night. Clouds blanketed its light, trying its best to keep the glow all to itself. All around the city, doors were being closed, candles were being lit, and prayers were being whispered. Kell Si slowly led Nikalas back to Fal Mor, the tower where he had been invited to dwell. It was the home of the elders. The most sacred place in the whole city.

As they strolled along the desolate streets, past the lanterns and the ponds that had been placed randomly, Nikalas found himself marveling at his newfound ability to really see things. For so long everything had seemed made of clay, including himself. But after today's test, the effect appeared to vanish. All was how it truly was. The buildings were organic, or at least they seemed to be. At all times they moved, back and forth, in small subtle movements. The sky— it was dark but that didn't seem to hide the details. Each cloud was as easy to spot as a red car in a lot full of yellow. Each creature that chose to travel at night was so vividly clear that one could almost see the very soul within them.

Kell Si paused as she realized she had lost track of her apprentice. Nikalas had stopped to admire a small glowing flower that grew taller as he neared it. She watched with curiosity as he sneakily neared the exotic plant. Holding out his hand, he gently rubbed his knuckles against the petals. He smiled as he noticed small amounts of neon specks littering the top of his hand. As he continued to rub the petals, the plant transformed, turning into a large bird with glowing wings and an elongated beak.

"Hey there," Nikalas whispered, rubbing the bird on the top of its head. The bird whimpered and lowered its head, rubbing it against his knuckles and continuing to simper.

Quietly, Kell Si neared, watching Nikalas with interest as he quickly adjusted to the strangeness he had just witnessed.

"What is it?" He asked in adoration.

"It's a Fadril," she replied as she knelt down. Even at this level, she still towered above Nikalas.

"They're shapeshifters. During the day, they look like birds, but at night, they can take on many different appearances."

A loud bell suddenly rang in the distance, stealing their attention and sending the Fadril taking off into the night sky. Nikalas slowly rose to his feet, looking back towards Fal Mor Tower.

"It seems it's time for dinner," Kell Si noted as she began strolling towards the looming tower.

With Nikalas in tow, she approached the building and came to a pause. She pressed her hands gently against the chilled matter that made up the building. It flinched, rippling away as if to flee the warmth of her skin. She smiled, the beauty of Cap Ti Mor never wore thin, even for those that had lived there all their lives. And she had. For twenty-six years, she had wandered this strange land. Grown with it, become bonded to it, loved it, and embraced it. And yet still, she never found herself taking any of it for granted. Each morning when she awoke, she found herself feeling a new appreciation for her home. She had heard stories aplenty of the other worlds — of Furlasia, and its dull scenery and twisted minds.

"Come here Nikalas," she whispered with a motion. He promptly approached and paused next to her. Slowly she reached down, grabbed his hand and brought it up towards the organic matter. He flinched.

"Do not feel pause. There is nothing to feel wary about. This is *Tinlen*, a gift from the fathers and mothers. It will not hurt you," Kell Si comforted. Without awaiting a response, or a sign of approval, she lifted and touched his hand to its surface. As before, it flinched, creating a ripple that glowed blue.

"Interesting," she whispered.

"Does it normally do that?" Nikalas questioned.

"Yes. But not for your kind." She continued to silently observe as he began to move his hands across the surface, having fun with it. It overflowed, spilling over his fingers, and over the back of his hand. With each movement, more blue hue continued to radiate.

"That's pretty cool," Nikalas laughed.

Wasting no further time, Kell Si pushed through, pulling Nikalas behind with a quick motion. As he reached the other side, he shuddered.

"You've traveled through this material before haven't you?" Kell Si grinned.

"Yea. But it's cold. I'll never get used to it. I don't get why you guys don't just build doors."

Kell Si smiled and proceeded forward.

"Doors are designed to keep people out Nikalas. Gnomes are always welcoming people in. How would one make new acquaintances if we put doors in people's faces?"

Together they approached a familiar large bubble. It was the very same one he had first entered with Talos when he had first arrived. Strangely enough, this strange orb of clear, soap-like material, behaved very much like an elevator. But it didn't just travel up and down, it also moved side to side. It was paramount because each floor in the building floated. There were no attached elements like in a traditional building.

"Are you ready to dine?" She asked, turning towards him with a serious expression.

"Oh yea," he happily replied.

Roros stood silently, draped with concern as he and the other elders looked at a large pool of water that contained a vision. In its ripples, they saw war. Terrible war. The war in Furlasia. Hand over mouth, the Gnome elders continued to observe the dark scene, offering very little in the way of reactions. Their eyes darted back and forth with rapid motions, quickly, like REM. In the vision, Emlin was being carried by a giant skeletal creature, while she screamed and protested. In the distance, there was an explosion of energy, magical energy. The skies were filled with Arnouts and deceased Phoenixes that somehow still managed to maintain their flames. Finally, Roros pressed his hand into the pool and waved it side to side, clearing the water of the vision.

"So it's started," El Dir whispered.

"Yes," Roros paused. "It would seem so."

He turned towards the others and let out a sigh.

"We took too long to bring Nikalas here," Fal bluntly stated. Fal was perhaps one of the oldest Gnomes in all of Cap Ti Mor. Her importance could not be overstated. In fact, the very building they occupied had been named after her. It was her that first decided the Gnomes should pay closer attention to the wars of the outside worlds. She was, like all Gnomes, rust skinned and quite tall. Her face had very few distinguishing features apart from wrinkles. Her eyes looked as empty as anyone's would after surviving for as long as she had. She was aged, but still quite spry.

"I don't believe that," Roros objected. "I believe Nikalas arrived here at the precise time he should have."

"But the war has started," Lorid Fen replied.

"Yes," Roros nodded. "It has. But we were never going to prevent it from starting. That was inevitable. But we can still help Furlasia, by helping Nikalas."

Lorid solemnly looked towards the pool and sighed.

"Do we tell him? Do we tell him the war has started?" She asked.

"Absolutely not," Roros sternly replied. "We must not allow him to have any knowledge of what is going on. If he finds out, he'll try to leave. And he's not ready yet. If he leaves now, he'll die, and we will have failed."

He slowly looked around the room, the seriousness in his eyes left little room for argument.

"Very well," Fal replied. "But you'll be the one to explain to him why his friends have died."

Roros nodded his head and bowed in acceptance. To him, the positives of this plan far outweighed the negatives.

"Tomorrow, I will train with Nikalas personally. It's time for him to learn who his true father is," Roros added.

The others in the room all nodded in agreement, before looking back to the pool of water. Silence filled the room like a cloud of poison.

***

Nikalas cheerfully took a bite of what looked to be some kind of dessert. It was red, fluffy and danced on his plate, not unlike jello in fact.

"You know we have something like this where I come from," he noted as he took a bite.

Next to him, Kell Si carefully used her powers to summon the food towards her mouth. The table was much too short for her height and bringing herself down to the plate seemed too much of a bother.

"I can't wait to learn that," Nikalas commented.

"You will, soon enough I'm sure," she replied.

Together, with few words said, they continued to finish their dinner. It was just the two of them. The room had been promptly emptied as soon as they had entered. It almost seemed to Nikalas like he had some kind of virus or cooties, he had never seen people scamper away from him before. He didn't mind though; the Gnomes were still a sight to get used to. A whole room full of them, well, that would be quite an adjustment indeed.

After the festivities had been properly devoured and all plates had been placed in the proper disposal location, Kell Si motioned for him to follow her. Nikalas shrugged, taking the suggestion with an optimistic excitement. They stepped into the hall, and she quietly led him past the various doors. As he continued to follow, he could feel exhaustion setting in. Sleep would soon find him. It had been a trying day for sure.

"This is your room," she explained as she stopped in front of a room that had nothing but a curtain for privacy. He looked at her and smirked. Of course he couldn't get a door. They didn't believe in them.

"Oh," she paused as she looked at his sarcastic expression. Quickly she waved her hands in front of the curtain, and with no effort at all, a door manifested.

"That should be more to your liking."

Nikalas shrugged and offered a wink.

"I'll see you tomorrow then?" He asked.

Kell Si shook her head.

"You will be making rounds with Roros tomorrow," she informed.

"Ah, well when will I see you again?"

"Very soon." And with that, she turned and made her way towards the bubble elevator they had taken earlier.

Nikalas pushed open the door and was greeted by the familiar sight of Fawn. He flew towards him happily and hovered at eye level.

"I missed you too," Nikalas smiled. As he held out his arm, Fawn happily climbed aboard and together they wandered over to the bed. It was large, a king-size from the looks of it. The sheets were red satin, and there was no shortage of pillows. There was even a television in the corner that had been mounted on the walls, although he couldn't imagine what the channels would be. As he continued to look around the room, it became very clear that it had been tailored just for his liking. Obviously, the Gnomes were quite familiar with humans and their habits.

He set Fawn on the bed and scanned the nearby dresser and desk for a remote. There was none to be seen. He began searching each drawer one at a time. Clothes that looked brand new and straight from Earth filled each shelf. There was everything he could ever need: socks, underwear, pants, and shirts. He beamed as he continued scanning drawers.

"Oh my," he paused as he pulled open a drawer that had a stack of magazines inside. On the front cover was a woman with large breasts kneeling in front of a naked man.

"They thought of everything, didn't they?" Nikalas laughed as he looked towards Fawn. He shook his head and pushed the drawer shut. As he pulled open the next drawer, his eyes grew wide with excitement. There it was, the remote.

He quickly pulled it from its nestled abode and plopped onto the bed next to Fawn. With an aim and a quick press of the button, the reflective screen came to life. On the screen stood a man on a stage with an orange spray tan and awful looking hair. He stood with his mouth wide open and a crummy trench coat as he held his hand up.

"I swear to uphold the values of America," the man said.

Nikalas turned and looked towards Fawn.

"Yeah right," he rolled his eyes. Quickly, he changed the channel and was suddenly greeted with explosive sound effects. On the screen, a man was running with a woman down a crowded street as fire chased them in the distance.

"That's better," he smiled.

The following day started just as he would've started any other day back home. Lying in bed and trying his best to recall his dreams. His parents only existed there now. He had to hold onto them. The dreams were all he had now. Looking around the room served as a reminder that he wasn't back home. That he wasn't in the Hall of Wizards. No, he was in a whole new place yet again. Life, it seemed, had become a literal journey lately. Lying next to him was Fawn, he was the one constant since arriving in Furlasia. He was the one thing he could count on. Like a dog, Fawn was already growing quite hastily, his new legs were almost fully grown, and soon he would be walking on four legs instead of just perching onto two. After that, it would only be a matter of time before he was rideable.

"Hey buddy," Nikalas whispered as he rubbed the back of Fawn's ears. The adolescent Grimwort gave a slight whimper and rolled over.

"Hey, if I have to get up so should you." Fawn continued to lie stagnant, ignoring his master's suggestions. Nikalas shrugged and stepped down onto the cold stone floors. The instant sensation of a chill quickly shot through his body.

"At least one thing is constant in my life," he laughed.

Approaching a wardrobe, he pulled it open to find something he never thought he'd see again. The clothes hanging inside were just like his back home. Baggy pants and all. Next to them, however, was his wizard attire.

"Decisions decisions," he whispered. His eyes darted back and forth as he weighed the options. He truly did long for his old attire but at the same time, he knew it would only make him look foolish in a land where everyone dressed with dignity and class.

"Fine," he sighed as he reached for the wizard attire.

Once he had gotten dressed, he stepped into the hall. Standing there, waiting patiently and creepily was Roros. He looked like a man with a purpose. He bowed as he glanced at Nikalas and Fawn.

"You're with me today Nikalas," Roros explained.

Nikalas faked a smile as best he could.

"Great," he replied. "So what kind of test am I going to have today?"

"There is no test," Roros replied. "Today, we search for knowledge and truth."

Nikalas silently shrugged and without any further conversation, they navigated their way towards the elevator bubble. Fawn chirped happily, as they began their descent from the upper floors of the tower. As the young Grimwort continued to grow, so did its chirp grow deeper. It now sounded more like a cross began a bird chirp and a young dog. It wasn't exactly the cutest combination of sounds.

The bubble reached the bottom floor with its usual haste, and Roros quickly stepped out into the lobby of the tower. As Nikalas followed suit, he caught a glimpse of Kell Si. She appeared to be engaged in a secretive conversation with one of the elders. He tried his best to make out what they were discussing, but for the life of him, he couldn't.

"Nikalas," Roros spoke softly. "Where we are going today, it might be best to leave Fawn behind. It won't be a place for such a young Grimwort."

Nikalas turned as Fawn let out a sigh of disappointment. Roros slowly led them through the exit and out into the fields where a young Gnome stood with a gathered group of Grimworts. As Fawn saw the others, his disappointment suddenly turned to excitement. Before they even reached the crowd, Fawn had already jumped from his shoulder and joined the others.

"How are the younglings doing?" Roros asked of the trainer.

"Exceptional. Many of them will soon be ready," the young trainer replied. She was far shorter than most Gnomes, likely due to her age although Nikalas couldn't determine how old she was just at a glance. Her skin was a lighter shade than the taller Gnomes though. He figured that had to be a giveaway.

"Take good care of him," Nikalas added from a distance. The trainer smiled and slowly approached, extending a hand out for a greeting.

"The name's Mar Ni Fal," she informed as they locked grips.

"Of course I'll take good care of him. Training Grimworts is what I do every day. He'll be fine."

Nikalas nodded and slowly leaned to the right, glancing at her and Fawn, who was already playing excitedly with the other Grimworts.

"We will be back in a few hours," Roros bowed and turned around. Nikalas shot one last glance towards his young pet and proceeded to turn around.

They wandered quietly through the ever-moving grass and returned to the stone path. There was little to be said as Nikalas followed the strange being known as Roros. Soon enough, they had entered the city district. Here the buildings were quite tall and far more impressive than any he had seen in Furlasia. Each one, like the tower of Fal Mor, was covered in the same organic material.

Roros waved at various citizens as they continued making their way down the busy streets. Everyone here moved with a purpose. They all seemed quite focused and interested in Nikalas. It was hard not to feel objectified as the Gnomes all continued to observe him with an almost awe-like expression. He kept his head down, and his eyes remained fixed on his feet and the stones beneath them. Ahead, he could just make out the heels of Roros, so he knew he was still on the right path.

They turned a corner, and suddenly, Nikalas found himself standing in the middle of an empty alley. Buildings lined it the whole way down, but as for the alley, there was nothing to be seen. And yet, there was something interesting about it. It was wide, and in the middle, it almost had a square shape. On the ground, in the middle of the strangeness was a large square brick that glowed and stood slightly higher above the ground than the others. Roros walked over to it and came to a stop.

"Come here, Nikalas," he instructed.

Now what? Nikalas thought to himself as he wandered to the stone. Without needing further directions, he stood atop the brick and looked towards Roros.

"When you first got here Nikalas," Roros began. "I told you that your parents were not dead and that the man you know as your father was not your real father."

"I remember," Nikalas replied, his heart beginning to beat faster.

"I have a request for you Nikalas," Roros paused. "We are going to take a journey. A journey that will give you the answers you have been seeking and in doing so, will help you understand who you really are."

Nikalas looked Roros in the eyes and gulped. He didn't know what to expect but he couldn't help but feel that what he was about to learn would shake the very fabric of his existence. Already he had been told that he was, in fact, from Furlasia all along. A truth that for some reason was fairly easy to accept. But would his father's true identity be as easy? What truths would he learn about his mother? It was time to find out.

He solemnly nodded and turned his gaze to the ground. Suddenly, the stone surface beneath his feet began to glow, emitting a cyan hue. It grew brighter and brighter by the second, blinding Nikalas completely. He quickly closed his eyes, but it was too late. The light had left him seeing nothing but white.

$\mathcal{C}$hapter 12

Kunklestick's staff sent a searing hot streak of white energy crashing towards Agavordis. It was met with quick resistance. As usual, an orb formed between the two spells and began to howl as it spun at breakneck speed. Next to him, Zanna swung her wand, trying with utmost persistence to hit Vigil, but she was a slippery foe indeed. Her icy form allowed her to slide around rather quickly, and this made her troubling to deal with. She continued to dodge Zanna's attacks, all the while sending ice shards flying towards her. Zanna could hardly keep up with the nagging pieces of ice that continually hurtled towards her, some of them even made contact, offering a small cut here or there.

Elsewhere, Didorumpus slowly sat up from the blood-soaked ground. He was distant from the others, Herratia had given him a powerful shove and sent him careening away. Luckily, he was able to produce a quick spell that absorbed some of the impact from the fall. As he slowly climbed to his feet, he scanned the battlefield around him. Herratia was nowhere to be seen.

"Where are you witch?" Didorumpus taunted. A bright light suddenly appeared from behind him. Her attack was swift, claws slashed quickly across his back, ripping his robes and digging into his flesh. He promptly turned around, grunting through the pain, but she had already vanished. Luckily, however, his maneuver did afford him the opportunity to be greeted by a Terrian ghoul who was charging towards him with berserkly swinging arms.

"Inginimo!" Didorumpus exclaimed, sending a streak straight into the head of the creature. It fell to the ground, with smoke drifting from the hole in its head up towards the chilly air. Next came an Akordan ghoul. This one was a tad trickier to deal with, as it approached armed with a typical Akordan blade, which was odd considering its lack of motor functions. He quickly brought his staff up, blocking the blade as it swung down above him. With him distracted, Herratia quickly seized the opportunity and came in for another swipe. Just as before, her claws dug deep, this time in his right arm.

"Ahh!" He roared as he dropped his arm, and dodged to the left. The Akordan's blade clashed against the ground, a narrow miss that would've likely rendered him headless. With his body in much pain, he raised his staff, bringing a hot beam of energy into the creature's chest, and with a quick upwards maneuver, sliced the creature's head in half. It was a gory sight, to say the least.

"Your spell is weaker, old man," Agavordis taunted as the orb between them continued to edge closer to Kunklestick. He was right, this head-on spell wouldn't work. Kunklestick madly lifted his staff towards the heavens, sending the two beams soaring into the skies above. With speed quicker than a man at his age could be expected to have, he charged at Agavordis, swinging his staff and knocking him upside the head.

Agavordis fell to the ground as pain radiated in the side of his head.

"You idiot!" Agavordis expelled. He quickly brought his legs out and tripped Kunklestick, bringing him down to the ground, and face to face with himself.

"Ugh," Kunklestick grunted as the impact traveled throughout his left side. On his lower leg, he could feel a slight sting, and as he looked towards it, he noticed a large rock underneath his shin. It wasn't broken, he was sure of, but there would most certainly be a bruise. Their eyes met, and as Kunklestick looked to his attacker, he couldn't help but see clear similarities in appearance to his former pupil. The ginger hair, the freckles, the pale skin. Everything seemed so remarkably similar, everything except the eyes. Even in his angriest days, Drachen never had red eyes. In what was certainly his least prideful moment yet, Agavordis spat at Kunklestick's face and then quickly rolled away.

"Disgusting," Kunklestick groaned, wiping his face and then standing up with frustration and contempt.

"Who even does that? We may be fighting, but we can at least show some dignity," he added.

Agavordis stared at him with a blank, emotionless face, slowly lifting his hand up and revealing a green ball of light. Kunklestick sighed, then gripped his staff, vanishing like a cloud in the wind.

"Coward!" Agavordis roared as he angrily scanned the field. Try as he might, there was no sign of the elderly wizard. He was just about to vent his aggression to another when an abrupt beam of energy came crashing into him, and like a lasso, contained him.

"That ought to slow you down," Kunklestick grinned, reappearing just a few feet behind him. Agavordis shook his head and then proceeded to phase downwards, into the ground like a ghostly apparition.

"Umm," Kunklestick muttered with surprise.

"Foolish child," Vigil taunted. "Did you really think you had what it takes to take on a servant of Undr? His power flows through my veins." She brought her hand firmly across Zanna's face, then quickly grabbed her by the neck. Her icy skin instantly left a rash, a burn that radiated and stung not unlike a burn from a flame. Zanna's heart ran rampant with consternation as she stared into the ice-filled eyes of Vigil. With no wand at her side, she was powerless to do anything.

"Evil witch!" A voice suddenly called out. From amongst the chaos, emerged a Tin Man. He approached wielding a mighty blade and swung it quickly towards Vigil. As she ducked, her grip on Zanna weakened, and eventually she dropped her altogether.

"Fuit!" Zanna exclaimed as she fell to the ground. Above her, the Tin Man brought his monstrously heavy foot down, trying with urgency to crush Vigil, but her icy form left her quite speedy. She slid back and instead of crushing her, the Tin Man merely cracked the ground.

Zanna looked towards Vigil and quickly jumped up. Her wand was nowhere to be found, but it needed to be—and fast. Her eyes carefully studied the carnage around her. The ground was littered with death, decay, discarded weapons, all things that she wasn't looking for.

"Where is it?" She muttered to herself. She grabbed a body, pushing it over, then another and another but still the wand eluded her.

"A staff is a wizard's best friend. A wand may be easy, but it's far less powerful and much less reliable."

Kunklestick's impartial words of wisdom rang in her ears as she continued to look around. In the foreground, she could hear the grunts of the Tin Man as he kept trying to defeat the icy Vigil. Her focus was unwavering. So much so, that everything around her seemed to vanish. Her determination to finding her weapon was so strong that she didn't even notice the large Akordan charging towards her, a Beacon in its hand and fury on its face.

"Die you vile scum!" The Akordan roared.

"Who are you calling vile?" Another voice bellowed. The Akordan turned in surprise just in time to be greeted by the sight of a large, burly Tin Man. Like Paul Bunyan cutting down a tree, he swung the blade towards the Akordan, but to his and Zanna's dismay, the beast jumped, high enough to avoid the attack altogether.

"Whoa," she whispered. The Akordan landed a couple feet back, aiming the Beacon forward and pressing the trigger with haste. The yellow ribbon of light came as advertised, piercing through the soldier's armor and leaving him in several pieces.

"No!" She yelled. It was in this moment of pure anger that she was finally able to spot a small tip of wood hiding quite well under the remains of an unfortunate ghoul. Its skin was black, and from each of the gaping wounds emerged hundreds of bugs and maggots.

Jumping towards the grotesque body, she quickly reached for the wand, and before she even stood, fired a spell towards the Akordan.

"Balathan!" She quickly called out. From the tip of her wand, emerged a twirling yellow light, it danced in the air like a ribbon in the wind until finally reaching its intended target. The result was unpleasant. It was a spell she had only used during training, and although in that instance the result was rewarding and granted them fuel for a fire, this time was far less pleasant.

"Ok that's just gross," she whispered. A groan of pain in the background ended her small victory. Standing up, she turned, looking towards Vigil as she gave the Tin Man an icy kiss. His skin went blue, and before long, his entire body was nothing more than an ice sculpture.

"That's it." Zanna declared, pulling on the wand and returning it to staff form.

"In the name of Undr, I declare you obsolete."

Vigil looked at her with a grin, then slowly knelt to the ground.

"Please," she whispered. "Don't hurt me."

Her eyes looked to Zanna with excitement, and she gently placed her hands on the ground. The surface quickly became ice, creating an obstacle for everyone in the surrounding area.

"Cyliamo Sensio," Zanna snapped, her staff began to glow, but just before she could complete the spell, an Arnout dove towards her, grabbing her and taking her up into the sky.

***

Herratia's shriek was terrifying enough to bring pause to all who heard it. Didorumpus continued to fire beams of energy all around, but as fast as he could cast the spell, Herratia was already moving. Her teleportation gave her an extreme advantage. Around him, the battle still lingered on. It was beginning to feel hopeless; the soldier's numbers were dwindling, which in turn, led to Agavordis' army growing. His only means of creating a distance was the occasional shockwave spell, which quickly pushed away all that attempted to approach, including, his own allies unfortunately. It bothered him, but he couldn't take the risk. It was far more important to eliminate Herratia, than the ghouls. Knocking down the ally soldiers was just an unfortunate side effect.

"Enough of this," Didorumpus whispered as he tapped his staff to the ground. Everything around him suddenly vanished. A haze filled the air, and a fog twirled around him like a dog desperate for attention. All around, he could see yellow spheres of light. He was in the Echo.

"Where are you, brother?" He whispered to himself. He began to frantically search the field, passing by the various balls of light and looking each of them over. To an untrained eye, they all looked the same, but not to him. Well—most of them did, but he knew how to spot his brother. He had used The Echo many times in the past to sneak up on him, as such, he had become quite familiar with how Kunklestick's form appeared within The Echo.

He continued to edge closer to where he imagined he had originally come from before Herratia's attack. It was a long shot, the landscape looked unremarkable in here, but with enough patience, he would soon find him.

A loud shriek suddenly erupted from behind him, and as he turned around, he found himself face to face with a beach ball-sized orb of energy.

"What the—"

He jumped aside, crashing against the rough ground. He'd be scrapped, maybe even bruised but at least he survived.

"How did you get in here?" He called out as he climbed to his feet and looked around.

"Into your precious shadow realm?"

Her voice traveled all around him. Like a mighty deity, her voice alluded to him, the words made their way to his ears but all other signs seeming mystical. She hardly seemed real— that is—until she was standing behind him, laughing and giving him a shove forward.

"Ugh," he moaned. His lip had begun to bleed, the impact of his chin against the stone was painful and in the back corner of his mouth, was the sensation of a tear in his cheek. He lay, holding onto his staff and focusing on the sinister sounds of her reptilian tongue. Closing his eyes and focusing his mind, he reemerged in the midst of the crowded battlefield, nearly getting trampled by the chaos.

"By Undr!" Didorumpus shouted as he jumped to the side. He turned, scanning around and smiled as he noticed a familiar white ball of light in the distance.

"Brother," he whispered to himself. He quickly skimmed the field, making sure Herratia had not followed. Nothing. Nothing except the spoils of war. He turned and began to run, dodging blade, energy, and ice, and although he wasn't looking for confrontation, he did give a few ghouls a good whoop across the head. He pressed forward, lurching like an ant in the middle of a crowded park. He kept his eyes on his goal, but just as he thought the danger passed, a familiar screech crawled into his ear. Herratia. She was back. This time, he opted not to look, instead, he continued towards his destination, using zigzag patterns to avoid any of the witch's attacks.

"You can't run Dido!" Herratia taunted. Didorumpus continued his pursuit forward and hastily retreated from the field, once again returning to The Echo.

"Roloman!" He called out in desperation. His loyal Grimwort had always been quite reliable, quick in his responses and today seemed no different. From the grey skies he dove, swooping down and presenting his master with a hasty escape.

"Go!" Didorumpus nervously pleaded as he settled onto his back. Into the air they soared, two desperate beings trying to outrun an abomination, a deformity unworthy of words. Herratia sneered as she looked up towards the sky, worry-filled and more determined than ever. She couldn't allow them to escape. She had to win. Not to help Septus, but instead to prove her worth to the world.

"You cannot escape me!" She roared.

With the possibility of losing her targets becoming uncomfortably real, she looked at her hands, willing energy to form, and then swiftly began hurling balls of energy upwards. Like a snot-covered kid in the midst of winter, she tossed the orbs of energy. Each attack seemed closer to hitting its mark than the one before, but Roloman was slick. He expertly swayed, avoiding her attacks like a car dodging cones. The space between them was beginning to grow. Each time she missed, the sour taste on her palate grew tarter.

"Keep going boy," Didorumpus said, gratefully patting his trusted pal on the neck. He looked around, scanning the field of yellow orbs and then pointed towards a tightly formed cluster that seemed to be moving every which way.

"There!" He declared.

Roloman proudly neighed, then began to dive. At last, he had found his brother, or at least he was hoping he had. His excitement began to boil over, the idea of splitting up just didn't sit right, not in a time like this. He tightened his grip onto Roloman and allowed himself to smile. They were still in the midst of a war, but at least being near his brother meant that they could protect each other. They continued to near the ground, when out of nowhere appeared a flash of light and an all too familiar shriek. There, standing with a broad smile, was Herratia.

"Fuit," Didorumpus muttered. "She's relentless."

"You thought you could outrun me?" Herratia whispered. With resentment filling her core, she summoned a ball of energy larger than any she had ever summoned, and quickly launched it into the air.

"Look out!" Didorumpus declared, but it was too late, the ball was far too large to avoid. It struck Roloman, sending a searing pain through the unfortunate Grimwort and left them both crashing towards the ground. The impact was hard; the sound of bones breaking filled his ears. Together in a twisted pile, they lay, their bodies aching, their hearts racing, and their minds filled with fear.

Walking with an air of confidence and bigheadedness, Herratia approached, kneeling in front of the dead Grimwort and grinning.

"For so long I heard about the powers and awesomeness of the wizards," she whispered. She slowly lifted her hand, running her claws gently through Didorumpus' hair.

"But now I've realized, you're more limited than I imagined."

"Do what you're going to do," Didorumpus tearfully demanded.

Herratia shook her head and climbed back to her feet.

"Oh, I'd love to kill you, but he has other plans for you," she replied. She looked down at the wounded wizard and brought her tail above him.

"You belong to Agavordis now." And with that, she forcefully brought the tail down, sending her defeated prize into darkness.

Chapter 13

Kunklestick fired a beam of energy towards an incoming Akordan. It quickly seared the armor and brought the creature down to the ground in a lifeless slump. His eyes scanned the field. There was no sign of Zanna or his brother. Their absence was starting to cause some anxiety, but he dared not let it show.

"Cyliamo Sensio," he proclaimed as he brought his staff to the ground with a firm thud. The shockwave quickly emerged, taking out a few more ghouls that had begun to approach. The air was filled with the music of combat. Whines from the Beacons, clinks and clanks from the swords, thumps from the footsteps of the giants. As he took a deep breath, he couldn't recall ever smelling anything worse than the way this field smelled at this moment. Rotted corpses—both fresh and old—lay scattered all over the ground. Blood pooled in various places, some of the pools large enough to be mistaken for a pond. It was a horrible and gruesome sight indeed.

Behind him, a loud wave of electric energy hissed in the air. He promptly turned to see Agavordis, floating in the air and firing steady streams of energy towards Cristol. His attack struck against the force field and sent out a resounding pop, similar to a highly charged static shock. But despite all the dramatic sound effects his attacks produced, the force field still held strong.

"Inginimo."

Kunklestick sent a beam hurtling towards Agavordis, but before it could land, Agavordis phased out of sight. His beam instead hit the force field with a loud thunderous crack. A sinister heckle filled the air as Agavordis sent another attack of energy heading towards the forcefield.

"Kunlestick look out," a voice suddenly yelled. He turned, just in time to see Vigil, sliding towards him on a steady stream of ice. Her impact knocked him to the ground.

A Tin Man quickly approached, swinging a sword towards the ice-covered sorceress. His effort was in vain, however, as his maneuver was quickly spotted, and countered with a blast of ice. The heavy mechanical suit instantly lost its heat, its gears froze, and it fell to the ground, taking its frozen passenger with it.

"Kunklestick. The stories do not do you justice," Vigil remarked. As he began to sit up, he slowly reached for his staff and vanished.

"Hmm," Vigil scoffed as she looked around. Suspiciously, she navigated the area, trying with the utmost intensity to locate the missing wizard.

"If I were an old coward past my day, where would I be hiding?"

Inside The Echo, all was silent, finally some peace. But it wouldn't last long, and he had no intention of lingering. This trip was purely designed as an escape. Slowly, he climbed to his feet, keeping Vigil's orb of light in his sight. He watched with curiosity as she navigated past the various balls of light. After just a few moments of peace, he took a deep breath and re-emerged onto the battlefield.

"Selaphat," he whispered as he moved his staff in a circle-like motion. A shield of white light suddenly emerged behind Vigil and slowly crept towards her.

"Hey lady," Kunklestick called out, beckoning her attention. She turned, coming face to face with the shield and in an instant, was sucked inside of the two-dimensional blob of energy. From within its prisonlike confides, she screamed and hollered, but her words were far too muffled for him to make out.

"You've joined the wrong side, my friend," Kunklestick sighed as he grabbed the now solidified mass of energy and tossed it into the air. It lingered in the sky for a brief moment, before coming to the ground and shattering into a million tiny pieces. Kunklestick looked at the pieces with a slight bit of regret, in one of the shards, he almost could've thought he saw her, but upon closer examination, it was vacant of all features. The shards remained on the ground for a few moments then quickly transformed into liquid and dissolved into the ground.

At that moment, a loud explosion filled the air, sending a shockwave that threatened to knock any unstable persons off their feet. Fortunately for Kunklestick, he had his staff for support. He turned, just in time to witness the demise of the protective barrier that had encompassed Cristol in safety. *Oh no*, he thought. In the air, Agavordis laughed before letting out an ear-piercing whistle. Kunklestick followed the necromancer's gesture and took notice of a large brute pushing his way through the crowd and heading towards Cristol's main gates. It was Killigan, or at least, the shell of Killigan. In death, he retained no personality but he did retain all of the strength. Running like a locomotive, Killigan crashed into the gate, knocking it down in a quick fell swoop.

Quickly, a massive horde of ghouls turned, bringing their attention to the newly revealed area, and began to charge the opening.

"Not good" Kunklestick muttered.

"Yogurn!" He called out. From high above, Yogurn impetuously dove, heading towards her master and paying little regard to the crowded skies. She landed on the ground with a bounce and swiftly lowered herself, allowing Kunklestick to mount atop her back easily.

"Let's go," he proclaimed with resounding effect. Together, they made a quick dash, getting airborne just in time to avoid an Akordan blade. The view from the sky was troublesome, looking down at the fields of Cristol, one would be forgiven if they felt suddenly devoid of all hope and optimism. Yes, from up here, Kunklestick could fully see the extent of the damage and the continuing destruction caused by the dead army. It was extensive. Perhaps, most upsetting of all was the fact that the living soldiers were now outnumbered by the dead. It certainly didn't bode well. Yogurn careened through the desolate skies and with a cautiously skilled maneuver, dove down towards the city.

Inside, madness had begun to spread like a virus. The dead ransacked buildings, pulling out civilians—both women and children—and killing them where they stood. Screams of terror filled the air as desperate mothers tried their best to repeal the attacks. All Arnouts were gifted with abilities, but not all were trained to use them, least of all defensively. This was the case with many of the Arnout mothers. They did their best. Adrenaline and parental love gave many of them a higher purpose and resolve, but before long, their demise seemed imminent. There were far too many ghouls, and far too few skilled warriors, and so, Cristol began to be overtaken.

"This is awful," Kunklestick whispered. He gave Yogurn a compassionate pat on the neck as he continued to scan the streets for Killigan. The beastly Adrasain was dead, his thought process literally nonexistent, and yet, he seemed quite driven. He had a mission, an order had been handed to him, planted into his mind, and Kunklestick had a pretty good idea what it was. After all, the Arnouts were the superior and most respected race in Furlasia; if they were toppled, it would prove Agavordis' superiority and would surely prompt a surrender. No one would stand up to an army that would wipe out a species so close to divinity, and with the armies of Morlay and Terria beginning to shrink, now was the time.

"Come on Yogurn. We have to find him," Kunklestick sighed. He kept trying his best to spot Killigan, but with so much chaos taking place below, it was proving difficult. Death and mayhem were peppered throughout, creating a canvas of blood and torn limbs. The ice ghouls were powerful. Their attacks brought quick pause to any Arnout that even began to consider revolting.

Hopelessness had begun to set in. The thought of failure had just found its way into his grief-stricken mental palace, when a sudden shriek caught his attention. His focus quickly shifted, and finally, he spotted him. There—just on the other side of the bridge to the palace was Killigan. In his hands, he held a head and in front of him stood an unfortunate guard. As the young guard toppled over, Killigan grabbed a mechanized cart, jumping aboard and heading towards the palace.

"Forward," Kunklestick ordered, giving Yogurn a light kick.. They quickly neared, and as they did, Yogurn descended, bringing Killigan closer and closer into view.

"Let's cut him off," Kunklestick suggested. Yogurn nodded, howling as she quickened her pace. Once they had gotten a good lead, she quickly performed a sharp turn, bringing them face to face with Killigan.

"Let's take him down," he whispered. Forward Yogurn went, and while she did her part—which was considerable—Kunklestick did his, firing blasts of jagged energy towards the mindless behemoth. The first few blasts missed. The jarring motion of Yogurn made a steady aim quite onerous. Alas, however, he finally landed a hit.

"Yes!" Kunklestick giddily exclaimed. As though reading his mind, Yogurn quickly landed, lowering herself to make his dismount easier. Kunklestick promptly hopped off, holding his staff close to his chest.

There was no sign of motion, no sign of life, or lack thereof. The cart hissed as it released a faint grey smoke into the air; it was completely destroyed, left in mostly shambles. With his staff raised and ready to fire, he carefully inched closer.

"Ahh," A loud voice roared from within the wreckage. Killigan emerged, throwing the wrecked cart into the water and locking eyes with Kunklestick. He looked onwards— then—like a bull in the arena, began to charge.

"Inginimo," Kunklestick called out. His staff had just begun to glow when it was suddenly ripped from his grasp by an unseen force.

He didn't turn to see what had caused it, there wasn't time. Besides, he had a pretty good idea. The heckling in the background was hard to mistake. He reached to his side, drawing his sword and held it outstretched in front of him.

"Haa," He bellowed as he swung towards Killigan. The blow landed just below the rib cage but did little to stop the impact of the large ghoul from crashing into him. Kunklestick flew into the air like a cheap toy, soaring clear over Killigan's head before crashing against the hard crystal platform.

"Ugh," he moaned. There were stars in his eyes and throbbing on his side. His bones ached as if they had been broken and his head pounded with the intensity of a high school marching band.

"Nice try old man," Agavordis laughed. He slowly hovered in front of Killigan and gently touched down on the surface of the bridge.

"She took the last leader's head," he paused. "Bring me hers."

Killigan nodded in compliance, then charged towards the main entrance. The door that led to the palace was enormous, thick, and intricately designed, but for Killigan, it surrendered, falling over as though it were nothing more than cardboard.

"You should know," Agavordis paused, as he reached down and picked up the orphaned staff Kunklestick had dropped.

"Killing Lord Fae is merely a formality at this point. My army has overtaken the free armies. In doing so, it has become even bigger, even more powerful than it already was. Victory is mine. Furlasia is mine."

Kunklestick slowly climbed to his feet, ignoring his body's nagging warning to stay down.

"Then why kill her?" He grunted. Agavordis shrugged with a smile and looked down towards the dark waters of Lake Cristol.

"Because I want to," he calmly replied. He grinned as he studied the details of the staff — then — with a quiet nod, he tossed it towards the wizard's feet.

"A duel," Agavordis taunted. "The old versus the new. The weak versus the strong. The worthy versus the unworthy."

Kunklestick waved, summoning the staff to his hand with a deep sigh.

"Wow, I really didn't know you had it in you," Agavordis remarked with an adoring smile. His hands began to glow green, a ball of sizzling energy forming in each palm.

"Ha!"

With little warning, he suddenly sent the energy careening forward.

"Inginimo," Kunklestick bellowed. Their spells met in the middle with a splash. The orb between the two streaks quickly turned green and began to make its way towards Kunklestick, whining as it continued to spin. The magical duel was futile, Kunklestick knew it. The talismans Septus had acquired had indeed given him a considerable amount of power. But with any luck, he might just be able to summon a spell that would throw him off guard. As he clenched his teeth, his eyes frantically searched for the talismans. But as hard as he tried, he could see no sign of them.

Through the shrieking sound of the orb, Kunklestick could just make out the heinous laughter from Agavordis. As the orb neared, the laughter grew louder. With a sudden quick motion, Kunklestick sent the spell to the left, letting it pull Agavordis' arm with a surprisingly firm force. With Agavordis disoriented, Kunklestick quickly collapsed his staff to wand form and fired off a series of small beams of energy. They struck Agavordis, and as they did, his anger began to grow. Like an apparition of the night, he phased through the bridge, vanished, and left Kunklestick alone with his thoughts.

"Your father wasn't so much of a coward," Kunklestick taunted. At that moment, the ground in front of him began to liquefy, and from within the puddle of prismatic liquid, emerged a pair of ghouls, each of them made of crystal.

"Great," Kunklestick sighed. He quickly held his wand forward, firing smaller beams towards them, but missing as they dropped to the ground. They looked at him, hissing for a moment, and then began to crawl towards him like a couple of vicious mutts.

"Balathan." He proclaimed. A twirling white beam of energy danced from his wand, making its way towards the beast with haste. The ghouls attempted to maneuver away from the heated ribbon of light, but alas failed, resulting in their quick demise.

Kunklestick breathed a sigh of relief, then looked around, trying to see any sign of his foe. There was none. *Lord Fae*, he thought. He hurriedly began to make his way to the entrance. He was mere inches from the door when at that moment, he found himself engulfed in a ball of energy.

"You stupid murdering fool!" Agavordis yelled from a distance. He waved his arms, mimicking the motion of dribbling. With each downward thrust, the ball of energy bounced, crashing against the bridge and disorienting the elderly wizard.

"You don't need to be this person," Kunklestick pleaded. His head was beginning to throb and his body, which was already quite sore, was starting to feel like putty. Dizziness set in and his heart began to race, each breath became harder to swallow than the one before.

Darkness seemed inevitable, death seemed on the horizon, and for a moment, he accepted it. He had lived when so many other wizards had perished, and for what? Why him? The prophecy? Surely there was someone else that could've done this. Why was he chosen to survive? How was he able to summon Yogurn without his staff that dreadful day? He closed his eyes, taking in the faces of those he had lost.

"I'm coming," he whispered. Suddenly, Agavordis stopped, allowing the encompassing ball of magic to dissolve into the air like a whispered secret.

"Do you see it now?" Agavordis questioned. "Your doom. The end. Do you see my father? Are you replaying the moment you betrayed him?"

He slowly sauntered towards Kunklestick with a look of disgust masking his face.

"Do you remember now how he came to you, begging you to help him get rid of the voices? And what did you do? You turned your back on him. Declared him unworthy."

Slowly he knelt down, lifting up the disoriented wizards head.

"No, my friend. He wasn't unworthy. It's you." The sound of glass breaking filled the air and sprayed down shards all around them. With a grin, he wiped himself off, looking up in time to see a head falling towards them. It landed next to Kunklestick with a bloody splash and rolled almost off the edge of the bridge. Lord Fae—like Lord Aldon before her—had been beheaded.

Kunklestick looked towards the decapitated remains of Lord Fae and with a deep breath, slowly passed out. Agavordis grinned and climbed to his feet. He quickly wandered over and picked up the head, looking into the eyes with a smile.

"You lasted as long as you could my queen," he whispered. He continued to look into her empty eyes, imagining for a moment what horror must've been captured in that final moment. Then, with a subtle wink, he leaned in, kissing her softly on the lips. As he pulled back, he could see the wrinkles that sat just below her eyes, an imperfection in her form that she had masked so well. With an overwhelming sense of satisfaction, he hovered into the air, making his way over the battlefield and looking down at his army and those Arnouts that still fought.

"Your queen is dead. Your city is breached, and your women and children are now my prisoners," he wailed. The fighting came to a quick halt, all looked up, growing silent like kids being scolded by a parent.

"Lay down your weapons. Surrender your forces, and I will spare the remaining forces. I am not the tyrant you believe. I am merciful. I believe in second chances. Lay down your weapons, and let's end this horrible conflict. As you've already seen, the more of you my army kills, the bigger it becomes. There is no stopping it. If you continue to fight, you will all die."

The battlefield grew stagnant as bleakness spread over the crowds, infecting them like a disease that had no cure.

"The age of kings and queens is dead and gone. Now is the age of peace, the age of unity. The age of Agavordis."

Part 2

Chapter 14

The ship made landfall almost exactly when they had expected it to. Standing on the upper platform, Sillimon, Penny, Methalda, and Articus all looked forward onto the land ahead. The journey had been far more tiring than they had anticipated; each of them felt an eagerness to step atop solid ground. More than anything, most of them wanted a bed that was wider than a few feet.

Adrasia. It looked like a mighty place indeed, a home of titans. In a way it was. Adrasians were unusually gifted with strength and agility, and some even seeme immortal. Those ones were called elites. Most of the country's top authorities were elites. They ran Adrasia, governing with an iron fist and a policy of fear, which nevertheless seemed effective. Not only was Adrasia a fairly crime-free nation, but most were quite content—happy—even, with their home.

As the ship neared port, a group of about twenty men stood waiting. All of them armed with swords and shields. Each of them donning elegant and recently polished armor.

The sun here seemed shy; it was hardly visible thanks to the fluffy clouds that were attempting to rule the sky. In the distance, the city expelled columns of smoke, mixing with the clouds and creating a rather gloomy atmosphere.

"Doesn't look like much does it?" Penny asked aloud.

"It's not," Jinn replied, sneaking up from behind. "Adrasia is home to the vilest and most disgusting people imaginable. It's a nation filled with violence. It's every man for himself here, so watch your back and don't go anywhere alone."

As the ship slowly neared the port, Idrix cautiously climbed the steps, her walk was shaky, but she had an eagerness about her.

"Easy now," Dorrin cautioned, as he followed behind her. She waved her hand back at him in a dismissive fashion. Once she finally reached the top, she paused and drew a deep breath.

The ship gently bumped against the dock, prompting the group of men to quickly approach.

"What brings you to Adrasia?" One of the men questioned in a loud, commanding tone.

"My grandma here is ill," Kadeen explained as she emerged from beneath the ship. "She is dying and has arranged to meet with an apothecary here who claims to have something that can help."

Idrix began coughing hectically and patting her chest.

"Who is this apothecary?" The man questioned.

"She called herself Dr. Chilten. Said she's about three hours from the port," Kadeen replied.

"Who are the rest of these people?" The guard demanded.

"Grandkids."

The guard looked at the group with skepticism. There was certainly a variety of people on board the ship, and not just the skin tones either, none of them really looked related to each other.

"Alright. Welcome to Adrasia mam," the guard replied. *Strength but no brains?* With that, the guards turned around and headed towards a small building that read *Gatekeeper*.

Idrix grinned and looked towards Jinn.

"Alright," Idrix paused as she looked around at the assembled crew. "Time to blow their minds." With that, she turned and made her way back towards the steps.

"What does that mean?" Penny asked, looking towards Jinn for some sort of reply.

"This ship has a few tricks up her sleeve," Adam replied. "Get downstairs and you'll see."

Articus looked towards Penny and nodded. Together, they descended the stairwell. Waiting at the bottom, in the narrow hall was Jinn and Idrix, who both wore excited looks upon their faces.

"What?" Articus asked.

Suddenly, the floor beneath them began to rumble, slowly at first, but then it became quite pronounced. They had started to move, somehow, however, the ship sounded different than it had previously. This time it sounded thunderous, and even more powerful. Articus continued to observe the curious expression on their two hosts' faces. At that moment, it became apparent. They were no longer in the water; they were now driving on land. Through the thin paneled metal, they could just make out the cries of shock from the guards at the dock.

"It's a vehicle?" Sillimon questioned.

"It's a vehicle," Idrix beamed. "We call her the Maratan. First of her kind, by land or by sea, Maratan will get you where you need to be."

Sillimon smiled and looked towards Penny with wide eyes.

"I'd love to take a closer look at her when we stop," he added.

"Of course," Idrix replied. "I'm always fine showing off this technical marvel."

Sillimon looked towards Penny with excitement, then turned back towards Idrix.

"Can I go up?"

"Have at it, but keep your head down. We are driving through desolate lands here."

Quickly, Sillimon turned, grabbing Penny's hand and pulling her up the stairs. Methalda looked towards Articus, they both shrugged and proceeded to follow. None of them had ever seen another continent before; it was admittedly exciting, even if it was in a land where every citizen had the strength to break your skull between their fingers.

As they emerged at the surface, they were shocked to find that they were not on a road at all, but off road, traversing through a thick forest filled with hills and rocks. The trees here were tall; they hid the sky and kept the air feeling cool. Scattered in various places in the forest, were statues, most of them run down and falling apart. Ancient history that was trying to linger on.

"What a strange place," Methalda remarked.

"I think it's beautiful," Penny retorted. They continued to observe the serene forest as the Maratan led them on a mysterious journey. They were here to find a jewel, one which belonged to the Arc Blade, but all they had to go on, were whispers. The whispers had led them to Adrasia, but where exactly, they did not know. But there was someone who might. That's where they were headed, to the *Boss*. The Boss was a legend among Adrasia. She was an older woman with decadent taste and more money than she needed. She had amassed quite the reputation. It seemed she had plenty to make her happy, and yet she wasn't, she was bored. *I have the jewel you seek*, she had said. The message had been sent to Idrix by raven only a few months ago.

The letter had initially been met with criticism, The Decoyers all thought it seemed too coincidental, but after learning more about the Boss, it seemed plausible. After all, her father had been the original holder of the Arc Blade.

The Maratan hit a bump that nearly caused Penny to lose her balance.

"Careful," Articus advised as he grabbed her hand. Now, they were in the middle of a clearing that was covered as far as the eyes could see with rocks of various sizes. A sea of rocks it seemed. It was the *Crag Exodus*, a barren land that no horse could travel and no ordinary buggy could venture, luckily for The Decoyers, Maratan was no average buggy. Its large wheels made the rocky terrain no bother at all. There was little life to be seen here. The sky had the occasional bird, but besides that, it was quite stark.

"I wonder where we're going?" Methalda called out over the loud sound of crunching rocks.

"I've heard of this place," Sillimon replied. "I heard it leads to a metropolis, one that is sealed off from the rest of Adrasia."

"Who would want to live in such a place?" Penny asked.

"People with something to hide," Articus spoke up. Penny shook her head and turned her gaze to the barren lands ahead.

"This place gives me the creeps," she whispered as she grabbed Sillimon's arm. He turned, looking at the dreadful expression that she donned and nodded in understanding. She wanted to go back below. One of the perks of a long relationship is the uncanny ability to read the other partner's thoughts. Penny didn't need to say what she meant, but through her expression and tone, Sillimon knew exactly what she wanted.

"We're gonna go back below," Sillimon explained as he slowly led Penny towards the stairs.

"We'll be down shortly," Articus replied with a bow. Penny and Sillimon vanished down the stairs, leaving Methalda and Articus to themselves. Together they continued to observe the scant landscape.

"Look," Methalda suddenly pointed. Articus quickly followed her finger, and his jaw dropped. Running along the rocky valley was a large creature, much larger than any they had seen in Furlasia. This creature bared a striking resemblance to a lion, only it was all grey, and its tail was wide like a handheld fan. It roared as it continued its wayward charge forward, paying little mind to the Maratan.

"What is that thing?" Methalda questioned with a hint of terror masking her face. "It looks to be thirty feet tall."

"I don't know, but I hope it's friendly."

The creature continued its path forward, eventually turning and heading towards them.

"Fuit!" Articus called out. He grabbed Methalda's arm and promptly led them towards the steps.

"Wait," she paused. The creature continued to near, but something in its eyes seemed friendly. As Methalda watched with curiosity, Articus tightened his grip, nearly crushing her fingers in the process.

The creature let out a mighty roar and leapt clear over the Maratan, skidding in the rocks before it continued on its way. Articus sighed in relief, as a single drop of sweat slowly crept its way down his face.

"That was cool," Methalda smiled.

It wasn't too much longer, and the wheels on the Maratan began to slow. They had cleared the rocky valley and were now on smooth, sandy ground, their destination closer now than ever. As they sat below, in the cramped dining room, The Decoyers all remained steadfast and focused. The newcomers from The Society, all sat in a group, keeping their eyes on their new hosts and making it quite clear they didn't quite feel at home yet. At the head of the table, sat Jinn, sharpening a dagger quietly, as though they were planning on finding a fight. The possibility of conflict seemed slim. Accoring to Idrix it wasn't supposed to be anything other than a standard heist. Her words of comfort did little to quell the concerns of The Society. After the last job, they learned, always expect the worst.

With a harsh pump of the brakes, the Maratan came to an abrupt stop. Dorrin excitetdly stepped from the control room, weaing a cheek to cheek smile.

"What?" Kadeen asked with a bolstering grin.

"Pretty good driving, ehh?" Dorrin coyly replied.

"Yes Dorrin," Idrix grunted as she maneuvered her way to the stairs. "But you need to learn how to use the brakes. I nearly hit my damn head." With Jinn right behind her, she climbed the stairs, disappearing to the surface of the ship. Dorrin quietly shrugged off the criticism, shedding it away like a coat when the weather had become too warm. With a confident smile, he looked at the newcomers and nodded towards the stairs. Articus looked at the crew and proceeded up the stairs.

The light from the day hit his eyes, revealing a beautiful day with a light breeze that smelled vaguely of caramel. As Methalda emerged from behind him, she let out a gasp of enthusiasm. The city in front of them was simple but full of elegance and class. Each house seemed perfectly maintained, each yard freshly cut and flowers lined the sidewalk borders. There were no extravagant buildings to be seen, this wasn't that type of place. It was a quaint city for those who wanted a quiet life. A city for those that had the money and power to isolate themselves from the rest of the country's inhabitants. There were all the necessities to survive; bakeries, markets, even the occasional tavern. On the outskirts, were a few farms, and even they seemed quite decent for what they were.

"Welcome to Olivium," Idrix explained with a sigh. The skies were filled the songs of birds, and the surrounding fields were filled with the neighs of the horses and cows.

"It looks amazing," Penny remarked.

"Most places with evil intentions look heavenly and welcoming on the outside," Idrix explained.

Their momentary silence soon came to an end, as Dorrin dropped a metallic ladder off the side of the vehicle. The others turned to him with a startle. "Shall we?" Dorrin asked, looking bashful.

Chapter 15

Vicham stood hushed as he looked out of the stained windows lining the bordering walls of Ramir Hold. The streets were solemn, devoid of any cheer — and people, for that matter. There were, however, plenty of Akordans. They patrolled the streets armed with their monstrous blades, some of them even carried Beacons. Despair had found Morlay. With Agavordis' victory, came occupation. Hundreds of Akordans had been sent to each of the cities to keep the residents in line. Then, of course, there were the undead. No one could forget them. They stood vacant of any expression at every corner, motionless and just waiting for an order. The eerie conditions left the streets mostly untraveled. People only left their homes when it was time to go to work. And even then, most traveled in groups. Safety in numbers, that was the thought.

"What do you see?" Linuk asked, as he quietly approached.

"Nothing," Vicham replied. His eyes scanned the streets once more. None but the Akordans and the undead could be spotted. He sighed and looked up towards the skies. They were dark, filled with clouds, had been since the occupation had begun. Furlasia was literally covered in darkness.

"Nevo is coming by today," Linuk informed. Vicham gulped as he turned to look at Linuk.

"And Herratia?" Vicham asked.

"I don't think so," Linuk replied.

Vicham turned back towards the windows and sighed. "Let's hope not."

Since the occupation, Nevo and Herratia had been making regular visits to the cities. Most of the times Nevo came alone, but when he did bring Herratia, it almost always ended with blood being split. For all their sakes, it was best if she remained in Cristol, the city she had been ruling over since the end of the war.

They stood in silence as they contemplated the incoming dread of Nevo's visit. He was unhinged. Violent, aggressive, and quick to snap. The death of his older siblings left him an Akordan with only one thing on his mind, killing.

"Sir," a voice called from behind. Unsure who the person was addressing, both Vicham and Linuk promptly turned around.

"He's entered the city," the servant said with shaking hands.

"Alright," Linuk replied. "Show him in." The servant looked towards Vicham with a gulp and then quietly bowed. As the servant faded from sight, Vicham reached toward Linuk, placing a hand gently on his shoulder.

"We have to play nice," Linuk lectured, sensing the disdain in Vicham's touch.

"We still haven't found her," Vicham sighed. "She's being held hostage out there. I was supposed to keep her safe."

They started walking towards the foyer. All around them, servants had begun to scatter, closing and locking doors behind themselves. Fear was running rampant in Ramir Hold. Together they walked towards uncertainty, the weight of the situation causing them both to drag their feet.

"We will find her," Linuk replied. "The scouts are still searching every day. Don't give up on them yet."

Vicham groaned as they stepped into the foyer, which now hosted over twenty guards. Linuk may have been stripped of his title, but that did not stop their loyalty. To them, and to the rest of Morlay, Linuk was still the king.

"It should be me," Vicham retorted. "I should be the one out searching."

Linuk shook his head as they came to a stop.

"I need you here with me. You've been through all this before. You know how to survive."

Dmitri emerged from a hall to their left wearing a long blue robe and resting his folded hands just below his navel. As he looked at Vicham, he cracked an unenthusiastic smile. In truth, he despised Vicham. Resented the way he had come into the city and stolen his friend's attention, loyalty and trust.

"Linuk," Dimitri said as he patted his friend on the back. He gulped with concern as he turned towards the doorway ahead of them. Silence filled the air like an unwelcome fart. It lingered, stealing all voices and sounds, leaving the ambiance quite dry and dreary. As they stood mutely watching the large wooden doors, the sound of voices began to seep through. Dimitri sighed as the voices continued to grow louder and louder. It was him. Nevo had arrived.

The door to the foyer pushed open just ever so slightly. Even to Nevo, the doors were an exercise in strength.

"Hello, hello, hello," he roared as he stepped inside. With a slow push, the doors fully opened, revealing a horde of undead ghouls that sauntered inside with slow dragging feet.

"Leave your pets outside Nevo," Vicham demanded.

Nevo laughed and motioned towards one of the ghouls. With a groan, the ghoul slowly limped over to Vicham, and stopped just a few inches shy of his face.

"Do they make you nervous Vicham?" Nevo asked. Vicham silently stared at the ghoul with disgust. Its breath stank; it had skin that hung loosely off its bones and wounds that were crawling with ants.

"Why do you bring them?" Linuk calmly questioned.

"They are a reminder," Nevo answered as he strolled over to Linuk and licked his lips.

"They are a reminder of what you can all become if you piss me off."

The ghouls quietly positioned themselves at various places around the room. The stationed guards quietly shifted, moving away as subtly as they could.

"So to what do we owe the pleasure of this visit Nevo?" Dimitri investigated.

"Agavordis wants an update on the new shipment. He wants Abbisal Keep fully steam-powered in the next two moon cycles."

"So you're just his errand boy?" Dimitri asked. "Here to pick up his slack."

Nevo scoffed and approached Dimitri. With a quick motion, he grabbed him by his chin, lifting him into the air and letting his nails dig slightly into his flesh.

"I'm here for the fun," Nevo rebutted.

"Nevo, please. Leave him alone," Linuk calmly pleaded.

Nevo continued to hold Dimitri above the ground for a moment longer, before finally letting go, allowing him to fall with a thud.

"It's remarkable how you knew what I was doing without even being able to see," Nevo remarked. He approached Linuk and observed the silk bandana masking the empty sockets where his eyes once were.

"Speaking of those messed up eyes of yours. Agavordis sent a gift. Extra security to help keep you safe from any dangers that might try to sneak up on you."

A set of heavy footsteps suddenly filled the room. Through the entryway, marched the dead remains of Killigan Knight. Dimitri's eyes grew wide with anger and he quickly pushed himself to his feet.

"How dare you bring him here?!" Dimitri bellowed.

Linuk grew nervous, even without the gift of sight, he had an idea of who had just stepped inside. Those heavy footsteps were hard to forget.

"Killigan?" Linuk questioned.

The dead traitor groaned and continued to march slowly towards them. The nearer he got, the more Vicham could feel his skin crawl. The ghouls were off-putting enough as they were, knowing that this one was capable of unimaginable feats of strength, made it all the more nerve-wracking.

"This is cruel," Linuk remarked as Killigan came to a stop. "Is he always so spiteful?"

Nevo looked towards Vicham with a look of dismay creeping across his face.

"You haven't told him huh?" Nevo smiled as he shook his head.

"Told me what?" Linuk questioned.

"That'll have to be a conversation for later." Nevo countered. "Take me to the pits. I want to see the workers."

Vicham quietly led Nevo and Dimitri along with a few guards and a couple ghouls through the desolate streets of Morlay. The pits were on the outskirts of the city, just on the other side of the wall, in an underground cavern that had been discovered well before the city itself had been established. In fact, one could say, it was these pits that led people to first flock to the location. The rocks and minerals found within the dark depths had a value that didn't take long to be realized. It was, however, many years later that the realization of the minerals' full potential came into mind.

They turned a corner and stepped into a grimy street riddled with puddles of cloudy water and the occasional unfortunate corpse that had yet to be claimed by Agavordis. What few living souls occupied the street, quickly scampered away upon seeing the dreadful Akordan Nevo. The occupation had barely started a couple months ago, and already, Nevo had amassed quite the terrible reputation.

"I love the smell of fear," Nevo remarked as he followed his hosts down the disheveled path. Vicham rolled his eyes and pressed forward, trying his best not to give into the overwhelming anger boiling within. In the not too far distance, he could make out a building that stood almost as tall as the bordering wall itself. Its front was metal-platted, it had no windows and apart from the door, there was no other way in. As they neared the entrance, Dimitri leaned closer to Vicham as if to tell him a secret.

"We can take him," he whispered.

Vicham slowly turned and looked at him with extreme skepticism.

"You must be joking," Vicham retorted.

"No whispering!" Nevo bellowed as he tossed a rogue stone towards Dimitri's unsuspecting head. It struck the back of his skull with a slight thud, then fell back to the rocky street.

Dimitri stopped in his tracks and turned towards Nevo with a look of hatred.

"You got something to say?" Nevo asked.

"You think you're so strong. You think you're invincible. Mark my words, you will lose. And when you do, I'll be there to drive the blade into your heart," Dimitri threatened.

Nevo laughed and scanned the street.

"You're a brave one," Nevo paused. "If only more of your kind were so bold." He slowly walked to Dimitri and placed a hand on his shoulder.

"You're always welcome to try," Nevo advised as he nodded towards the sword on his hip.

"Take it. Take it and use it to kill me."

Dimitri looked at the blade over as sweat began to form atop his brow. He wanted nothing more than to make this vile reptilian beast pay for all he had done in the past few months, but the Akordans calm demeanor did little to inspire inner confidence.

"Oh well. Maybe you're not as brave as I thought," Nevo sighed. With his hand still atop Dimitri's shoulder, he quickly pulled him, turning him around, and gave him a shove forward.

"Open it," he ordered.

His hands reached for the handle, and with a slow turn, the door pushed open, revealing a dimly lit room and in its center—a large hole. From within the hole, the sounds of voices and pick axes crashing against rocks could be heard. The sounds traveled up, filling the room with an almost orchestra-like melody.

"You first," Nevo demanded, nodding towards a ladder that led down into the crater. Dimitri looked nervously at Vicham, who simply nodded his permission. Wasting no time with arguments, Dimitri began his descent down into the darkness of the pits, followed by Vicham and then Nevo.

As they reached the bottom, the vastness of the pits came into full view. It was as massive as the length and width of a football field. The walls were lined with sharp bits of glowing rocks. *Ramite.* It was one of the most important minerals in all of Furlasia. Its strength and flexibility offered numerous uses. Buildings, weapons, tools, and that's just what had been thought of so far. In Morlay, Ramite was heavily used in creating the various steam-powered contraptions that littered the city.

Nevo grinned as he observed the hundreds of children that tirelessly swung their pickaxes into the embedded rock.

"As you can see," Vicham paused. "They are working quite hard."

"Is this all the children the city has?" Nevo questioned pointing to an area that had no workers. "Why isn't that area being mined?"

"The rest are far too young to be of any use down here," Vicham replied.

"So there is more then?" Nevo replied. "I want them brought down here and put to work. Agavordis will not accept delays or excuses. If they are old enough to walk, they are old enough to mine."

"You piece of fuit," Dimitri scowled. "If it matters so much, send your Akordan children!"

Nevo glared at him with vengeful eyes, then sauntered towards an enervated teenager who had sat down to catch his breath next to a pile of harvested Ramite.

"Why have you stopped child?" Nevo asked, coming to a halt in front of the young man. He was grimy, covered in sweat, and reeked of urine and feces.

"I'm tired," the boy panted.

"Do you think Agavordis cares about your exhaustion? The fate of Furlasia hangs in the balance. He's trying to fix a broken land full of corrupt leaders and liars. He can't do that without the necessary tools. So tell me, do you not respect your new leader's vision for a brighter future?"

The boy looked towards Vicham and Dimitri, who were both staring at him with concern.

"Of course I do," the boy replied as he climbed to his feet. "But he needs me alive. If I die from exhaustion, that's one less worker."

Nevo shook his head in understanding as a grin crept its way onto his face.

"A few more moments then," Nevo instructed. With that, he turned towards Dimitri and approached.

"These boys need someone to keep an eye on them. Make sure they are working their hardest. Who is in charge down here?"

Dimitri solemnly scanned their surroundings, looking for the oldest of the children.

"There," he pointed. "His name is Goat."

Nevo followed the finger and squinted his eyes as he observed the unassuming, ginger-haired boy.

"You there," he called out. "Goat."

The young man turned and even from this distance, his nervousness was evident. He hesitated for a moment, perhaps contemplating ignoring the intimidating Akordan, but ultimately, he set down his pickaxe and approached.

"Yes, sir?" Goat asked as he glanced at Vicham and Dimitri for a sign of what to say or do.

"You're in charge down here are you not?" Nevo asked.

"Yes, I suppose," Goat stuttered. "Although, I don't really think of myself as a boss. I'm working just as hard as the rest of them."

Nevo looked around the cavern at the various children, all diligently working, even perhaps harder than normal.

"Agavordis is displeased with the production and the amount of product coming out of here," Nevo explained.

"I....I"

"Excuses won't be tolerated. He has expectations, and if your team isn't going to deliver, there will be consequences." Nevo elaborated.

"Do you understand?"

Goat looked once again at Vicham, who simply shook his head, opting, it seemed, not to interfere with the conversation.

"Yessss ssssiiir," Goat replied.

Dimitri and Vicham quietly approached the gates of Morlay, a sour taste filling their mouths as they trailed ever so slightly behind Nevo. The streets were just as deserted as they had been earlier, the desire to travel, even for food, had been stripped by the presence of the ghouls. No one felt comfortable when the dead were constantly lingering around; they were unpredictable and capable of abruptly attacking at any moment. It wasn't a chance most wanted to take, despite the overflow of Beacons that had taken over the streets and dark corners of the city.

"I will return at this same time in one week's time," Nevo paused in front of the gate and turned towards his escorts.

"Unless you want the children slaughtered, things had better pick up."

Without another word, he sauntered through the gates. As they slowly closed, Vicham let out a deep sigh.

"We can't keep living like this," Dimitri groaned. "We have to fight back."

"We will. We are not going to end up like this." Vicham calmly replied.

"How do you know that?" Dimitri questioned as a ghoul caught the corner of his eye.

"Because Nikalas is out there somewhere, and when he finally comes back, Agavordis and High Mother will be in for one hell of a fight."

Chapter 16

Nikalas stood atop a soaring mountain that was covered from top to bottom with smartly maintained neon blue grass. Next to him stood Kell Si. Together, they overlooked the city of Cap Ti Mor with a sense of pride and wonder. Kell Si had lived in Cap Ti Mor her whole life, but only a handful of times could she actually admit to making this journey. A truth she was regretting at this moment. Nikalas seized a deep breath and looked down, watching the blades of glowing grass dance in the wind like ballerinas on the stage.

"It's amazing up here," he smiled.

A gust of wind suddenly swept in front of him, nearly causing him to lose balance. Luckily — Kell Si quickly grabbed his shoulder, pulling him back from the edge.

"Careful," she cautioned. "It would be a shame if the savior ended up falling to his death. It would be rather perverse indeed."

"Savior," Nikalas laughed aloud. "I don't feel like that."

"That's good," Kell Si replied. "If you walked around thinking of yourself as the savior, it would be most ugly indeed."

Nikalas nodded in agreement and returned his attention to the skies above. In the air, Fawn confidently soared, flying alongside his fellow kin with joyful satisfaction. He had grown considerably in the past couple months. His second set of legs had finally emerged, and he was looking more and more like an adult Grimwort. As the Grimworts circled the skies, Fawn let out a proud neigh and went into a tailspin along with the others in the pack.

"His growth is nearly complete," Kell Si observed.

"Finally, I'll be able to ride him. No more horseback rides to get where I need to go," Nikalas replied.

Kell Si smiled and looked towards her feet with a bashful grin.

"What?"

"You won't be needing to ride atop Fawn, Nikalas," she replied.

He quickly turned, looking at her with a bit of confusion that slowly turned into a coy smile.

"Do you mean I'll be able to fly?" He ecstatically bellowed.

"But of course," she replied. "Your true father was an Arnout. It is your destiny to take to the skies."

"Ah yes," he nodded. At that moment, his mind crept back to that day in the alley, where he had been shown the truth of his parentage.

***

Down the silent corridors of Nasleigh Keep wandered a simple, yet quite intelligent maid. She had many duties; laundry, cleaning, and even occasionally helping out in the kitchen. But none of her duties seemed as important as her favorite task of all, making the king's bedchambers. Often times, she would catch him before he left to do whatever it was a king did. He was friendly, talking to her and regaling her with tales of his adventures and his past. The more of him she learned, the more she fell in love. Yes, she was in love with him. But there was one major problem. The King was married to a lovely young woman named Venora, who was beautiful both in appearance and personality. She knew she couldn't compete with such unequivocal beauty, but that didn't stop her mind from wondering.

With an arm full of sheets, she approached the royal chamber, nodding at the guards that stood just outside the door.

"Is he in there?" Trisna questioned with her typical soft tone.

"Yes," the guard replied. "I haven't heard a peep in there. He may still be sleeping."

"Oh," Trisna paused. "Well, I'll probably just go in anyways. It's time for him to get out of bed anyways."

The guard bowed and stepped aside. Red-cheeked with nervousness, she approached the door and gave a light knock. No response. Looking towards the guard, she shrugged and then pushed the door open. Inside was dark, the curtains had been pulled tightly shut, only a sliver of light managed to enter, and it did little to remedy the situation.

"Your Highness?" She called out to the darkness. Looking towards his bed, there was no sign of him. If he wasn't sleeping then where was he? She was filled with concern because this was unusual, even for him. Dwennon was very often quite predictable, so where had he gone?

"Your Highness?" She called out again. Still nothing. Not even a whisper. Her eyes looked towards his private lavatory. *Could he be in there perhaps?* As she pulled open the door, she was greeted with dimness. Only a single candle was lit and a red satin curtain had been pulled tight, sealing away all other light. Her eyes scanned the room, towards the tub, and towards the toilet. Still, there was no sign of him.

"Where is he?" She asked aloud. Turning around, she quickly made her way back to the main quarters. She had just begun to head towards the door to summon the guards, when something made her pause. A wardrobe. It was large, dark-stained, and decorated with rustic flowers that had been carved into the wood. It was Venora's wardrobe. She knew this. She had often accessed it to place garments inside. She looked around the room one last time, then quietly approached it. With a light pull, the doors swung open, revealing a plethora of majestic outfits far too pricey for her to ever contemplate owning. One by one, she looked them over, pausing with wide eyes at a white gown with gold stitching and embroidered with various insects. Venora always had been a lover of nature.

"What can it hurt?" She whispered to herself. Carefully, she pulled the dress from its hook, looking it over with excitement and bringing it to the main bed. She laid it across the fine, satin comforter and began to gingerly undress. In the emptiness of the royal chambers, she stood in nothing but her knickers. *Just do it*, she thought to herself. Swallowing all fear, she lifted the dress, and carefully lowered it over the top of her. Her heart raced. It was exciting, the idea of almost walking in the skin of the woman who got to sleep with the man she loved. Exciting, yet dangerous. The penalty for being caught would surely be severe.

She stood in front of a tall, white framed mirror and looked herself over with a quaint smile.

"Wow," she whispered to herself. She looked better than she could've ever imagined, and to her dismay, the dress fit perfectly. Venora — it seemed — was the same size. Her eyes meticulously studied the different details of the gown. The various insects all seemed to be strategically placed. They told a story. A story of the world Venora had left behind when she married the King. She kept her gaze fixated on the gown, when suddenly the window facing out towards Tordenth, creaked open. Her heart jumped into her throat. Quickly, she stole her attention from the mirror and aimed it towards the window. There was nothing there.

"Strange," she muttered. With a bit of nervousness, she quickly moved towards it, slowing down a bit, as she got closer. As if by some form of magic, a figure began to appear in front of her. On its back was a large set of wings, its eyes were blue and filled with lust.

"Venora," the voice called out. As the figure continued to materialize before her eyes, the full identity became clear. Lord Aldon of Cristol.

"Lord Aldon," Trisna replied with a startle.

"You look ravishing my dear. Tell me, are you wearing that gown because you knew I was coming?" Aldon questioned.

Trisna stood still, her mouth was devoid of any words. Try as she might, she could find no strength to speak. Aldon prudently made his way closer to her, coming to a brief pause, before he leaned in and kissed her passionately on the lips. As he pulled back, he could see the tremble in her hands.

"My dear," he paused. "Why do you shake?"

Still, she could find no words. The whole situation was startling. She was stuck, a prisoner of trespassing, and a prisoner of the lie she had just discovered. Venora had not been faithful. *How could she do this?*

Using a gentle touch, he slowly led her towards the bed, and as her knees found the surface of the mattress, she carefully sat down.

"I've missed you," Aldon whispered, pushing her down against the comforter.

***

Nikalas sighed as he recalled the story, it wasn't exactly one he had wanted to know. But it did explain quite a bit about who he truly was. An accident. A result of an adulteress relationship.

***

Trisna sat quietly, surrounded by darkness and cold. The slums were no place for a pregnant woman — and yet — that is exactly where she found herself this night. She couldn't bear to remain at the palace. Not after what she had learned of the queen. It was undeniably shameful, and for each moment she spent with the King, the truth threatened to come out.

"Are you okay mam?" A longhaired, smelly drunken man questioned as he stumbled by.

"Yes," she whispered. "I'm fine."

"Can I buy you a drink?" He sloppily asked.

"No thank you."

The man angrily shook his head and began to walk away.

"I don't need anything from a pregnant whore anyways," he muttered as he continued on his way.

She looked up, staring at the man with anger as he continued to saunter further from where she sat. Getting up took a bit of work, the pregnancy had added quite a bit of strain, but stand up she did. She wanted to hit him. Wanted to knock him off his wobbly feet and watch him faceplant into the wet concrete. There was fire in her steps; anyone paying attention could've seen it. She reached down, picking up a loose rock, and continued towards the drunk as he whistled and sang a tune aloud.

"I knew a whore, yea, I knew a whore. Her name was Molly. She liked 'em all. She liked 'em all every night. Yes, I knew a whore. She once made love to a boar. Anything for chitte. Anything for a bang."

She raised her hand, preparing to throw the rock when suddenly, a hand grabbed her, causing her to yelp. "What are you doing?" The man asked as he shook her hand, triggering the rock to fall.

"I was gonna teach that creep a lesson," Trisna retorted. The man looked down at her protruding belly and shook his head.

"You're pregnant," he noted. "I don't think you should be looking for alleyway fights in your condition." He looked her in the eyes, as he did, she saw something remarkable. Compassion. Innocence. Things she thought she would never see again. Somehow, in this unassuming and nerdy looking man, she found them.

"Come on," he grabbed her shoulder and turned her around. "Let's get you out of this cold."

Carefully, he began to guide her down the alley, being sure not to move too quickly

"I'm Stephen," he said as they continued to walk.

"Trisna," she replied with tearful eyes.

***

Nikalas opened his eyes and beamed into the lavender breeze as it rushed like a stampede of horses through his hair.

"Nikalas?" Kell Si questioned.

He turned towards her with a confident smile and without warning suddenly thrust himself over the edge.

Air rushed all around him, wrapping him in its grasp like a mother to her child. It brought with it, a sense of urgency, but somehow he felt no fear. His eyes remained focused on the surface above, at Kell Si, as she stood at the edge with her hand over her mouth. *I can do this*, he thought to himself.

His descent to the ground halted suddenly. Keeping his eyes trained on Kell Si, he began to imagine himself flying back up, and to his dismay, he began to rise. Higher and higher, he climbed until he was hovering over the ground, prompting Kell Si to step back. As he released his focus, his feet found the soft grass.

"Nikalas," Kell Si laughed, patting his chest with pride.

"What?" He coyly asked. "You told me I could fly."

Kell Si looked at him with a hint of awe, then squinted her forehead in confusion.

"What is it?" Nikalas asked.

"I assumed that like all Arnouts, you would need wings to fly. Yet you did that without having any."

"Well to be fair it wasn't really flying," Nikalas explained. "It was a spell."

Kell Si nodded her head in understanding and took a seat in the grass. She timidly motioned for him to do the same.

"You know of your heritage. You know of your ability to use The Echo. But you have not unlocked your full potential," Kell Si lectured.

"If you're going to defeat Agavordis, it'll take all you have. It's time to awaken the Arnout within, only then, can you become truly powerful."

"How do I do that?"

Kell Si looked towards the ground and with her left hand, drew a circle in the grass that suddenly began to glow a faint yellow hue.

"Many years ago, the mother of the Arnouts gifted her children a bit of her power. Pomari was her name. She was miraculous indeed. She blessed the bloodline, ensuring all descendants would have the same power she had," Kell Si explained.

Within the circle emerged an image of a young boy being led to a glistening body of water, an old man stood at his side.

"While the potential is buried within each and every Arnout, their skills are locked away until they reach the proper age."

The elder Arnout grabbed the boys head and thrust it deep into the picturesque waters of Cristol. From within the depths, the water began to glow, filling the sapphire waters with a light hue. When the boy emerged, a pair of glorious wings had sprouted from his back.

"The ritual unlocks the powers. The ritual is how the Arnouts gain their powers."

Nikalas continued to watch the image as the boy, now fully powered, took to the skies with a beaming smile.

"That's Cristol, isn't it?" He finally asked.

Kell Si shook her head.

"So are we going back to Furlasia?" He questioned.

Once again, she shook her head, this time in the opposite direction.

"But how?"

Suddenly, the circle filled with water, sapphire blue water. Nikalas' eyes widened with shock—on his chest—he felt something cold suddenly come to a rest upon his skin. Upon looking down, he noticed a strange necklace had appeared. The very same one the boy from the vision had worn.

"How did you do that?" He inquired. Kell Si offered no answer. Instead, she quickly grabbed his head and pushed it down into the window of water. He choked and struggled to be free, but Kell Si would not let him up. Her grip on the back of his head was strong. She watched mercilessly as he struggled to breath, and as expected, all around him, a light began to glow. It was bright, so bright she had to shield her eyes using the one hand that wasn't preoccupied. He continued to struggle, tapping his hands on the ground as if to beg for mercy, but Kell Si offered none.

After he had finally stopped resisting, and the light began to fade, she lifted her hand. Nothing. There was no movement. He was perfectly still. Instantly, he shot up and began to cough out water. Slowly, the window of water closed, leaving nothing but the neon glass in its place.

"What the hell?" He wailed as he continued to choke on the water that had filled his lungs.

Kell Si looked at him with a smile.

"You think you're funny? I almost died!" Nikalas hollered. As he looked in her eyes, he realized she wasn't looking at him, but instead past him, at something behind him. In a quick motion, he whipped around, catching a glimpse of something.

"What was that?" He pondered.

Once again, he quickly turned around, getting yet another glance at something that was fair colored and nearly translucent.

He tried again, and again until alas, he finally threw his arms up in frustration.

"Ok, what's going on?" He finally asked. With a broad smile, Kell Si pointed behind him yet again.

"You have wings," she replied.

"What?" Nikalas said with dismay. "Wings? Like a fairy?"

Kell Si shook her head.

"Well, that's just great," Nikalas sighed.

Chapter 17

Emlin sat on the cold, porous, floor, holding—in her hand—a sponge. Her circular motions did little to improve the overall appearance of the floor, yet her captor cared very little. Sitting on a throne, watching with an all-too-satisfied grin, was Agavordis. He watched contently as his former friend worked diligently to clean a floor that would never be clean. Her spirit was strong. She would not break. For weeks now, he had forced upon her pathetic chores like this one, offering an end to it if she would only say one phrase, *I love you*. She refused, spitting at the offer every time it came up.

"Emlin dear, you missed a spot just over there," Agavordis pointed towards the feet of a ghoul who had just vomited a bit of black goo onto the floor. She looked at the mess, then shot him a glare of contempt.

"I could always have one of the maids clean it," he offered. Keeping her eyes trained on him with a hatred she had never known, she climbed to her feet. Without a single word of protest, she wandered over to the ghoul and knelt down with the sponge and bucket. Agavordis sighed with disappointment as she began to clean the grotesque mess quietly. Footsteps from down a nearby hall began to travel towards their ears. Emerging from the hall, were a couple Akordan soldiers, as well as Zanna. Her hands and feet were bound with chains, and her attire left something to be desired. Her hair, which was usually freshly maintained, was a disheveled mess.

"She's refusing to do her chores sir," one of the Akordan guards croaked. He was large, but hardly the biggest Akordan. His mouth was missing several teeth, and he had scars running horizontal across his eyes. Grayden, was his name. His presence in Solarian was on his own accord; when the fighting had ended, many grateful Akordans pledged themselves right then and there.

"Zanna," Agavordis called out as he jumped up from his throne.

"What's the problem?" He walked towards her with open arms and an insensitive smirk. He came to a stop a few inches shy of her and shook his head.

"What will I do with you?" At that moment, Zanna pulled back her hands and brought them down on Agavordis' head. He dropped to his knees as the chain began to press against his neck.

The maneuver didn't last long, however. Grayden promptly put an end to it. All it took was one strike to the head to get her to see things a bit differently.

"Well that was rude," Agavordis accused as he quickly phased backwards. Grayden firmly gripped Zanna's hair and lifted her head, forcing her to look at Agavordis.

"You didn't really think that would work, did you?" He calmly asked.

"No," Zanna replied. "I just wanted to see how fragile you really are." Agavordis cocked his head, looking towards Grayden with surprise.

"And?" He asked. "What did you think?"

Suddenly Zanna's expression went maniacal.

"You're weak and flimsy, just as I expected," she laughed, spitting a splotch of blood at his feet. Agavordis looked at her with concern, she seemed unhinged. Maybe even broken . Had she broken already? It hadn't even been that long. He had expected to toy with her for a bit longer. As Zanna beamed, he continued to silently observe her, pondering what was the best course to take next.

"Grayden," Agavordis paused as he turned and looked towards Emlin.

"Zanna seems tired. Perhaps she needs a rest. Take her to the dungeons; we'll give her a break."

The battered Akordan nodded his head, and then grabbed Zanna firmly by the arm as he led her to a stairway on the far side of the foyer. As they vanished from sight, Agavordis approached Emlin and stood with his weight leaning on one side and his hands placed confidently on his hips.

"You like the way the power makes you feel don't you?" Emlin scoffed.

"I like it better than how I felt when your father had me banished," Agavordis retorted.

As Emlin climbed to her feet, she let out an extended sigh of disgust.

"How long are you going to hide behind that one moment in your life?"

She paused a few inches shy of his face.

"Your father cost me everything. Were it not for him, none of this would've happened. We would be happy."

"The ugliness I see before me, it was always there, and one day it would've come out. My father didn't create this darkness, it was already there," Emlin roared as she took a step closer.

"We would never have worked. I would've seen the real you eventually and ended it."

Agavordis peered at her with hatred in his eyes, then, suddenly in a moment of emotional rage, he brought his hand across her face. The sound of the slap echoed throughout the room, repelling off the bricks and filling the room with treacherous noise. Emlin stood still, red-faced and filled with shock. As he looked at her, he knew he had made the worst mistake of all. He had struck the woman he professed to love. There was no coming back from it. It happened. It was done. The moment would be forever embedded in their history.

"Emlin," Agavordis paused.

"Stop," she coldly replied. She held her cheek and turned towards the direction of the dungeons.

"Where are you going?" Agavordis called out.

"To the dungeons," Emlin called out.

"Where you keep all your victims," she whispered.

Her words landed hard. Like a blade to the gut, they burned. Searing his heart and mind with a wound that felt like it would never heal. Once she faded from sight, he was left with nothing but his guilt. His guilt and contempt.

"Fine," he muttered to himself.

"Am I to assume this means you've finally given up on this ridiculous crusade?" A malevolent voice suddenly crawled into the air like a rodent seeking scraps. Epard. Always Epard. He was an expert at showing up when least wanted.

"She'll never take you back now," Epard laughed. "Not after that."

Agavordis turned to see him emerge from a side hall filled with burning torches.

"How much did you see?" Agavordis questioned.

"Enough to know you just blew your last chance," Epard scoffed. He entered the foyer with a pleased grin and looked around as if expecting someone else to be in the room.

"It's time Septus. You've won your war. You rule these lands just as your father would've wanted. And now," Epard paused.

"It's time to make good on your word. On your father's word. I need to get back. I don't belong here. I never did. I need to get back to Cap Ti Mor. There are some people I need to have words with."

Agavordis stared at the floor, taking in the sight of every pore in the stones. Was he truly ready to lose his mentor? He wasn't sure. Insecurity had found him and left him mute. Silently, he continued to reflect on his life. On the path that led here. Epard was a continuous key throughout all of it. It had been *he* that found him when he was at his weakest and most frail moment. *He*, who transported him out of the forest and to Solarian.

"Are you sure you must go?" He finally asked, looking Epard firm in the eyes.

"I don't belong here Septus. I've been trying to get back to Cap Ti Mor since before you were born. I will return to my home and exact my vengeance."

Agavordis looked Epard in the eyes, into the soul, and saw his words rang true. He had a plan, one he would see through even if it meant his very own death.

"Alright," he said, shaking his head in disappointment. "I'll give you what you need to find the entrance."

Without another word, he turned, heading towards a stairway. His steps felt heavy as he began the climb, it was as though he wore weights on each foot. It was draining, just getting up the steps was an exercise in persistence and strength. When he finally reached the top, he turned and looked towards Epard, who stood with a wicked grin. Clearly, the gears in his head were spinning, Septus couldn't read minds, but in this case, he didn't have to. Dark things were coming to Cap Ti Mor, that much he was certain of.

After another flight of stairs — this one winding — he finally arrived at his quarters. Inside was a room that seemed more like storage than a living quarter. Boxes upon boxes were stacked atop each other, but in the center of it all was a bed. A bed that at this point seemed too large. He glanced at it for a moment, taking in the memories of the nights he had spent with Vigil. It seemed he was destined to live his days without a companion. Emlin rejected him, and Vigil had been killed in the conflict.

"I miss you," he whispered as he glanced at the spot on the bed where she had been. Their time together had been all too brief. With that, he shrugged off his emotions, pushing them aside like unwanted clothes and approached his desk. Sitting atop were a few glass beakers filled with various liquids of different colors, and in between them all, was a Shewglomus.

"Don't forget Septus, the transfer must be completed soon," a voice in the air warned. It was faint now, far less prevalent that it had previously been. His father's soul was fading. With each passing day, the likelihood of bringing him back became grimmer.

"I haven't forgotten. The ritual will be soon. I'm just looking for a suitable host," Agavordis explained.

"I haven't got time for you to leisurely shop for a body!" The voice roared.

"It's getting harder and harder to see you; soon I will be lost here."

Agavordis shook his head in understanding, and then picked up the Shewglomus.

After a few moments, it began to emit a light blue hue.

"Septus?" The voice questioned from within the orb. It was High Mother, his guardian both spiritually and physically.

"Yes," he paused. "It's me."

He looked around, scanning the room with paranoia, then brought his face right up close to the glass.

"She won't take me back. No matter what I say, I can't win Emlin's heart. I don't know what to do. It's driving me crazy," he whispered.

"If she won't be with me then I'll just kill her."

"Septus," High Mother paused with a sigh. "You can't really expect her to be with you after all you've done to hurt those around her. Come now. You killed her father. You killed her best friends. You killed her people."

"I had to. Hervott left me no choice. He forced my hand. He ruined my life." Agavordis bellowed in a screeching tone that bounced against the permeable walls.

"Why her Septus? Why does it have to be Emlin? There are so many women for you to pick from. Why do you cling to this one person so desperately?"

He closed his eyes. In his mind, he saw a girl. Beautiful yet terrifying. Elegant yet fierce. Smart yet merciless. He kept his eyes tightly shut as he continued to watch her stroll through the darkness of his mind. Here, she was calm. Here, she still loved him. Here, he could still see her entrancing smile.

"Septus?" High Mother questioned.

He heard her words. He knew he had to answer, but he didn't want to. Opening his eyes would bring him back to reality. To a reality where Emlin loathed him. It wasn't a place he wanted to be.

"She's the only one," he finally replied. "She's the only one in this world for me. The others are just mirages, faint traces of the female form. None of them will ever hold my heart. None of them will ever understand."

"You drive yourself mad, Septus," High Mother replied. "It's not good for you, and it's not good for the people."

"The people?" He questioned.

"Yes. You have a duty. A responsibility to make Furlasia a better place. Your father didn't start a war just so he could rule this land. He started a war because he truly believed he knew what was for the best," she explained.

He quietly sat back in his chair and bit his lip as he looked up towards the ceiling. It was unsightly; thwarted from greatness, but the unkind effects of time. Wood rot had taken over in an awful way, yet it mattered very little at this point.

"It's time to rule. To fix this land and shape it in a better way. They don't know what is best for them Septus. But you and I do. Together, we will bring greatness to Furlasia."

As he listened to her words, a grin formed on his dry, chapped lips. In his mind, a painting began to unfold. A land where poverty was a thing of the past. Where fear was a thing of the past. Where crime was all but eliminated. As he continued to envision this new land, he couldn't help but imagine Emlin at his side. Helping him shape Furlasia in a positive way. Perhaps such a role would give her a new purpose. Perhaps, if she saw the good he was doing, she might take him back.

"What do I do first?" He inquired.

"Start with Terria. For too long, that city has been hindered by crime, poverty, and corruption. You can do something about that. With an iron fist, you can turn that city around. They will fight you. They will try to resist. People don't like to be controlled, but that doesn't mean they don't crave it."

"Go there. Unlock the Beacons. Give them to the people. Free the prisoners that have been kept locked up far past their sentence. Kill all those who stand in your way. Eventually, they will submit. And when they do, that's when Terria will truly be saved."

"Yes," he smiled as he stood from his chair and approached a window that overlooked the former courtyard of Abissal Keep.

"If I save Furlasia. If I fix this broken place, she'll have to take me back. She'll be so grateful that she'll run to me with open arms."

"Septus," High Mother paused.

"Yes?" He replied.

"Never mind," she sighed. Without a moment's notice, the Shewglomus went dark. She had left, leaving him alone with his thoughts and his hopes.

Chapter 18

"That boy is an idiot," High Mothered sighed as she turned and looked at Jacob with a disappointed gaze.

Jacob wore a bulky and metallic brace on his leg, but it served its purpose well. It had been a few months since Kit had shattered his knee, and yet, the pain still persevered. It held onto him with dear might, begging him to surrender. Unfortunately, there was no time to rest, no time for relaxation. Not when one was serving the High Mother.

"What do you mean my lord?" Jacob inquired.

"He's letting his obsession with this insignificant girl cloud his mind. I'm not sure how much use he'll be to me at this point, but hopefully, with any luck, he'll follow my advice."

Jacob took a step closer, limping on his left leg with each passing movement.

"You really think he can unite Furlasia?" He asked.

High Mother looked at him before bursting into an exorbitant cackle.

"Unite Furlasia?" She continued to laugh.

"Yes my lord."

As she saw the seriousness in his face, her laughter quickly ceased. Turning her chair, she stood up and sternly approached.

"No," she simply replied.

"Septus isn't here to save Furlasia. He's here to help me ruin it. Whether he realizes it or not."

Jacob looked at her with dreadful turmoil.

"My lord?" He pondered aloud. As he continued to look at her face, he saw in her eyes a glimpse of someone completely stripped of love. Someone who was completely lacking in empathy or sympathy. Darkness. There was darkness in her eyes, perhaps even all the way down to her soul.

"Septus will fail. All he will accomplish is further muffing things up. And when he does, when it all falls apart, my brother will come. And that's when I'll kill him."

Jacob shifted his weight and then took a leisurely step back. High Mother grinned at the subtleness, then turned back towards her chair.

"The great feud is coming, Jacob. Soon I will reveal my true identity to the world."

She plopped into her chair and gazed at him.

"But for now, it's time to get our guests to start pulling their weight. Bring them to the sacrificial chamber," she instructed.

Tricia and Stephen Noise silently followed behind Jacob as he led them through twisted corridors lined with metallic thorns. Along the ceilings — placed sporadically about — were the skeletal remains of beings long gone. It was a truly heinous place. It seemed almost intentionally dark and morose. This wasn't meant to be a home, it was a lair. A lair belonging to someone who wanted to remind all who visited of just how dangerous she really was. Two of the High Mother's red slaves followed behind them. As always, they were silent, offering no noise at all, not the sounds of their footsteps, nor the whimpers of their breath. Their presence did little to disturb the environment around them.

After a nerve-wracking tour of the dreaded fortress, they emerged in a large room that reeked of smoke and an unknown mixture of chemicals. Each wall was decorated with torches and in slap dab in the middle of it all — was a large pool of red liquid. Jacob quietly led them towards it, as they drew nearer, smoke could be seen rising from the mystical substance.

"What are we doing in here?" Tricia asked aloud. Jacob remained silent, coming to a stop outside the pool and slowly turning around. In his eyes, there was a hint of something she couldn't quite make out.

"Welcome to the Yoke Pitt," a voice called out. Tricia jumped with startle as a looming shadow began to grow on the floor in front of them. Slowly, in an almost angelic quality, High Mother touched down to the floor. She peered at them with a bothersome smile, then slowly sauntered towards them.

"This is where you will learn to serve me without question, without hesitation, and without rebellion," High Mother motioned to the slaves that stood just behind her two guests. They mutely nodded, then grabbed ahold of both Tricia and Stephen with a grip much stronger than one would expect from such petite women.

"Why are you doing this?!" Tricia demanded.

"Because dear," she paused. "Because I hate you. And because I want to hurt Nikalas. When he sees what you've become, mindless slaves who can't even remember him, it'll break him. He'll fall before me without me having even to lift a hand."

Tears filled Tricia's eyes as the words slithered to her ears like a duplicitous serpent.

"Take me," Stephen whispered as he looked to the floor.

"What was that?" High Mother croaked.

With red eyes overflowing with anger, Stephen looked up.

"I said take me you bitch."

High Mother tilted her head dauntingly, her eyes fixed on him with malice. Without another word, she motioned towards the slave. The bare skinned woman nodded and began to push Stephen forward.

"No!" Tricia hollered. Towards the pit, the slave continued to guide Stephen, until they came to a stop just in front of Jacob.

"Stephen Noise," Jacob halted. "The High Mother appreciates your sacrifice. You are serving a purpose higher than any mortal can comprehend. In these mystical waters, you will be transformed into a devoted servant of the goddess Gravi. You will speak no words; you will remember nothing of your past. You will live only to serve our lord."

As he looked towards Stephen with a bit of regret, he nodded, and the servant began to push him up a small stairway. There were only three steps in total, so the trek to the water was brief. From the sides of the room, emerged three more slaves, each of them carrying a rock and a small amount of rope. As with the others, they offered no sound, no noise, no proof of their presence. They sauntered over to Stephen, and began to tie the rocks onto his limbs one at a time. One on each wrist and one on each ankle.

"Stephen!" Tricia called out one last time. He froze.

"I will always love you. No matter what they do. She can't erase our love."

High Mother gave a slight shrug of amusement.

"Actually I can."

Without further ado, the slave guided Stephen to the water's edge, and then slowly, they walked inside. Immediately, smoke began to rise, heavier and thicker now than it had been before. He winced as the water grew deeper, with each passing moment, the pain grew more severe. Behind him, Tricia, who was held, stood with tears, her sobbing filling the cavernous room with its melancholy tone. It was music to High Mother's ears.

Soon Stephen had vanished from sight, and from the pool, the slave emerged. As she stepped out and onto the small stairwell, the cryptic liquid dripped to the floor with a sizzle.

"And now we wait," High Mother sighed.

Seconds turned to minutes, and before long, almost ten minutes had come and gone. High Mother finally nodded towards the slave, and back towards the pit, the slave went. Time seemed to slow down. As the slave reached down into the water, Tricia struggled, trying to get an early glimpse of what had happened. Slowly and silently, Stephen emerged.

He turned, splashing through the water and then came to a stop atop the quaint stairway. As with the others, his skin was red from head to toe. All his hair was gone — burned away — along with his genitalia. He was a sexless shell of the man that had once been Stephen Noise.

High Mother clapped with joy as he began to wander towards her with empty eyes.

"Yes, yes," High Mother smiled. "Excellent."

He came to a stop in front of her, and she looked him over with satisfaction.

"Let's get you dry," she winked.

She looked towards the floor, then promptly lifted her arms, sending a cloud of red smoke circling him. Tricia gulped as she watched, dumbfounded by the terrifying display of power. There was heat to this smoke, enough that even standing few feet back, she could feel its warmth.

"You'll burn him!" Tricia exclaimed. High Mother ignored her concerns and kept her focus locked on her newly acquired slave. Panic took over, a fear that would not be quelled. She had to be free. She quickly looked towards the slave that held her. He was gargantuan, his arms as big as her whole head, and his grip so firm she was sure to have bruises. The chances of escape seemed slim, but she had to try. With a grunt and a groan, she wiggled, trying her best to shake the silent man off.

As High Mother heard the struggle, she dropped her spell and turned to see what was happening. *Wham!* She was greeted with a slap to the face. Somehow, Tricia had managed to break loose of the slave's grip. Tricia reared her hand back, preparing to take yet another swipe, when suddenly, Stephen approached. Looking at her with hollow, emotionless eyes, and then lifted her by the neck, holding her as high as his arms would allow.

"Stephen it's me," she choked.

High Mother cackled maniacally as she clapped with joy.

"Take her to the pit," she ordered.

Tricia's face was beginning to turn red, the tight grip around her throat threatened to strip her of her consciousness. Everything began to blur as she faultered under Stephen's awesome new strength. She knew at that moment the man she loved was gone. However she couldn't help but hope. It was all she had at this point.

"Stephen, stop this," Tricia pleaded. Ignoring her remarks as if they were just faint whispers, he turned and began carrying her to the pit. Her vision continued to blur, unconsciousness was in her cusp, and soon darkness would take over. Behind her, she could hear the distant laughter of High Mother. Her cruelty and malice had no limits and no conscience. No—she was much too filled with hate to feel anything other than pleasure watching the suffering of others. As he reached the top of the stairway, he carelessly threw her still body into the water.

Sleep had gotten her. Darkness had found her, and so, she could do nothing but float. In her mind, perhaps she was somewhere pleasant; at the beach with Stephen and Nikalas, sharing a pizza at the park, riding the tram around the city. Perhaps she was outside of her body, looking at all this from another plane of existence. Wherever she was, it was quite clear, she wasn't here—not anymore.

Slowly she rose from the water. Her hair and all signs of her gender were gone. She turned around, nodding silently at Stephen, and trudged her way through the murky bath. High Mother smiled as the pair of new slaves made their way towards her. As before, she quickly sent a funnel of red smoke circling around Tricia, and before long, the procedure was done.

"Jacob," High Mother turned towards the cowering servant, who had rushed to the far wall.

Quickly, he rushed back towards the center of the room and looked at the two latest members of the staff.

"Yes, my lord?" He replied.

"Take these two and put them to work in the fields," High Mother instructed.

"As you wish," Jacob bowed. "Come along you two. There is work to be done."

The three of them silently made their way across the large room and faded from sight as they passed through the doorway.

"This is all going much smoother than I expected," High Mother said to herself. Her focus suddenly shifted to the pit, it was still now, back to the way it normally was. She slowly wandered towards it, coming to a stop at the first step. Sighing, she began to ascend the stairs, the sound of her heels filling the otherwise silent expanse. She paused, looking the water over with a satisfactory twist of her lips. As she continued to study the mystifying liquid, she reached down into her dress. Her hands felt around for a moment, and then, from the shadows of her gown, she withdrew a blade. It was an intricate blade and sharper than most. In its hilt, was the familiar depiction of a serpent devouring a skull.

"Soon," she whispered to herself as she hurriedly pressed the blade against her wrist. With a quick pull, she sliced deep into her skin, allowing a bit of her energy to pour through the gash and into the pit. As the energy hit the water, it sizzled, bringing a generous amount of red smoke into the air.

"I'll see you soon brother."

In the smoke, the shape of Undr suddenly appeared. His human face peering at her with contempt and disappointment.

"And you will lose," Undr whispered. His voice was faint. So faint, she questioned whether or not it had in fact been real. In the distance, she heard something, something that stole her attention from the familiar shape. She turned, scanning the opening of the room and shrugged at its empty appearance. She had just begun to turn her focus to the pit when something caught her eyes. Standing up and wedged firmly into the floor, was a sword.

Grinning, she summoned a cloud of red smoke and let it carry her to the floor below. Once her feet had landed, she leaned in to examine the phantom weapon. It was impossible not to smile as she beheld its elegant architecture. Her fingers gripped the handle, and with a quick and effortless pull, she lifted the sword from its confinement.

Chapter 19

Olivium had much to offer. It was a fairly secluded city. A city for people who didn't wish to be bothered by the politics of the larger cities. Here, one could actually feel free. Together with their newfound companions, Articus, Sillimon, Methalda, and Penny wandered the streets, taking in the sights. It was difficult not to be impressed. There was money in this city, that much was clear. The shop windows were filled with items of value, all of them appealing and tempting. As Articus passed by a shop that sold handbags, he looked at Methalda and smirked.

"Maybe on our way out," Methalda whispered. Articus nodded with a grin and returned his attention forward.

At the front of the group, were Jinn and Idrix, serving as the guides. Neither had been to Olivium before and yet, both seemed to have a pretty good idea about where they were heading. After all, the destination wasn't exactly hard to spot. The Boss had a flair for elaborate things. So, when they spotted a house that sat on the edge of the city and stood a few stories tall, it was all too clear. Little was known about their mysterious host—if that's what you could call her— but to Idrix it was clear, she couldn't be trusted.

"Have you ever seen such a bunch of self-entitled fools?" Idrix whispered to Jinn.

"The Kajj would never live in such a manner," Jinn replied.

Idrix turned and looked at her with a smile.

"I hope one day you allow me to meet your people. See where you came from."

"We should never write off anything as impossible," Jinn said, keeping her gaze trained forward.

They continued to make their way down the pristine streets, getting stares and gossip all the way. For as wealthy of a city as it appeared Olivium was, it seemed surprising how simple the clothing of its citizens was. None of them looked fancy; none of them looked like they were on the higher end of society. Perhaps, the money was better spent on more important things than one's clothes. That had to be the case, because many of the Decoyers even had better attire, and *that*, was saying something.

"Feels like we are in a lucid dream," Penny muttered to Sillimon, as a woman carrying a bag of groceries stopped to stare.

"They look at us like we are the strangest thing they've ever seen."

Sillimon nodded, taking notice of an elderly man who pushed in front of him a cart.

"Perhaps we are," he replied.

"Can I interest you in some oysters?" The man with the cart called out. Penny jumped, startled by the man's abrupt tone.

"She doesn't like oysters," Sillimon turned and replied. His comment earned him a stern glance.

"Don't speak for me," she glared. The elderly man smiled and opened the top of the cart to reveal its contents. Sitting inside, nestled nice and tightly, were dozens of sealed oysters. She carefully at looked them. Some of them were smooth, while others had a rather rough texture.

"I'll take just a couple," Penny replied. At the front of the line, Idrix and Jinn had stopped, turning to see what was causing the holdup. They were on a tight schedule after all. As Idrix took notice of the transaction, she giggled slightly and then, proceeded towards the elderly man.

"I thought you didn't like oysters. Every time I've suggested them you act uninterested," Sillimon remarked. His comments only served to dig a deeper hole—once again—Penny shot him a furious glance. Without giving him a response, she reached down into the cart and pulled out two of the largest oysters she could find in the bunch. As she withdrew her arm, Sillimon's eyes widened. They were monstrously large, not exactly the best endeavor for a first time eating oyster experience.

"Here," the elderly man paused as he reached into a sheath on his leg. "Use this."

He carefully handed a long blade to Penny, and she quickly pried the oysters open, revealing their gooey inner contents. She looked at the old man with uncertainty.

"You just put it to your lips and tip your head back and suck the meat down," he instructed. Nodding, Penny looked towards Sillimon, who looked at her daringly.

She quickly did as she was told, tipping her head back and taking down all the viscous contents. Sillimon went silent, hoping—nay—expecting a reaction of disgust.

"Wow," Penny replied. "That was so......interesting."

"It's an acquired taste for sure," Idrix added as she came to a stop. She leaned over, looking into the cart at the batch of oysters.

"How fresh are these?" She questioned.

"Just caught them this morning my friend," the man replied.

"I'll take a dozen," she ordered. With a smile she turned, looking towards the group.

"They are rumored to be good luck. We should all have one," she explained.

Articus looked towards Methalda with skepticism as the elderly man reached inside and began handing out oysters. Sillimon grabbed one, as did Jinn, Kadeen, and Dajreem. But Methalda and Adam seemed none too interested. Idrix paused, looking at the two holdouts with disappointment.

"Come on," she paused. "I used my own money to pay for these."

Looking at each other with obvious disgust and vacillation, the two grabbed an oyster and glanced at the rest of the members with an awkward smile.

"We traveled a long way in search of something that is going to save the world. Everyone here is important, and a part of something that goes beyond the understanding of most people," Idrix proudly looked at the group as she held her oyster in front of her.

"I'm proud of all of you."

With that, she quickly brought the oyster to her lip and sucked down the contents. The others immediately followed suit, although Methalda did need a slight nudge of an elbow to finally take the plunge. As the last of the gooey texture slithered down her throat, she shuddered and tossed the shell to the ground.

"Never again," she said, shooting Articus a look of annoyance. He returned the look with a wink and then tossed his shell to the ground as well.

The journey across the city continued, each of the members finding something to enjoy. After another fifteen minutes of slow, strenuous walking—mostly due to Idrix—they arrived at the outskirts of a very large mansion. It was guarded by a rather large gate that was comprised of very intricate metal rods, each of them twisted all the way up. At the top of each rod was a golden sphere. It was hard to make out if it was in fact real gold or not. But Articus certainly found himself studying them rather closely.

Outside the gate, at a spot that presumably served as an entrance, stood a single guard with a spotless uniform and a black top hat. He didn't look like much, but given that he was placed at the entrance of the largest building in the city, one could safely assume he could handle himself.

"Welcome to The Cone. How can I help you?" The man asked. Dajreem scratched his head, perplexed by the off naming.

"The cone?" He asked. "But it's a rectangle."

"Yes, it is. The mam thought it reminded her of a cone, in the sense that its most interesting point is at the very top," the guard explained. He was older, perhaps midway into his years, his skin was brownish, and his eyes were jade green.

"I received a personal invite from The Boss," Idrix added, cutting past the mild small talk.

"She told me to inform you that it always smells like sulfur here just before it rains."

The guard looked at her with a smile and nodded. Stepping aside, he pulled on a sturdy bar, once it was clear of its containment, the gate slowly glided open. Once the gate was fully opened Idrix stepped inside. She stepped towards uncertainty, towards possible danger, but if their host was being honest, towards vengeance as well. Into the unknown she continued, her loyal comrades following closely behind her. As they took in the sights, it was hard not to be awestruck.

"The Cone," Jinn whispered. "I bet that's a clue. The most interesting point is at the very top? I bet that's where she's hidden it."

"Let's not make presumptions," Idrix replied, brushing her hand in the air as if to swat at her words.

Preceding the entrance to The Cone, was an elaborate, and tightly maintained garden. It was lined on both sides with hedges that had been pruned into the shapes of various animals. Perhaps the most interesting of all was a two-legged creature that stood upright and had small arms sprouting from its chest. Its face was elongated and from its head protruded long feathers. It was — suffice to say — not a commonly seen species. In fact, none of the group appeared familiar with it.

"I don't know what that is," Penny whispered. "But I don't ever want to meet one."

"Same," Sillimon nodded in agreement.

As unsettling as some of the pictured species were, it was hard to deny the calm and intrigue in seeing them formed into hedges. The path towards the entrance was lined with white rocks that sparkled in the light of the sun, and growing neatly next to them were red roses. They offered their pleasant aroma into the air like a gift that could be seen but not touched.

The door to The Cone opened as soon as they had cleared the garden path and standing in the doorway was a tall fellow with a lumpy build and golden tanned skin. There was something in his expression that made one feel pleasant, even before he opened his mouth to offer his personality.

"Welcome my friends," the man said.

"I am Daolin, I look after The Boss' affairs while she is out."

Idrix looked towards Jinn, then shot the man a perplexed stare.

"She'll be back soon, she ran to town to gather ingredients for tonight's dinner," he quickly explained.

Idrix let out a light sigh, then nodded towards the cheerful fellow.

"I must say I didn't quite expect you to bring so many with you. How many of you are there?"

"Ten in total," Idrix replied. A sudden tickle in her throat prompted a cough. It sounded hoarse, perhaps painful even. Once she had finished, she looked at the host and smiled.

"I did mention to her that I had my extended family coming along."

Daolin looked at the group and then quietly shrugged.

"Ehh. Who am I to protests such things? Come on in, I'm sure you're ready for some cooler air."

Idrix stepped inside, and sure as he had said, the air was noticeably cooler. It was strange actually. The room was dim, shielded from the sun, but it had a cooler feel than just a shaded room. With the others all gathered inside, Daolin carefully closed the door. The latch rang into the air with a loud click as the door came to a full close.

"Now then," he paused. "Let's get you all sorted."

Without further conversation, he proceeded to the front of the group and led them towards a flight of stairs. It was steep, much too steep for Idrix, luckily, an elevator was close by. The technology was simple enough, yet oddly, hadn't made its way to Furlasia. If it weren't for the fact that Idrix was well traveled, she might not have known what it was. Daolin stepped in front of the gate and pulled it open. It was roomy, but for ten people, that remained a mystery.

"Can it hold all of us?" Idrix asked. "Safely?"

"I'm not looking to die today," Daolin replied with a smirk as he waved them inside. Articus looked at Methalda with a mixture of confusion and awe, then followed Idrix inside. Once they were all inside, Daolin pulled a nearby lever and up they went. The technology was reliable yet primitive, and it was dreadfully noisy. All the way up, the sound of clicking gears fought—nay—barged its way into their ears. By the time the elevator had come to a stop on the fifth floor, everyone but Daolin was feeling a mild case of headache. With the gate pulled open, Articus, along with the other Decoyers, all eagerly piled out.

There was something different about this floor; it was an eye sore to say the least. With white walls and close to a dozen doors, the whole thing looked like the entrance to a doctor's office, a doctor with no decorative taste whatsoever. Daolin carefully weaseled his way past the group and made his way to the front.

"What is this place?" Dajeem asked. "It's hideous. Surely our host has better taste than this."

"This is the game floor," Daolin cheerfully replied.

"The game floor?" Penny questioned. Daolin silently nodded his head, then led them to a door that was smack dab in the middle of all the others. With a quick turn of the knob, the door creaked open, revealing a room of extraordinary magnificence. The game floor sure lived up to its name. There were tables spread all around, and each table featured a different game. There were marbles, chess, a game with blocks, and lots more. Idrix and the others all followed Daolin inside, looking around the room with curiosity. The walls in here were painted a bright combination of blue and pink. And on them, intricate decorations and strangely unique paintings were hung. One odd thing to be noted, however, was the fact that all the decorations were hung crookedly. Each of them was titled just ever so slightly. It seemed deliberate.

"What are we doing in here?" Idrix questioned.

"Mistress Lana wanted me to offer you the chance to play and enjoy your visit whilst she is out running her errands," Daolin explained.

"Her name is Lana?" Jinn asked. Shaking his head in disappointment, Daolin nodded, bumping his open palm to his forehead as he did.

"She wouldn't want you to know that," he whispered. "Take care to keep that bit of information between us."

Jinn looked at Idrix, who shrugged and turned her attention to a table that had a game of chess set up. The pieces were already moved; it appeared a game had already been started.

"How long will she be gone?" Idrix asked.

"Not long at all," Daolin replied. He looked at the group then bowed and made his way to the door.

"I'll have her come up here just as soon as she returns."

And with that, he was gone through the door from whence he had come, leaving them alone with their thoughts and confusions. There was an unsettling idiosyncrasy to everything about this place. It didn't make sense. Nothing seemed to match. From the ground floor up, there was nothing predictable. There was a lot to be told about someone, based on how they lived, how they decorated, the things they acquired. And The Cone, told a story that Idrix found most troubling.

"I don't like this," she finally admitted.

"Which part?" Methalda sarcastically asked. "The creepy animal hedges, the strange butler or this ridiculous game room?"

"None of it," Idrix sighed. She turned and approached Jinn.

"What game do you think she is playing?"

Jinn closed her eyes, trying to form a picture in her mind. Trying to understand their host, to know what made her tick, and what really prompted the invite.

"I suspect, she knows who we really are. And what we are here to do," Jinn replied.

"I think this is an observation. She's probably watching us right now. Trying to see what we will do. You can tell a lot about someone from the games they chose to play."

Articus looked around the room, taking in the various types of games. Most he had heard of, but there were some that looked a tad foreign. Perhaps they only existed in Adrasia. As he took notice of a board game with nothing but simple squares and two different game pieces, he leaned towards Methalda.

"I don't think they know what they're doing," he whispered.

"What gave that away?" She retorted.

"So what do you think we should do?" Jinn asked as she glanced at the rest of the group.

"Play a damn game," Idrix replied.

After what seemed like a good hour, the entrance door opened and in stepped a woman with what had to be the tackiest floral pattern dress Penny had ever seen. Her hair was tied up in a curly mess, her glasses were tacky, and her skin had an artificial golden hue to it.

"Hi y'all," she exclaimed with a smile. "It looks like you're all having fun."

Idrix looked up, setting down a wooden block, and peering at the outlandish woman with annoyance.

"Please tell me she's here," Adam huffed. "I can't take any more of this waiting."

The kooky woman laughed as she took a few steps inside. Grinning from ear to ear, she observed the room, paying close attention to where everyone had positioned themselves.

"Well, of course, she's here silly," she replied. "I'm her."

"You're The Boss?" Dajreem queried skeptically.

The woman nodded and smiled broadly.

"I'm so pleased to see you all made it safely. The Peridian Sea is not the easiest water to travel."

Idrix studied the woman, then carefully pulled herself from her chair, bumping the puzzle as she did.

"Oh shoot. I'm sure you worked hard on that," The Boss commented with upside down pursed lips.

"Not as hard as I worked at bringing my family all the way over here," Idrix retorted.

Suddenly, the woman's obtuse smile faded, giving way to a much more serious, if not sinister expression.

"Let's not pretend this is your family," she beamed. "I know a crew when I see one."

Idrix's eyes opened with shock, and once again, the smile returned to The Boss' face.

"We can talk all about how you plan to steal from me later. But first, let's get some supper in our bellies."

Chapter 20

"Bordium!" Nikalas called out. From his hands, a steady beam of energy appeared, blasting, a hole in a nearby tree with ease. He smiled with childlike enthusiasm and canceled the spell.

"Amazing," he exclaimed. "All this time I've been dragging around a staff, and the truth is, I didn't even need it."

Kell Si looked at him cautiously and shook her head.

"Wrong, Nikalas. There are still many spells an Arnout cannot perform. If you wish to have full use of the magic The Echo has to offer, you'll still need your staff. It's still the most capable way of harnessing the energy."

"So you mean Gnomes are more powerful than Arnouts?" He sighed.

She shook her head and smiled.

"It's not about which species is more powerful. It's about how capable you are of tapping into The Echo, and how much energy your genetics allows you to process," she explained.

Expelling a huff, he peered into her eyes, raising an eyebrow as he did.

"Ok fine," she paused. "I'm more powerful than you."

"Damnit!" Nikalas hollered. He looked at her with a suave simper, then looked up towards the sky. In the air, circling in an almost territorial-like way, was Fawn.

"Hey boy," Nikalas called out with excitement. With a mighty neigh, Fawn dove down, coming to a firm thud against the neon grass. The ever-cheerful Grimwort dashed to his side, lowering his head in hopes of being rubbed. Kell Si chuckled as Nikalas began to rub behind Fawn's ears. What little hair the creature had, all began to stand up. The sensation was all too exciting. Grimworts craved nothing more than the approval of their master, and the touch of their hands. It was such a simple existence. Not unlike a dog.

"He likes this," Nikalas explained with a smirk.

"I see that," she remarked. Slowly, she approached while keeping a watchful eye on the creature's reaction. Unlike Nikalas, who barely stood as high as Fawn's belly, Kell Si soared high above. She studied his reaction a bit further, then finally decided to go for it. Her large hands were quite capable indeed. She could reach far more area at one time. Fawn shook his head with enthusiasm, taking deep breaths all the while.

"You have an incredible bond with this creature," Kell Si observed. "He loves you."

Nikalas looked at Fawn with a proud smile.

"Yea I suppose he does. The only sad thing is that I no longer need him. I mean, I have wings now."

Kell Si promptly shot him a furious glance, and then continued to gently rub Fawn's ears.

"Just because you have wings, that doesn't mean you don't need him. Fawn will be a friend for life if you let him be. Have you not heard the stories of the final battle with the necromancer? Yogurn saved Kunklestick in the midst of certain doom."

Nikalas nodded as he recalled the story. A terrible story it was. Furlasia was on the brink of certain doom, all was seemingly hopeless until Yogurn swooped in, narrowly saving the day. As he thought back to that day, he suddenly found himself thinking of Emlin. He thought of the vision the corpse of Drachen had shown him. It was dreadful. Terria was in shambles and Emlin….Emlin was dead.

"That cannot happen," he whispered.

"What?" Kell Si questioned.

"The vision," Nikalas paused. "I can't let it happen."

Suddenly he turned, looking over the landscape, and took a deep breath.

"I think it's time for me to go back," he proclaimed. "Septus is dangerous. He has unchecked aggression and an extraordinary amount of power. That's a bad combo if I ever heard of one."

Kell Si nodded, then slowly strolled towards him, her feet sinking into the moist grass with each new step. Standing next to him, she looked towards the tall tower of Fal Mor shining under the sun. It served as a constant reminder of how far the Gnomes had come. After all, it wasn't too long ago that the Gnomes were not much more than a primitive species living off the land in caves and huts. Now they were a technical marvel, and more attuned to The Echo than they had ever been. And what made them so powerful was their constant sacrifices, their selflessness, and their ability to see the bigger picture.

As she looked over the landscape, she could feel a bit of guilt building up inside her. She knew. The elders had already told her. Agavordis had won. He had brought war down upon Furlasia and killed thousands. To prevent *that* war, Nikalas was already too late. She looked at him, silently pondering his reaction when he realized the secrets they had all been keeping from him.

"Nikalas, you're not ready yet," Kell Si informed.

"To hell, I'm not," Nikalas retorted. "I can fly, I can summon magic with or without my staff. I can go in and out of The Echo at will. Septus can't do those things. I can beat him."

Kell Si looked him over, summing up her thoughts and trying her best to stomach his egotistical response.

"Your reply just now is why I know you're not ready," she replied.

"You have skills, and you have unlocked a lot of power deep within you. But your anger, and your ego is still there. In that regard, you and Septus are no different."

Nikalas opened his mouth to protest, but Kell Si quickly lifted her finger.

"In a battle of magic, you are equally matched. If you want to defeat him and save Furlasia, you need to be more in control than he is. Only then will you have the upper hand."

He sighed as he realized the trueness of her words. Even now, he could feel it, that compulsive need to be the best. To get revenge on the bullies who jumped him. To fight fire with fire. He wanted to hurt Septus. He wanted to kill him. Deep down, it felt like if he could defeat Septus, then he could defeat his own insecurity. *My parents left because of me.* The idea had been tormenting him the past few years. It drove him, pushed him, controlled every part of him. This undying and possibly false guilt had turned him from a loving and compassionate boy to an emotional and spite-driven one.

"We need to do more mediating and focus training," Kell Si briefed.

An hour later, he found himself sitting inside a darkened room that was sorely lacking in furniture. The *Meditation Chambers.* Silently, he sat on the floor; legs folded, eyes shut, trying his best to follow his mentor's instructions.

"Silence your mind. Only then will you be able to access all the secrets that have eluded you."

He grinned as he sneakily opened his eyes, taking notice of Kell Si's strict focus as she sat across from him. *I'm hungry,* he thought to himself. *I wonder how long she expects me to do this. What's Emlin doing?*

Clarity seemed impossible. How could someone so molded by past events clear his mind of the memories? Why would he want to? After all, it was in the past where his parents existed, where Emlin was, where home was. Why focus so hard on the present if it stripped all those things away? It didn't make sense. It seemed nonsensical.

He let out a frustrated sigh, as he tried to bring his focus back to the task at hand. *This is stupid,* he thought to himself. Shrugging his shoulders with aggravation, he opened his eyes, ignoring his mentor's instructions with little remorse. As he opened them, he found himself staring at something rather unexpected. Nothing. There was absolutely nothing. No Kell Si, no door, no sounds, just nothing.

"Hello?" He called out. He pressed his hands onto the white, marble floor, leaving a print behind as he pushed himself upwards. He was surrounded by infinity. A room that appeared to have no beginning or end.

"I should be used to this kind of shit," he whispered. He quickly felt his clothing, searching for the one thing that kept him feeling in control—his wand. However, with each pass over the fabric landscape, it became quite clear, his wand wasn't there.

Silently, he continued to wander, exploring a place that had nothing to see. Seconds turned to minutes, minutes turned to hours, and still, he remained trapped, surrounded by an infinitely empty room, filled with unbelievably hollow thoughts.

"Why can't I just wake up?" He whispered to himself as he lay on his back. His eyes studied the ceiling above. It was familiar, decorated with unsightly drop boards that served a purpose but lacked fashion. Hundreds of holes covered each one, each one offering plenty of distractions from the meaningless dungeon he currently occupied.

"Nikalas," a mysterious voice called out. He swiftly sat up, looking around filled with a mixture of excitement and unease.

"Who's there?" He queried.

In the ceiling, a face appeared, a man with river blue eyes, bony cheeks, and long, brown hair.

"You've wasted too much time here, son," The man disappointingly replied.

"You're him, aren't you?" Nikalas questioned, with a tilt of his head.

"You're my father."

"I am," the man confirmed. At that moment, the ceiling began to liquify, and from the white puddles of goo, emerged the figure of Lord Aldon. He slowly dropped down, landing elegantly mere inches from Nikalas' face.

"I saw you in the water fountain," Nikalas announced. "Only you looked less alive."

"Yes, you did see me," Aldon replied. "And I saw you. I saw a boy who had no idea about who he really is. I saw my son."

"Your son?" Nikalas questioned. "You were a cheater. So was Venora. You're not my father. You didn't raise me."

"It's funny how you think you know everything about a situation," Lord Aldon replied.

"I think I know where you got that from."

Aldon turned around, waving his hand and summoning before him a sturdy looking, metallic chair with sapphire cushions for comfort.

"Things weren't easy back then Nikalas. It was.....how would you put it? Disturbing."

Aldon shook his head with unease, then summoned yet another chair opposite him. This one looked cushier and far more functional. Nodding reluctantly, Nikalas accepted the gesture.

"You didn't use to be able to love who you wanted to love. You didn't use to be able to marry who made you happy. Venora and I loved each other very much, we had such a strong connection, but they wouldn't let us be together. Society mocked us, threatened us, tried to use its laws on us."

Nikalas' mind began to grow heavy as the story of star-crossed lovers manifested in his mind. It was a struggle all too familiar.

"I wanted Venora to be happy. I wanted her to be well provided for. So I arranged a chance encounter for her to bump into Dwennon. All it took was a small push, and a little bit of magic to seal the deal. With him she would be safe, and she would have riches that I would never be allowed to give her."

Nikalas sighed as the movie continued to play out.

"What we did was wrong. I used Hervott as a means to protect the woman I loved. She never wanted to be with him. She loved me. That night with your mother, that was the night that convinced me I had to rescue Venora."

Aldon's eyes grew tearful as he looked towards the floor regretfully.

"I knew you were my son. As soon as I saw you looking down at me in the water, I knew."

"That's messed up man. Where I come from, they are pretty much that stupid as well. I think they're working on it though. The whole equality thing. Maybe I'll have to rescue that place next," Nikalas smirked.

"So what are you even doing here? How are you here?"

"Our species is a unique one son. We've always been able to hear the thoughts going on inside the mind of others. More than that, we can talk to them," Aldon explained.

"Telepathy, huh? I didn't know I could do that," he grinned.

"What else can I do?"

"A great number of things, my son," Aldon replied. "If you let me help you, I can show you all that hides within."

"Furlasia is in peril. A terrible sickness is spreading over everything that you have come to care about. You need to get back there."

"They won't let me go back," Nikalas retorted. "They say I'm not ready."

Aldon nodded in agreement, as he climbed to his feet.

"You're not ready. I agree with the gnomes on this matter. But with my help, you will be."

"For starters, we can work on teaching you how to communicate with the minds of others."

Aldon approached Nikalas and held out a piece of paper in one hand, and a pen in the other.

"What's this?" Nikalas scoffed.

"It states that as of right now, you're going to drop the sarcastic attitude and lone wolf act and do as I instruct so that you can defeat the darkness in Furlasia."

Nikalas glanced at him, stunned by the sudden switch of tone.

"You just sign here," Aldon instructed. With the pen, he pointed to a line with an asterisk next to it.

"Umm," Nikalas gawked.

Slowly, he reached for the pen, looking at Aldon with admiration, and then brought it down to the paper.

Chapter 21

Dark clouds swirled in the air, bringing with them a chill that summoned goosebumps to the poorly dressed. The very breeze that at once felt so pleasant now just brought with it hopelessness. Vicham rode morosely atop his confident stallion. Next to him, on a horse far less enticing, was Dimitri. They had left Morlay only a day ago, but already the journey was wearing him thin. Dimitri — as it turned out — was dreadful company. He relished in complaining, arguing and not much else. It was all Vicham could do, to not knock the whiny brat into the mud. Like him or not, he needed the extra set of eyes. They had no destination, no real bearing for where to search, but something compelled him to head towards Rangmar.

"Those ruins must hold some kind of secrets," Vicham had *said.* That was almost three days ago, back when he was trying to explain to Linuk why he had to leave Morlay.

"I have to find Kit. I can't leave her to be a victim to High Mother."

Now here he rode, heading towards Rangmar, not really knowing if there was anything to be seen or not. He couldn't explain why, but something about that direction gave him hope. He was a pretty well-traveled man, he had seen much of Furlasia, and as such, he understood its hiding spots. Certainly, Solarian could've been where High Mother had taken her hostages, but Vicham thought not. He argued strongly for Rangmar, and so, that's where they headed. To be truthful, bringing any old Tin Man would've been preferable, but Linuk insisted on Dimitri. Why, however, was anyone's guess. Clearly, this man had no experience in the outside world. No skills that would be useful. *Oh well*, Vicham thought as he tugged on the reins to slow his steed.

"Are we nearly there yet?" Dimitri exhaled in a nagging tone.

"Not quite. We are nearing a small settlement that used to be home to some of the Delopar outcasts. We will stop there for rest. With any luck, there will be a warm meal waiting for us," Vicham replied.

"Delopars?" Dimitri gulped. "You mean the cat people?"

"Yes," Vicham replied. "The cat people. And in the name of Undr, please don't call them that."

They pressed on just a tad bit longer, and as soon as the trees started to have thorns and the ground felt squishy, Vicham pulled the reins and brought his horse to a stop.

"We're here," he proclaimed as he jumped off his horse. Sure enough, the ground here was quite moist. His feet sunk into the mud, and while something like this would normally annoy him, he had left his nicer shoes behind, so instead, he just shrugged it off.

"It's a swamp," Dimitri pointed out. "They actually live here?"

Vicham shook his head and exhaled. Carefully, he led his horse through the soggy soil to a nearby tree. Reaching for his sheath, he quickly withdrew a sword and began chopping off some of the thorny branches. Once he had cleared a spot, he brought the reins closer and secured the horse.

"Bring your horse," he instructed to Dimitri.

Dimitri quietly nodded, and gave his horse a light kick. Slowly they walked over and once Vicham had secured the reins, he hesitantly climbed off.

"So what now?" Dimitri asked. Quickly, Vicham brought his finger to his lip, urging his companion to be silent. After a prolonged eye roll that didn't go unnoticed, Dimitri shrugged.

Vicham kept his sword drawn as he began navigating the trail, keeping his eyes darting between the treetops and the path ahead. Delopars were climbers, good ones at that. It was common practice for them to have a lookout or two stationed in the upper limbs, ready to pounce and attack if needed. Having his sword drawn did present a slight risk, it could be seen as a threat, but he decided it was worth it.

They pressed onwards, not altogether silently either. The moist ground didn't promote stealth. It squished and splashed with each new step, making a true covert approach impossible. But despite the sound of deep breaths, wet footsteps and rubbing fabrics, they didn't seem to be setting off any alarms.

Forward they pressed until they came to a wide opening with a gruesome sight. In the center of the clearing, was a pile of slain Akordans, each of them missing their heads and tails. A gag-inducing sight indeed.

"What in the name of Undr happened here?" Dimitri choked.

Vicham shook his head in uncertainty as he carefully approached the slaughter. As his eyes neared the scene, the source of this carnage became abundantly clear. Delopars. Each of the Akordans had deep claw marks decorating various parts of their lifeless bodies.

"Ya!" A loud voice suddenly bellowed into the air. Looking up, revealed a young Delopar, blade raised, and heading down towards them. He quickly jumped back, and the Delopar landed atop the pile of carnage. She was young, but nonetheless, she appeared deadly.

"Die!" She hollered, as she leapt off the pile and headed towards Vicham. He quickly lifted his sword, just narrowly deflecting her attack. Their eyes met, and suddenly, she flipped back, bringing her sharp feet tearing across Vicham's chest. Luckily, his armor was far tougher than the claws of a junior Delopar. She swiftly tossed her blade to the ground, and dropped to all fours, letting out a low growl as she studied him with anger.

"I'm not here to hurt you," Vicham called out. In a fury of emotions, she charged towards him, and then, right before she reached him, she leapt into the air.

"Behind you," Dimitri warned. Quickly, Vicham turned around, just in time to be greeted with a paw and a set of mean claws. He lifted his hand, grabbing her paw, and then quickly twisted her arm. The maneuver did nothing other than annoy her. She quickly cartwheeled into the air, freeing her arm at the same time.

"I'm not here to hurt you," Vicham reiterated. "I'm merely tracking a woman who took two of my friends hostage."

The Delopar landed in the mud, sliding a few feet and then brought out her claws. She roared, much like a lion, and then darted towards him once again.

"I'm looking for the High Mother," Vicham explained. The Delopar crashed into him, knocking them both into the mud, and then suddenly, grew calm. Lying atop him, she looked him in the eyes with curiosity and intrigue.

"The High Mother?" She whispered.

"Yes," Vicham replied, looking around as the moisture of the mud made its way into his hair. "You've heard of her?"

"Oh yes," the Delopar sneered. Suddenly, she back flipped and landed in the mud. She looked at Dimitri, who stood shaking as he held a tree branch in front of him.

"She passed through here a few weeks ago, killing my family in one swift move."

Vicham crawled to his feet and looked at her with remorse.

"I'm sorry," he replied. "She's a vile woman, to say the least."

The Delopar sneered.

"That's one word for her."

Vicham looked towards Dimitri and then towards the pile of dead Akordans.

"My name is Vicham. My companion is Dimitri. What is your name?"

"Wexel," she replied.

Dimitri suddenly furrowed his brow.

"Isn't that a boy's name?"

She looked at him with disdain.

"Isn't Dimitri a fool's name?" She snickered.

As he looked the young Delopar in the eyes, Dimitri found himself feeling suddenly quite silly.

"What happened here? Did you kill all these Akordans?" Vicham questioned. Wexel turned, looking over the mass of carnage and a cold grin suddenly came across her face.

"Yes," she replied.

In the background, Dimitri gasped. Not out of fear, but out of awe. There were at least a dozen in the pile of dead.

"You're a weapon," Dimitri remarked. "Come with us. We could use someone with your skills."

Vicham shot his comrade a look of aggravation, then turned his attention to the pile.

"What happened?" He quietly asked. His eyes continued to study the massacre, trying to answer his own question. In his mind, he imagined her surrounded on all sides, and like a warrior of the past, taking them all out in a single maneuver.

"They were with her. The — High Mother — as you call her. She killed my people, leaving these fools behind to eliminate me."

She looked at the rotting massacre and sneered with satisfaction.

"They all underestimated me. I was taught by one of our finest warriors. I can take on as many as they can throw at me. But magic," she paused.

"That's a different story," she explained. At that moment, tears formed in her eyes, trickling down and absorbing immediately into her fur.

"Only a coward fights with magic."

Vicham slowly neared, keeping his steps far apart and his hand near his sword. Finally, he came to a stop in front of her, looking her carefully over, before gently placing his hand on her shoulder. She flinched, the urge to attack boiling its way to the surface, begging and nagging her to rip his throat from his neck.

"Did you see two people with her? A man and a woman?" Vicham questioned. Wexel slowly nodded her head.

"Good," he whispered.

"Good?" Wexel questioned.

"They're still alive, that's the best I could hope for," he replied. Looking at Dimitri, he pulled his hand back, turned around and faced the pile of death.

"I won't ask you to come with me, this fight is mine, but if you could point me in the direction they went," he paused.

"I'll show you where they went," she whispered. "But only if I can come with you. I need to kill her."

Vicham shook his head in protest.

"She's not a mortal like you or me, you can't kill her. No one can. Not without the Arc Blade."

She scoffed and reached towards her sword.

"I haven't met a foe, I couldn't kill yet," she rebutted.

"Now, do you want to know where they went or not?"

Vicham sighed as he played out all the reasons it was a bad idea in his head. She was clearly young, and unaware of the extreme danger that they were heading into. And yet, who was he really to deny someone their shot at vengeance. Besides, he could deal with that when the time came, he obviously wouldn't let her jump into harm's way, but she didn't have to know that.

"Alright, you can come with us," he reluctantly replied.

"But we have to be smart. High Mother has more power than you could possibly imagine. She's dangerous."

"So am I," Wexel replied.

The debate didn't last much longer. Wexel had gathered some supplies, and then, riding along with Vicham, they took off. Their destination took them towards Rangmar, but Wexel had warned that the journey wouldn't end there. She had tracked High Mother for some time before returning to bury her family — as a result — she had a pretty good idea where to go, and it wasn't Rangmar. Nevertheless, journeying there was still their best idea. As it turned out, there were more Delopar to be found there. Many more in fact. As they continued their journey, Wexel explained all about how some of the Delopars had returned to the ruins, trying their best to distance themselves from the worries of Furlasia.

"So they just sat back and watched the war?" Dimitri barked.

"When has your species ever helped ours?" Wexel retorted. "Where were the men when Rangmar was destroyed? Where were the elves or the Arnouts?"

"It was a difficult time," Vicham explained. "Besides, you're too young to even know about what happened."

"Well please," Wexel paused. "Enlighten me."

Vicham offered no reply, instead he pointed ahead.

"We're here," he announced.

Staring back at them, in grandiose fashion was Rangmar, or what remained of it. It looked still and if there were Delopars hiding out here, they would be well hidden. Wexel's eyes grew as she took in the sights, one never did outgrow the shock of seeing the ruined city. Once they neared the outmost tattered building, Vicham pulled the reins and quickly brought his horse to a stop.

"I don't like it," Dimitri remarked as he scanned the apparently vacant surroundings.

Slowly, Wexel departed the back of the horse, followed quickly by Vicham. Together they began to search, peering inside ruins, looking for signs of life. But there were no signs to be found. Behind them, Dimitri wandered, his hand firmly grasping a Beacon. It wasn't exactly the most gracious way to enter someone's home, but then again, Dimitri was anything but decent. Vicham continued to look inside the various ruins with Wexel keeping close by. The air was dry, the swift breeze littered their eyes and mouths with sand, threating to choke and blind them. Even for Wexel, the sensation was unpleasant.

"Where are they?" Vicham asked. At that moment, an arrow soared by his head and got firmly wedged into a nearby brick wall. He quickly turned, the sun was blinding, but there was almost certainly the shape of a Delopar heading his way.

"What are you doing here?" The silhouette hissed. Vicham nervously looked at Wexel and nodded silently.

"Kadem Sa Vets brronks," Wexel calmly replied.

"Sava non?" The figure questioned as it finally came to a stop.

"We are tracking a woman who came this way with two prisoners," Wexel explained.

The Delopar nodded, looking at Dimitri and Vicham with doubt and disgust.

"You are not welcome in the sacred city," the stern looking Delopar jeered. He shot Wexel a glance of frustration, then shook his head.

"You can go no further."

Moments later, the three found themselves being escorted through the grim remains of a once great metropolis. As Vicham took in the sights, it became abundantly clear just exactly why the Delopars were at one point the shining example of evolution. They had a grasp of architecture that none of the other species seemed to possess. Before the ruins had returned under Delopar's occupation, it was quite common for scouts and builders to visit in a bid to understand the techniques, and to also try to figure out how to emulate their success, but those days were gone. The Delopar controlled this land now, and they had no intention of letting it go ever again.

"What was that?" Dimitri suddenly exclaimed, pointing his index finger at a bit of sand that had just rustled about. The Delopar host stopped, turned and followed Dimitri's shaky finger. His eyes narrowed as he began to sniff the air. He lifted a sword, edging closer to the spot, when suddenly a loud thud from their left stole their attention. Dimitri pointed again, this time at a large stone that had fallen, creating a small cloud of dust. The strangeness continued. All around them, the sand appeared disturbed, and bricks continued to fall. The four of them stood, weapons drawn and ready for a fight.

Suddenly, many hands began to emerge from deep within the dark sands. The skies above turned a startling hue of green, and a swift gust of wind swept between the pillars, bringing a sand wall hurtling towards them.

"It's him," the Delopar observed aloud. A loud screech abruptly filled the air, and suddenly, before they knew it, a small battalion of ghouls erected before them. Their eyes glowed, their mouths hung open, and their arms twitched, as though a current was pulsating through them.

"Septus," Vicham whispered under his breath.

"You led him here," the Delopar accused, shooting the three of them a cold stare. He lifted his sword, and without any further words, charged towards the terrifying crowd of the dead. Delopar by the looks of them. Remnants from the original war. His blade swung fast and true, quickly dispatching a couple of them, but a backhand from a much larger ghoul, sent him careening off his feet and into the sand. From beneath the sands emerged — once again — a set of arms. They grabbed him, holding him down with spectacular strength.

"Ha!" Wexel exclaimed, leaping into the air and landing on her hands in front of the remaining ghouls. With her legs standing upright, she began to spin, bringing her feet claws tearing across each of the ghouls' faces, then she quickly shot up, landing firmly on her feet. She looked around with a satisfied grin, then grabbed her sword and plunged it quickly into the downed ghouls.

"Not so bad," she remarked. Her boastfulness was quickly cut short, by the sight of the ghouls slowly climbing back to their feet.

"What?" She bleated.

As fear and confusion set it, she stumbled back, unsure of what to do. The ghouls continued to approach, when from the side, a sword quickly swung, removing their heads in keen fashion. Each of the removed skulls fell into the sand, rolling back and forth before quickly eroding in the wind. Standing with a determined stare, was Vicham, holding an outstretched sword.

"You have to remove their heads," he explained.

"You've put us all in danger!" The Delopar host accused, storming towards them with a bitter glare.

"He's watching you. He's watching all of you."

"Oh please don't even start with that," Dimitri groaned. Vicham turned, looked at him and shook his head with a pleading stare.

"His gaze fell upon Morlay and now we are all slaves. The women, the children, all of us are forced into his service. I'll take a few ghouls over that any day."

"Did you take any ghouls?" The host questioned. "From what I saw you simply stood there like a scared little girl."

Dimitri looked towards the ground bashfully and kicked a bit of sand.

"Well, you got knocked down," he muttered.

"What was that?" The host queried.

"Follow me."

Quickly, he turned around and continued stampeding through the sands, coming eventually to a tall hill. Climbing was a struggle, each step forward sent you half a step back, for the three of them it was quite the hassle. Their host — on the other hand — scaled the hill with ease.

"We weren't hiding," he called out.

As they came to rest at the very top, the host pointed towards the clearing down below.

"We were preparing."

Dimitri looked down into the clearing, gulping with awe. It was a metropolis. A sanctuary they had not expected to find. Hundreds—nay—thousands of tents were spread about. Walking all around the valley were Delopar, many of them donning battle armor, and armed with swords and shields.

"By Undr," Wexel whispered. She turned, looking towards Vicham with pride and smug satisfaction.

"Why didn't you help us?" Dimitri asked. "If you had all these people, why didn't you come help?"

"The Delopar will not sacrifice their lives unless we know there is a certain chance of winning," the host replied. "We were not trained properly, nor were our numbers great enough."

Dimitri shrugged, not really grasping the meaning behind the response. To him, it seemed an army that could've helped sat idly by while their troops were beaten. Vicham, on the other hand, looked onwards with understanding. The war had come swift, Agavordis hadn't exactly given a notice, defeat was inevitable, and like Nikalas, it seemed the Delopar wanted more time to prepare, even if it meant letting Furlasia fall. It was a hard call. A sacrifice that likely didn't come easy.

"This gives me hope," Vicham replied with a smile. The Delopar host turned to him with esteem and nodded a grateful glance.

"The answers you seek lie down there. The woman you track, we know of her. If you want to find her, you'll need to speak to our elder. She has the answers you seek."

Vicham continued to observe the spectacle then nodded.

"Well let's not waste any time," he declared.

$\mathcal{C}$hapter 22

Kunklestick looked over the icy field of Solarian, the bitter cold made its way up under his robes and towards areas he'd rather not chill. His hands shook, his teeth chattered, and his temperament was sour at best. He was restrained, his hands bound by a thick chain, it was heavy and cumbersome but not restricting. No, he had plenty of ability to swing his pickaxe. All around him were scattered bits of ice and black rocks. To his left, was a large pile he had been adding to.

In the bitter cold, under the watchful eyes of the ghouls, Kunklestick and Didorumpus tirelessly worked. They were both swinging their pickaxes at the ice, trying to dig beneath the surface at the valuable minerals below. Before Solarian was an icy and desolate wasteland, it was a thriving kingdom filled with lots of potentials.

This particular portion of the icy field was at one point, home to a mine with rocks that were quite useful in the creation of dark objects. Agavordis had wasted no time in sending a revolving set of slaves out to help mine the ice for these valuable bits of stone. Kunklestick paused, dropped his axe onto the icy surface and looked around at all the unfortunate captives that Agavordis had mining the field. Many of them were red-faced and shaking, some of them, looked like they were a few inches from death. If one of them started moving too slow, the ghouls would approach, threatening them with their rented power.

"Get back to work vermin," an Akordan guard demanded. Kunklestick turned and looked towards the reptilian beast. He stood arms crossed, encased in a small bubble of warmth that was mostly clear apart from a light red tint—a gift from Agavordis.

"It's cold," Kunklestick replied. "I can barely feel my fingers."

The Akordan charged towards him aggressively while sporting a frustrated expression.

"I don't remember asking about your fingers," he barked. He swiftly brought the back of his hand up and swung it firmly against Kunklestick's cold cheek. The impact was jarring, and on top of that, his balance was shaky, a side effect of the icy winds barking up his legs. Like a house of cards, or a senior citizen that had lost his cane, he toppled, landing in a patch of snow that only further added to his discomfort.

"Stop it," Didorumpus demanded. He quickly rushed to his brother's side, grabbing him and giving him a firm pull.

"It's freezing out here. You're sitting in a warm spell, but the rest of us are on the brink of death," Didorumpus barked.

"That's how he wants you," the guard replied. Didorumpus stood to his feet and took a step closer to the guard, close enough in fact to feel a bit of the warmth of his spell.

"Step back," the guard demanded.

Didorumpus continued to look the Akordan in the eyes, letting the warmth wash over him.

"Brother," Kunklestick chimed in. Didorumpus took a few steps back and wandered back over to his pickaxe, keeping his eyes trained on the Akordan all the while.

"That's what I thought," the guard mocked.

After another hour or so, the guard blew on a horn that had been tied to his belt, signaling the end of their shift. It was time to return to the dungeons. The captives all eagerly dropped their axes and began to form a line. As the Akordan guard patroled, everyone threw their eyes to the ground, everyone except Kunklestick and Didorumpus. They kept their heads raised and their eyes trained firmly on him. Once the guard reached the front of the line, he huffed and began to lead them towards the rear of the castle. The sun had just reached mid position. It was noon. The next shift would start, with another guard taking his place.

Through the ice and wind, the line of workers sauntered, trembling all the while. As they neared the rear door, it slowly began to lower, revealing a new crowd of workers awaiting their turn. They walked past each other like players on the football field. Each of the workers coming out grew nervous as they saw the disheveled appearance of those coming in.

"Zanna?" Didorumpus called out. Standing in the line of the next batch of workers was their fellow wizard, her hair was a mess, and there were bruises under her eyes.

"What in the name of Undr happened?"

She glanced up for just a moment, and then quickly put her eyes down. Didorumpus paused, holding up the line.

"Zanna," Didorumpus demanded. "Did he do this to you?"

"Keep moving!" A guard yelled. Didorumpus shrugged off the remark and leaned closer, pressing his forehead against Zanna's as he grabbed the back of her head.

"I can't talk," she whispered. "They'll beat us if we don't keep moving."

"Did Septus do this?" Didorumpus repeated. She shook her head and quickly glanced at a large Akordan guard that was hurrying his way towards them.

"It was the Gnome."

Rage filled his heart and mind as he pulled back, taking another look at her bruises. It wasn't just on her face; her arms had bruises and cuts as well. He turned to his brother with a heavy anger lingering over him.

"I said keep moving," the guard repeated, giving Zanna a firm shove. She stumbled forward, then continued. Didorumpus looked at the guard, contemplating some form of retaliation, but what? Unarmed and without his staff he was nothing, especially against a large beast like the one standing before him. Pushing away his desire, he continued to move forward.

"Where is Nikalas?" He whispered under his breath.

"He'll be here," Kunklestick replied. "He'll be here."

They continued forward until they entered the warmth of the castle — well actually — the castle wasn't very warm, but it wasn't nearly as cold as where they had just been. As they stepped inside, they were greeted by a dozen or so Akordans, all of them looking rather serious. One by one, they inspected the workers, gauging whether or not they would need a trip to the infirmary.

"This one's hand is frostbit," one of the guards remarked. He grabbed the man's hand, holding it up for the others to see.

"There's no saving that," another guard replied. "Oh well. More meat for his pets."

The worker's eyes widened, and he began to tremble.

"No, please. It's not that bad," he pleaded. The Akordan guard pulled him from the line, pushing him against a nearby wall, and then returned to his inspection.

The scrutiny continued for a few moments longer, and while most were fine, a total of three did end up pulled away, whisked to an unknown fate. Kunklestick drew a sigh of relief as the procession got back underway, grateful that neither he nor his brother was harassed.

Through the stark halls, they trudged, keeping their heads down. Ghouls were placed sporadically about, most of them huddling around the various torches that were hung on the walls. It seemed like a typical behavior for the dead — standing near light sources — it was a very interesting trait, especially to Kunklestick.

A smile crept across his face as the familiar sight of his cell came into place. It was large, holding up to three prisoners at once, and although it was normally nothing to be excited about, today he couldn't help it. The frigid fields of Solarian had proven so trying that even confinement seemed a winning option.

The Akordan guard pulled the cell doors open one at a time, and with a firm shove, placed the workers in their respective places. Kunklestick and Didorumpus had mercifully been assigned to the same cell, as they stepped inside, the elder wizard found himself stumbling to the floor.

"Are you ok brother?" Didorumpus asked, kneeling down next to him.

"Oh yes, just a bit tired," he replied. His face was flushed, his hands still shook, and his skin looked cracked and dry. He reached for his pad, gripping the itchy blanket with gratefulness.

"You wouldn't lie to me would you?" Didorumpus questioned.

"No no," Kunklestick replied. "What did you make of Zanna? How is she holding up?"

Didorumpus rose to his feet and looked around the cell, pausing as he took in the sights of their third cellmate, a large fellow with a curly mustache named Riley.

"I'm worried about her," Didorumpus replied. "I worry she's snapping."

Kunklestick rolled over, looking towards the wall and their cell mate. They didn't know much about him, only that he was a blacksmith in Terria before the conflict started. Like so many others, when the call to arms went out, he ardently replied, leaving his wife and kids behind. A decision, he had since admitted to regretting.

"She's far tougher than you think," Kunklestick replied. "She has a force to her, unlike any woman I've ever met. I think she'll be fine."

Didorumpus wandered slowly to the bars, pressing his head and hands against them.

"I hope so," he whispered.

The next morning, they awoke to the sounds of swords being dragged across the bars of the various cells. Numerous Akordans wandered the cells, summoning their attention.

"Time to wake up," one of them yelled. Behind him, wandered another guard, who carried with him a basket of bread and fruit. He stopped at each cell, tossing inside a loaf of stale bread and severely bruised fruit. The prisoners all quickly jumped towards it like hungry dogs, ignoring the unpleasant condition of the scraps they were being given.

"Agavordis wants you to see you two," a large guard said, coming to a stop outside their cell. His name was Roth, and he appeared to be one of the head guards. Kunklestick and Didorumpus stood from their beds, shooting each other a concerned look and then quietly approached the bars.

"What's it about?" Kunklestick investigated.

"Do you think he tells me?" Roth sneered. He reached to his side and pulled out a set of keys. He inserted them into the lock, one at a time, until he got the right one. The door swung open with a screech, and he motioned for them to step out.

"You stay here," Roth demanded as he pointed towards their other cellmate who had started to approach. The shy man nodded and returned to his mat.

There was a sense of urgency in Roth's steps as he led them through the winding halls, past the ghouls and cells. As they neared the throne room, Kunklestick could make out a set of voices. They seemed raised, an argument perhaps? His heart began to race as they neared their destination. It had been many years since he felt this vulnerable and was at the mercy of an over-emotional necromancer.

As they entered the throne room, they were greeted with the sight of Agavordis, Epard and Emlin all standing over a dead body. Kunklestick looked towards his brother and then quickly made his way over.

"She succumbed to the cold it seems," Agavordis explained. Laying on the ground — looking quite blue — was Zanna.

"No," Didorumpus roared, dropping to his knees and lifting her hand. It was cold and stiff. Kunklestick looked towards Emlin, who seemed blank and broken. Her eyes were fixed on the sight, but she remained mute.

"Bring her back," Kunklestick demanded.

"The Sea of Souls is not an easy place to navigate," Epard chimed. "One could easily get lost, or worse, bring out the wrong soul."

Agavordis looked at Zanna, a hint of remorse riding on his face.

"There's no room in Furlasia, in Solarian for weakness," Agavordis declared. "She had a poor temper and thought she could beat me. Now nature has beaten her, how ironic."

Emlin turned towards him, her eyes piercing him with a look of disgust. Suddenly she lifted a hand, bringing it up to his face in a firm and direct strike. The slap echoed against the hollow walls, causing everyone to pause.

"You make me sick," she hissed. Agavordis grabbed his cheek and held it as his face heated up.

"You'll soon change your mind my sweet, I promise," he replied. Emlin shook her head and cleared her throat, launching a large wad of spit onto the floor.

"You're losing your grip on reality son," Kunklestick noted. "Your father has twisted your mind and turned you into nothing more than a common psychopath."

Agavordis looked at him with a content smile and dark eyes, then turned to Epard and nodded.

"Today you are all going to bear witness to my skills as a leader. Starting with Terria, I am going to turn this land around and give it a sense of normalcy it so desperately needs," he announced. With a quick snap of his finger, a yellow portal opened, bringing a howling wind careening across the room.

"Step into the light, and you will see my awesome ability to unite this broken land."

"You broke it," Didorumpus yelled. "It wasn't broken before."

Agavordis shrugged, then quickly lifted his hand. From his palm, came a yellow, nearly translucent beam of light. It wrapped around Didorumpus, holding him perfectly still.

"You've been gone a long time, buried in the darkness of that dreadful cavern. You don't know what you're talking about. You haven't been here to see what's been going on, but trust me, it isn't working."

He brought his arm towards the portal, sending Didorumpus careening into it, then turned to Kunklestick.

"I'll walk," Kunklestick said, raising his hand with concern. He winked at Emlin and, then strolled over towards the portal. Taking a deep breath, he stepped inside, and before he knew it, he was standing next to his brother.

Terria looked different than it had when he last saw it. There was a grimness to it all, the streets were mostly empty, and ghouls stood silently about, rocking back and forth as they struggled to stay upright. There were a few Vanguards standing idly by, and next to them, were some Akordans. It appeared they were allowed to patrol, but only under the supervision of the Akordans.

"I say we run," Didorumpus whispered. Kunklestick shook his head.

"We can't. In case you didn't notice, we are surrounded on all sides."

Didorumpus looked at him, taken back by his neutral mentality.

"Why have you become so complacent?" Didorumpus questioned.

"Because he's smart," Agavordis said quite suddenly. Both wizards jumped with a startle, only to turn around and be greeted by the dark necromancer himself and Emlin. As Agavordis came to a stop, he waved to a nearby guard who silently bowed and sauntered over.

"Have they gathered?" Agavordis asked.

"They have sir," the Vanguard replied. "They await you at the town center."

Agavordis bowed, then turned to his guest.

"Shall we?"

They strolled through the city streets under the watchful eyes of a couple Akordan soldiers. The city smelled different than usual; it smelled of soot rather than sweetbreads. As Emlin took in the sights, she could feel the wave of disappointment washing over her. It weighed her down like a belt of rocks, reminding her of her inferior leadership skills.

Through the desolate streets they continued to stroll, the nearer they got to the city center, the louder the sound of voices became. Before long, they emerged at the foot of the palace where a large crowd had gathered, a morose group at that. Agavordis looked at Emlin and nodded.

"Now you will see my vision for Furlasia," he declared. He looked to the sky, and then floated upwards, towards the palace stairs. Gasps came from the crowd as children pointed towards the unusual spectacle.

"Silence," he roared. His voice filled the area with tremendous bass and resonance, a trick from his powers.

"My name is Agavordis and I am the bringer of peace to Furlasia." The crowd went silent, and Kunklestick looked at Didorumpus skeptically.

Chapter 23

Articus stood quietly atop a desolate building looking through some magnifying lenses towards The Cone. It looked nearly impossible to scale, but that would hardly be a deterrent. The Society had encountered more exciting challenges than this bizarre bit of architecture. As he studied the layout, he whispered, making mental notes to himself and occasionally setting the lens down to take notes. His notebook looked like the ramblings of a mad man, but that's how he liked it. He couldn't have neat and organized notes. Unless there was chaos, there was no order. That's how he felt.

He reached for his paper and began to scribble down an observation. Just behind the building were some hills, mountains actually. They seemed like a viable option. In his notes, he doodled a sketch of the mountains, then walked over to the building's edge. Standing on the ground, was Sillimon. He was dressed in loose fitting cloths that heavily resembled nightwear, but was considered casual attire here.

"Those mountains," Articus yelled. "They are kind of interesting aren't they?"

Sillimon looked towards them and nodded.

"I bet a lot of unique things can be found up there," Sillimon replied. Without another word, he exited the alley, walking across the busy street towards a tea shop. It was quiet inside; the ambiance was calm and the air smelled of cinnamon and perhaps a bit of mint as well. Sitting at a table silently reading a book entitled, *The Black Forest* was Penny. She was dressed in a white dress and wore a hefty hat that was covered in flowers of all colors. He smiled, then approached her table.

"Is this seat taken?" He asked with a smirk. Penny looked up and smiled.

"I don't have any company. No one seems to want to talk to a young woman who can read," she replied.

A young man at a nearby table suddenly perked up, lifting his head away from his studies and looking in her direction. Sillimon took notice and subtly nodded at him.

"Well, I am going to order a drink for myself," he declared. With that, he strolled away and approached the counter that was manned by a helpless looking elderly woman. With the coast now clear, the young man jumped to his feet and meandered towards Penny.

"The Black Forest," he softly remarked. "What would make an innocent looking woman like you read such scary stories?"

He approached the empty seat and slowly sat down.

"I don't scare easy," Penny replied with a simper. "All the best books are a little scary."

The young man carefully placed his book down. *Dawn of Batharen*. Penny looked at the title and lifted her eyebrows.

"What is Batharen?" She asked.

"He was an ancient being who could control the sands," the young man replied.

"The name's Nate." He held out his hand and offered a comforting grin.

"Penny," she calmly replied. She turned her head, glancing towards the counter and noticed that Sillimon had moved on, likely using the back entrance to scoot out.

"You're not from here," Nate observed.

"How can you tell?" Penny chuckled.

"Because the girls here don't quite dress like that," he smirked. Penny looked herself over, and suddenly her cheeks went red with embarrassment. She had seen the outfit in one of the local shops and had thought it best to blend in. Apparently though, that didn't pan out.

"Well I like to stand out in a room," she retorted.

"I doubt that's a problem," he replied.

***

Sillimon waved up to Articus, who was still atop the building scanning the surroundings. It took a couple attempts and a loud whistle, but he finally robbed his attention from the lens and brought it to him.

"What?" Articus called out.

"Let's take a walk," Sillimon replied, taking a quick sip of his piping hot tea. Articus shrugged and proceeded to gather his belongings.

As he patiently waited for his partner to make his way back down, he took in the sights. It was truly an exotic location. There were far more pigments to the citizens of Adrasia, at least in this region. Living in Morlay, it was uncommon to see those with a darker complexion, but here, it seemed like a normal occurrence. He nodded with satisfaction as he observed the citizens making their way through the day. There was a sense of business that really kept the whole place buzzing. As he watched, he found himself trying to guess what each person's role in the city was. What they contributed. It was a fun game that he and Penny often played when arriving at new places.

"Where is Penny?" Articus questioned as he approached.

Sillimon turned, offering a lighthearted bow.

"She's in there," he pointed. "Having tea with a local."

Articus looked around his friend, towards the teashop, and shook his head.

"I don't know how you can stand it," he replied.

"It's for the job," Sillimon defended. "Besides, I know I can trust her."

Articus expelled a deep breath and shrugged as he turned his focus to the mountains ahead.

"Well, let's get moving.

Together, they ambled through the streets, being sure not to aggravate any of the residents. Looking at them, everyone seemed so normal that one could almost forget that everyone here, even the children, likely had more strength than them. They weren't in hostile territory so to speak, but they were in a place where if things did turn hostile, it would be extremely dangerous. Luckily, staying low-key was an easy trait to them. Thieves — after all — worked mostly in the shadows.

It didn't take long for things to take a derelict turn once they left the confines of the city. Much like the route they had taken to arrive, things were stark, and covered in dust. The sun was quite hot, and the air lacked much breeze. Articus looked towards the mountain, trying to swallow the challenge. It was steep but not jagged and covered in red dirt and loose rocks.

"Why do we do this again?" Sillimon asked.

"I really don't know," Articus laughed. He shot one more glance at the mountain, and together they proceeded to climb.

***

Jinn silently floated down the halls as she followed Idrix and The Boss towards something she assured them *"would really be something."* It was cryptic, a part of Jinn thought it seemed fishy, in fact, she had told Idrix to decline, but The Boss was quite convincing and clever. Under much duress, and with overflowing reluctance, Idrix agreed to follow her. The other Decoyers went back to the Maratan, but Jinn opted to tag along. If there was some kind of a setup, Idrix would certainly need her help.

"This is the first room I decorated," The Boss explained as they turned a corner. "It holds a special place in my heart."

"Mmmhmm," Idrix sighed. The lighting in The Cone was quite murky. For someone who praised their home and its interior decor, The Boss sure didn't seem to be making it easy for people to observe it. As they continued to make their way forward, she found herself feeling quite stiff, letting out a whimper or two until they stopped at a set of winding stairs.

The Boss turned, looking at Idrix with concern as she realized the enormity of the steps. They weren't extremely tall, but it wouldn't take much for someone in Idrix's condition.

"Can you make it up these steps?" She asked. "I'm afraid my lift doesn't go any further."

Idrix looked the stairwell over and nodded.

"Good, we're nearly there," The Boss disclosed. She turned and began to make her way up the stairs, followed by Idrix and then Jinn, who opted to stay behind to keep a watchful eye.

The Boss came to a stop as she reached the top of the stairs, turning and looking down at Idrix and Jinn and feeling a bit of anguish for her elderly guest's struggles. Age seemed far harsher on Furlasians than it did on those who were born in Adrasia.

"It's just over here," she happily informed as Idrix reached the top.

"Good," Idrix exhaled, pausing to catch her breath.

"We have wonderful apothecaries here Idrix. You really should visit one of them. Perhaps I can arrange a visit," The Boss offered.

"That would be most gracious indeed. I'm not the young woman I once was," Idrix replied.

The Boss shook her head in understanding and turned towards a door with a handle unlike anything they had ever seen. It was neither a lifting nor a turning handle — no — this was a square metal frame, with an opening in the middle.

"What kind of handle is that?" Jinn puzzled.

"This is a special handle that requires a certain sequence of turns in order to open," The Boss replied. She reached inside the handle, then turned to look at her guests.

"Could you turn away for a moment?"

"Of course," Idrix replied, offering a subtle wink to Jinn. Gripping the cold metal handle, The Boss began to turn the handle in various directions, all the while, Jinn focused, listening to her motions and recording them in her mind. It was a rather unusual skill and one of the many reasons she was known as the best thief in all of Furlasia.

"Ok, I'm done," The Boss informed as the door clicked open. Idrix looked to Jinn, who offered a slight bow of her head, and then into the room they proceeded.

"Welcome to the top of The Cone. I call this room the most interesting room in the entire house," The Boss clarified.

Idrix looked around. The room was startlingly white. There wasn't so much as a single decoration in the whole space. Not a piece of furniture. Not a light. It was the most empty and awkward space she had ever seen.

"Is this some kind of joke," Idrix accused. "You had me climb all those stairs to show me an empty room?"

The Boss smiled and walked towards the front of the room. Suddenly, the floor started to shake, and a pedestal began to rise from the floor. Idrix watched the impressive demonstration with bejeweled eyes. Like the rest of the room, the pedestal was white, but what was sitting on it more than made up for its boring appearance. It was a glass display case containing a small jewel not much bigger than a nickel. It was silver and had a glow to it.

"My father was an explorer of such," The Boss explained. "He was gone all the time, but he always brought me a present whenever he returned. One day, after an unusually long period away from home, he gave me this. I didn't think much of it, in fact, I thought it was boring compared to some of the gifts he had given me, but then something unusual happened. It began to glow. Not long after the legendary freezing of Solarian in fact. It wasn't until much later that I realized what I truly had."

She reached into her pocket and pulled out a single white glove. Carefully she slipped it onto her left hand and reached for the display case. As if by magic, the lid popped open and she cautiously reached inside, grabbing the jewel as gently as she could.

"You've got to be careful when handling it. The power contained in this thing is pretty hazardous. I won't ever touch it without this specially layered glove."

She turned to Idrix and held it up.

"This is why you're here, isn't it?" She smiled.

"Of course. You sent me a message telling me you had it," Idrix replied. "The real mystery is how did you find me? And how did you know I was searching for it?"

The Boss nodded with excitement, raising a finger and bringing it towards Idrix.

"Now you're asking the right questions." She turned around and smoothly placed the jewel back onto the pedestal. As she swung around, the floor began to shake, and just as quickly as it had appeared, the jewel vanished, returning to its resting place beneath the floors. The Boss looked at Idrix and removed the glove, stuffing it messily into her front pocket.

"I have a lot of friends that live all over Daulest. Lots of connections. Lots of ears to the ground. You weren't hard to find. Royalty might have been stripped from you, but you'll always be the princess of Solarian. Your reputation precedes you, probably to your disadvantage, but we'll see."

Idrix glanced at Jinn, who remained quite stoic despite the passive-aggressive nature of the conversation. Jinn was never good for support in times like these, her talents lie elsewhere, in more mysterious affairs.

"There's something else you're known for, a talent I doubt even Jinn here knows. It's that talent that prompted me to invite you."

Idrix shifted her weight.

"You're a lover of games that challenge the intellect, are you not?"

Idrix silently nodded her head. It was nothing to be ashamed of, yet for some reason she was. This wasn't a part of her she wanted others knowing, least of all the Decoyers, this was her personal treat. She glanced at Jinn once again, who appeared thoroughly unamused.

"I am prepared to give you this jewel. Hand it over without any questions or fuss, if you would just partake in a challenge of minds."

Idrix peeked at Jinn, looking for a response, hoping her wise friend would have some counsel. She may have been the leader of The Decoyers, but the decisions didn't just belong to her, Jinn was also a crucial part. They had always made decisions together. She counted on this, her input helped steer her in the right direction and kept her grounded, lest she gets sidetracked by her desire for vengeance.

"I would like to talk it over with my associates," Idrix finally replied. She looked at The Boss who smiled ecstatically.

"Absolutely. You should definitely do that," she replied.

***

Articus placed his hands on his knees, trying desperately to retrieve the breath the mountain had stolen from him. It wasn't nearly as subtle a thief as he was. The mountain was obvious, sucking away his strength and energy in a rather quick and noticeable maneuver. He had often enjoyed a hike or two up a summit from time to time, but under the grueling sun, the enjoyment seemed lost.

"You're out of shape my friend," Sillimon remarked, looking down at Articus with a smile. His remark earned him a stern glance and an eye roll. Once the air had begun to climb its way back into his lungs, Articus straightened his posture. Reaching towards his pack, he pulled out the lens he had used earlier and began to look towards The Cone. The rooftop looked quite problematic. Dark brown wooden shingles were placed carefully all the way up, creating what looked like a slippery surface. He squinted, furrowing his brow as he tried to take in every detail. After a few moments of uncomfortable silence, he lowered the lens, keeping his eyes on the roof ahead.

"I don't think this method is going to work," he informed.

Sillimon sighed and reached towards the lens. Articus looked at him with dismay, a part of him wanting to pull back and tuck them away. *That's childish*, he thought to himself. He glanced at the lens for a moment and then handed them over to Sillimon who was grinning broadly.

"They are kind of heavy," he said with surprise. He carefully lifted them and squinted as he pressed the eyepiece against his left eye. It was just as Articus had said. The roof was quite precarious indeed, but no more so than he had expected. It was a cone, after all, one had to expect a tricky ascension.

"I see what you mean," Sillimon added as he handed over the lens. "Although it's not impossible."

He peered towards the small window that was on the backside of the upper point. It was quaint, tiny as a matter of fact, but it would work.

"Did you not notice how small the window is?" Articus retorted, taking another look through the lens. He shook his head, turned and looked towards Sillimon with skepticism.

"I'm pretty skinny in case you didn't notice," he said, as if reading his companion's mind.

"Mmmhmm," Articus shrugged. "The climb looks extremely tricky as well."

Sillimon laughed.

"I've climbed weirder angles than that," he rebutted. "I can do this. I can do the climb. I can get in the window. I can get that jewel."

Chapter 24

The sky seemed angry, dark clouds loomed above with echoes of thunder hiding under its breath. Through lightning covered skies, Nikalas and Aldon soared, dodging the electric streaks with beauty and grace. There was a chill in the air at this height, but luckily, Aldon had taught him how to wrap himself in warmth. It was an easy skill to pick up, and immensely useful. Nikalas looked towards the ground below; the mountains looked malevolent from this view. Their sharp, jagged peaks looked like weapons of the land. A loud crash of thunder erupted, shaking him from his comfort and making him paranoid.

"Couldn't we practice over a warm beach?" Nikalas called out.

A bolt of lightning suddenly careened between them, striking the mountain peak with a furious and impressive display.

"When you go after Septus, he's gonna pull out all the stops. He's gonna turn the very environment against you. How is practicing on a beach going to help you with that?" Aldon retorted.

He quickly dove, heading towards the mountaintop. Nikalas sighed and followed. Perhaps he made a good point. Septus did have all three talismans now. He was a challenge already—now—having had time to perfect his craft, he would be a terrifying foe indeed.

His legs nearly buckled as he landed atop the mountain peak, his time in the air had made him forget the sensation of physical matter underneath his feet. It was a common occurrence for those that spent too much time in the skies. It was that reason that Aldon had lectured that they should not spend too much time in the air.

Come down frequently, he had said.

"You nearly got hit by that bolt up there," Aldon announced. "What happened? Where did you go?"

"I was thinking about something," Nikalas replied.

"What? What was more important than paying attention to the weather around you?" Aldon snapped.

A flash of his mother suddenly appeared before his eyes. She was in the kitchen, her hands hidden behind a stained-glass bowl as she kneaded oatmeal cookie dough. He watched from a distance, the scent of cinnamon filling his senses and making his stomach growl.

"Can I have some now?" Nikalas asked.

"No, honey, there are raw eggs in this. I can't have my strong boy getting sick," she replied.

"It won't happen again," Nikalas replied. Aldon's eyes were filled with frustration as he studied Nikalas, still trying hard as ever to figure him out. On the surface, Nikalas looked like an incapable adolescent but there had to be more, right?

"You have to focus, you can't be traveling off in your mind like that," Aldon explained.

He approached Nikalas and handed him a wand.

"He's coming. And you better be ready."

Nikalas slowly grabbed the wand and looked around. The mountain peak was rigged, its ground uneven and its surface slippery. Just being atop it presented certain doom, a hazardous situation. He nodded in understanding and searched the horizon. Nothing but mountains could be seen, the wind made sure of that. Snow filled the air like sand, encompassing the landscapes and blinding his eyes.

"I don't see him," Nikalas sighed. His eyes turned to Aldon, at that moment, two small red lights caught his eyes, they were far, piercing through the snow like a knife through the heart. Gulping with unease, he began to extend his wand into staff form.

"Stop that," Aldon snapped. "You have to let that fear go. Let it go, or throw down your staff and surrender. You will never beat him if he holds any power over you."

Nikalas nodded with understanding and closed his eyes. Agavordis stood with a smile over the slain corpse of Emlin. It was the vision. The same one he had months ago. He watched the blood seep from her neck, but then suddenly, the river of blood began to flow backward. The blood was hastily returning to Emlin. Once the wound had healed, Emlin stood up, and turned, quickly thrusting a blade into Agavordis' neck. He roared, his screams of agony filled the air like a powerful bass line, then, the form that was Agavordis, disintegrated.

"Inginimo!" Nikalas called out as he opened his eyes. The spell careened from the top of his staff with startling speed. The green aura dashed like a dog in the snow towards the red eyes but was suddenly met with a thunderous clash. Agavordis bellowed into the bitter air, it was quite distant, but the cold breath of the mountain echoed his shout towards him.

"You cannot defeat me Nikalas!" He yelled. The energy between them was dangerously strong but that wouldn't stop him. Forcing himself to summon more power, Agavordis edged his way closer, closing the gap and shrinking the spell between them. Nikalas looked towards Aldon, who stood idly by. In his eyes, it was clear, he had no intention of helping. He had to do this on his own.

Nikalas turned his attention forward and suddenly felt something. It was deep within, hard to spot really, but it felt strong, like energy. He needed it, needed to embrace it if he were to truly find his power. His mind wandered, his thoughts left the battle and went elsewhere, into the maze that was his soul.

As he navigated his internal labyrinth, his spell weakened, giving Agavordis just the opportunity he needed.

"Haa!" Agavordis crowed. His spell had begun to win the duel, a fact clearly demonstrated by the furiously spinning green orb that edged closer to Nikalas.

"There!" Nikalas exclaimed. Waiting patiently in a golden room filled with portraits of the past, was a golden orb of light. He dashed towards it, grabbed it swiftly and then reemerged from his mind and back into the battle. Agavordis was near now, near enough that he could see the confidence masking his pale skin. He looked at his foe with poise and began to spin his staff.

"What is that supposed to do?" Agavordis mocked. "You mean to defeat me with theatrics?"

Lifting his free hand, he menacingly fired another beam that quickly joined with the other, giving his spell more power. The orb between them grew, from the size of a basketball to that of a beach ball, a jumbo beach ball made of raw energy, with one target in mind — Nikalas. The anomaly was a bit distracting, it hid both of them from each other, and while one could guess what the other was thinking, focusing became a bit tricky.

"You can do this," Nikalas whispered to himself. The air around them had begun to clear as the radiating heat filled the breeze. He kept his focus, pushing the sensation of fear away and ignoring the massive orb. Gripping his staff with both hands, he began to trace out a square. Over and over he repeated the motion until suddenly, the heat from the orb had vanished. Nikalas rotated his staff in a square like motion, over and over again.

"You will die Nikalas!" Agavordis sputtered. With a forceful push, the orb careened forward, hideously heading towards Nikalas. But suddenly, Nikalas reached out, grabbed the orb and held it tight in his hands.

"How?!" Agavordis shrieked. "How are you doing that?"

"What's the matter Septus?" Nikalas grinned.

"I am not afraid," Nikalas whispered. He pulled his arms inward, then, in a quick motion, sent it soaring towards Agavordis.

"Nikalas," a voice suddenly called out. Up in the sky, a bright glow appeared and within the glow were two enormous eyes.

"Nikalas," the voice repeated.

"What in the-

He slowly opened his eyes. They had been closed for so long that crust had begun to form on the outer edges. His legs were crossed as he sat on the floor— across from him—sat Kell Si. She wore a satisfied look on her face.

"You were gone a long time," she smiled. "You've gotten pretty good at meditation."

Nikalas rubbed his eyes, pushing out the crust and wiping away the tears that had formed. His heart was still racing. Lately, he was spending so much time in his mind world that it was beginning to feel like that was the real existence and this was the dream. He grunted and slowly pushed himself to his feet.

"Where did you go this time?" Kell Si questioned. She too, stood up, towering above him as always.

"Did you see your father again?"

Nikalas nodded and wandered over to the edge of the mountain they were currently on. The neon grass blew calmly in the wind, and the breeze had hints of salt hiding on its breath. In the skies above, flew Fawn. He seemed to be rather enjoying his newfound friends.

"I think I found a new energy," Nikalas said with his eyes fixed on the city.

"An energy? Perhaps the second flower?" Kell Si replied. She slowly strolled towards him, coming to a stop to his left. He turned and gave her a quiet nod.

"This is excellent."

His eyes squinted as he took notice of a cluster of people gathering in the streets down below. The city seemed eager like it had a tale to tell and even from this distance, they could hear the whispers of concern.

"What's going on down there?" He questioned.

"The elders are holding a special gathering. There's an important matter to be discussed," Kell Si informed.

"Well, should we be there?" Nikalas asked.

Kell Si shook her head.

"I don't think Roros would want you getting distracted by things that don't matter to you."

"Don't matter to me? I've been here for months. Believe it or not, I do care about what happens here," he retorted. Without uttering another syllable, he leapt into the air, pushed his wings out and sailed towards the city.

In the air, he soared, passing by Fawn, who screeched with excitement and decided to follow. In midair, the two danced around each other like performers in a ballet. Their movements were fluid, precise, and majestic. Nikalas smiled as he continued towards the city, racing Fawn as best he could, but try as he may, Fawn was still faster.

"You've made your point!" Nikalas called out as Fawn vanished into the distance.

"Still can't beat a Grimwort," he whispered as his eyes studied the city layout. He needed a vantage point, a spot that would allow him to listen in without being spotted. The crowd had gathered in the midst of the business district, which naturally had plenty of tall buildings. His eyes continued to skim the city until he finally found a place that looked perfect. It was on the far side of the crowd and had a roof decorated with ornamental grass.

"That's the spot," he whispered. With a sneaky maneuver, he flew over to the building, landed and quickly moved to the edge to listen.

"Something has happened. Something that we all need to be aware of," Lorid Fen announced. He turned towards Fal Mor, gave a polite nod, and motioned for her to step up. At this point, the crowd was intrigued. As the eldest Gnome took center stage, whispers began to form. Nikalas leaned his head a bit farther over the edge, paying no attention to the dreadful height and hoping to hear some of the gossips.

"A disturbance has been felt, my friends. The Echo is out of balance, and we fear that it is at risk of tearing," Fal Mor announced.

"Tearing?" Nikalas whispered to himself. "How is that possible?"

"It's Agavordis, isn't it?" A gnome in the crowd called out. "Who else could achieve such unnatural talents?"

Nikalas continued to observe the gathering when suddenly he felt a large hand grab ahold of his shoulder and pull him back.

"You shouldn't be here," Kell Si sternly lectured. "Eavesdropping on Gnome business is inexcusable. If Roros found out, he would have you tossed out at once."

Nikalas rolled his eyes and wandered towards the center of the rooftop. There, looking mighty relaxed indeed, was Fawn, along with another Grimwort he had never seen.

"Doesn't it suck to *need* one of those to fly?" He questioned, rubbing Fawn's ears with a firm motion.

"No offense boy," Nikalas grinningly added.

"Gnomes rather enjoy the bond they share with their Grimworts. It's a symbiotic relationship." She replied.

"So no….it doesn't suck."

Nikalas continued to caress his Grimwort companion, bringing his hand slowly towards the mid back and then eventually, to the tailbone.

"Fal Mor was mentioning the possibility of there being a tear in The Echo," Nikalas paused. "How is that possible?"

Kell Si sternly approached him and pulled him towards her.

"Listen," she paused. "You should not be thinking about this. You need to focus on your training. Not on the concerns of the Gnomes."

"The Echo is my concern," he rebutted. "It's literally where I get my power from. If that's in danger, how the hell am I supposed to fight Septus?"

"The Echo is an ancient realm, it's been here far longer than any species, and it'll be here long after we are all dead," Kell Si explained.

"Then why the concern about a tear?" He countered.

Kell Si sighed and shook her head, shooting him a fierce glare of disapproval. His pestering and nosey way, was—as always—quite aggravating. But alas, something in his eyes, demanded honesty. Compassion perhaps? Genuine care? It was hard to determine.

"The Echo is filled with many doorways. Including one to here," she whispered.

At that moment, Nikalas knew exactly what the elders feared. She needn't say no more.

"Epard?" He nervously asked.

His words hit the air like a hammer to a nail, landing hard and twisting her posture. And like a bent nail, she grew weak, her hands trembling as stories of the past rushed to her mind. The name brought fear. She feared him. She feared a man she had never even met, and yet, it didn't matter. His hatred and actions were well documented. His threats against the species, against all she loved, were finely chronicled. He may have been a fable, he may have been a myth, she didn't know for sure. And that's what troubled her the most.

"Tell me about your meditation," she replied, quickly changing the subject.

"The energy you found. Was it a flower?"

Disappointed by her inability to divulge, he approached the edge of the roof once more. By now, the crowd had begun to disperse, the meeting was done and the elders were quietly sauntering back to the tower of Fal Mor. They were discussing something, but it was hopeless trying to figure out what.

"Nikalas," Kell Si barked. "This is serious. I'm trying to help you."

"Yea," he replied. "It was a red lily."

Kell Si nodded with a satisfactory grin.

"The second flower. Perfect," she smiled. He shrugged and sauntered towards Fawn. As he neared, Fawn lowered his head, ready and willing—nay—hoping for a petting. Nikalas smiled as he carefully ran his hands along the backside of Fawn's neck. The Grimwort shuddered with satisfaction as he neighed.

"There's just one more for you to find within yourself. When you do, you'll have more control over your power than Septus," Kell Si beamed.

"You're so close Nikalas."

"That's a good boy," he whispered into Fawn's ears. "You're a boss."

He slowly swung around, and in an instant, his eyes widened with fear. Standing in front of him, with a malevolent grin, was Agavordis. He lingered still and pointed slowly at a corpse that lay at his feet. It was Zanna.

"No," Nikalas bellowed as tears formed in his eyes. The small streams of saline slowly flowed towards the edges of his eyes, as they trickled down his cheek, they froze instantly. There was a loud scream in the air; it was rather distant and quite reminiscent of a town siren during a storm.

"Help me!"

The words floated into the air like an unwanted odor. The sight was heinous, he knew it wasn't real, but his sight couldn't be stolen. The vision held his full attention, filling him with fear and grief. It was powerful, so strong that it made his knees weak. They buckled, sending him collapsing onto the glass rooftop.

"Nikalas?" Kell Si exclaimed. She rushed to his side, dropping down and putting her hand against his.

"What happened?"

He didn't answer, his breathing was too rapid and his mind too distraught to reply. He looked at the rooftop, peered down at its glass exterior and tried to see through it. There were faint shapes and colors but overall it was too distorted to really make anything out.

"Since I'm telepathic," he paused. "Is it possible for me to see the future?"

"No," Kell Si replied. "That's not possible."

He shook his head as he continued to study the surface. No matter how hard he focused on the obscurities in the glass, all that filled his mind was the image of Zanna.

"If I didn't see the future that means what I saw has already happened," he whispered. His eyes finally found their way upwards, and with tears filling them, he looked at Kell Si.

"I have to go," he whispered. "He's got my friends."

His wings began to flap, lifting him to his feet in a quick fell swoop. The roof seemed unstable, his legs — evidently — still felt weak. He kept his wings flapping, using their gust to keep himself upright.

"You're not ready yet Nikalas," Kell Si shook her head. His eyes met hers; there was a seriousness, unlike anything she had ever seen. Something told her this was it. There would be no talking him out of it this time. Whatever he had seen, whatever the vision was, it was the straw that broke the camel's back. As she studied his expression, she sighed and shook her head in understanding.

"Alright," she exhaled. "But we can't tell Roros. If you need to go, we need to just do it. I can take you to the gate."

She looked at him, sighing at the sight of his persistently serious expression. Her words held no ill effect over him. With nothing other than a nod, she knew his mind was made up.

"You've learned a lot Nikalas. Maybe not everything I had hoped, but you have truly made an impressive amount of progress," she paused.

"You will save Furlasia. I just know it."

"You've been a great teacher," Nikalas replied with a tearful smile. He held out his hand, offering an earthly sign of acceptance. She looked down, unsure what to do — then — she held out hers. He swiftly brought his hand to hers and embraced it with a firm grip.

"Thank you for all you've done."

Kell Si smiled and began to lift her arm up and down in very large and unconventional motions. The gesture was so strong that Nikalas couldn't help but erupt in laughter. In the background, Fawn began to neigh and stomp his feet with excitement. Nikalas shook himself free of the odd handshake and turned towards his faithful companion.

"Let's go home, boy."

Chapter 25

Things were going quite well in Neveraus since the end of the war. Herratia sat atop a throne, not unlike the one she was used to, and there seemed to be a general calm among the Akordans. Being the sudden dominant species suited them well. At last, they were free to travel the land, they were the ones in charge, not the Terrians, not the Arnouts, and especially not the Delopar. She looked at her children with maternal love. They may not have looked like humans, but she was still their mother. Actually, it was quite the concept to wrap one's head around.

Neveraus Hold had been given a Terrian touch ever since she arrived, and things looked a little less grim. There was a much-needed feng shui now present. She liked the new look, but the Akordans seemed decidedly less impressed. Nevertheless, this was her kingdom, her domain, and they were her subordinates, so they quickly accepted it. They had no room to offer protest. One thing she had learned quickly was that Arnouts were ill-tempered and in need of a harsh touch. Since her return, she had already killed six of her precious children, all in the name of making an example.

Much had changed in her mood since the new occupation of Agavordis. She now had a better understanding of her role in this world, and the choices that led to where she was. Her use of dark magic had at one point seemed like a curse, but now, she considered it a blessing.

Today was to be a special day. She had an assignment, one that she was eager to complete. The kingdoms were all under Agavordis' rule, but they still needed regular maintaining and supervision. Nevo had been tasked with Morlay, and she had been tasked with Terria. Agavordis had opted to control Cristol on his own—it was—after all, his pride and joy, his prize. And what a prize it was. Terrorizing and belittling the once powerful species was so extremely satisfying.

She grinned as the thought of stepping into Nasleigh Keep crawled into her mind. She wondered how it looked, and how much had changed. It had been more than twenty years since she lived there. Dwennon had moved on, remarried, and even had another daughter. So much time had passed. As her mind filled with excitement, her eyes took notice of an Akordan that was running a mop over the porous stone floor. It was pointless, and she knew it, but it was tasks like these that taught them patience and obedience, while taming the animal.

"When you're done with that go turn my sheets and pillows," she ordered. The Akordan looked up from his chore and nodded.

"Of course mother," he replied. Her cheeks grew warm as she smirked, they were so compliant, it was hard not to feel proud.

She jumped to her feet and strolled towards the main doors, prompting the two idle guards to hastily pull them open. As she stepped into Neveraus, she took a deep breath. Despite being hidden in a mountain, devoid of all sunlight, it was undeniably beautiful. The hard-pointed ceilings had an art-like quality to them, and the air smelled like freshly dried clothes. As if the ambiance wasn't impressive enough, Neveraus also had all the features of a functional city. There were stores, schools, homes, spas, and even a combat arena.

Her eyes studied the steps that led down, and then suddenly, she phased to their bottom. Teleportation was without a doubt, her favorite new skill, it made everything else so much easier. As she began to stroll through the business district of Neveraus, she was greeted by bows and nods. Children stopped and waved, and shop owners desperately tried to steal her attention. She was truly a celebrity. If she wanted someone's lunch, they handed it over. If she liked someone's weapon, they offered it. No one denied her anything.

"Hello, Mother," a shopkeeper called out. She turned and looked in his direction. He immediately grew excited and began to wave at her persistently. In a quick instant, she was in front of him, looking at his display with curiosity.

"I make some of the finest handbags in all of Neveraus," he proudly declared.

"Are there many makers of handbags in Neveraus?" She sarcastically questioned.

"Well, there's me," he replied with a pointed finger. His aim was in the direction just across the path.

"And then there's that lady. She won't give you the same quality I can."

Herratia swung around and studied the shop across the path. The woman was large, looking mostly the same as any other male except for some spots under her eyes. As she took notice of Herratia's gaze, she grinned and began to wave her over.

"Well, I must say these do seem to be quite elegant," Herratia replied as she turned around.

"Which one is your favorite?" The shopkeeper asked. She looked at the display carefully. There was an impressive selection, especially considering the obvious handicap of having long claws at the end of each finger. Finally, she pointed at a dark grey one that had a couple pockets on the side and a picture of an Uborox embroidered onto it. Without hesitation, the shopkeeper lifted it and handed it to her.

"It's yours," he smiled. She looked it over, and a wave of guilt washed over her.

"I can't just take it; you worked so hard on it. I mean seriously look at your fingers," she nodded towards the claws.

"I can't believe you could even stich something so decorative."

He shook his head in refusal.

"I'm sorry, mother, but I won't accept any payment from you. It's but a small token of my appreciation for all you had to endure in your life."

She looked him over with dismay and then gracefully nodded.

"Thank you so much. What's your name, my child?" She questioned.

"Kent, your highness. My name is Kent," he bowed with a huge smile.

"Well thank you Kent," she replied. After offering one last smile, she turned and continued on her way. Everything seemed to be running smoothly. There was the occasional guard randomly stationed to ensure peace, a useful idea she had come up with after noticing the frequent street brawls. She understood there was a natural aggression to the species, they were *her* children after all, but Neveraus needed order. She would allow the arena to stay open since that was the only place where violence was allowed in the city. If any Akordan broke this law, they were brought before her and swiftly executed.

She continued her travels, making her way up and down the various paths and into the various districts. She was an attentive leader; she didn't just simply sit upon a throne, she regularly sought to check on the well-being of her people. Were it not for her homicidal tendencies, one could almost call her compassionate.

Each district appeared to be in working order. The guard station was filled with recruits, the market was bustling and filled with energy, and the children seemed content with their studies and free time. There was a part of her that was almost disappointed it was going so smoothly. Killing something sounded like fun right about now. She yawned and thought of Terria. Surely, there would be someone there who was in need of punishment.

"Where are you Nevo?" She whispered aloud. Her mind began to travel, scanning through Furlasia's every nook and cranny like a satellite. Everything was visible, every person, every animal, nothing was safe from her gaze.

Suddenly, she zoomed in on Nevo, who was standing on a street corner, dragging King Linuk in chains behind him.

"Now what are you doing?" She muttered. Her eyes went white, and in an instant, she was standing in front of Nevo, causing the nearby guards to startle.

"What are you doing with him?" She questioned. Nevo looked at her with a scowl and then pulled on the chains, forcing Linuk forward.

"He was undermining my authority. Whispering secret commands to the Tin Men and attempting to plot a coup," Nevo accused. Herratia looked at Linuk, skepticism filling her mind as she looked at the blind, helpless man.

"Is this true?" Herratia asked. Linuk looked around, unsure about whom to respond to. She carefully lifted her hand, placing it softly against his cheek and turned him towards her.

"He's paranoid," Linuk gulped. "I fully accept Agavordis' claim to the city and Nevo's right to patrol and monitor it."

"Then what were you doing?" Herratia questioned. Linuk paused and took a deep breath.

"He asks too much of the children in the mines. I wanted some of the Tin Men to keep watch, make sure they aren't being abused," Linuk explained. Nevo pulled on the chains and forced Linuk to the ground.

"So you admit to trying to undermine me?" He growled. "The children in the mine belong to Agavordis. Not you. Their lives are forfeit to his will."

Herratia shot Nevo a stern glance.

"Come Nevo," she replied. "I need to speak with you."

He looked at her, and after sighing frustratingly, dropped the chain and followed her around a corner.

"I understand the need to feel in charge," Herratia whispered. "The Akordans have played second fiddle since the dawn of their birth. But we won, Furlasia is our playground now, there is no need to belittle them. Linuk has endured enough."

"You sympathize with him?" Nevo scoffed.

"There is a time and a place for subjugation. Morlay seems to be under control. You've done very well," she replied. She turned her head and began to survey the city streets, taking in the sight of its desolation and defeat.

"Come with me to Terria. I am going to be checking on them to see how they are coming along," she suggested. "I could use a touch like yours."

He grinned at her.

"Playing to my ego, huh?" He laughed. "It's a good approach."

She smirked and held out her hand.

"Are you ready?"

He calmly nodded, in the blink of an eye, they found themselves standing before the stairs to Nasleigh Keep. Her eyes narrowed as she took in the familiar sight. It was like déjà vu. So little had changed, even the moon atop the roof was still there.

"You actually lived in that monstrosity huh?" Nevo observed. She quietly nodded her head, and in the corner of her right eye, a tear began to form.

"Seems barbaric," he added. She laughed, looking at him with a rarely seen smile.

"Barbaric," she laughed. "And Neveraus Hold is pleasant?"

Her focus speedily veered to the surrounding streets, which were filled with a surprising amount of diligence. Everything appeared to be business as usual. The adults worked, the children played, and bravely enough, some of them even approached the ghouls, throwing taunts and stones.

"You're dead, you're dead, you're dead," they would chant. Herratia watched the adolescent behavior with a twisted expression of vexation.

"What wretched little brats," she whispered. She turned towards Nevo with a scorned look on her face.

"I can't wait till one of the ghouls grabs a child and rips its face off," she quipped.

Nevo looked at her, admittedly taken back by her comment.

"That's dark," he twistedly replied.

"It's no more than they deserve," she responded. "Come on. Let's get moving."

She began to lead them through the streets, paying particular attention to some chanting that took place in the distance. Her curiosity suddenly got hold of her, and before she knew it, she was approaching the barracks. Her arrival, however, prompted a speedy end to the chants. The crowd looked up from their task and eyed her nervously.

"Good," she whispered to herself. What was once a mighty training ground filled with weapons, armor and targets, was now just farmland. There was no need for warriors anymore. Agavordis had ordered the soldiers to build gardens and provide food. The few warriors he allowed to patrol were not gifted with Beacons—no—those had all been given to the citizens instead.

"You have nothing to fear from me," she addressed. "So long as everyone is doing their part to keep the wheel moving, there should be no need for violence."

She approached a younger man and carefully went down on one knee.

"Do not worry. This is for the best. Just look at how much more peaceful things are here. Everyone is working towards a common goal. Subjugation suits you all so very well. Furlasia has never seen so much peace."

The young soldier looked at her with trembling hands and nodded.

"Yes, mam," he whispered. Beaming widely, she rose to her feet.

"Where are the remaining Beacons?" She queried. At that moment, the headquarters' door creaked open and out stepped the former Colonel, looking a little worse for the weather. Defeat—it seemed—had not been kind to him. His eyes were darkened, his hair was a mess, and his new beard looked thoroughly unkempt. With his eyes locked forward, he walked towards them, swaying and dragging his feet with each step.

"What are you doing here bitch?" He declared. "I mean witch."

Nevo roared and charged towards him, lifting him off the ground in one quick one handed-motion.

"I meant witch I said," Sabasio restated.

"Put him down Nevo, he's clearly had a few ales," Herratia explained. Nevo looked into the eyes of the disgraced colonel and swiftly dropped him in the mud.

"Jeez," Sabasio said as he picked himself up. "I've been treated better."

"Agavordis wants to know where the Beacons are. He wants the supply shut down. And I'm here to make sure it happens," Herratia explained.

Sabasio looked at her with belligerence, anger on the tip of his tongue and hatred swelling up in his fist. But rather than letting these emotions bring about a disaster, he politely nodded and waved at them to follow him.

"The Beacons were made in the slum district of Terria by a man named Falker Squarleff. If that name rings a bell to you, it's because he raised Septus into the charming man he is today."

They made their way past the bakers, the tailors, and the candlestick makers and arrived at a point where the pristine cleanliness of the road, seemed to fade rapidly. Here, the air smelled like piss, shit, and vomit. Had she not known such desperation, Herratia might have been judgmental about this place. Unfortunately, she knew this lifestyle all too well.

"This is it," Sabasio explained, as he looked at her. She gave him a nod, and after a long sigh, he knocked on the wooden door. From inside, bangs, clangs, crashes, and pops were heard.

"Ish coming," a voice cried out. The door opened revealing Falker, looking far frailer than he ever had. His frame was thinning and his eyes appeared slightly sunken in. Herratia looked at him and surmised almost immediately that the man was terminally ill. Standing behind him were two ghouls, they peered into the streets with open mouths and blank expressions.

"Colonel? What brings yoush here?" Falker asked, as he looked the two Akordans over. With a nervous smile, he offered them his shaky hand.

"Ish not taking any new ordersh at the moment, but ish always willing to meet new people," he added. Nevo clenched his teeth, even to a primal species like Akordans, the lisp was quite unpleasant.

"I'm actually here to make sure the Beacons are no longer being produced," Herratia explained. "We can't allow you to make them anymore."

"Ah," Falker shook his head. "So my shun sent you." He turned around and waved them into the shop.

"Out of all the folks living in Terria, only I know how to make these tricky weapons. Godly, they are. Perhaps that's why sheptus doesn't want me making any more."

He hobbled over to a back room and flung a door open. Inside, sitting like a lonely bird that was forgotten, was a single Beacon. It sat isolated atop a deformed table, covered in dust and cobwebs. Herratia looked at it with admiration and wandered towards it, tuning out the creaky floorboards as best as she could.

"It's crystals that give these weapons their energy, isn't it?" She asked. Her hands reached down, wiping off some of the dust before picking it up.

"Yesh," Falker replied. Her eyes glanced over its simplistic design; it really was quite an impressive feat. Falker seemed so feeble, so incompetent, and yet, clearly he was a near genius. Suddenly, the Beacon dissolved into dust, leaving nothing but the crystal, which dropped to the floor.

Sabasio's jaw suddenly widened.

"Did you see that?" He asked Nevo.

"Enlightenment can give you a great many abilities," Herratia explained. She slowly knelt down, picking up the crystal and looking it over.

"Where did you find these crystals?" She questioned. She quickly swung and looked towards Falker.

"I uhh," he muttered. In a quick instant, her tail sprung to life, extending long and grabbing ahold of him in a firm squeeze.

"Mother?" Nevo confusingly questioned.

"Silence," she hissed. Her grip on Falker grew stronger, his bones beginning to give way.

"Where do I find them?" She repeated.

"The Hills of Edmere," Falker stuttered. "Theresh a mine there thatsh full of them."

She looked at him with a twisted smile and relinquished her grip.

"I want you to take me there," she ordered.

"But mother, why?" Nevo questioned. "Why do you want these crystals?"

Herratia looked towards the pile of dust that was once a Beacon. Her mind began to race, ideas dashing into her head like gnats to an eye. *Septus is but a boy*, she thought to herself. *A pretender holding onto power that doesn't belong to him.*

"I want their power," she whispered. She closed her eyes, envisioning the boy that she had followed into battle. Perhaps one day, he would serve her.

"Their power?" Nevo perplexed.

"Yes my child, their power."

Chapter 26

Vicham, Dimitri and Wexel slowly worked their way through the crowded camps of Rangmar. Nerve-wracking was the best word to describe it. It wasn't exactly enemy territory, but it wasn't friendly territory either. Delopars were naturally on edge and mistrusting, and that's without being wronged. It was this delightful personality trait that made them such fierce allies, and such awful enemies. If personalities were inherited, then whoever the first Delopar was must surely have been through some awful times. Vicham kept this in mind as they wandered the camp, keeping as close to the others as he could. He studied the surroundings with adolescent curiosity. The tents looked small, each of them holding not more than two or three Delopar. In between each tent were racks filled with weapons of different shapes and sizes. Clearly, this wasn't an ordinary camp.

As Wexel led the way, she began to branch out, approaching various Delopars and asking for directions to the Elder. Vicham watched with awe and interest as she started conversation after conversation. She seemed a natural, not letting the fact that she hadn't met them before bring any pause to her words. They were an interesting species. Old, wise, and governed by a strong belief in Acumen — the day of the All Father.

Past tent and barricade they continued, taking note all the while of the number of warriors that trained. There seemed to be many that were actively working to improve their craft. It was encouraging, especially to Vicham. Their strict regimens and disciplined behavior was something the Vanguard army could use. As he continued to follow, he made a mental note to mention his observations to Emlin because it would be useful if they ever regained control of Terria. Eventually, the tents became larger, indicating an area of particular importance.

A little further ahead, they neared an area that was filled with torches, each of them featuring a perfect red flame. With each blow of the gentle breeze, they flickered, sending tiny red dots floating up towards the sky. The torches were lined up in order to present a pathway, and at the end of it was a tent that featured two guards.

"That's gotta be it," Wexel pointed. She proceeded forward, and as they neared, the guards raised their blades and furrowed their foreheads.

"What purpose does a man, a Terrian and a pipsqueak have with The Elder?" One of the guards demanded.

"We were directed to speak to her about a woman we are tracking that traveled near here," Vicham replied. "It's rather important I find this woman. She is dangerous and has two of my friends held hostage."

The guards looked at each other, then turned towards him with disgust.

"We care not about your problems or your needs," the left one sneered.

"That may be, but your elder might," Vicham retorted.

Wexel stepped forward, stopping just a few feet shy of the two guards and put her hands on her hips.

"This is one of those moments where you can save yourself some embarrassment, or spend the rest of your days humiliated. Because if you don't let us through, I'm going to beat you both senseless and you'll spend the rest of your lives remembering the time you were bested by a pipsqueak," Wexel threatened.

The two guards erupted in laughter, and withdrew their blades.

"Let them pass," a voice bellowed from within the tent. The guards looked at Wexel draped in disappointment.

"Pity," the one on the right said as he stepped aside. "I would've loved to teach you some manners."

Wexel smirked as she stepped past the two guards, offering them an innocent curtsy before she stepped inside.

"She doesn't speak for all of us," Dimitri quietly added, before he and Vicham stepped through the curtains.

If the rest of the Delopar camp was New York City, this tent was Paris. Everything about it seemed highly maintained and perfectly tailored. Each chair looked fit for a queen, and each table looked prepared to feed an army. Lying in the middle of the tent, with her legs pointed up, and her arms spread wide, was The Elder.

"Welcome to what remains of Rangmar," she greeted. Letting out a chuckle, she jumped up, landing on her feet and facing towards them.

"I am Rashik. I am The Elder. Although truth be told, I'm actually quite young."

There was a surprisingly friendly quality to her that made her almost come off as unusual, especially compared to the other Delopar.

"I'm Vicham of Terria. This is Dimitri of Morlay and Wexel, from I don't know where."

Wexel looked at Vicham with a coy smirk and extended her hand towards Rashik.

"I'm from the former village of Frand," she informed. As Vicham heard the name, he turned towards her. Frand. There was a name he hadn't heard in a while. It was at one point one of the largest settlements of the nomad Delopars, but Septus had quickly ended that title. He hadn't seen the carnage first hand, but the descriptions painted a pretty vivid picture. It was here that Septus first revealed himself after the banishment.

"I'm sorry to hear that," Rashik nodded. "What happened there was terrible. Unforgivable."

Rashik pointed to a table that had an outstretched map lying across it.

"Our army has been building up for some time. Delopars from all over Daulest have been trickling in, answering the call. The necromancer's actions here are well known, even beyond the lands of Furlasia," Rashik explained.

"So you mean to retaliate?" Vicham questioned.

"Oh yes," Rashik nodded. "The Delopar will have their day on the battlefield."

She began dragging her finger over the outstretched map, pointing towards Cristol, Terria and Morlay.

"The problem is we can't do it alone. We need the occupied cities to rise and fight when the time comes."

Dimitri flashed a look of dumbfound at Vicham.

"How do you propose we do that? Our armies were defeated. And those that lived long enough to surrender are all captives. Living in camps and forced into slavery," Dimitri barked.

Rashik calmly approached him and placed a gentle hand atop his trembling hands. With a calm demeanor, she began to rub, while breathing deeply.

"The prophecy is real," she whispered. "The one called Nikalas Noise will free the armies. He will unite the land with his newfound powers."

Vicham suddenly went alert, the mention of his former friend's name brought butterflies into his stomach.

"What do you know of him?" He asked.

"We know his return is almost near. Soon the call will echo throughout the city streets, forest, and village alike," she replied. A wide smile crept across her face.

"It's actually pretty exciting."

Dimitri groaned and turned towards the tent's entrance.

"Where are you going, my friend?" Rashik called out. "Don't you want to know where the goddess has taken your friends?"

Vicham's eyes suddenly widened as he looked at their host with astonishment.

"You know about her?" He asked.

Rashik smiled and neared a chest that sat on the ground. It was large, made of ramite and contained a twist lock that looked like it was made of gold. She swiftly dropped to her knees and lifted it open. From within, an orange hue emanated, filling the tent with its radiant light. Dimitri paused, the phenomenon holding his interest enough to halt his retreat.

She reached into the chest and pulled out a large orb that glowed orange. Vicham smirked as the familiarity caught his eyes. A Shewglomus.

"I can see from the look in your eyes that you know what this is," Rashik summarized.

Vicham nodded yes, and gently approached.

"This Shewglomus is no ordinary Shewglomus. This is the first one ever made. The very same one that Undr himself once used. This Shewglomus does more than provide communication. It has been known to show visions to the right person. It was in this holy device that I was able to keep track of Gravi. And it was in this device that I learned of her whereabouts," Rashik explained.

"She's smart though. Somehow, she found a way to block its gaze from seeing her. But nevertheless, I already know where she resides."

She carried the Shewglomus over to the map and set it down. With an extended finger and claw, she pointed at a place that was just past Rangmar. A region called Sanlorus. Vicham looked down and sighed as he noticed the destination she had pointed at.

"Sanlorus," he whispered. "Makes sense."

"What is Sanlorus?" Dimitri questioned.

Rashik waved to Dimitri, summoning him over to the table and directed him to the Shewglomus. She placed her hand carefully above its glass — then — as soon as he had brought his attention towards it, pulled it away. From within the glass came a vision. A land that was dark, riddled with rock and covered in a seemingly never-ending dusk. The sky was filled with swirling dark clouds, and the ground was teeming with different manner of beasts. As he took in the sights, he could feel his hands beginning to shake. His lips quivered, and his feet were starting to feel numb. In the center of it all, near a dark bubbling river, stood a tall fortress, which gave a large beam of light from its rooftop.

"Your path takes you into one of the most dangerous regions in all of Daulest. A place outside of Undr's care. Here, in this soulless wasteland, Gravi reigns. She controls all and knows all. Everything there is subject to her control, even the wind and the soil beneath your feet. If her gaze falls upon you, she will rain fire down upon your heads," Rashik grinned.

"Do you still want to go find your friends?"

Dimitri looked at Vicham who still appeared determined as ever. Dimitri on the other hand was as white as a ghost. The little courage he had within him had vanished at the sight of Sanlorus.

"I'm out," he barked. "There is no way I'm going there with you."

Wexel glanced at Vicham and gave him a comforting nod. A nod of approval and a nod confirming her participation.

"Yes. I must go," Vicham replied.

"I knew you would say that. There is a conviction in you. One that I sense won't be stopped," Rashik smiled. "I will have a few of my men lead you to where you need to go. They will go as far as the border of Furlasia, but after that, you're on your own."

Vicham bowed in understanding.

"Thank you," he whispered.

Rashik sauntered over to the chest once again, this time retrieving two daggers, and quietly handing them to Wexl and Vicham.

"These are the daggers of Fendel. My father. Rumors say that they were blessed by Pomari, goddess of the Arnouts and that when times are particularly dark, they will prove stronger than most."

Vicham looked at the blade and nodded. It looked rather simple. Curved towards the top and obviously quite sharp. The hilt was wrapped in leather and upon the blade was an inscription that read *Si Paay Lemol*.

***

It had been nearly two hours since they had left the camp of Rangmar. Now — without Dimitri — Wexel and Vicham pressed forward. Furlasia was officially behind them. A place of the past, filled with darkness and painful memories. A place filled with the dead. On the back of a couple horses, they carefully traversed the region known as Sanlorus. It was every bit as ghastly as the vision in the Shewglomus had shown. Whatever this place used to look like, it had become truly forsaken.

There was a hum beneath their feet, a tremor that felt similar to the ones that had plagued Furlasia before the war had started. Vicham kept his eyes to the ground, concerned the tremble would worsen, but so far, it remained nothing but a hum. Wexel rode nervously atop the back of her horse, or rather Dimitri's horse. She had confiscated it during a rather entertaining argument. The young Delopar had fortitude, that much could not be denied.

The clouds in the skies danced with passion. Twisting and thrusting like the dancers of Swan Lake. Soaring in between the frightening pockets of condensation, were black birds with red eyes and long, sharp beaks. They were the *Scorns*, legendary spies of Gravi. As their calls filled the air, Vicham looked up, gulping at the sight of the terrible creatures.

Distant howls echoed on the wind's breath, playing in the breeze like a far off record player. A wolf, a bear? Vicham, sighed with unease as they continued forward.

"Sounds like a Worthiar," Wexel proclaimed. "Those are a fun kill indeed."

Vicham pulled on his reins and gave his horse a light kick.

"I'd prefer to just take you at your word with that," he called out.

Wexel grinned and gave her horse a kick as well.

Through the dark and grimy atmosphere of Sanlorus they galloped, and the further into the region they got, the more noticeable the scent of acid had become. Ricter. Such a dreadful and strange substance, surely a product of evil rather than divinity. To see that it existed here, made sense in the most obvious way.

"Do you smell that?" Vicham questioned.

"I perceived it awhile back," Wexel replied. "It's Ricter."

"Yes," Vicham agreed. "We must be getting near."

As they continued making their way, a large beam of light began to creep from the horizon. It climbed to the sky, crafting a magnificent spectacle of glowing clouds.

"Whoa," Wexel whispered.

The two horses pressed onwards, as the tower came into sight, they began to slow down.

"That's it," Vicham sighed. Lingering on the horizon like an unwanted pimple, stood Gravi's tower. At its top was the beam of light and circling the upper portion of the tower were various dark shapes with large wingspans.

"Now there's a sight I never wanted to see. The very origin of evil itself," Vicham informed. Their eyes widened and their nerves trembled as they continued moving forward.

"Those are Arnouts," Vicham exclaimed, pointing up towards the tower. "They must be under some kind of mind control."

"Mind control?" Wexel remarked. "How are we supposed to get into the tower with those things circling above?"

Vicham silently looked towards the tower and summoned his horse to a halt. Wexel quickly followed suit.

"If we go on foot, we can use the rocks as cover," Vicham explained. He carefully climbed off his horse, trying his best to ignore the panic in his stomach. Sighing with remorse, he gave the horse a firm slap on its butt.

"Go on now," he called out. "This is no place for you."

The horse lifted its front legs, letting out a loud neigh, and then dashed towards the horizon. Wexel urgently climbed down from her horse and did the same.

As their last hope for a quick escape faded from sight, the two of them exchanged a silent glance, then proceeded forward. Time passed by, their feet grew tired, and the air continued to reek of acid. Traveling had at one point been one of Vicham's favorite hobbies; there were so many things to see in Furlasia, so much beauty. Here, however, the sensation was lost, and he found himself wondering if it would ever return. Can one return to normalcy after witnessing the chaos in the world?

A sudden deep tremor beneath his feet made him pause. He stopped, looking around and planned for the worst.

"What is that?" Wexel questioned. Vicham looked ahead, offering nothing except a faint shrug of his shoulders.

"Let's keep moving," he whispered. His legs popped as he crouched down, doing his utmost best to remain unseen by the soaring Arnouts. He quickly waved at Wexel, then proceeded forward. With his heart in his throat, the tremors below seemed like they had vanished. Nothing mattered more than getting inside that tower. He couldn't fail her. Not again.

They stayed down, hiding behind boulders whenever they became available. As his skin pressed against the porous stone, he couldn't help but smile at the warmth each seemed to contain. The sensation was almost freakish, so unlike anything he'd encountered. The Arnout spies looked attentive, changing directions every couple of minutes and occasionally looking in their direction.

"Hold up," Vicham would warn with each occurrence. Wexel was quick to respond each time. She would swiftly drop to all fours, scanning the area with maximum concentration, and quickly leaping up once the *all clear* was given. Their approach seemed to be going smooth, far smoother than either had expected. The terrain — while terrifying — did provide quite a bit of cover.

There were a few hundred yards away, when all of a sudden, Wexel began to slow down, her nostrils flaring as she sniffed the air. Vicham halted, turning towards her with wonder as she continued her animalistic display.

"What's going on?" He asked. She lifted her hand, crawled towards a nearby pile of rocks and climbed up. Her paws gripped each stone like velcro, allowing her to scale atop with ease.

"What do you see?" Vicham questioned.

"Akordans," she whispered. "Hundreds of them."

She turned around and grinned as she began to slide back down the mound. As she came to a stop, she stood, shooting Vicham an unsettling smile.

"Why are you smiling?" He queried. "Akordans are bad news."

She huffed and brushed past him.

"Akordans are practice."

Vicham stood mystified by her ignorant sense of risk and adventure, then headed towards her.

"I think we should find a way around," he muttered.

Wexel looked at him, scratching her head.

"How many detours are you trying to take?" She sneered. Laughing, she turned and began to crawl towards the tower once more. She had barely moved ten feet when another tremor began to shake the ground. It felt stronger, more pronounced and this time it sounded like the source was near.

"What the heck is that?" She pondered. Turning around, she noticed that Vicham had stopped in place. His skin appeared pale, and his fingers twitched rapidly against his legs.

"Vicham?"

His hands continued to tremble as they slowly moved towards his face. There was a strange faintness to his eyes and he seemed quite focused on the ground beneath his feet.

"He's here," he whispered. Wexel cautiously approached, keeping her hands planted readily on her blade.

"Who's here?" She questioned.

Vicham looked up, his jaw had widened and his eyes were now entirely black.

"Undr."

He urgently began to push aside rocks, tossing them every which way as he aimlessly dug towards the unknown. The further he dug into the pile of rocks, the more violent the tremor became. Soon, it became plainly clear that something had vexed her friend. But who or what remained to be seen.

"Vicham stop!" Wexel protested. She reached towards him, but before she could land a hand, he gave her a firm shove. Into the dirt she crashed, humiliation and surprise finding her thoughts.

"Hold on," he bellowed. His hands continued to plummet towards the rocks, pushing them aside as hastily as he could until alas, he came upon a door. Small—its size seemed rather similar to that of a cabinet.

"What is it?" Wexel nervously asked as she approached. Vicham shook his head, looking at her and returning to the familiar.

"You're back to normal," she remarked.

"I think he took over me," Vicham shakenly whispered. His eyes peered down at the door, towards the light that seeped from around its hinges. As he continued to study its simplistic design, he knelt, pressing his hand slowly to the handle.

"What are you doing?" Wexel questioned. "You don't know what's in there."

Vicham nodded in agreement as his conversation with Linuk played through his mind. The *Pocket Doorway*. Was it the product of a father trying to entertain his son? Or was it real? There was only one way to be sure.

"It's the Pocket Doorway," Vicham replied.

Without another word he gripped the handle, giving it a firm twist. Moments later, the door flung open and a yellow beam of light emerged from within. It landed on the ground in front of them and formed into a familiar shape. A human. A tall man with blond hair and broad shoulders.

"Uh oh," Wexel whispered.

Chapter 27

The silence of Abissal Keep offered nothing but despair. As Agavordis sat at his desk, poring over charts and incantations, he continually felt the sting of loneliness. Emlin was back in the dungeons, a choice she had made. He had offered her time and time again a place at his side, but she refused. It was disheartening. He had done so much to try and please her. The situation was beginning to seem hopeless.

All he had now was the voice of his father, who continued to insist that he proceed with the ritual. As much as he longed to see his father again, the idea of actually bringing him back from the Sea of Souls made him hesitate. Right now, he was in charge. He was the leader, Furlasia was *his* to make as he wished. If Drachen returned, that would all change, suddenly he would be taking orders. And what would happen to his power? The power and his father's soul were tied to the rings, and although he could free the soul, would that also take away the power? The more he pondered, the less interested he was in completing the ritual. He hadn't told his father that of course, instead, he pretended to be going through all the necessary motions.

Today was the day. The day he would bid farewell to his friend and mentor, Epard. And although he was not looking forward to it, that had always been part of the plan. For months now, he attempted to find The Wall of Truth, but unfortunately, his efforts were in vain. The Gnomes were clever in their paranoia; the gateway to Cap Ti Mor remained an impossible destination to find.

However, in his research, he did discover something interesting. If Furlasia was plentiful in anything, it was in stories of The Echo. To some, they were merely folklore, while to others, they were hard and true. And if one could sort out the differences, it would be easy to learn the truth. Normally, one had to have a bond with the creatures native to the realm in order to enter, but if his studies were correct, there might have been a way to open a small tear, a doorway to the limitless.

The details to the spell were well hidden, wizards far older than Kunklestick had seen to that, but as with all knowledge passed down, eventually the secrets spilled out. As it turns out, the final piece of the puzzle was found at the very same place that began his journey. Undr's Temple. Fate was not without irony, that much was clear.

Day in and day out, he had worked to enter the godly realm, but no matter how hard he focused, the spell simply would not allow him to step inside the tear. The results were maddening, but despite his frustrations, he did feel quite confident in Epards ability to enter. Once inside, the back door into Cap Ti Mor would be quick and easy to locate.

He continued looking over some documents that sat atop the desk, rereading the incantation and necessary steps to open the breach. As boredom took hold, his eyes began to wander, and after observing the stark appearance of the room he occupied, he looked at his rings, the true source of his power. They sat on his fingers as a constant reminder that his power did not belong to him. But why? Why could he not harness The Echo's energy? Why was his father able to, but not he? In truth, he wanted very much to be rid of the rings, he hated them. They were bulky, unappealing, and just plain annoying.

"Why can't I own this power for myself?"

He jumped to his feet and began to pace back and forth. With each pace, he visualized everything he had done to this point. The good, the bad and the ugly. His focus was unwavering, so much so that initially he didn't hear the knock at his door. Suddenly, it flung open, revealing Herratia and Nevo who were looking quite serious.

"What are you doing here?" He demanded. "I didn't summon you."

Herratia smiled and stepped inside with Nevo following closely behind.

"I didn't know I had to be invited to visit," she replied. "We are allies, aren't we?"

She looked at Agavordis amusingly. He looked disheveled, weakened, and emotionally drained.

"Now's not a good time," Agavordis sternly responded.

"I've seen that look before," she grinned. "It's the very same look I had when I was trying to summon skills I wasn't meant to have, night after night, day after day."

She stepped closer, prompting him to take a side step. There was something strange in her expression. He watched her with interest.

"What spell are you struggling with?" She questioned.

He looked to her with unease, and shook his head.

"There's no spell I can't pull off," he assured. "Why are you here?"

He looked at Nevo, who looked oddly stoic and calm.

"I went to Terria and did a patrol. Things seem under control," she explained. "Your father has halted production on the Beacons and the Vanguards' moral seemed quite broken."

Agavordis nodded.

"I was there just yesterday," he replied. "The Beacons are in the hands of the people now. Order is coming to Terria."

"Oh," she remarked. "I hadn't realized you were checking on Terria."

He shrugged as he recalled the occasion. It was successful in the sense that he eased the minds of some of the people, but a failure in terms of winning Emlin's affection.

"Terria is my home. It will always be of the utmost importance to me," he replied.

"Did you think I did all this just to flex some muscles? I really do want to bring justice and balance to Furlasia."

Herratia looked towards his desk and caught the faintest glimpse of the incantation he was trying to work on.

Quickly, Agavordis darted towards her, blocking her gaze as promptly as he could.

"I was thinking the other day about something you once told me," she smiled. "Your power comes from the rings, doesn't it?"

She casted her eyes on him and noticed the sweat dripping down his forehead.

"The rings contain the soul and power of my father," he replied. "Why?"

She reached into a pouch that she wore and carefully opened up the flap. From within its depths, she withdrew a crystal, a rather familiar crystal, in fact.

"Where did you get that?" He nervously questioned.

"I found it in the mountains," she answered. Suddenly, something caught his eyes. On the floor, just under the pouch, was a bit of blood. In fact, as he retraced her steps, he noticed that there were specs of it leading all the way to her.

"What's in the bag?" He demanded.

"Allow me to show you," she coyly replied. Her hand reached inside once more, this time pulling out the bloody remains of a severed head.

"He talks and talks but his voice sounds so bad, his lisp so strenuous, that I just had to shut him up," Herratia explained. Agavordis looked with panic at the severed head of Falker. Despite all the death and carnage he had seen and caused, nothing could've prepared him for this. To see the ravaged remains of the man who raised him from infancy, made him sick. As he fought the urge to hurl, he observed Falker's vacant eyes. They remained wide open and glossed over. Baby blue jewels of decay.

"Why?" He tearfully asked.

Herratia dropped the head onto the floor, letting it roll towards his feet.

"I said why!" He roared. In that instant, she vanished, leaving Nevo standing there with a beaming smile.

"I told you I would kill you," he laughed. He reached down and withdrew his blade.

"We don't need you anymore."

Quickly, Agavordis pushed his hand forward, sending Nevo crashing like a rag doll into the bed behind him. He had just begun to relish in his quick handling when a loud screech suddenly filled the air. It was agonizing, threatening to destroy his hearing with each passing second. Tears formed in his eyes as blood began to seep from his ear canals and finally, he could take no more. He dropped to his knees, summoning a cloud of energy around him. The screech vanished. He could hear nothing now but the sound of his breath as he attempted to retrieve it.

"This partnership isn't going to work," Herratia explained, as she appeared before him. In her hands, she held a weapon, unlike anything he had ever seen. It resembled a Beacon, but the barrel was far larger and the size was decidedly bigger. With a firm squeeze of the trigger, a powerful and profound beam of light emerged, tearing towards his shield and quickly shattering it.

"Move!" Drachen bellowed from above. Agavordis nodded, acknowledging the persistent voice and leapt into the air.

"I should've left you in that cocoon," he scorned, hovering in the air with crossed arms.

"Yea," Herratia sighed, as she aimed the weapon and fired another shot.

"Prolly would've been a smart call."

Once again—however—he was able to evade the attack.

"You really thought you held power over me?" Herratia sneered. "I helped you only so that you could clear the field of my enemies."

Her words surged through his ears like poison through a vein, filling him with resentment and hate. His eyes began to glow red, and from his hand, green energy began to emanate.

"This time there won't be anything left to resurrect," he whispered. With soulless eyes, he lifted his hands, sending a beam of burning energy towards her.

"Imbecile!" She roared as she grabbed the ribbon of energy. She held it in her hands like a toy and began to assemble it into a sphere. Once it was complete, she chucked it forward and knocked him out of the air.

"Ugh," Agavordis sighed as he hit the floor.

"My turn," Nevo remarked. He approached with a bolstered grin and his sword held high above his head.

"Foolish boy," he roared. He brought the blade down with a furious force. However, just before it landed, it stopped.

"What?" He asked confusingly. The blade was ripped from his hands, and rocketed forward with near instantaneous speed. Herratia quickly flung her arms, summoning an invisible energy that swiftly turned the blade into dust.

"Don't worry Septus," Herratia smiled. She nodded at Nevo and then quickly brought her tail swinging around and crashing into Agavordis. The impact sent a radiating pain through his chest, surely there would be a bruise, if not broken ribs. With a slow push, he climbed to his feet, trying his best to remain steady. As his eyes adjusted, he noticed Herraita had once again acquired the weapon.

"Boom!" She heckled.

***

"Did you hear that?" Didorumpus suddenly whispered. Kunklestick looked upwards, towards the ceiling and quietly nodded.

"It sounded like an explosion," he remarked. "What do you think it was?"

Didorumpus rose to his feet, wandered over to the nearby wall and pressed his hands gently against it. There was a slight hum, a vibration, mind you. It was faint, almost unnoticeable but clearly, something was happening. He turned and looked at his brother with a shrug.

"The tremors maybe," he replied.

"You mean Undr," Kunklestick retorted. Yes — they had both been informed about the near certainty that the tremors were not tectonic plates, but instead Undr, the guardian of Daulest. Didorumpus shrugged and returned to his bed, plopping down and allowing a feeling of dread to come over him.

"I can't stay here anymore. Where is Nikalas?" He huffed. Kunklestick looked at the outer bars, towards the ghouls that lingered nearby and shook his head with uncertainty.

"You must remain strong brother," Kunklestick advised.

"Strong?" Didorumpus questioned. "Strong is what I stayed for twenty years in that cavern while you were up on the surface drinking and having a merry old time."

Kunklestick looked at him with a squint. It was an unfair remark. He hadn't known that his brother had survived. If he had, then he most certainly would have plummeted into the darkness to find him. How was he to know a miracle had occurred?

"Don't even start that again," he warned. "I didn't drink to have a merry old time. I drank out of grief. A grief so strong that for the longest time, I didn't even have access to my powers. I spent each day staring at the painting of us, regretting and wishing that it had been me that suffered your fate."

"But you didn't," Didorumpus returned. "You led us into a fight with Drachen, knowing fully well that he outpowered us. You doomed us all that day."

Another loud rumble filled the air, causing specs of dust to sprinkle down atop them. In the halls, the guards began to grow restless, nervousness setting in.

"We don't always know what we are walking into," Kunklestick replied. "But we had to try. Freedom is worth the fight."

Another loud rumble filled the air, and suddenly, the ceiling began to tumble down.

"Watch out," Kunklestick warned. Didorumpus quickly pushed himself against the back wall, gracefully avoiding the incoming heavy rain.

"What's going on? What are you two up to?" An Akordan guard roared. He approached the bars and pushed his sword towards them.

"What sorcery are you pulling?"

Didorumpus shook his head and snickered a bit.

"We don't have our staves idiot. We can't use magic," he retorted.

The guard roared and reached towards a key ring. It was a wide loop and filled with many keys that looked to be quite ancient.

"Um, what do we do brother?" Didorumpus nervously asked as the guard fidgeted with the various keys.

Kunklestick looked at the guard with apprehension, then looked down towards the direction of one of the fallen bricks. His back hurt and his knees popped and cracked as he reached down, but that didn't stop him. With a grunt and a slight accidental fart, he lifted a brick and held it above his head.

"You think that is going to save you huh?" The guard taunted. Suddenly, an invisible force pulled him back, slamming him into the wall and knocking him unconscious. Kunklestick looked at Didorumpus with dread, and together they both prepared. The ground continued to shake, dust continued to rain down and suddenly the gate flung open. The ghouls turned, looking at a cloaked figure and suddenly, their limbs began to twist.

Kunklestick gulped, preparing to launch the brick as best as he could. From the darkness of the halls, emerged a familiar shape dressed in wizard's garments. It was Nikalas. With his staff in his hand and a proud smile on his face, he approached the cell.

"Nikalas," Didorumpus called excitedly.

He darted towards him, gripped him in a quick hug, and then pulled back as he noticed the wings.

"You're an Arnout?" He questioned.

"Half," Nikalas replied. He looked at Kunklestick, who, smiling, dropped the brick to the floor.

"Is this you?" He asked, pointing towards the damaged ceiling above. Nikalas shook his head.

"No," he replied. "Agavordis is fighting with some weird looking woman. We need to get out of here before they tear the whole place down."

Kunklestick and Didorumpus nodded in agreement and stepped out into the halls.

"How many prisoners are there?" Nikalas queried.

"Hundreds," Kunklestick replied.

"Ok, we need to get them out," Nikalas added. He reached to his side and pulled out two wands, handing one to each of them. Kunklestick smirked and extended it to staff form. He sighed with relief upon realizing it was his actual staff. He looked at Nikalas and beamed.

"It took you long enough."

***

Agavordis summoned a shield, blocking Herratia's assault just narrowly. She was fast, clever, and psychotic. Each time he thought he had gotten track of her, she would teleport and vanish into The Echo. The fight was far more challenging than any of the wizards had proven to be. But then again, this was Herratia, a witch who needed no staff to use her powers since they were rooted in darkness, disdain, and misery.

Her screeching filled the air, but she was nowhere to be seen. He looked around; the battle had been moved from his quarters to the roof of Abissal Keep. It was frigid, the blistering air ferried towards him, threatening to cut through him like a serrated blade. She was nowhere to be seen, but her screech could be heard from miles away. He quickly brought his hands up, trying his best to shield his ears from her ear-piercing howl.

"Where are you?" He called out. "Stop hiding and fight me!"

"With pleasure," Herratia replied. Like a flash of light, she appeared, quickly bringing her claws lurching towards him. They were sharper than that of any animal in Furlasia, to be caught by them would be an agonizing wound indeed. Luckily, he was able to summon an armor just in time. Her claws crashed into the buffer of yellow light, sending a glow echoing from end to end.

"Ha!" He roared as he pushed his shield forward. She fell back in surprise and began to slip on the ice-covered shingles.

He looked at her with a satisfied smirk, then waved his hand upwards, sending her flying into the air and holding her in place in front of him. Her eyes were filled with anger, ferocity and from this angle, perhaps jealousy. His confidence had never been higher, she was a formidable foe indeed. With his hand still raised, he began to rotate them, causing Herratia to start spinning slowly.

"Ahhhh!" She screeched.

Chapter 28

The night air was filled with cheers, applause and paper lanterns. Tonight was a joyous occasion, the birthday of an elder always was. There would be dances, parties, drinking and sex; all the usual customs would be present. The town's residents filled the streets, talking and socializing amongst each other about matters mostly unrelated to the actual occasion. Almost every man and woman held a drink in one hand and a paper card in the other. As The Decoyers looked out on the city, they felt fairly certain that they were witnessing the beginnings of a death cult. There was so much joy and euphoria that it seemed bizarre. There was an erotic hue to the air, and each of the townspeople looked hungry for connection. Articus looked at Methalda, who was standing silent with nervous eyes and an open jaw.

"Well," Sillimon paused. "I suppose everyone has their own customs." Penny looked at him with surprise, then gave a subtle wink. He smirked as he noticed the gesture, then returned his attention forward.

"I have heard of such customs," Jinn whispered. "But I never expected to witness it myself."

As the music in the streets sped up, some of the citizens began to dance, many of them pressing themselves against others in a rather suggestive way. Penny gawked with surprise and took a step closer to Sillimon.

"What is this festival called again?" Methalda asked.

"It's the Tides," a nearby man informed. He approached them with an arm full of glowing vines and held them outright for them to see.

"Can I interest any of you in one of these?" He questioned.

In the foreground, the citizens had begun to kiss, with many of them kissing multiple people at once. Penny shook her head with surprise and grabbed hold of Sillimon's arm.

"What are they?" Jinn asked.

"Neorbs," he replied with a sound of surprise. "You've never seen these before?"

He looked around at The Decoyers, all of whom shook their heads *no*.

"Bunlets! Where are you lot from?"

Jinn hovered towards the man and paused. He quickly looked her up and down and then, with large eyes of confusion, looked back down.

"Bunlets!" He exclaimed. "How'd you lose your feet?"

"I am a Kajj. We were the first species to walk these lands," she replied. He looked down and shook his head in disagreement.

"Not with that situation going on," he barked. "You didn't walk anywhere."

Kadeen chuckled and reached for her pouch, pulling out a few coins and handing them to the dirt-ridden man.

"How many will this buy me?" She questioned. The man looked over the coins and was suddenly ecstatic. Without saying another word, he tipped his arm downwards, letting all the vines fall to the ground.

"Bunlets!" He exclaimed. "You can have em all."

Suddenly, a howling firework shot up into the air, exploding and creating an almost phallic shape. As Penny looked up, she blushed, and expelled a bit of laughter.

"You folks sure have a lot of money. If you need anything else, you come find me. I'm by the building with the painting of a giant—

Another firework shot up, this one exploding in dozens of smaller streaks, and dancing across the sky. This tantalizing spectacle was certainly far more glamorous than any they had ever seen in Morlay or Furlasia for that matter. Even the Arnouts, with their gifts and natural talents, didn't have this type of thing.

As the party continued to escalate, and the eroticism continued to rise, Jinn had finally seen enough.

"We need to get back to the Maratan," she informed.

"Fine by me," Methalda replied.

They maneuvered through the crowd moving past the adultery, inebriation, and sin, until alas, they reached the outskirts of this suddenly very strange town. The Maratan waited just ahead — from within — there were lights that shone into the dark night like a beacon of hope.

"Well, that was certainly something," Adam declared. The others stopped, looking back at him disappointingly.

"You want to go back, don't you?" Jinn guessed. Adam nodded his head with a grin.

"Fine," Jinn sighed. "Go ahead, but make sure you are back by morning. The plans begin at dawn."

Adam gleefully turned around and began to jog forward.

"Wait for me," Dorrin called out. Jinn pondered his eagerness and looked at him with disheartenment, then finally, waved him on.

"Perverts," Methalda whispered as she watched the two vanish towards the festivities.

"We all must choose our own path in life," Jinn replied. "So long as they are ready and able tomorrow, I don't care what that path is."

She looked towards the city once more, the music was louder than ever and the fireworks and lanterns continued to rise. Shrugging with understanding, she turned and climbed the steps that lined the side of the Maratan. The others quickly followed. As they sealed the door to the entrance, they expelled a breath of relief.

The following morning, Articus awoke to find himself being pelted in the eyes by a sliver of light. The shade that blocked off his window had just been left open a tad. It was a welcome sight; however, the sliver of light brought warmth and perhaps even a sense of calm. Outside, he could hear the banters and conversations of the others that wandered the ship, most likely heading towards the dining area. He stood up slowly, letting his muscles stretch and adjust to the day, then sauntered over to the door, pushing his ear against the cold metal.

"Oh, it was fantastic," Adam explained to someone. "Those cards everyone was holding, let's just say they contained very particular instructions."

"How interesting," Sillimon replied. Articus lifted and pulled on the lever that sealed his door and slowly pushed it open.

"Rise and shine buddy," Adam exclaimed with a grin. "Today's the day. I hope you guys are up for it."

Articus nodded and headed towards them, scratching his head as he neared. A door behind Sillimon suddenly pulled open, revealing Penny, looking fresh and ready as ever. She looked at everyone with excitement and put her arm through Sillimon's.

"Get to the dining area," Idrix ordered, her voice loudly filled the air as she croaked into the vocal piping system.

Wasting no further time, they sulked down the hall and turned to the opening on the right. Idrix and Jinn sat inside, holding a cup of tea and Danish cheese in each of their hands. Sitting atop the table were five cups of piping hot tea and danishes for all. As everyone promptly took a seat and grabbed their meal, Idrix looked around with an unapproving glare.

"What?" Dorrin finally asked.

"You two," she pointed. "Should have come back with the others. Do you know the risk you took going back to that perverse party?"

"You mean the risk of getting some sexual gratification?" Adam retorted. "Excuse me but I've been traveling with The Decoyers for some time now, loneliness happens from time to time."

"These are Adrasians," Idrix reminded. "Each of them has the strength to turn your skull into powder. This is something neither of us can afford to forget. Interactions need to be kept to a minimum."

She looked around the table, receiving nods of understanding from all except Adam.

"Now then," she paused. "Articus and Sillimon have come up with a plan that I think we all need to hear."

She nodded towards Articus and took a sip of her tea.

"Well," he cleared his throat. "The mountains behind provide a good way to reach the top of The Cone. Sillimon has volunteered to make the climb. Once up there, he's going to squeeze through a window, and that should get him into the room."

"The Boss wears a special glove to handle the jewel," Jinn added. "We will need to procure that so that he can handle it. That's where I come in."

"Dorrin and Adam," Idrix pointed. "You two are our honeypots. You like fornication, well now's your chance. The Boss needs to be distracted. You will both lure her out of the home and to one of the local clubs."

"Yuck," Adam shrugged. "I'm not doing anything with that old woman."

"You don't have to," Jinn added. "You're just a distraction."

"Methalda and I are going to clear a path inside The Cone, take out the staff and make sure we are all alone," Articus added.

Everyone looked at each other and nodded as they came to understand their roles.

"What am I doing?" Penny asked

"You have the most important job of all," Idrix replied. "You're going to keep me company."

Penny suddenly felt a blanket of disappointment fall on her. She had wanted to be involved. After all, The Society always worked together. She quickly stood up in anger and pushed her chair back.

"I will not stand idly by on this ship while Sillmon goes and risks his life."

"Besides," she replied. "I was always the better climber."

Sillmon turned towards her with a cheerful beam and winked. She smiled back at him, then crossed her arms and firmly nodded towards Idrix.

"Well ok then," Idrix sighed.

The remainder of breakfast was filled with tales of their previous adventures, each member of The Society taking a turn to brag about an accomplishment. Once the food had been consumed and their moods were in an upswing, Idrix dismissed everyone, and off to fulfill their jobs they went.

The city felt less alive today, most of the citizens walked around as though bricks were tied to their feet. Faces were flushed, moods were sour, and conversation seemed quite infrequent.

"Ah, I remember those days," Adam remarked. Methalda looked at him, confused.

"Hangovers. Looks like there's a lot of people feeling the wrath of the devil's poison."

Articus looked to the ground with a smirk; it was riddled with trash and loose debris from the previous night's shenanigans. Just a couple years ago, he too would've been excited to indulge in such a provocative party, but not anymore. Not since age had caught up with him. Nowadays, a silent night at the tavern with a beer sounded much more exciting than one of those loud taverns. No—he preferred a slight bit of background music just for ambiance. Nothing annoyed him more than not being able to actually have a conversation.

As they neared The Cone, they came to a halt. Dorrin and Adam looked at each other with mischievous expressions. All they had to do was take the old lady out for a day of fun, it seemed all too easy.

"Are you sure you want to go up there?" Methalda asked as she approached Penny.

"I'll be fine," Penny laughed. "Besides, I've got Sillimon with me. He wouldn't let anything happen to me."

Methalda looked at Sillimon and pointed a stern finger.

"We aren't losing any more members of The Society. No carelessness," she ordered.

"Well, believe it or not," Sillimon paused. "I'm not suicidal."

Articus nodded with satisfaction and looked at Jinn.

"You'll be able to get in there? That glove is paramount. Without it, the whole thing is a wash."

"I am a Kajj. There is no task I cannot achieve," she replied.

"Well, couldn't you just phase through the door and get the jewel?" Adam questioned.

"You idiot," Idrix lifted her cane and smacked him in the leg with a rather firm swing.

"If she could've just phased through the door, we wouldn't be doing all of this."

Articus looked up towards the sky, noticing the distinct lack of clouds, then looked towards the mountain behind The Cone. On his hip, he carried a club, the very same one Methalda had as well. With any luck, it would be quite useful for relieving unsuspecting guards of their conciseness. On the other side of his belt, he carried something a bit more peculiar. It was small and looked not too different than a table paddle. Fortunately, it was hardly that modest, anyone it touched would be jolted by a quick surge of electricity. The only problem was that it only had a couple uses, so it had to be saved for the direst conditions.

"Get a move on everyone, and good luck," Idrix bowed and turned around. Quickly, Penny and Sillimon looked at one another and then started off for the mountains. They both carried a harness, rope and a few pegs on their backs. In addition to the climbing gear, Sillimon carried a bow.

It had earned them a few odd glances as they strolled through the streets, but the hangovers left no one interested in questioning them.

"The rest of us will head inside," Jinn remarked.

Onwards they went, all of them remaining quite mute. There wasn't much to say. Their plan was dangerous; it left all of them feeling a tad on edge. As Jinn led the way, she recalled the peculiar offer Idirx had received. It seemed too good to be true. It seemed like just a game. But still, a part of Jinn wondered if it wasn't the better option.

As they entered the gardens of The Cone, the tension began to rise. Articus gulped with each step they took. His eyes looked at Methalda. Was she truly ready to be doing another heist so soon? So soon after losing Josiah? He carefully observed her as she walked, looking for any reason to tell her to go back. But to his dismay, there was a determination in her eyes.

"Hide," Jinn ordered Methalda and Articus. Together, the three of them retreated behind a section of large bushes, leaving Adam and Dorrin to approach the door. Articus looked outwards, trying his best to see what was happening. Adam and Dorrin appeared to be talking to someone, but he couldn't see the person.

They remained hidden for a few moments longer, and then suddenly, Adam and Dorrin turned around with The Boss walking right behind them.

"It worked," Methalda whispered. "How did those idiots convince her to leave?"

"They may look stupid on the outside, but those two are master manipulators," Jinn explained.

Once Adam, The Boss and Dorrin had exited the gardens, the three of them stood up, looking around the entrance for any leftover issues.

"Ok," Articus paused. "We know she has one servant for sure. But I doubt he's the only one. We'll keep you clear while you search for the glove."

Methalda glanced towards the entrance and giddily cracked her knuckles. There was a crazed look in her eyes, and suddenly, Articus knew why she was so calm. She wanted revenge. Vengeance against anyone she could. *Undr help whoever gets in her way*, he thought to himself.

They carefully exited the bushes and sauntered towards the entrance. In the distance, they could just make out the final bits of conversation from Kadeen and Adam, but it was clear they were getting further away. As they reached the door, Jinn halted, lifting her hand and urging silence. Suddenly she floated upwards, towards an open window and floated inside.

"No wonder they call her The Dark Thief," Methalda whispered. Articus smirked and looked at Methalda with a bit of concern.

"Are you alright?" He softly asked.

"Yea. Why wouldn't I be?"

"Josiah," he shrugged. "All of this. Is it too soon?"

"No," she replied. The door suddenly opened, and standing there, looking humorless as always, was Jinn. She lifted her finger to her lips, encouraging silence, and then turned around. They quickly stepped inside, closing the door softly behind them. Their focus quickly turned to the various doors that populated the room. It wouldn't be easy to search them all, least of all together.

"We should split up," Methalda whispered. "We can cover more ground that way."

Articus nodded in agreement and began to approach the left side of the entryway. Metalda approached the right side, and Jinn headed upstairs.

His fingers nervously gripped the brass painted handle and gave it a slow turn. It squeaked just a bit and then he pushed it open. He sighed as he stepped inside, instantly concluding that this was not the room. It looked like a large walk-in closet. The walls were filled with coats and cleaning items. He looked around, pushing past various coats and tools, and then finally decided the room was a bust.

As he stepped out into the entry, he noticed Methalda. She too had emerged and with her back to him, was entering the next door over. She was a tough woman, always had been. One of the toughest he had ever known. She could best even the strongest of guys, but still, he couldn't help the feelings of nervousness, concern and worry. As she disappeared into the next room, he sighed, pushing his woe aside and returning to the task at hand.

The next door opened considerably smoother, but once again, it seemed like the wrong place. A pantry, a place for overflow and rarely used dishes. This time, he didn't even waste his time stepping inside. It was obvious this wasn't right.

As they finished searching the last of the doors, Articus and Methalda slowly ascended the stairs. The next floor was not unlike the one prior, filled with doors that likely were all pointless, and yet, they had to search every one of them. Going their separate ways, they began scanning each area, learning quickly that the rooms offered no sign of the object in question. As Articus closed the door on the last room, he turned around and squinted at a rather peculiar observation. There hadn't been a sign of a guard or servant thus far. In all his years of thieving, there was almost always resistance to be met, so something about this certainly raised a warning.

"Where is everyone?" He whispered. Methalda cocked her head as the realization hit her.

"Maybe we just got lucky," she whispered. Of course, in the thieving world, there was no such thing as luck. She and Articus both knew this quite well. However, what she really meant to say was, *You're right, something is up.* She wandered towards the staircase and nodded at him.

"Shall we?"

Articus shrugged and began to follow her up the stairs. Waiting at the top, with a frustrated stare was Jinn. She hovered with crossed arms, and that look of hopelessness they had come to know so well.

"I think she knew we were coming," Jinn informed. "I think she let us in here."

Articus glanced at Methalda as they reached the top of the stairway.

"Why would she do that?" He pondered.

"She's a gamer," Jinn replied. "She enjoys playing games and toying with people."

"Well if this is a game. Then we should at least have some fun," Methalda added.

She turned and pushed open a door that was decoratively painted with flowers, red flowers with glowing blue stems. Inside the room was a large collection of books. Storming inside, she approached the shelves and began pulling out books. Filled with frustration, she tossed them to the floor, giving little regard to their placement in the shelves.

Across the hall, Articus searched an apparent guest room. It was quite extravagant. It had a large wardrobe, queen-size bed, candles, incense, and an excellent view of the open plains. Yes, it had all the makings of an excellent place to stay, but it didn't have the glove, and so, he pulled the door shut and stepped out. The three of them met in the middle foyer once more, looking around with dismay and concern.

"Well," Methalda paused. "Might as well keep going." She looked towards the stairs and began to ascend slowly. As they continued their short journey up the stairs, it became clear they were each feeling something different. Each of them was here for a different reason. What had led Jinn to becoming The Dark Thief? What made Methalda join up with Josiah? What kind of misfortunes really led someone to a life of crime? Did being a criminal make one inherently bad? Or is it just a chemical reaction to an infection, the infection of life?

As they continued their way up the various levels, the floors became smaller. Eventually, they came to a floor that contained only one door. Articus cautiously approached and gave the knob a turn. With a loud click, like that of a roller coaster, the door swung in. Methalda stepped behind and sneered. It was a bedroom, the master bedroom from the looks of it. In the center of the room sat a massive bed, draped in fine pink satin that hung over the top and almost isolated the bed. On the wall next to a large vanity, was a portrait of a young couple smiling proudly as they looked happily at each other.

"She used to have a husband," Articus remarked. "I wonder what happened to him."

"Prolly lost the game," Jinn replied.

Articus leaned closer to the portrait, something in its details stood out to him. It was The Boss, on her right hand, there was a small ring with a jewel that looked remarkably like the one they were supposed to be chasing after.

"She's wearing the damn thing," Articus replied. "It's not in a safe. It's on her bloody finger."

Skepticism painted its way onto Jinn's face. Closer she leaned in, studying the portrait with determination.

"But she showed us the jewel," she whispered. "She reached into the safe and showed it to Idrix and me."

Jinn turned, her thoughts filled with turmoil. Then suddenly, she looked towards the stairs.

"So what's really in that room?" She questioned. Without a moment's hesitation, she floated upwards, phasing through the floor and quickly vanishing from sight.

Articus and Methalda quickly looked at each another, then dashed over to the elevator.

"This better not be another trap," Methalda exclaimed as she pulled the gate to the elevator shut. With a heavy breath, she stepped back, leaning against the bars and letting out a worried sigh.

Chapter 29

Linuk awoke in a sweat, the same way he had for the past few months, enclosed in a hollow darkness and surrounded by noise. He was miserable. He hated it. In his mind, he would imagine that the sounds he was hearing were sounds of laughter and that the conversations were of love and compassion. It helped to make crawling from his bed just a tad easier. In these days of trepidation, it was all he had. Things were bad, and there was nothing he could do about it. Even if he had his eyesight, there was little he could do against such malevolent forces. Now – blind – he felt completely helpless.

He rolled over and searched with his feet for the edge of the bed. His heavy blanket stifled his attempts, but eventually, he found the edge he so hesitantly sought. He threw his legs over, allowing them to dangle above the floor. The air was cold. His servants had been tasked with doing chores in the service of Agavordis. Because of this, the fires remained out. There was no more warmth to be found in the palace. He shivered as his feet hit the stone floor. The darkness was an enemy; it taunted him with each step he took.

"Ouch," he whispered as he bumped into a table. Shaking off the pain, he lifted his arms and began to feel around.

"Ahh," he yelled. His room was quite bare, his father's things had been stolen and ransacked, all that remained was his wardrobe. His skill of using sound was still quite limited, but each day he was finding himself a little bit better at finding his way to the wardrobe.

"Ahh," he cried out once more. He cocked his head, searching for the point where his voice encountered resistance. *Just up ahead and to the left*, he thought. Slowly, he sauntered in the direction he had thought was correct. For a brief moment, he could feel the warmth of a carpet beneath his feet. He nodded his head with satisfaction as he realized he was indeed going the right way.

As he stubbed his foot, he realized he had reached the wardrobe.

"For the love of all things," he muttered. His hands reached forward and pulled open the door. Unfortunately, his selection was depleted; it was empty save for a robe, which he certainly wasn't going to wander around Ramir Hold in nothing but that.

"Perfect," he whispered to himself. "Guards!"

He turned around and started strolling blindly towards the exit, hoping perhaps that there would be an idle guard waiting around. He pulled open the door and was suddenly hit with a foul odor. It smelled like that of decay. He could feel the breath of an undead ghoul against his skin. And from the position where the breath was hitting, it was clear that this ghoul was quite tall.

"Morning Killigan," Linuk snickered. He reached out and pushed the ghoul to the side, stepping out into the halls.

"Hello?" He called out. With no response, he began to make his way down the halls, behind him, he could hear the footsteps of Killigan. He shuddered, the thought of his escort made him nauseous. He wanted to kill him — well — kill him again. After all, it was Killigan that had blinded him, not to mention, nearly killed him.

"Is there anyone here?" Linuk called out. In the distance, he could hear several pairs of heavy feet marching towards him. Akordans. He gulped and came to a stop, Killigan stopping directly behind him.

"What's all the racket about?" one of the Akordans named Rangle demanded.

"I have no cloths, clean cloths," Linuk replied. The Akordans all exploded into laughter and took turns spitting in his face.

"You think we care about your clothes?" Rangle laughed. "Killigan. Show this fool back to his room."

Killigan let out a low groan and reached for Linuk's shoulders.

"Get your hands off me you dreadful abomination," he demanded. In a quick motion, Killigan lifted Linuk, tossed him over his shoulders and then began marching back towards the royal chambers.

"Put me down you slime!" He hollered. In the background, he could hear the laughter of the Akordans.

As Killigan entered the room, he released his grip, letting Linuk fall to the floor with a hard thud.

"Ugh," he grunted. Killigan groaned and left the room.

Hours passed, and still, Linuk remained trapped in his room, no food, no water, and no escape. Time had begun to feel like just another enemy. As he sat quietly in solitude, he found himself longing for the company of Dimitri. *Why did I send him off?* He wondered.

"Oh, yea. He's supposed to help find some strange woman I've never met," he sarcastically whispered.

"Stop it Linuk, that's selfish thinking," he said to himself.

"Still," he paused. "I hope she's worth it."

He climbed to his feet and wandered towards the window. Getting there took some trial and error, a couple bumps and maybe even a bruise, but finally, he felt the chill of the glass against his fingers. He pushed it open and took a deep breath. The breeze washed over him like an ocean wave, bringing with it the sound of despair. In the far distance, he could hear screams, cries of protest and even a couple scuffles.

"My poor city," he whispered. Tears began to form at the edge of his eyes as he let the pain of the citizens wash over him. He imagined the children, being forced into slavery in the mines. He imagined the housewives, being turned into maids and entertainment. He imagined the soldiers, being turned into drones.

"I can't do this anymore," he muttered. "I can't continue letting this city down."

Suddenly, something caught his attention. A woman, an elderly woman by the sounds of it. She was nearby, perhaps in the alley, or maybe even in one of the buildings across the way, although where she was didn't matter. What mattered were the raspy, yet, beautiful words that poured from her mouth.

"Where are you? Where are you? Why have you gone, so far, beyond my sight? Where are you? Where are you? When will we meet again? When will we fly? I have waited days and days and counted all the ways that you could save the day, but you don't. I have waited days and days, to give my life away, but I know that won't stop all the pain.

Where are you? Where are you? We need your hope, your love, your strength, and your mind. Where are you? I can't find you. I peer in the skies, to look, for your sign. I have waited days and days and counted all the ways that you could save the day but you don't. Why have you run away? And left us feeling gray, when will you bring your light to this day? Where are you? I can't find you, but I need you. But I need you. Where are you? Please help me. I need you, yes, I need you."

Linuk smiled, wiping a tear from his cheek as the last syllable left her soft lips.

"Please no!" She suddenly cried out.

"You like singing huh?" A coarse voice croaked. "Well come on. My boys are just aching for some entertainment."

"Please," she begged. "My children need me."

"Agavordis doesn't care about your children," the Akordan rebutted. He firmly grabbed her and began to drag her down the streets, ignoring her constant cries of discomfort.

"Damnit," Linuk muttered. "This has gone on long enough,"

As the screams of the woman faded, he turned around and started making his way back towards the exit carefully.

"I'm leaving this room!" He yelled. His anger fueled him, giving him the courage he hadn't known he had. *I'm the king*, he thought. His fingers gripped the handle and gave the door a firm pull. There it was again, the odor. It reeked, but this time, it smelled even worse than it had earlier. He coughed as he covered his mouth. He swung his free arm forward, feeling for the grotesque murderer he knew to be standing idly by. He winced as his hand brushed against a heavy armor, and like an eager mouse, he darted towards the left. Killigan groaned and turned towards him. It was like a game of cat and mouse, if the cat was just simply following the mouse.

He dashed forward, hoping and praying that he didn't run into any walls. The deep breaths of Killigan became less noticeable, and he knew that he had succeeded in putting some distance between them.

The world was a cavern, a dark cavern with no hint of light. He imagined himself as an explorer, an explorer whose torch had blown out. *I'm not blind*, he thought to himself. *I'm just wandering in a dark cave*. It helped somehow, the notion gave him a boost, a little bit of confidence.

In the distance, he could hear the chatter amongst the Akordans, they were in the hall to the right, towards the main entrance, but that's not the direction he intended on taking. No—he was much more interested in the secret door he had so often used to sneak out of the palace as a child. It was a servant's exit, hidden by a painting and located in the far west corner of the dining room. He had explored the secretive tunnel many times as a kid. Growing up, he so often wanted to leave, he abhorred being kept confined all day. And yet, here he was, grown and now leading a kingdom, but still confined.

His fingers ran along the walls, giving him some type of guidance. His heart raced each time he felt a familiar object; the statue of his father, the ornamental pot, the statue of Zalep. They all reminded him of his path, his destination.

"Hello?" He called out to the empty dining hall. His voice echoed into the dark, coming back to him like a boomerang to its thrower. Behind him, there were slow footsteps. Killigan was still stalking him.

"Time to get out of here," he whispered. His legs carried him faster than his mind had time to process and observe. Against chairs and carts, he bumped, but it didn't deter him. His mind was far too focused on his escape to care about a few bumps and bruises. The door would be toward the back of the hall, near the portrait of his mother.

He came to a stop, feeling the soft fabric of the painting and quickly ran his fingers along its border. The groaning and deep breaths suddenly made its way to his ears. Killigan was in the room. The painting of the Zalep was encased in a finely carved wood frame. As he ran his fingers along its edge, he felt a splinter or two, then suddenly pulled the frame firmly.

He closed the entrance behind him, taking a deep breath of relief, then turned and slowly sauntered his way down the tunnel. Even with his eyesight, this tunnel was always quite dim, as such, he felt more comfortable in here than he had ever felt out there.

As he reached the end of the tunnel, he gave the door a firm push, and a rush of fresh air swam towards him. He took it in, and for a moment, he thought he could taste the salt in the air from the sea that bordered the city.

"At last," he smiled.

***

Dimitri Slauters approached the gates of Morlay and paused. Just ahead he could see the shapes of the city's new occupants. The Akordans, and, of course, the ghouls. He looked onwards and expelled a deep sigh. He had to get inside. He had to get to Linuk. But how was he going to get past all those Akordans. Surely, they would capture him, and throw him in a dungeon — or worse — into the mines. He furrowed his brow, as he looked forward, trying to piece together some kind of plan.

Morlay was quite impenetrable, King Ucertine had seen to that. In fact, it was the last time a necromancer caused havoc that prompted him to order the abominable wall to be built. Now here they were, twenty years later, he was dead, and the wall continued to stand. Agavordis hadn't needed to break it down to get inside. The Tin Men bowed and opened the gates. The fall of the Arnouts — of Lord Fae — really was the end of Furlasia.

He crouched down and began to sneak his way towards the wall, he had a plan, one that if done wrong, would end with him being a corpse, but he had to try. On the far side of the city wall — the side that faced the sea — was a purposely made trail of protruding bricks. Most didn't know about it, and those that did knew it was a perilous climb, for there wasn't much to grab on to. But as it turns out, Dimitri and Linuk had at one point been quite fond of climbing. *Sure, it was mostly trees but the wall shouldn't be too much different*, he thought.

The fields surrounding Morlay were mostly bare, just the occasional tree and bits of tall shrubbery. There wasn't much cover, but he would have to make do. He pressed his back against a tree and took a deep breath. His palms pressed against the bark and a bit of its wood flaked onto his skin. He peeked around the trunk and noticed a few ghouls that were mindlessly wandering around the wall.

"Move," he whispered to himself. Suddenly, he felt something give him a shove. He stumbled forward and paused, turning to see what had happened. There was nothing.

"What in the name of Undr was that?" He questioned himself. He shook off the uncomfortable feeling and began to dart towards the wall. As he reemerged into the field, he was greeted by the sight of a few more ghouls. These ones were quite far decayed, they were now mostly skeletons. Goosebumps covered his arms and for a moment he thought he might retch.

Fear grabbed him and held him still. Briefly, he felt like he was in a trance. How could this possibly be? How could he be looking at a walking skeleton? In real life, that is.

Sure, every child has heard a scary story from time to time, but this wasn't a story. Tears formed in his eyes as he watched the ghoul continue to stumble its way towards him. Finally, he shook off the feeling and charged forward.

"Ahhh!" He yelled, crashing into them. As they fell to the ground, he began to stomp on them, breaking their bones and leaving them in shambles.

"Get out of my city!" He yelled. Up and down, his feet continued to pummel the ghouls, until they were totally motionless and in shambles.

"Who's there?" A distant voice called out. He quickly looked up, pushing the hair out of his eyes and scanned ahead. A couple Akordans were walking around, blades raised and ready to kill.

"Oh fuit," he whispered. Keeping low, he charged towards the wall. His heart raced and his mind preached doom, but he kept moving. Once he reached the wall, he pressed himself against it and held his breath. The voices in the distance continued.

"I don't see anything!" One of the Akordans yelled.

"I know I heard something," another replied.

"Well, then you come look!" The other retorted.

Dimitri waited for a moment longer, then turned his attention to the wall at his back. His eyes scanned up and down, looking for the protruding bricks he had heard of. Finally, he spotted them. They were indeed protruding, and like he imagined, looked dangerous. Suddenly, he found himself debating his entire plan. But, just as he began to question the entire idea, his mind raced to his friend. To Linuk. His blind, helpless friend who was all alone in a hostile city under occupation. He had to do it.

His fingers gripped the first brick, as the roughness dug into his skin, he gave himself a firm pull. Quickly, his feet found the next brick, and onwards he continued. It hurt, each brick only stuck out just enough to allow the tips of his fingers to grab on. As he continued his passage up the wall, he kept his mind focused on Linuk. At one point, he had schemed to steal his spot on the throne, a move he had since begun to regret. Their friendship had lasted a long time and Linuk had seen him through many hard times. Perhaps it was jealousy that inspired the attempted coup. Perhaps it was resentment that Linuk had so much power while he had so little. Whatever the reason, it was childish and irrelevant.

Maybe it was his guilt or his childhood love of scaling tall objects, but against all odds, he reached the top. His fingers burned, blood even leaked from a couple of them, but he had made it. That in itself was a victory. He looked the city over, Akordans and ghouls were constantly patrolling, it wouldn't be easy remaining undetected.

"Seems worse than before," he whispered to himself. Suddenly, something caught his eyes, a figure wandering from the backside of the palace. It was Linuk. He moved slow, waving his arms back and forth.

"Oh no," Dimitri muttered. He began to dash along the top of the wall, trying to keep low and stealthy whilst keeping his eyes on his friend. Linuk continued to wander, but his progress was slow due to the handicap Killigan had inflicted upon him.

"Linuk," Dimitri whispered as he neared his friend. Linuk paused, looking around with interest.

"Linuk what are you doing?" Dimitri queried.

"Dimitri?"

Dimitri scanned the surrounding buildings and then swiftly leapt towards one. He landed hard, as he stood up, he could hear the voices of the people inside.

"Stay there," Dimitri whispered. He walked to the edge of the building and looked down. It was high — the fall — while not deadly, looked painful. Biting his lip, he looked around, searching for options, but there were none. Taking a deep breath, he leapt, landing on the ground with a slight roll.

"Did you roll?" Linuk questioned.

"Yea," Dimitri replied. He climbed to his feet, as he did, a sharp pain surged through his leg.

"Ahh!" He yelled.

"What's wrong?" Linuk whispered.

"I think I hurt something," Dimitri replied. Again, he attempted to stand, but just as before, the pain was stifling. He dropped to the ground, whimpering in pain.

"I can't walk," he muttered. Linuk knelt down and quietly inspected his friend's leg. All seemed normal until he reached the Achilles tendon.

"Ow," Dimitri exclaimed, shaking his head in frustration.

"Look at us. A blind guy and a crippled guy," he laughed. He looked at Linuk and let out a sigh.

"I tried to convince the council to replace you." Linuk calmly nodded his head.

"I know," he replied. "I've known you were jealous for some time now."

"And yet you let me stay around?" Dimitri questioned.

"Of course. We've been friends for a long time. I'm not about to let a little bit of misplaced envy ruin that."

"Misplaced?" Dimitri retorted.

"Have you seen my job?" Linuk chuckled. "No one should want it."

Dimitri pondered the notion for a moment, then quickly realized his feelings actually lined up with the statement.

"I'm sorry buddy. I'm sorry this happened to you."

Linuk lifted his hand, searching in front of him and then gently placed it against Dimitri's warm cheek.

"If you want the throne, you can have it."

Dimitri's eyes widened with surprise, for a moment, he thought to jump at the offer. Then, with a sly grin, he shook his head and brought his hand up against Linuk's.

"Nah," he replied. "I'd rather help you do the job you were born to do."

Suddenly, footsteps and the sound of clinking metal neared them.

"Your Highness," a harsh voice sneered. "How did you get out?"

The Akordan lifted his blade and held it high above him.

"My orders were clear, Nevo said to kill you if you try to escape."

Dimitri sighed and pulled himself closer to Linuk. He carefully wrapped his arm around him, then closed his eyes.

"By order of Nevo, you are sentenced to death."

He swung his blade down, but something suddenly stopped it.

"What?" The Akordan exclaimed. The blade was quickly ripped from his fingers, as he turned around, he saw a man hovering in the air like an angel.

"It's time for your kind to leave," Nikalas whispered. He waved his wand towards the Akordan, in an instant, his head twisted full circle.

Dimitri opened his eyes, letting go of Linuk and turning towards him.

"It's time to take Morlay back," Nikalas instructed. He reached down and offered a hand. With a grin, Dimitri accepted.

"I thought you'd never come."

Chapter 30

Solarian was in disarray as Herratia continued her attack against Agavordis. Everything had been thrust into chaos. Even Abbisal Keep was in near shambles. On the icy, crack-ridden ground, the two continued to fight; tossing magic spells at each other in spectacular fashion. Herratia was tough, her speed and connection to darkness were quite clear. Agavordis, on the other hand, was inexperienced, but despite that, he was proving himself a worthy foe.

As he sent a streak of green energy towards her, he felt disappointed. He had thought he had found an ally in Herratia, in the Akordans. But now, it seemed they were just another powerful foe that would need to be dealt with.

She quickly repelled the beam, as it darted back towards him, he quickly formed a shield. It struck against it with a bright flash, and then dashed towards her once more. Again, she sent it back, but this time, rather than reflect it straight at her, he aimed it to the ground beneath her feet.

It crashed into the surface, cracking the ice and leaving an opening underneath her. With surprise, she yelled, and for a moment, disappeared into the waters below. He grinned at his mild victory and began to creep backwards, trying his best to filter out the sounds of the wind. She would be back, he was sure of it. Looking into the snowy winds, he decided it was best to prepare.

"I know you," he whispered. In his hands, he quickly formed a blade and began to spin around slowly.

"Come on!" He exclaimed. "Show yourself."

The sound of cracking ice came all too quickly, and suddenly, he found himself plunging downwards. The frigidity of the water nearly stopped his heart, breathing became difficult, and his limbs began to numb. Staring at him with a chilling grin was Herratia. She nodded, then quickly brought her hands up, grabbing onto his head and squeezing it on both sides. In torment, he clenched his jaw, bringing his hands up and trying to pry hers off, but her grip was too strong. The more he struggled, the larger her grin became, and the more obvious her satisfaction was.

His eyes were starting to get blurry, with each passing second, Herratia was slowly fading from his sight. He knew his end was close and so he closed his eyes and allowed the pressure on his head to act as a final comfort. *What a peaceful death*, he thought to himself.

The next instant, he found himself being pulled back onto the surface by a lasso made of energy. His back scrapped against the ice and air found his lungs once again. He coughed, expelling an eruption of ice water, then quickly rolled over. The coughing continued, as he lay, he noticed a small figure standing over him.

"Where is she?" Epard questioned.

"She's in the water," Agavordis weakly replied. Epard approached the hole, looking down into it and shaking his head with disbelief.

"I don't see her," he replied. He turned, moving towards Agavordis and tossing a warm spell over top of him.

"I always thought it was foolish to trust such a vile creature," he lectured.

"She gave me an entire army," Agavordis replied.

"She also nearly killed you," Epard retorted. "She's more powerful than you, and she knows it. It was only a matter of time before she made a move."

Agavordis rolled onto his back, looking up at the massive clouds that seemed unwilling to let the sun shine through.

"We have to kill her," he sighed.

"Not just her. All the Akordans must be eradicated," Epard replied. "If you kill just her the Akordans will be coming for you. You have to kill them all. A total cleansing of Furlasia."

Agavordis shot up, looking at him with disillusionment.

"Have you lost your mind? Destroy an entire species? That's insane."

Epard sighed and waved his hand, lifting Agavordis into the air and facing him.

"You have enemies on all sides of you now. Your only allies are the dead. Imagine how powerful an army you would have if the Akordans could be fully controlled."

Suddenly, a light went off. Agavordis, at that moment wore an expression of excitement.

"Yes, you're right," he agreed. "But how? I can't storm Neveraus on my own."

Epard shook his head with aggravation.

"You won't be alone my boy. I'll go with you. Together, they won't stand a chance."

"But Cap Ti Mor," Agavordis paused. "I thought you wanted to go back."

Epard nodded and slowly lowered his apprentice back down to the ground.

"Nothing will stop me from getting back there, not even death. But the gates to Cap Ti Mor aren't going anywhere. It can wait," Epard smirked. Agavordis nodded and climbed to his feet. His arms trembled, his head throbbed like a million tiny needles had been placed inside his skull and shaken repeatedly. With cloudy eyes, he looked at the remains of Abissal Keep. The destruction was significant. Silently, he began to walk towards the dreary fortress, afraid of what he might find.

The rear entrance door and the wall surrounding it had been destroyed. He moved inside, stepping over some scattered bricks and pieces of wood. His eyes narrowed with concern as he observed the wrecked halls and battle-damaged ceilings.

"What are you doing?" Epard questioned. "We need to finish her off."

"I need to see this," Agavordis replied. He continued down the halls, making notes of the considerable wreckage and remembering where he was when it occurred. Their battle had gone through many parts of the castle; it was remarkable that any of it remained standing. However, the castle was not his concern—no—he was far more interested in his prisoners.

As he neared the dungeons, he began to slow down, letting out a long sigh as his worst fears were finally realized. They were all gone. Each cell had been seemingly ripped open by something rather strong. Stronger, he thought, than any human hand could be capable of.

"These cells were ripped open by a spell," he whispered.

"But they didn't have their staves," Epard pointed out.

"That's correct. And that means someone with a staff rescued them, took them all, including Emlin." He turned with a dark expression and looked at his miniature mentor.

"Nikalas."

Epard brought his finger to his chin and began to ponder. The boy from the prophecy had returned. But from where? Why had he been absent during all the conflict?

"If you're gonna fight the savior," Epard paused. "You're gonna need a bigger army."

He took a few steps closer to Agavordis and grinned.

"Let's go get you one."

Chapter 31

Jinn quickly inserted her right hand into the strange lock that guarded the *interesting room*. Her wrist twisted back and forth like a dog watching cars, as she worked out the unique sequence of turns.

"Hurry," Methalda urged. Sweat was starting to form on her forehead, as thoughts of a worse time filled her mind with dread. She feared the worst. Feared they would lose yet another friend.

As the lock clicked, the weighty door began to swing outwards. Standing inside, looking rather confused, was Sillimon and Penny. On the floor beside them was their climbing gear and in their hands, each of them held a sharp pick.

"What are you doing?" Methalda demanded.

"What are we doing?" Sillimon asked.

"What are you guys doing?" Penny added. "Why do you look like you've seen a ghost?"

Methalda looked at Articus who gave a subtle gesture of discretion. She nodded in understanding, then returned her attention to the odd couple that stood before them.

"This room is bogus," Methalda explained. "The jewel isn't in here. The cunne is wearing the damn thing on her hand. We looked right at it and didn't realize it."

Sillimon turned and looked at Penny with frustration.

"Are you serious?" Penny questioned. Methalda quietly nodded.

"Then why did she show Jinn and Idrix this room? Why show them a bogus jewel?" Penny asked.

"Because she already knew we planned on stealing it," Jinn explained. She turned towards them and shrugged.

"She knew we were a crew."

"So this is all just a game then?" Articus investigated.

"It was entertainment," a boastful voice said from behind them. Standing in the doorway was The Boss. Her expression spoke volumes. She was overflowing with both humor and pride.

"The game hasn't started yet," she subtly added.

Methalda looked at Articus with a vengeful stare, then stomped towards The Boss with her club raised.

"They could've died," she yelled, pointing to Sillimon and Penny.

"But they didn't," The Boss quickly retorted. "You guys are every bit of what I've heard. Remarkable. Every last part of this plan was stunningly executed."

She stepped inside and smiled.

"Luring me out of the house, scaling that mountain, memorizing the combination. Wow," she exclaimed.

"I am awestruck."

Methalda brought her empty hand up, and swiftly went in for a well-timed slap, but just before her hand made contact, it was caught. Her grip was strong, dangerously strong. The Boss firmly held her hand, keeping a cheerful smile all the while. Methalda looked at her with concern. For a moment, she had forgotten where they were, but suddenly, it became clear. Adrasia was not home to traditional men and women. Here they all possessed uncanny strength. Each of them, including the children, were dangerous. Even the elderly woman known as The Boss was likely to be capable of killing them all with great ease.

"Don't be so emotional," The Boss cautioned.

"How can you expect us not to be?" Penny questioned. "You've been playing games with us since we arrived."

The Boss released her grip and gave Methalda a firm glare. Stepping inside, she walked past them, towards the spot with the hidden stone.

"I'm very much into games. As a matter of fact, I offered to hand the jewel over with no questions asked, if your boss Idrix could best me in one," The Boss explained.

Methalda looked at Jinn, who silently nodded in agreement.

"What kind of game?" Articus questioned.

"A game of the mind," The Boss replied with a smile. "One of the most intense games I've ever played."

"What do you get out of all this?" Jinn questioned.

The Boss turned towards them with a sigh.

"An actual challenge," she replied. "I have played almost every game I've come across, challenged the best players of each of them, but no matter what, I always win."

"I'm bored of these victories. I want someone to beat me. I want to meet a mind more brilliant than mine."

Articus and Methalda looked at each other, each of them looking dumbfounded.

"I'm willing to hand over the jewel in exchange for a defeat."

Footsteps and heavy breathing in the distance seized their attention. Each of them turned towards the entrance. Idrix was hobbling towards them while relying heavily on a cane. She walked inside, coming to a stop in the center of the room and looked at The Boss.

"What's the game?" Idrix sighed.

"It's called Yorolla," The Boss responded. Idrix looked towards the floor and took a deep breath.

"Fine," she muttered. "You have a deal. We can play your game. But if I win, I want more than just the jewel."

The Boss perked up with excitement and smiled.

"I want each member of my crew to get 5,000 chittes," she declared. The Boss looked around, studying the complacent faces of the group of disheartened thieves, then nodded her head in agreement.

A couple hours later, Idrix found herself sitting in a room that was quite cozy. It was decorated all around with a sort of middle age Victorian look. There was a fireplace, tall bookshelves and in the center of it all was a hand-carved wooden table. Atop it sat a wooden board, and resting still atop the board were two intricately carved pieces. Each piece had been shaped to look like an animal. One looked quite similar to a Grimwort, and the other looked like a lion. The two pieces sat idly by at the start of a longboard filled with various squares. In between the squares were different lines, each line offering a different path. And handwritten onto each square were various words, with each word indicating a particular challenge.

As Idrix looked the board over, she couldn't help but admire its craftsmanship. It was quite meticulous; whoever designed this board knew their craft. This was no mere game; this was a rite of passage. A calling. To look at the board almost signified royalty.

Standing behind her, pressed against a brick covered wall, was Jinn, and next to her stood Articus and Methalda. The others had been sent back to the Maratan, but these three had been allowed to remain. Were it up to Idrix, the whole crew would stay, but The Boss insisted that they keep the audience at a minimum. Standing on the opposite side of the room, pressed against a very similar wall were two boisterous women with tacky clothing and too much makeup, sisters from the look of it. Their small lens glasses sat perched at the very end of their pointed noses.

"Yorolla," The Boss paused. "It's a game of the mind and a game of strategy. The objective is to reach the other side of the board before the other player, but it's not an easy task by any means. Each player will roll a die, and that die will allow you to move a certain number of spaces in any direction, so long as you are moving to a square that has a line drawn to it. Once on this square, you will pick up a card that is associated with that square. Each card will offer a challenge, and if you complete it, you stay on the square. If you fail, then you go back and the other player gets to roll twice."

Idrix nodded her head in understanding.

"The cards are as follows." She reached for a stack and picked one up. "Anagram, the unscrambling of words. Trivia and Logic. Once you reach the last row, the challenge is increased with a special round."

"Are you ready to begin?"

Idrix turned and looked at Jinn. Her companion nodded silently.

"Let's get this over with," Idrix replied.

***

"What do you think the game is?" Kadeen questioned as she took a drink of her ale. Adam hiccupped, then took a swig of his as well.

"I bet it's a spelling game," he replied.

"I don't know why we don't just cut the ring right from her self-entitled fingers," Dorrin added.

"I have one thought," Sillimon said, promptly getting the attention of everyone

"Well, we are in the middle of a city full of overly strong beings. Not to mention, we are outsiders. She's likely to have a lot of friends who would come to her aid if need be."

"So in other words we'd get our asses kicked," Dajreem laughed.

"Yes," Sillimon replied. "To put it bluntly, yes."

"He's right," Adam added. "Even that old woman could prolly kill us all."

"We are like fish surrounded by sharks."

"Only here the sharks won't just eat you," Penny remarked. "They'll play with you first."

"I wouldn't mind being played with," Dorrin smiled.

"I don't think you'd like the kind of playing they like," Penny replied. "But I'd love to see you find out."

Dorrin looked at her with surprise, then turned his attention back to the cards in front of him.

"That's cold Penny," he muttered. She looked at Sillimon and shrugged.

"Four," Dorrin declared as he looked down.

"Go fish," Adam replied. Dorrin shook his head and reached towards a flipped over deck of cards. One card after another he continued to flip, until alas, he came upon a four.

"What do you think the game is?" Penny questioned. Sillimon shook his head with uncertainty.

"The whole thing is weird. Why have we traveled all this way just to play a board game?" Sillimon pondered.

"Well, Idrix is one of the most skilled players in the entire world," Dajreem answered. "For someone looking for a challenge, you can't find much better."

Adam and Dorrin looked at him with surprise. The realization that he had known something about Idrix that they didn't clearly took them by surprise.

"I'm not worried about it," Adam added. "If Idrix doesn't win, we'll just get the jewel some other way."

Sillimon rolled his eyes, then motioned for Penny to step out into the hall. She nodded in agreement and quietly they strolled from the room.

"Don't like our game?" Dorrin called out. No response. The door was closed behind them, leaving just the three Decoyers remaining in the room.

"How could you not like go fish? It's such a classic," Dorrin muttered.

In the hall, Sillimon led Penny, holding her hands firmly as they looked at the various doors lining the surprisingly spacious corridor. He came to a stop two doors from the last on the left side of the hall and smack dab in the middle of it all. Releasing his grip on Penny, he turned the handle on the door and pushed it open. Inside, lay a couple beds stacked atop each other. He turned towards her once again, grabbing her hand and leading her inside.

"I have a bad feeling about this," he whispered as he pushed the door shut behind them.

"We've already been played for fools once. What's to stop her from doing it again?"

Penny looked at him and smiled. His cleverness and the way their thoughts always seemed to line up were just one of the many reasons she was madly in love with him. Sure, they had their quirks and arguments from time to time, but there wasn't anyone else she'd rather spend her days with. For Penny, that was enough.

"Something tells me this is real," she replied. "This was her plan all along. Why she let us try to steal it is a mystery, but I'm pretty sure this is what she wanted."

"However," she paused. "We need to come up with a real plan in case this is just another trick."

"Exactly," Sillimon replied. He walked over to a case that he had packed and slowly pulled it open. Inside was an array of strangely matched clothing with a single flower sitting on top of it all. "When Articus and I were surveying the job I found this," he reached inside and pulled it out. "It looks a lot like a Perrim, doesn't it?"

Penny giddily reached for the dried plant and lifted it to her nose.

"Yes it is," she laughed. "All the way out here huh?"

"Remember that time we accidentally smoked one of these?" Sillimon asked. Penny began to laugh as the memory rushed back to her. It was a few years back at this point, they had only just met, but for some reason Sillimon had wanted to take her out to look at the moon after inhaling some herb. It didn't go as planned.

"How could I forget? It was the moment I knew I had to keep you," she smiled.

Her mind continued to recall the night. He had promised her an enlightened experience, a truly spectacular view of the moon. Instead, they woke up the next morning feeling groggy and quite frail.

"Do you think it would work on her?" Sillimon asked. "On an Adrasain?"

Penny continued to study the particular details of the plant, then quietly nodded.

"How do we get it into her system though?" She questioned.

"The same way we got it into ours," Sillimon replied. Penny looked to him with a smile, and began to laugh.

***

Tension filled the air like a humid Florida day. All eyes were intently fixed on the match of Yorolla that was taking place between The Boss and Idrix. Each of their pieces was near the halfway point, but The Boss' piece was just a couple squares further. Still though, it was anyone's game.

"It happens when you least expect it. It ends when you least want it. There are rough edges all around and it's mostly filled with ups and downs," Idrix read aloud. She raised her eyebrow, then gently placed the card facedown.

"A relationship I'd gather," she skeptically announced. "Although the rough edges part is a bit perplexing."

The Boss quietly nodded.

With a satisfactory grin, Idrix picked up the die and handed it over to The Boss, who quickly tossed it back down. Four. Her eyes lit up as she looked up at Idrix. Holding her breath, she gripped her piece and began to move it. Two to the left, one up, then once to the right. Idrix mutely picked up a card and handed it over.

"It's an anagram," The Boss remarked. She set the card atop the table and nodded towards Idrix, who swiftly flipped over an hourglass. In silence, The Boss studied the card, whispering only occasionally as she attempted to work out the solution. Her fingers gripped a nearby pen as she began to jot down various possibilities.

"Time," Idrix announced.

"What?" The Boss gawked as she looked up with dismay. Indeed, the hourglass had run out. Idrix nodded towards The Boss' piece, and with a sigh of disappointment, The Boss moved the piece back where it had previously been.

"You got lucky," she remarked as she handed over the die. Idrix gripped it, blew into her hand, and then tossed it down. Six. The Boss moaned with annoyance as Idrix began to move her piece. Two to the right, three up and another two to the right.

"Keeping to the far side of the board, ehh," The Boss remarked. "That won't save you."

Idrix ignored the taunt and flipped over a card. Her eyes widened with curiosity as she read its contents.

"Well, what is it?" The Boss impatiently blurted out.

"It's a logic puzzle," Idrix replied. She carefully handed over the hourglass and signaled for The Boss to flip it. As the sands began to pour, her eyes studied the ink, and with a silent grin, she grabbed a piece of paper and scribbled something down.

"Here," she said as she handed the paper over. The Boss clutched it in her hand, then silently read the response. She looked at the card and shook her head doubtfully, then reached for the answer deck. It took a minute to find it, there were many logic cards and each one had a corresponding answer card, but eventually, she found it and as she flipped it over she began to shake.

"Your answer is correct."

Chapter 32

Vicham stood silently next to Wexel as the man before them quietly surveyed the horizon. In the not too far distance, was the tower belonging to High Mother.

"Time to put an end to this," the man whispered. He turned towards them and nodded with appreciation.

"You have done well Vicham. You have followed your destiny to a tee, now, go back to Morlay. There is nothing for you here," he instructed.

"What are you?" Wexel questioned. The man took a couple steps towards them. He looked young, his skin was pale white and his hair was dark brown. There was compassion in his eyes but anger on his forehead and despite it all, he seemed genuine and pure.

"My name is Undr," he replied.

"By Undr," Vicham whispered. The man cocked his head with confusion.

"Such a curious expression. I've noticed your species uses it a lot when you don't know what to say."

"Is there a better response to meeting a God?" Vicham questioned.

"I doubt it," Undr replied. He turned his focus back to the tower.

"Get out of here. Things are about to get ugly. My sister has wreaked havoc on this planet long enough."

"What are you going to do?" Vicham questioned.

Undr turned towards him with a serious expression.

"I'm going to kill her."

Suddenly, he began to grow. Taller and taller. First six foot, then seven, then eight and before long he was well over three hundred feet tall. A giant. A massive giant.

"Well that's weird," Wexel remarked, turning and looking at Vicham.

"Gravi!" Undr bellowed. He began to march forward. Every step he took shook the ground, it was like the tremors all over again.

"You wanted me. Now here I am."

Vicham kept his eyes glued on the tower. Kit was still in there. He had to reach her. Sure, the God he had spent most of his life praising told him to turn around, but he couldn't, he did not come all this way just to turn around. He began to move forward.

"What are you doing?" Wexel exclaimed.

"I'm not leaving here without Kit," Vicham replied. Feeling a sudden sense of urgency, he began to run.

"Gravi!" Undr roared. Vicham and Wexel continued to charge forward as a small figure emerged from the tower in the distance. They continued their forward march and suddenly, the small figure that had appeared from within the tower, became a very large figure.

"Today just keeps getting weirder and weirder," Wexel huffed. They kept moving, keeping their eyes pinned on the two gargantuan beings in front of them.

"Brother," Gravi called out with a mischievous smile. "Like what I've done with the place?"

She took a few steps forward, shaking the ground in the process.

"You've tried your hardest to ruin my planet but so far you have failed," Undr accused. "You're still just as weak and petty as the last time I saw you."

"Why is he taunting her?" Wexel questioned. Vicham kept his eyes forward as they drew nearer to the tower.

"She's been taunting him for years," Vicham replied.

"This ends today," Gravi exclaimed. She reached to her side and withdrew a sword, massive in length and width, it shimmered under what little light the sky could afford. Undr grinned and suddenly, a mace and chain appeared in his hands.

"Haaa!" Gravi bellowed as she swung the sword forward. It crashed against the handle of the mace with a thunderous boom, sending a shockwave traveling across the sky.

Vicham paused as he neared the entrance to the tower. Standing idly in front of the door, were two red beings. They wore no clothing, yet they didn't seem nude, as there was no genitalia, all was just red. In their hands, they idly held blades. Their eyes were fixed on them and as he continued to observe the strangeness, Vicham could feel a pit forming in his gut.

"What the heck are those things?" Wexel questioned.

Vicham shrugged with uncertainty, then withdrew his sword with shaking hands.

"Well they're in our way," Wexel added. "Let's kill them."

She growled and began to dash towards the door on all fours. As she neared them, she leapt into the air, withdrawing her blade, and crashing into them in spectacular fashion. All three of them tumbled, rolling down the short stairwell and onto the gritty, hard surface. She quickly jumped up, paying little mind to the pain, and then swiftly brought her feet tearing across the face of one of the beings. To her dismay, this strange red being didn't react. Not a cry, nor a whimper, nothing.

She studied the strange creature with disappointment, then turned her attention towards the other. Her animalistic instincts took over, and like a bull charging at the matador, she jumped head forward, slamming the sentinel in the gut. As the two of them stumbled forward, Vicham finally arrived. He looked towards the being whose face had been gashed and raised his sword. With blood slowly pouring from the wounds, the sentinel raised its blade and swung it towards him. The two blades met with a hard crash, prompting sparks and sending Vicham a couple steps back. In the background, the battle cries of Undr and Gravi tore through the air like an angry wind. He was curious and wanted to look, but the strange shell of the person in front of him seemed more pressing.

Vicham pulled his blade back, bringing it quickly forward for another strike. Once again, his blade was met with metal rather than flesh and as his sword quivered from the impact, sweat began to form on his head.

"Ahh!" He yelled.

With a surprising amount of courage and speed, he swung the blade downwards, cutting deep into the sentinel's leg and causing it to collapse to the ground. Wasting no time, he seized the opportunity. As his blade cleared its way from one side of the neck to the other, the head fell, rolling towards him and spraying blood all around. Even in death, the eyes remained open. They looked up with an accusatory stare. For a moment, Vicham almost thought he could see traces of an actual person hiding in them. A sudden streak of light suddenly filled the sky. He turned, and his mouth fell wide. One beam came after another, each of them coming from Undr's palm. He furiously fired them towards Gravi, but she dodged them all, allowing them to pass over her and into the sky.

"Are you seeing this?" He asked aloud. Behind him, he could hear Wexel grunting.

"I'm a little busy," she groaned. Freeing himself from his dismay, he turned around and thrust his sword into the gut of the sentinel. It fell backwards and began to twitch as the blood left its body.

"I had that," Wexel protested. Vicham continued to watch the being squirm and twitch until finally, all its movement stopped. He quietly stepped over the body, being sure to avoid the various pools of blood, then pushed open the door. Just as he entered the tower, he stopped. Standing in front of them was a dozen more of the red beings. Fear held him captive, hopelessness held his hand and worry welcomed him into its arms.

"This should be fun," Wexel remarked. "I'll take the ones on the left side. You take the ones on the right."

He slowly turned towards her, looking at her as if she was insane. She returned the expression with a shrug.

"What's the problem?"

He quietly shook his head and lifted his sword. After a deep sigh, he began to march forward.

"Ha ha ha!" Wexel exclaimed. He turned, at that moment, she was nowhere to be found. *She left me*, he thought. Just as the final syllable of the thought entered his mind, he looked up towards the ceiling, and there, crawling like a frog, was Wexel.

"Aye ye ye ya!" She howled as she dropped down into the crowd. Her blade quickly found its way into the torsos of some of the sentinels, and one at a time, they began to drop. Vicham smiled. Even in the face of insurmountable odds, she still managed to remain courageous and full of wit. It was admirable, if not stupid.

"For Kit," he whispered to himself. He charged towards the crowd and began wildly swinging his sword, hoping with all his heart that one of the frantic maneuvers would do some damage. It might not have been the most effective technique, it certainly wasn't the way of a great warrior, but it did yield some results. As he slayed a couple of the beings, he looked at the remains and grinned coyly.

"Wow," he whispered.

"Don't mess with a Delopar unless you want the claws," Wexel laughed. Vicham looked in her direction and shook his head disapprovingly. Wexel, being as overconfident and naïve as he had mostly gotten used to, had tossed her blade to the ground and was merely using her claws to swipe at their throats.

As he watched her in the heat of battle, he couldn't help but be reminded of Inca. She seemed so very much like her. Her personality, her skills in combat, and actually even her appearance were on point. *I wonder*, he began to think to himself.

Shaking off his thoughts, he turned his attention back to the task at hand. His sword danced through the bodies like a tiger through the tall grasses of Africa. One at a time, he slayed his attackers, finding a bit of comfort in the unexpected ease of it all. He had just begun to think of himself as a masterful warrior, when suddenly, a large fist loomed towards him, knocking him to the ground with a breath-stealing impact. He lay on the ground with stars and flashes filling his eyes. Breathing was hard, and his ribs begged for comfort with each new breath.

"Wexel," he muttered. Her laughter was a distant song, a far-away melody in the musty, blood-filled air. A large sentinel reached down, picking him up and holding him high above its head. Panic kicked in, and he began to squirm about, trying with what little remaining strength he had to be free. But try as he might, the sentinel was far too strong.

With a forceful toss, Vicham careened through the air, landing on the crowd and falling at the bottom of it all. A dozen legs threatened to trample him, blood from Wexel's kills threatened to gag him and a strong foot to the throat threatened to end him. His eyes widened as he began to choke, desperately trying to stay conscious. The Sentinel was strong, its foot came down like a hammer to a nail. His face went red, and his eyes began to water. Coughing seemed like his only move.

"Ha!" Wexel exclaimed as she swung her claws across the sentinel's gut. Intestines began to pour out, landing atop Vicham and creating a most unappealing sight. He began to gag as he attempted to clear himself of the repugnant debris by wiping himself off. Wexel looked down at him, then swung her leg around, kicking the sentinel and sending it crashing into another.

Quickly, she reached down, offering Vicham an eager hand.

"Try and be more careful," she cautioned. She reached to the ground and retrieved his fallen sword, holding it out towards him, before leaping into the air with an animalistic growl. Vicham looked onwards with despair, then turned towards an incoming sentinel.

"Not this time!" He roared. His shoulder crashed towards it, knocking the creature down in an instant. With manic eyes, he lifted his sword, bringing it down over and over. Blood seeped from the various wounds, and before long, the body looked like swiss cheese.

"This is for Pip!" He roared. Wexel turned, looking at him with concern as he continued to pummel the creature with the blade.

"I think you killed it," she announced. Vicham paused, looking around the room and noticed that all the sentinels had been dealt with. He looked down, at the twitching body, and then shook himself free of his madness.

"Are you ok?" Wexel questioned. Her eyes looked at the hole-ridden body, bringing a sudden discomfort to her normally calm demeanor.

"Come on, let's find your friends," she sighed, shaking off her concerns.

They made their way forward, stepping over the mess and entered a hall decorated with many doors. One at a time, they pushed them open, and each time were met with disappointment. Eventually, they traipsed into a large room with a pool of red, smoky liquid at its center. It reeked like melted plastic and presented a fume that stung the eyes. Vicham covered his mouth as approached the pit, but as he stepped closer, the air became more and more unbearable.

"What is that?" Wexel questioned. At that moment, a door to the right flung open revealing two more battle ready sentinels.

"I've got it," Wexel informed, but as she began to saunter towards them, something made Vicham pause. There was something strange going on. Could it really be a coincidence that these beings were the very same color as the ominous red pool that sat before them? Vicham began to wonder, as he did, he found himself unable to shake an anxious feeling that was creeping into his gut.

"Wait," he called out. Wexel stopped, looking at him with confusion.

"I think these are her victims," he whispered. As the realization hit him, he began to feel a swell of guilt and nausea. His face went pale, and soon, he found himself unable to hold onto the sickening feeling brewing within him. With watery eyes, he brought his hands to his knees and began to vomit.

"Yuck," Wexel remarked. She turned towards the sentinels and began to charge, leaping into the air just before she reached them.

"Wexel no!" he called out.

It was too late, like a lion to a gazelle she crashed down, bringing her claws across the face of the leftmost one. Flesh lodged under her nails, blood began to seep, and excitement flowed through her. Slowly, with a dead expression, the other sentinel began to rise, turning towards her and giving her a mighty kick. The impact sent her sliding across the floor and into the rear wall. She crashed with a thud as dizziness began to set in.

"Wow," she whispered.

"Are you deaf?" Vicham exclaimed. "We can't kill them. These are her victims. She turned them into this."

From above, a loud rumble materialized, and moments later, the roof began to crumble, revealing the large face of a vengeful Gravi.

"There you are," she roared.

Chapter 33

Nikalas sat quietly in a room filled with nothing but old books. In front of him was a table holding a heap of documents and a couple maps. He silently studied the maps, a look of concern masking his face. Sitting and surrounding him in anticipation, were Kunklestick, Didorumpus, Emlin, Linuk and Dimitri; each of them was waiting with curiosity. Finally, Nikalas stood up and looked at Kunklestick.

"I think I have a plan," he calmly informed.

"It's about time," Dimitri muttered. Emlin quickly and firmly nudged him, shooting him an angry look and then turned her attention forward.

"We're all ears," Kunklestick replied.

Nikalas looked down at the maps once more, shook his head and then looked back at them.

"Alright," he paused. "Firstly, let's start with what went wrong. How was Septus able to get ahold of the cities?"

He looked around the room, being met only with blank expressions.

"Cristol. He took out the Arnouts. Taking them out took away Furlasia's most powerful force."

He looked around once more, pausing as he glanced at Emlin.

"We need to recapture that city."

"How?" Dimitri loudly questioned. "It's surrounded by dead things. And not just dead people. There are animals and more importantly, giants."

"Well," Nikalas paused. "There happens to be more than a few men here who would love the chance at some revenge, the Tin Men. We're going to rescue them."

"Most of them are currently prisoners in the dungeons," Linuk said. "Those that aren't are in the pits with the children."

"Yea," Nikalas smiled. "We can take care of that."

"I assume you have a plan?" Didorumpus questioned. He looked at his brother and shrugged.

"Well we have a pretty good lineup here," Nikalas explained. "I think the three of us can get it done."

He looked towards Emlin and nodded.

"You and Dimitri will rescue the soldiers from the pits while we create a diversion."

Emlin smiled as their eyes met. He seemed so different, so confident, and so in control. He seemed nothing like the boy she had watched ride off into the sunset all those months ago. *What happened?* She wondered.

"What good am I going to be?" Dimitri bellowed. "I'm not a warrior."

"Lucky for you I am," Emlin grinned. She turned and smiled at the sheepish Dimitri.

"I'll keep you safe."

Dimitri looked at her with hesitation, then silently sat back in his seat.

"I can take care of myself," he muttered.

Nikalas turned his focus to Kunklestick and Didorumpus.

"I need to know everything about what happened while I was gone."

***

An hour later, the six of them emerged from the council chambers, each of them breathing just a little easier. Sure, things were about to get very dangerous, they were about to attempt an overthrow of the Akordan occupation of Morlay, but still, things looked optimistic. Nikalas had spent the last hour learning of the war and explaining what he had been through. The latter seemed the reason for the easy breathing. Yes, everyone seemed very interested in the revealing of his true parentage. It made them gasp and even caused a bit of laughter in the chambers. Nikalas kept his eyes fixed on Emlin as she walked carefully next to Linuk, letting him rest his hand on her shoulder and acting as a guide. Even though the reason for him getting to touch her was downright awful, he couldn't help but feel jealous.

"Emlin," he called out. She stopped, almost causing poor Linuk to stumble and turned towards him.

"Could I talk to you?" He asked. Emlin smiled and looked at Linuk and then Dimitri.

"Can you help him?" She asked of Dimitri. He nodded and grabbed his friend's hand.

"Come on bud. These two need privacy," Dimitri smirked. He led the two of them forward, leaving the hall empty save for Emlin and Nikalas.

"I'm sorry I wasn't here sooner," Nikalas explained, taking a couple steps towards her.

"There's no need to apologize. In war, sacrifices must be made most times." For a moment, she relived a few of the heinous deaths she had witnessed, then she quickly shook it from her mind.

"So you understand why I had to leave?" He asked. Emlin nodded and stepped closer.

"It was very brave of you. I'm sure it wasn't easy."

Nikalas shook his head and walked a few more steps.

"It was impossibly difficult. I wished every day to see you again," he replied.

Suddenly, Emlin stopped, feeling caught off guard.

"Me?" She inquired. "Why would you wish to see me?"

"Isn't it obvious," Nikalas retorted, taking yet another few steps closer.

"Nikalas, you barely know me. Don't pretend you have feelings for me," she warned.

"No one's pretending," he replied. He took a final few steps closer and paused a few inches shy of her.

"You were my reason for even going and meeting Kunklestick. You were what drove me every day during my training. You're what pushed me to enter The Wall of Truth, and you're what brought me back."

"I love you."

Emlin took a step back, pressing her hand to her mouth as she contemplated the life-altering three words. Then, suddenly, her mind raced to Septus. *Love.* He was her first taste of the strange phenomenon, her first dance in the dark, and her first kiss. He was everything that made her childhood great and now everything that made adulthood awful. *Love.* The word put a sour taste in her mouth. She thought of spitting. Thought of turning away, but there was something in his eyes that commanded her attention. He had changed so much.

"Nikalas," she paused. "I can't give you what you're looking for."

He looked at her with confusion and took a couple steps back.

"You don't feel the same?" He questioned.

Emlin looked towards the floor, as she looked down at the masterfully cleaned tiles, she began to feel sadness and regret.

"You're special to me. Perhaps one of the most special people I have ever met."

"But," Nikalas dragged out.

"I know this seems impossibly stupid. I know it. But for some reason, I'm still hoping to fix Septus. I loved him at one point. And love doesn't let you give up on someone."

"Emlin. He killed your father and Inca and Broli and thousands more. He's a murderer," Nikalas explained.

"Yes," she nodded. "And he should be punished. To spend the rest of his days in the dungeons would be merciful compared to what he deserves."

Nikalas studied her with confusion, hoping that at some point something she said would make sense.

"But what if it wasn't him? What if those talismans are poisoning him?"

"There's no walking away from this Emlin. The things he's done, no one is gonna care about the reasons. They are gonna want justice. They are going to want him dead."

"I know. But I can't help but think about how his eyes turn red when he's using his powers. It's as if it's no longer him."

Nikalas shook his head in disbelief, and then began to walk ahead, scooting around her with frustration.

"Nikalas," she called out. "We can't kill him. We need to free him. Free him of the poison."

Nikalas stopped, turned and looked at her with disappointment. How naïve could she be? To have been through so many hard times, to have seen so much darkness and atrocities committed all by him, how could she believe anything positive existed?

"I can't promise anything," he replied. With that, he turned around and made his way out of the halls.

"She loved you," Emlin called out.

He stopped, keeping his eyes ahead.

"Zanna was in love with you," she added.

**

Nikalas, Kunklestick and Didorumpus carefully strolled down the streets of Morlay. They passsed the hopeless street dwellers, the undead ghouls, and even the occasional inattentive Akordan. They stuck to the shadows as best they could, and when it came to areas where that wasn't possible, a simple shortcut through a building always came in handy.

"I can't believe she thinks we can save him," Nikalas muttered as they stepped into a run down, and battered clothing shop.

"What are you talking about?" Didorumpus asked.

"Emlin. She thinks that we can save Septus. That he's under the influence of the talismans and that he's not thinking clearly," Nikalas replied.

"She may be right," Kunklestick retorted. He turned a corner and pushed open a rear exit door. The three of them stepped out into the alley and continued their journey towards the pits.

"Even if that's true, and I mean *even*, there is no scenario where the people of Furlasia will agree to let him live," Nikalas explained.

"Is that what this is really about? Or is it about something else," Kunklestick whispered, shooting him a suspicious glance. Nikalas shrugged off the remark and returned to silence. He was right, it hurt to admit, but he was admittedly quite bitter. He wanted her affection, he had longed for it since he first laid eyes on her. Since the day he saw her emerge from the tree line with that bow, armed and ready. He knew right there that there was something special about her. He sighed as his thoughts came to the hard truth. She loved Septus. Beyond all logic, she still loved him. It was almost troubling to consider.

As they made their way into the run-down districts, they could hear the whisper of Akordan soldiers. Kunklestick raised his hand, summoning them to stop as he caught a glimpse of the nearby guards. There were six in total, certainly nothing for the three of them to be able to handle. A tall wall holding a large metal door stood on the other side of the guards. It led down underneath the wall and into the pits. Kunklestick looked around, scanning the area for further threats.

"Alright," Kunklestick whispered. "Time to get their attention."

He turned around, looking at Nikalas, and then past him. In the window of a nearby tavern he could see a candle burning. It was Emlin. She and Dimitri would wait for the three of them to create a diversion, and then once they had, they would sneak their way down into the pits and free the soldiers and children.

"Follow my lead," Nikalas instructed. He took a step from the shadows and emerged into the view line of the entrance.

"Hey, crocodile dudes!" He called out. "I bet you can't catch me."

The six soldiers looked at each other and laughed. Suddenly, they sprang into action, mindlessly taking the bait just as predictably as he had hoped for.

"Here they come," Didorumpus warned. He firmly gripped his staff and prepared for the oncoming battle. As the Akordans neared, Nikalas flew into the air, scanning the area and aiming his staff at the ghouls that had begun to wander towards them.

"Inginimo," he proclaimed. His beam of energy crashed down to the ground like a bolt of lightning, hitting the ghouls and quickly leaving them in a pile of smoking ash.

"Whoa," Didorumpus gasped. With an Akordan nearing, he raised his staff and began to mutter under his breath. In front of him, an orange wheel of light appeared. It spun, slowly at first, then faster and faster. With a quick flick of his staff, the wheel launched forward, cutting off the head of one of the Akordan soldiers and causing the others to panic. They halted for a moment as they watched their comrade drop to the ground, and then quickly continued forward.

Kunklestick excitedly grinned and began to twirl his staff. Didorumpus looked over, as he noticed the maneuver, he quickly stepped back. The shockwave tore through the air like an angry hurricane, sending the Akordans flying backwards.

"Levomente," Nikalas whispered. He extended his arm out towards the flying Akordans and began to pull them towards him. Into the air they drifted, getting higher than any Akordan had ever done. With his wings still fluttering, Nikalas observed his prey. They drifted towards him looking as helpless as a cat suspended in zero gravity.

"It's time to leave," he proclaimed. His eyes met with the nearest Akordan to him, and for a brief moment, he could see their panic and vulnerability. He almost felt a bit of guilt, but that was quickly erased when the Akordan suddenly snapped his jaw at him. He shook off his remorse and flung his arm upwards, sending them tearing into the sky and over the wall.

"He's gotten powerful," Didorumpus remarked as he looked up towards Nikalas.

"He's our best chance to end all this darkness once and for all. I knew it from the moment I saw him. He's our liberator, our salvation, our savior," Kunklestick whispered with awe. Nikalas carefully landed in front of them and looked around with satisfaction.

"That was too easy," he remarked. As if by some act of irony, the sound of metallic boots suddenly pummeled the air, soaring towards their ears like an infant desperate for attention. Nikalas squinted, looking into the distance, and began to grin.

"Like I said," he paused. "Too easy."

Didorumpus and Kunklestick turned around, gulped, then looked forward with their hands firmly gripping their staffs.

"You guys can do this," Nikalas remarked. And without further notice, he leapt into the air, letting his wings carry him towards the crowd.

"For Morlay?" Didorumpus questioned.

"No, for Furlasia," Kunklestick replied. He gripped his staff and dashed forward, with each step he took, a bit of dark mist began to surround him. It was The Echo. His connection to it was—in that moment—stronger than it had ever been. A small battalion of Akordans galloped on the horizon, with each of them holding a sword and shield. His staff began to glow and just as he reached the wall of opposing forces, he swung it upwards, and in an instant, sent two soldiers flying.

***

"They're going to die," Dimitri whispered as he and Emlin looked out the window towards the slew of chaos.

"If they perish, so shall we," she replied. She firmly grabbed his hand and gave him a pull.

"We're going out there now?" He questioned with distress.

"Yes," she replied as she continued to pull. "It's the diversion they were talking about."

He shook his hand free and continued to follow her down a creaky flight of stairs that led down to a glassmaker's workshop. The room was dark, the business had long since been abandoned. As she reached the door, she took a deep breath and pulled her bow off of her shoulders. Summoning a courage she had not needed to put in use for some time, she tugged the door open.

Anarchy filled the streets ahead of them; beams of energy flew from one side of the alley to the other. As she looked onwards, she couldn't help but re-live that dreadful day on the battlefields of Cristol.

"Where to now?" Dimitri queried. Her eyes scanned the surroundings and suddenly, she had an idea.

"You're not going to like this," she replied. She took off, heading straight towards the crowd.

You can do this Emlin, she thought to herself. Now just a few feet shy of the nearest Akordan, she let out a pronounced whistle. A couple Akordans quickly turned around and beamed with satisfaction. She lifted her bow, quickly firing an arrow into the eye of one of them and then, from the skies, came a beam of energy that took down the other.

"Go!" Nikalas called out. She looked up with appreciation and began to charge forward. With Dimitri in tow, they began to make their way along the sidewalls of the surrounding buildings. Nikalas, using his powers of telekinesis, kept the pathway clear for them. He flung aside all the Akordan, one after the other, finally finding a good use for his newfound powers. She wanted to breathe a sigh of relief as they made their way to the other side of the horde, but she knew now was not the time.

"Come on," she ordered Dimitri. He looked faint, his skin had turned pale, and his cheeks were now red, but without any protests or snide remarks, he nodded.

Their feet moved with more haste than ever. The wizards were outnumbered; they needed help, and fast. Her hands gripped the hot handles of the metal doors and gave them a quick pull. She was just about to charge forward when Dimitri placed his hand on her shoulder and nodded downwards. She gasped with surprise as she noticed the perilous drop down.

"Thanks," she whispered. Dimitri nodded with satisfaction, and the two of them made their way down the ladder. As Emlin's feet hit the bottom, the loud clamor of pickaxes being crashed against stone filled the air. There was no time to waste, that luxury had been long spent. With her bow in hand and an arrow in the nock, she lurched forward. There were dozens of children, and even more dozens of grown men. Standing in the middle of it all was a couple Akordan guards and roaming slowly down the narrow walkway were a couple Delopar ghouls.

"Ok," Emlin whispered to Dimitri. "We need to take out those Akordans first."

She slowly reached to her side, withdrew a short sword and handed it to Dimitri.

"I should be able to handle it, but if I get in trouble, step in," she looked at him and nodded. He gulped as he accepted the responsibility hesitantly, and with that, Emlin sauntered forward. She kept her eyes fixed on the two Akordans ahead; they were heavily armored in all places but their face. It was a poor design, but then again, these were Akordans, complicated thought and problem solving wasn't their specialty.

She lifted her bow, aiming at the back of the Akordan on the right. Her heart raced. Once she let the arrow loose, she would have the full attention of every servant of Agavordis occupying the pit. She had to be sure, had to have a plan. She closed her eyes and began to imagine the ensuing conflict. *Get his attention, hit him in the face and take him out, then quickly do the same to the other.* Seemed simple in her mind, but even Emlin knew, things never went as smooth as they did in the imagination.

"Here buddy," she called out.

"Huh?" The Akordans asked in a stumped tone. She released the arrow just as soon as she could see his eyes. It soared through the air, cutting through it like butter and offering a faint whistle to anyone who cared to hear. The arrow looked set to hit its mark, when suddenly, the Akordan brought up his wrist, letting the arrow deflect against his armor.

"Fuit," Emlin whispered.

"My turn," the Akordan sneered. They both unsheathed their swords and charged at her. She quickly fired another arrow, which bounced against his armor and fell to the floor.

"Ahh!" The Akordan roared. His blade crashed against the ground, shaking the steel and sending a hum up his arm. She speedily reached to her boots, putting her fingers inside the cuff and withdrawing a small dagger. In a panicked frenzy, she brought the dagger up, just barely scraping his face. As the small wound began to bleed, he looked at her with anger and swung his hand, hitting her across the face. She fell to the ground with a hard thump, and moaned as the pain burned through her cheeks.

"Dimitri," she called out.

You've gotta help her, he thought to himself. He looked onwards and jumped up, raising the sword and charging towards the attackers like an angry spartan. Fear coursed through his veins, but courage filled his heart. He had been on the sideline of life long enough. Now was his chance. His chance to fill the void he had left vacant for so long.

"Get away from her!" He roared. He had no form, no real experience with a sword, but that didn't stop him. He swung the blade forward, crashing against the armor and leaving an imprint. Adrenaline filled him, giving him a skill he had never known he had. As the second Akordan came towards him with his sword, he brought his up, catching it and then gave him a firm shove.

Emlin climbed to her feet, looking at him with surprise, then reached for the dagger that she had dropped. Dimitri continued to block the attacks, showing skills not unlike a warrior of the olden days. She looked at the other Akordan and furrowed her brow. She didn't like her chances, but the dagger was all she had. Making use of her agility and youth seemed her best option. She jumped back, narrowly missing a swinging blade, and then leapt into the air and kicked him in the chest. The impact stung, as the strength of the metal pushed back against her like an angry bull. Luckily, the push went both ways. He flew back, crashing to the floor in a messy heap of metal.

Emlin looked on, at Dimitri and the Akordan that he was fighting. Her knee hurt, her legs felt like they could buckle, but that wouldn't stop her. With one eye shut, she threw the dagger. It found its mark and the Akordan went down. Dimitri, stepped back as he reeled from the shock, then looked down.

"Ahh haa!" He yelled, bringing his sword down and severing the head of the Akordan in one quick movement.

"Holy crap," he whispered. He dropped the sword and looked at Emlin.

"How did I do that?"

***

Kunklestick lifted his staff, and looked towards the battalion that had quickly come to surround them. They fought as best as they could, their spells doing as much damage as one could expect, but still, it wasn't enough. Even Nikalas, with his newfound skills, was beginning to feel the sting of combat. He stood with his back against Kunklestick's and looked with frustration at the wave of Akordans.

"This is what you call a rescue huh?" Didorumpus laughed. He rapidly rocked his wand at the crowd, sending a hot gas cloud headed towards them. It engulfed them, causing their skin to start burning, then, before long, they dropped to the ground with bulged eyes.

"It's a constantly evolving plan," Nikalas retorted. *Wait a second*, he thought to himself. Suddenly he closed his eyes and focused. In an instant, he was surrounded by darkness with chilly mist scattered all around him and small yellow orbs of light hovering nearby. There was almost beauty in it all. Of course, the unfortunate reality was that all but two of those alluring yellow balls of light were Akordans. He took a few steps forward, hid behind two of the orbs, and then focused.

"What the?" Kunklestick barked with surprise. Nikalas reached out, grabbing two Akordans by the collar and suddenly his hands began to glow red. Within seconds the armor had melted, leaving them exposed and vulnerable.

"Feeling naked?" Nikalas questioned with a smirk. The Akordans swiftly turned around, and with lightning fast reflexes, he caught both arms and leapt into the air.

The breeze brushed against his hair, ruffling all the separate hair follicles and tickling his face. He smiled as his wings carried him high above the battle.

"Put us down," one of the Akordans hollered.

"Oh I plan to," he retorted. The glow returned to his hand and before long, the Akordans were entirely engulfed in balls of green and blue flames. In a quick motion, he launched them towards the ground. As they shattered against the ground, the embers spread, bringing fire to at least a dozen others as well.

Kunklestick looked at Didorumpus, surprised by the stunning display of power, it was almost ruthless. As the enflamed, Akordans took off running with screams, the others grew clearly restless. And it was at that moment that a series of loud thumps filled the air. They turned, looking towards the pit with curiosity.

"Atta girl," Didorumpus whispered with pride. Marching towards them were dozens of soldiers — Tin Men — devoid of armor but they did have Beacons.

Tiny beams of energy sailed through the air, piercing the Akordan army, and making quick work of the extermination process. Kunklestick and Didorumpus stood idly by, encompassed in a protective barrier as the surrounding Akordans met their grisly demise. It didn't take long. Soon, the odor of death littered the street.

"That's more like it," Nikalas remarked as he came down against the ground. Emlin and Dimitri slowly strolled towards them, each of them wearing a satisfied smirk.

"Good job Emlin," Kunklestick added. Emlin looked at Dimitri who simply shrugged.

"Actually, we have Dimitri to thank," she responded.

"Really?" Kunklestick questioned with surprise. Emlin nodded a simple *yes* and winked at Dimitri.

"Now what do we do, sir?" One of the soldiers asked. All eyes suddenly turned to Nikalas, who looked around and nodded with satisfaction.

"Gather the rest of the men and retake this city," he instructed. "Kunklestick, Didorumpus and I have another stop to make."

"Where?" Didorumpus queried.

"Terria. We're gonna need all the men we can get if we are gonna free Cristol," Nikalas retorted.

"This shit's just beginning," he said with a smile.

Chapter 34

It was quiet and still in Neveraus Hold, there was little chatter to be heard. There was only the prolonged breath of Herratia. She sat on her throne, digging her claws into the chair's stone exterior, keeping her eyes focused on the floor ahead. To her left, stood Nevo. He watched her with a calm demeanor, making sure not to say anything that would set her off.

"I don't like this," she finally muttered, ending the almost thirty minutes of silence.

"This waiting for him."

"You're so sure he's going to come?" Nevo asked. He slowly strolled over to her and paused.

"Of course he's coming," she replied. "He would be a fool not to."

She jumped from her chair and began to wander back and forth.

"I can't believe I let him escape."

Nevo cringed and darted over to her, quickly grabbing her shoulders with a firm pull.

"He's nothing. He's just borrowing his power. If you take those rings away, he's just a useless, cunne Terrian," he sneered.

She nodded in agreement and took a step back, freeing herself from his grip.

"But his power is too great," she whispered. "That gnome has taught him well."

"Then we'll kill them both," Nevo roared. "The Akordans are done serving others, we are the superior species. There's nothing that can stand in our way."

Unexpectedly, a low hum began to make its way to their ears. It was coming from outside the keep. Herratia turned towards Nevo and tilted her head slightly right.

"What is that?" She whispered. Nevo shrugged and steadily approached the door. The sound was louder now, in fact, it no longer sounded like one sound. It sounded like many. Like a hundred screams all crying out at once.

"Wait," Herratia called out. "What if it's him?"

Nevo twitched his shoulders and strongly pulled against the handles. There, in the middle of a crowd of Akordans, was Agavordis. He stood still with red eyes, firing beams of energy towards anything that moved. Nevo calmly withdrew his sword and stepped out of the doorway.

"Don't," Herratia pleaded. "This isn't something that can be fixed with a sword."

"I have to try," Nevo replied. With that, he darted out through the doors and down the steep stairs.

With the light of Neveraus shining against her skin, Herratia stood suspended, frozen in a mental prison that had no doors or windows. On the walls in front of her was everything she had ever done; the good, the bad, and the heinous. All of it played like a film, filling her with as much regret as it did pride. Hervott, the baby, all those she had ever wronged stood, beckoning her with black eyes. She shook it off, opening her eyes just in time to hear the cries of children as they were being slaughtered. He was going after them all, the women, the children, the elderly. It would be genocide.

"I ruined everything," she whispered to herself. Her mind took another trip as tears began to fill her eyes. This one was to a much darker place; a place she had only been to once before. It was in this place, this section of her mind, that held the ultimate truth. The terrible fact.

***

There she stood, in the middle of a room that was empty of everything but a single table. On this table, sat a couple vials. With the pages of a textbook flipped open, she tirelessly worked on replicating the recipe she had discovered. It would be the miracle cure. One that would ensure long life and good health for Alora. She was the first born, she deserved all the best. It wasn't very often that a princess was born.

She wiped her brow, and looked to the corner of the room. There, sitting in a manger, was Alora. She was quiet, quite well behaved and perfectly content watching nothing but the light dancing on the ceiling. Her laugh was sweet. There was purity behind it.

"You having fun over there?" Herratia asked with a smile. Alora replied with a simple giggle. It said so much, by saying so little. She smiled and looked back at the small mixing bowl that was in front of her. Gripping a small lizard, she cut its head and carefully drained the contents into the mixing bowl. Next came, a few of Alora's hairs, crushed dragon teeth, and a bit of soda. As the mixture began to bubble, she looked at Alora with excitement.

"You're gonna be such a healthy girl," she laughed. Suddenly there was a small squeak, it was faint but not faint enough to be missed.

"What's that?" she whispered, turning towards the sound. Unfortunately, her maneuver was sloppy, which consequently led to the table rocking, and causing the experiment to fall. Glass crashed to the floor, returning as close back to sand as it could, followed by the candle, and then the mixing bowl.

"No!" She hollered. As the mixing bowl crashed to the floor, it cracked in half, spilling its contents all over the floor and erupting into the air in a fine mist.

"By Undr!" She hurriedly wandered to Alora and picked up the manger. "Mommy messed up. We'll have to try again later."

She reached the door and gave it a one-handed pull while balancing Alora with the other. As they stepped out into the hall, Alora offered a simple cough and returned to her joyful laughter.

**

"It wasn't your fault," she whispered to herself. "It was mine."

As the cries of the Akordans continued to populate the air, she opened her eyes and looked towards the opening. In an instant, she teleported forward, exiting the hold and scanning the city. There, firing off beams of energy towards her children, was Agavordis and Epard. As she looked ahead, she could just barely make out the remains of Nevo. Scorched and smoking like an overcooked turkey.

"Where have you been Herratia? Mother of the Akordans!" Agavordis taunted. He looked towards a child huddled over and sent a quick fireball heading towards it. She teleported forward, appearing just in front of the deadly duo.

"Why?" She quietly asked. "Why kill a whole species because of the actions of one person?"

"Because," Agavordis explained. "I had to make sure you learned a lesson. And Akordans are so much more obedient when they're dead. Honestly, I don't know why I didn't think of this before. I never needed you to get the Akordans on my side. I could've left you in that cave."

Epard stood with a content smirk as he watched the realization of defeat make its way across her face. She had once been mighty, strong, powerful, and full of potentials. But now, she was nothing.

"You will not rule this land Septus," Herratia whispered. "You can kill me, you can gather an army of mindless slaves, but you will never rule this land."

Agavordis sneered and slowly approached, his red eyes causing her to feel unsettled.

"I saw him you know," she added. "The boy from the prophecy."

She looked at him with an extraordinarily uncharacteristic smile.

"He's going to destroy you."

Agavordis looked at his hands as they began to emit a green hue.

"I'll give you one last chance," he offered. "Serve me or die."

She went mute, looking into his eyes, those empty red eyes. Was she looking for something? Perhaps a sign of a conscience? Perhaps she was looking for hope, or maybe she thought there would be a reflection. Whatever she was looking for, it wasn't there. She dropped to her knees and lowered her head.

"Do it," she demanded.

Wasting no further time, he lifted his hands to her head, letting the flames spread. Her screech of pain bounced against the rocky walls, encompassing them in a cacophony of racket. Her skin seared, sizzling and popping as the flames continued to pierce the layers. He released his hands, stepped back, and seconds later, she toppled over, her head continuing to burn for a few more moments.

"No!" An Akordan yelled from the distance. Agavordis turned, looking at an opening, and smiling as he noticed a few more Akordans standing idly by.

"Let's finish this," Epard remarked. They looked at each other for a moment and then slowly walked forward with arms raised.

"Ha!" Agavordis roared as he sent a beam of green energy tearing through the air.

Chapter 35

As the match neared its conclusion, Idrix found herself just narrowly behind her opponent. There was so much on the line, losing was not an option. She needed this jewel. She needed it to fulfill her lifelong goal of revenge against Gravi. It was her main purpose for existing. For so long, her priority had been gathering the necessary weapons to kill her. It hadn't been easy. She had scanned through rumors, trying to sort out fact from fiction. So much had gone wrong, and yet, now, she was closer than ever. The thought of cleansing the world of such a powerful evil brought her purpose, helped her sleep at night and kept her pushing through her old age.

The familiar sound of the die roll traveled down to her ears. *Two*. The Boss carefully moved her piece. Two spaces to the right. She was dangerously close to the opposing piece. If Idrix rolled anything higher than a four, she could knock her back the number of spaces based on the die number. But, if she didn't, well, the finish line was in sight. She carefully flipped over a card and looked it over.

"The result of this mixed with two parts didil juice and the pollen of a chrolax plant yields the chemical compound known as *Hais*."

She looked at Idrix, who appeared pleased with this question, then closed her eyes as she scanned her mind, hoping to find some illumination. Tension was in the air. Behind Idrix, stood, Jinn, Articus and Methalda. She looked at them, reading their nervousness and grinning excitedly. She was so close. Her title of being the most brilliant game player would soon be cemented in the histories of the world forever.

"Wiffle," she calmly answered. Idrix nodded and reached for the coordinating answer card. As she flipped it over, she sighed, looking towards The Boss hesitantly.

"Wrong," she exhaled. "The correct answer is Cavipill."

The Boss looked at her with dismay, and then reached for the card.

"Let me see that," she demanded with an accusatory tone. As she quickly grasped the card, she flipped it over and let out a rather noticeable groan. The card indeed read *Cavipill*.

"Living a life of high end luxury, you've probably never had to make your own Hais. But for folks that can't afford soap, this is an essential recipe," Idrix explained.

"You were a bloody princess," The Boss sternly replied. She grabbed her piece and moved it back to where it had been. "You lived a high life as well."

"Not anymore," Idrix retorted. "Now everything I do comes from hard work and sacrifice."

"You mean stealing," The Boss added. With one last angry stare, she handed the die over to Idrix and sat back in her chair.

"Step away from your amenities and you'll learn so much about the world around you," Idrix lectured with a smile. She gave the die a quick roll. *Four*. The best path was going to be towards the right side of the board. Keep chasing The Boss. If she caught up, she could knock her piece back. It was as good a strategy as any. Knocking her back would buy her room for some wrong answers. Her fingers gripped the piece and she moved three spaces up and one to the right. Her piece was now directly behind The Bosses. With slow optimism, she flipped over a card and gave it a silent read.

"Anagram," she said, giving The Boss the go-ahead to flip over the hourglass. As the sand began to flow, she quickly began jotting down possibilities. The Boss watched curiously as Idrix whispered to herself, writing down various options with impressive speed. The sand was nearly out when she handed over her answer. The Boss tensely gripped the paper and looked at her response. Then, she flipped over the coordinating answer card.

"Idirx," The Boss paused. "I must say, I am truly amazed by how your mind works."

She flipped over the answer card, offering Idrix a grateful sigh of relief.

"Nice," Articus whispered in the background.

Idrix turned towards him and shook her head.

"Silence is required in the game room," The Boss spitefully said. Articus grinned at Methalda. The Boss was on edge, perhaps even nervous. The match was closer than anyone had expected. They were both prevalently brilliant. Methalda grinned with satisfaction, then the two of them returned their attention to the game.

"One," The Boss sighed, moving her piece one spot forward. She slowly exhaled deeply and reached for the coordinating card.

"Where was the first recorded instance of sephmill found?"

Idrix flipped over the hourglass and began to silently tap her fingers.

"Ah, believe it or not I remember this well. You should too, actually. Both of us have been around for quite some time," The Boss explained.

"New Bamont."

Idrix flipped over the answer card and silently nodded.

***

Another hour passed and although each of them had taken several turns, the progress seemed at a standstill. Each time any of them made progress forward, the other would come and knock the person back. It was tedious and beginning to wear out everyone in the room. They were mentally matched, that much was clear. Now, after five hours, they had reached the point of certain victory. Each of them was now less than five spaces away from the other side of the board. It was anyone's game but luckily, it was Idrix's turn to roll.

As the six appeared at the top of the die, she smirked with satisfaction and moved her piece to the finish line. The Boss shifted her weight, clearly feeling the sting of possible loss. She contently observed as Idrix flipped over a card and set it down for all to see.

"At the time of the Great Fall, *he* led the charge to recover the lost items of Loren," Idrix read. She closed her eyes and focused. The Great Fall was certainly a well-known event. It had been nearly fifty years, but it still remained a vivid part of Adrasian history. Idrix never considered herself an expert on the subject, but she did try her best to be well-educated in all important events in Daulest.

"I believe it was Zalindorf. General Zalindorf," she announced. The Boss nodded and flipped over the card. As she looked at the answer, she smiled, setting it down for all to see.

"You are wrong my friend," she informed. "Zalindorf was instrumental in the recovery but it was not he who led the search. It was a man named Xor Proin that was responsible for the recovery."

"No," Jinn whispered with disappointment. The Boss looked up, lifted her finger to her mouth and hushed her.

Looking Idrix in the eyes, she rolled the die and let out a cheerful giggle. *Five.* It was the exact amount she needed. Her piece moved forward with ease, hitting Idrix's piece and knocking it back a few spaces.

"Why do that?" Methalda whispered. "She could've crossed the line."

"I've asked the three of you several times now to cease your talking. Now, it's time for you to step outside," The Boss demanded. Idrix kept her eyes forward, focusing only on The Boss as the others filed their way out of the room. With the room to themselves, The Boss picked up a card.

"In modern science the word for any animal with only two legs is Duelongs. What was the previous name for such an animal?"

She set the card down and Idrix promptly flipped over the hourglass. The sand began to hastily trickle down. It seemed loud, almost like the loudest sound in the world. It was all she could hear. With her eyes closed, she scanned the immensity of her mind, the areas where she filed away all her important knowledge.

Idrix watched the hourglass as she gently tapped her fingers along the table. The sand level was getting low. She leered with hopefulness as the tiny crystals of destiny continued to diminish into the pile waiting on the other side. This was it. The Boss didn't know the answer. She would win the next turn and secure her lifelong goal to eliminate Gravi.

"Bilong," The Boss declared. Suddenly, Idrix felt the excitement in her heart diminish. Her hands reached for the answer card, trembling all the way, and as she flipped it over, her heart sank. She looked up with heavy eyes and flipped over the card.

"It seems this victory belongs to me," The Boss happily exclaimed. Idrix rose from her seat and quietly bowed. Everything was ruined. She would spend her last days filled with regret over this moment. The moment she failed to fulfill her lifelong promise. She peered at The Boss with humiliation and slowly turned towards the exit.

"Where are you going?" The Boss questioned.

"You won," Idrix replied. "There's nothing left for me to do besides return to Furlasia."

"Stop," The Boss demanded. Idrix paused and turned around.

"You are the most capable opponent I've ever faced Idrix. Your intelligence is remarkable. Your logic, your strategy, everything about the way you play is simply inspiring."

She sauntered over to her with a broad smile and wide arms.

"I know your story Idrix. I know your cause. I know what it is you're trying to do, and I think it's remarkable and brave."

She threw her arms around Idrix and gave her a firm squeeze. Idrix stood still, dumbfounded and stiff as the fierce woman embraced her in an unusually drawn out hug. Finally, she pulled away, giving Idrix one last squeeze on the shoulders and then, she lifted her hand and began to pull on her ring. Idrix's eyes narrowed with dismay, and moments later, she found herself holding the jewel she had sought for so long.

"But I lost," Idrix whispered.

"I always planned on giving it to you," The Boss replied.

"So this was all just another game? Everything?"

"It was a test. A test to see if you were worthy," she replied.

Idrix looked the ring over and studied it. It was elegant to say the least. The silver band glistened under the light of the sun. The pink jewel at its center was cloudy, but not to the point where you couldn't see into it. And within its center were tiny specs; flakes of an unknown substance. It was likely a substance no one in Daulest could identify.

"If there really is a threat out there, you and your team seem very capable. But be wary. Fighting with Gods and Goddesses is not meant for mortal men. Even Adrasians with their enhanced strength and vitality would find themselves out of place in such a conflict," The Boss explained.

Idrix studied the ring a moment longer, and then looked at The Boss with admiration and glee. She shifted her cane to the left hand, placing all her weight on it and extended her right hand outwards.

"Thank you," she calmly replied.

***

Not too long after the match had ended, The Decoyers found themselves shuffling into the Maratan. Idrix intended to be crossing the sea by nightfall. The jewel was theirs. The mission had been a success. Ironically, it turned out The

Society hadn't been necessary at all, but how was Idrix to know the jewel would just be handed over?

As Articus stepped into the Maratan, he turned around, pulling the door upwards and giving the handle a firm pull. It locked with a loud click and once again, they found themselves in the dark metallic canister they had all become so fond of. He turned around with a satisfied beam, and was greeted by the smiling faces of Methalda, Penny and Sillimon.

"What?" He asked as they all stared at them.

"We wanted to thank you," Sillimon informed.

"Thank me?" Articus questioned. "For what?"

"For all of this," Penny replied.

"For stepping up and being a leader," Methalda added.

Articus looked at the three of them with red cheeks as a proud feeling crept into his heart.

"I only did what I thought Josiah would've done. We only all know each other because of him," he replied.

"Regardless," Sillimon halted. "We achieved a great thing here today. We're a part of history. And it's because of you."

Articus looked at them and nodded appreciatively.

"What are you guys doing out here?" Dorrin blurted out. Sillimon turned and looked down the hall at the messy man they had come to appreciate for his ill-timed remarks.

"You guys aren't having a moment are you?" Dorrin questioned.

"Yup," Methalda sighed with exasperation.

"Well, hurry it up. Idrix wants to go over the plan," he retorted.

Chapter 36

Nikalas, Kunklestick and Didorumpus landed smack dab in the center of Terria. The streets were familiar, but there was an obvious gloom that was cast over the citizens. As they jumped from the back of their Grimworts, they shooed them back into the air, and began to march down the streets to the barracks. With a staff in each of their hands, they rambled through the streets, inspiring a bit of hope with their presence.

"We are going to be in for another fight," Nikalas warned. "Stay behind cover whenever possible. This time we might be facing Beacons."

"Akordans don't use those types of weapons," Kunklestick countered.

"They didn't use to. But then again, they didn't use to freely wander the surface either. All bets are off teach," Nikalas retorted.

Kunklestick looked at him with annoyance, then chuckled lightly.

The barracks of the Vanguard looked unrecognizable. It was comprised of mostly gardens that were maintained by former soldiers and being watched over by Akordans and ghouls. Nikalas halted, looking forward and counting in his head.

"Well, it doesn't seem too bad," he whispered. "But then again, neither did Morlay."

"Exactly," Didorumpus chimed in. "Let's assume nothing."

Nikalas looked at them and smiled.

"I would never," he replied. Suddenly, he leapt in the air, letting his wings carry him high above the courtyard.

"He really is a show off isn't he?" Kunklestick groaned.

"He learned from the best," Didorumpus replied. A sudden streak of energy soaring from the sky ended the peacefulness of the homestead. As the Akordan guards looked up, they began to dash towards a cart, and one by one, they each grabbed a Beacon.

"Attack!" One of them bellowed. They aimed the weapons at the sky and quickly began to fire at the floating entity. Nikalas laughed and fired another beam towards them. It crashed down in front of them, burning the grass adjacent to them and causing a roaring fire.

"He's gonna get himself killed," Kunklestick said as he ran into the courtyard.

The beams of the Beacons continued to fly into the air, and as the chaos continued to pick up, so too did the noise. Before long, more Akordans began to shuffle towards them with raised swords and angry faces.

Didorumpus turned and sighed at the oncoming swarm of Akordans and ghouls.

"This is what I get for tagging along with these two," he muttered under his breath. With a quick swing of his staff, he sent a beam of energy tearing across the ground, sending rocks and debris flying towards his oncoming attackers. The rubble slammed into the looming Akordans, knocking a few of them down, but leaving plenty standing and ready to fight.

As the horde closed in, he gripped his staff and collapsed it into wand form. He placed it carefully in his left robe pocket, and then returned his attention towards his foes. With his hands now free, he began to move them about, tracing the shape of a square over and over until alas, a spinning wall of light emerged.

"Charge," one of the Akordans ordered. The Akordan soldiers promptly pushed forward, raising their swords and shields, but it wasn't enough. With one touch of the energy wall, they found themselves soaring back, and landing with a hard thud while a jolt of electricity coursed through their body. Didorumpus grinned as one after the other, they met the same fate. It seemed at some point, they would know not to approach the energy, but to his dismay, the logic was lost on them.

Elsewhere, Nikalas remained airborne, swooping down and giving an energized fist to whomever he could. There was something so utterly satisfying about using his actual hands to deliver an attack. It seemed much more personal and left him feeling like a bad-ass; like someone who could finally take whatever a bully could throw. He continued the skirmish, dealing haymakers and left hooks like Mike Tyson in his glory days and before long, the air was clear of Beacon blast. He looked down at the Akordans that he had taken out, noticing the burnt and peeling skin each of them had. It was a monstrous sight, but as he looked at the remains, he couldn't feel anything but pride.

"Shouldn't I feel guilty?" He whispered to himself as he continued to observe the aftermath of his attacks. For so long, everything that had happened felt like a game. An intense virtual reality starring just him, but it wasn't a game. This was real. Every one that he had slain was once a real, breathing being. He was now judge, jury and executioner, a role he would have to live with for the rest of his days.

"Hurry on," Kunklestick hollered.

Nikalas turned, looking at Kunklestick and smiling excitedly as his mentor freed the shackles of each of the Vanguard hostages.

"Get the others!" Kunklestick ordered to the newly liberated colonel. Sabasio lifted his hand, gave a quick salute and motioned the freed Vanguards to follow him.

"Nikalas," Didorumpus called out. "A little help."

He turned towards the entrance, noticing the white wall of light that was repelling the oncoming Akordans. Sending Kunklestick a proud nod, he leapt into the air, charging his powers until he was fully in vibrant blue energy.

"Coming through," he called out. Like a comet in the sky, he zipped past Didorumpus, plowing into the wave of Akordans and ghouls. As his energy crashed into the attackers, a large explosion of fire hurdled into the sky.

"There will be more," Kunklestick warned as he arrived at his brother's side. They nodded at each other, and turned their focus ahead. Dozens of ghouls had begun to approach, each of them boasting glowing red eyes and wide-open mouths.

"No," Kunklestick whispered. He lifted his staff, bringing the end out towards the ghouls and drew a shield with the glowing end. Icy beams soared from within the mouths of the ghouls, crashing into the shield and raining water down on the ground, cold water that eagerly became slush.

Nikalas stood in the middle of a swarm of Akordans holding an energy sword in each hand. Just another one of the neat little tricks Aldon had taught him. For an absentee father, he was proving quite useful. Their sessions together had so far been invaluable. Each time he entered the dream realm, his fighting became a little more refined.

He eyed the Akordans with a persistent stare, taking obvious satisfaction in how easily his blades of heat cut through theirs. It was definitely a one-sided fight, but that was hardly of any concern to him. All that mattered was victory. He needed Terria's army to launch his final attack. It all hinged on this city.

"Com'on," Nikalas taunted as his blades sliced through theirs. "Give me a real challenge"

Loud footsteps loomed in the distance, as he shifted his attention, it seemed his wish had been granted.

"Ahh!" A woman screamed, pointing towards the city gates. Kunklestick and Didorumpus speedily looked towards the distressed woman, then followed her gaze. A giant loomed in the distance; it sauntered with a heavy gate, rotted skin and reddened eyes. The city entrance toppled under the weight of its monstrous foot, and towards the city center, it moseyed.

"Shit," Nikalas whispered with a gulp. Reaching into his robe, he pulled out his wand and extended it out. The head of his staff began to glow as he aimed it at the incoming foe.

"Inginimo," he proclaimed. The beam shot through the air, hitting the giant square in the chest, and although it wailed and swatted, it did little to deter its steps.

"Ahh!" Nikalas roared, focusing all his will into the spell. His concentration was absolute, nothing but his goal filled his mind. In fact, he was so preoccupied with powering the spell that he failed to notice an Akordan soldier creeping up from behind. Luckily for him, Didorumpus was decidedly more alert, sending a large blue fist careening towards the Akordan and causing it to crash into the others. The impact caused a chain reaction, an impressive one at that. Like dominos on a table, the Akordans fell, landing on each other and creating a deafening ruckus. Nikalas nervously turned his head, just enough to use his peripherals to see what had happened. He let out sigh of relief, and brought his focus back to the goliath ahead.

"I could use a hand here," he called out.

Kunklestick swung his staff, prompting an invisible force to crash into an Akordan, then looked up towards the sky.

"Yogurn!"

The call was answered just as quickly as always. The ever reliable Grimwort quickly dove from the clouds, emerging with a proud neigh as she continued her persistent descent into the chaos. She was no fool; the situation was quite obvious, even to her animalistic mind. Aiming at a crowd of ghouls, she extended her legs, plowing a path through them before coming to a stop.

"Good job girl," Kunklestick praised as she stopped in front of him. He carefully sauntered over to her, and began to earnestly rub her ears.

"Very good indeed."

She neighed with excitement, then brought her front legs down, allowing her master an easier climb. Kunklestick smiled and carefully gripped her fur, pulling himself up as gently as he could. Once he was properly seated, he gave her a soft tap with his feet, and moments later, he found himself high in the skies, looking straight at an unsettlingly tall ghoul.

"Keep it steady," he instructed.

As he released his grip on her fur, he tightened his legs, using them as an anchor while he collapsed his staff to a wand.

"I don't normally do this," he muttered to himself. As the mammoth ghoul locked eyes on them, he hurriedly raised the wand, aiming it straight at the creature's face.

"Magnificant!" He loudly expelled. The tip of his wand began to glow white and with a bright flash of light, sent a beam careening towards the deceased goliath. It crashed into it, forming a tight lasso that held the giant in place. The next step brought just the result he had hoped for. The giant toppled, crashing hard against the ground and sending a tremor that was felt across the entire city.

"Now's your chance," Didorumpus informed to Nikalas.

"I saw something like that in a movie once," Nikalas laughed. He brought his attention towards the toppled giant, then, using his powers, surrounded himself in flames. Like a bull to red, he charged, crashing into the giant's skull and causing the whole thing to explode with flames.

As the flames crept high into the air, Didorumpus smiled, then quickly brought his attention back to an incoming crowd of Akordans.

"Inginimo imphis," he declared. This time the energy from his staff sent out multiple beams, hitting three Akordans with scorching heat and causing them to drop lifeless to the ground.

"Nice," Nikalas complimented as he wiped himself free of some ash. His eyes studied the remaining Akordans, as the blue glow of fire began to surround him, they willingly threw their arms up in defeat.

"It seems they've had enough," Didorumpus remarked.

"Yea," Nikalas sighed. His eyes looked up to the sky just in time to see Yogurn heading straight down towards them.

"Hey I'm standing here," he laughed.

As the city began to return to Vanguard control, Nikalas summoned the soldiers into the center courtyard. Chatter and celebration filled the area with an enthusiasm that had not been felt in some time. Now — however — was not the time for celebration, not by a long shot. Floating into the air, he lifted his arms, asking for silence as best as he could. His influence was absolute. All grew silent.

"Terria is ours. Any ghouls and Akordans that remain will be promptly hunted and destroyed," Nikalas announced. Applause and cheers suddenly erupted, but as it did, Nikalas disapprovingly shook his head.

"We're not out of this yet," he explained, effectively ending the bliss.

"We still have a fight ahead of us. I know no one wants to hear this, but we need to overthrow Cristol. We need to get Agavordis, and his minions out of there and free the Arnouts."

"The Arnouts just gave up!" A soldier yelled from the crowd.

"That's right they did," Nikalas nodded. "But that's because they believed a stupid concept that once your leader falls you lay down your arms."

He looked around the crowd and then towards Kunklestick and Didorumpus.

"I've never heard of something more stupid in all my life!"

Cheers and applause overtook the crowd once again.

"So we have to go save them. We have to convince them that their power lies not with their leader, but within their resolve."

"But how?" A soldier loudly asked. "How are we going to succeed when we failed so badly before? Our numbers are far less now, so many have been lost to his army."

"This fight will only be a small part of the conflict. The real fight will be between him and I. Defeating him will end it all, I'm sure of it," Nikalas explained.

"How can you be so sure?" The soldier retorted. Emlin emerged from the palace steps. She was dressed in a white gown and donned a crown on her head, an attire she would've normally detested, but in this case, the people needed it.

"We need to trust him. He's got us this far. One city at a time he has freed us, given us back the means to fight. I am your queen, a queen I hope you trust. And if you trust me, I'm telling you, we must follow Nikalas."

Her voice carried weight, she had a way about her that hadn't ever been there before. As Nikalas watched her, the way her eyes studied the crowd, the way her hands moved, the different elevations in her tone, he knew she was now, a true queen.

Once the speeches had ended and the plans had been laid out, the Vanguards began to trot out of the courtyard, many of them returning to the barracks, while some went to their homes. Her words had succeeded, a new feeling had overtaken the soldiers. They wanted revenge, they wanted to end the darkness and eliminate the threat of magic once and for all. Nikalas watched with satisfaction as the soldiers strolled away, many of them whispering words of excitement.

"You did well Emlin," he said with a smile. "I'm sorry about your father by the way."

He turned to her, looking her sternly in the eyes.

"I don't want you to kill him Nikalas," she firmly whispered.

"I'll do my best," he sighed. "But you know, if we do manage to separate him from the rings, he can't stay here. He'll have to leave Furlasia. The only ending the people will accept is his death."

"I can get him out of Furlasia," Kunklestick added. "I know a place where he can live out the rest of his days. But

Emlin, you need to understand, it may not work. We might not be able to strip him of his powers. If we can't, then he'll have to be destroyed."

"Just do your best," Emlin replied. She looked at the three wizards, offering each of them a serious expression.

Kunklestick silently nodded, with that, Emlin turned around, heading up the stairs into Nasleigh Keep. As she vanished from their eye line, the wizards all looked at each other and shrugged dismissively.

Chapter 38

The air reeked of death. The sky was filled with red clouds and the sun seemed content hiding behind them. The Maratan crashed into the waves, offering a taste of seasickness to anyone that was susceptible. Morlay was in the distance, but there was something off about it. There were no smoke rising, no loud whines of steam, and no clicking of metals.

"It looks different," Articus remarked, his eyes studying the skyline with concern.

"Perhaps we are too late," Penny replied. She shuddered as a breeze brought the rancid scent of decay with it.

"What is that smell?" She asked.

"That my friends, is the smell of rotting meat," Dorrin announced. He stopped at the top of the stairs and placed his hands on his hips.

"It's the smell of war."

Penny looked at Articus and Sillimon with a growing nervousness about what they were going to find. As the Maratan crashed against another wave, Methalda found herself running to the side railing, throwing up the salted fish they had consumed the night before. Her head hang over the railings as her hands gripped them with all the strength she could find.

"You ok?" Sillimon asked.

"Do I look ok?" Methalda yelled.

"You've looked worse," Sillimon replied. Penny shot him a stern look before she punched him in the shoulder with a surprisingly strong jab.

"The city is filled with death. Gravi's will has been done. By now, she will have fought Undr. We can only hope he was victorious," Jinn explained as she floated up the stairs.

They were close now, less than a couple miles from shoreline, as the sight of the city grew larger, so too did their fears. Uncertainty awaited them, but their escapades in Adrasia gave them all a bit of hope. They had been victorious, The Boss had handed the jewel over despite winning the match, and once Idrix inserted the jewel into the hilt of the Arc Blade, it began to glow. A warm blue light that was bright enough to illuminate even the darkest of nights. Hope was on the tip of their tongues, courage was in their back pocket and fear was tucked securely out of sight.

The Maratan let out a loud hiss as the wheels below began to emerge, once they hit the shoreline, the tires began to spin quickly. Loose rocks and sand slowed their progress, but only for a moment. With a quick jerk, the wheels gained traction and the Maratan was on land once again. They hurried past the rear seaport and headed towards the main streets. The odor was stronger now, dead bodies littered the streets and smoke in the distance made them pause.

"This is awful," Penny whispered. Onwards they pressed, heading closer to the smoke, which brought them seemingly to the city center. There, in the center of it all was a large pile of bodies that were being burned by the Tin Men. Standing idly by was King Linuk and next to him a couple guards and of course, Dimitri.

"Looks like we won," Sillimon remarked. The Maratan began to slow down, and moments later came to a full stop.

"Why are we stopping?" Articus questioned.

"Because we need to find out where she went," Idrix explained as she hobbled up the steep stairs. Her breathing was heavy and her hands were trembling, but she had a youthful glow that none of them had seen before. On her hip, she wore the Arc Blade whose glow had been diminished by the sheath, but if one paid close attention, you could just make out a hint of blue by the top of the hilt. She was dressed in armor now, as if she planned on fighting the battle herself. It was a thin, mesh type metal that was colored red and gold. On the chest were two intersecting birds, their feet pressed against each other's and their wings expanded.

"Whoa," Dorrin remarked as he looked her up and down. Idrix paused at the top of the stairs and looked over the ledge, towards the smoke and the king. With a determined step, she approached the railing and firmly gripped her hands against the metal.

"Where is the High Mother?" She called out. The soldiers turned towards her, lifting their Beacons up and aiming.

"High Mother?" Linuk whispered to Dimitri.

"What do you want her for?" Dimitri called out.

"Many years ago she committed a terrible crime. She destroyed the hard-working kingdom of Solarian. I intend to get justice for her crimes," Idrix loudly replied.

"Who are you?" Linuk questioned.

"My name is Idrix, and I am the princess of Solarian."

Linuk furrowed his brow, as he tried to look towards Dimitri.

"She's not here," he replied. "She's left, taking two innocents hostage. A Terrian named Vicham left a couple weeks ago to track her down. He hasn't returned yet."

"The Terrian is likely dead," Jinn whispered to Idrix. She nodded in agreement, keeping her gaze firmly aimed at the young king.

"Which way did he go?" She questioned.

Dimitri looked at Linuk, and sighed deeply. *Is there no escape from this?* He thought to himself.

"He traveled north. Towards Rangmar," Dimitri replied.

Idrix nodded and quickly turned around, vanishing from sight just as fast as she had arrived.

"How do you plan to fight her?" Linuk called out. "She's not a mortal."

The Maratan's engines began to roar, and suddenly, they were moving forward, leaving Linuk with his unanswered question. As they traveled down the streets, they continued to observe what looked to have been a fairly interesting battle. The occupation had ended, but yet, people were still hesitant about returning to their normal lives. Staying inside with their heads down was still the preferred option. And really, with the unpredictable climate, who could really blame them?

Without waiting for any kind of permission or assistance, the Maratan plowed through the city gates, leaving behind two very confused Tin Men. They attempted to yell, but their words were lost in the roar of the engines.

Next, was the forest of Roo. It was quite dense, not exactly the ideal location for such a large vehicle, but that seemed of little concern to Idrix. As the forest path began to narrow and the trees started to become a bother, a large beam of light emerged from the front of the Maratan. It stuck the trees, knocking them down instantly, and with that, they kept moving.

"What the heck is that?" Sillimon questioned.

"You've seen Beacons, right?" Dorrin asked.

"Yea. Do you mean..."

"Yup," Dorrin inserted. "That's a mega Beacon."

"Where do The Decoyers get all this technology?" Articus questioned.

Dorrin looked towards Jinn and offered her a subtle nod. She returned the gesture, and moved closer towards them.

"My people were the most advanced civilization in Furlasia for a long time," Jinn explained.

"So the Kajj gave you guys this technology?" Methalda asked.

"Idrix's mission is honest and true. My people were more than happy to assist The Decoyers in any way we could," Jinn replied.

Another beam of light filled the air, its light was so bright, it left one seeing blips of color.

"I'd love to meet your people," Penny said with a smile.

"The Kajj are extremely private. They only allow outsiders to enter their domain once every twenty years," Jinn rebutted.

"How long has it been since Idrix met them?" Sillimon asked.

A sudden bump in the road ended the small talk. It caused everyone on deck to fall, all except for Jinn, who opted to hover instead. The Maratan had stopped moving, it looked like it was stuck. The screeching sound of spinning tires in the distance seemed a suitable indicator for this theory.

"Sorry!" Adam called out from below. Articus grunted and slowly climbed to his feet, offering Methalda and Penny a hand.

"I'm fine," Sillimon laughed. "Don't worry about me."

Penny turned around and offered a hand. He smiled at the gesture and gratefully accepted it. With everyone now back on their feet, the sound of arguments below grabbed their attention.

"I only looked down for a moment," Adam explained.

"Sounds like a good time to stay up here," Dajreem remarked.

"Everyone get out. We need to get this thing unstuck," Idrix demanded. Dorrin and Dajreem turned towards each other, shrugging and letting out a sigh.

"You go first," Dorrin insisted.

"No way, mate. I'm not walking by Idrix when she's cranky and carrying that crazy sword," Dajreem retorted.

"Move," Methalda huffed, pushing past them and heading towards the stairs.

Darjreen and Dorrin turned to Articus, both of them shooting him a look of bewilderment. He gave them no reply, instead, he moved forward, following Methalda down the steps.

As they stepped outside the Maratan, it became instantly clear what the problem was. They were indeed lodged against something, but it wasn't at all what they expected. Methalda and Articus looked under the tires and shuddered at the sight. There, lying underneath the tires was a large pile of ghouls. They had been crushed, but their bodies still provided resistance for the tires. As if the heinous sight of rotted corpses wasn't enough to set their teeth on edge, the rear tires had apparently sunken into a pool of murky, red mud.

"Who did this?" Methalda asked loudly.

Articus continued to study the surroundings, shaking his head as he observed the sights.

"It seems deliberate, doesn't it?" She pondered.

Articus looked at her with dread as his mind contemplated the possibilities of her words being true. His eyes scanned the forest line. There were no signs of a threat, no whispers or rustling in the leaves. It was just the familiar sound of the birds singing amongst each other. He drew a deep breath, letting his senses grab hold of all the sensations he could.

"What is it?" Jinn asked, hovering gracefully towards them.

"Bodies," Articus replied. "Lots of them."

Jinn floated down, bringing herself face to face with the gruesome sight, but still managing to avoid touching the ground. Articus watched her with admiration and maybe a tad bit of jealousy. She was like an apparition; Here but not here. Able to do things only spirits were thought to do. And yet, here was this living, breathing woman, who could float at will.

"We must hurry," Jinn declared. She lifted herself back upright, hovered through the Maratan and brought herself down towards the corpses. Fading halfway into the ground, she lifted her hand, and gently touched the pile of corpses. The effect of her touch was instantaneous, the pile of ghouls faded to dust.

"Uhh," Articus stammered in dismay.

"You will never know all the abilities of the Kajj," Jinn calmly said as she floated back towards them. Without another word, she floated back up the stairs and into the

Maratan. Moments later, Adam hit the accelerator, and after some seconds of resistance, the Maratan jumped forward and out of the mud.

Articus looked at Methalda and shrugged, together they made their way back on board. Idrix stood in the hall looking agitated like never before. Her hands were on her hips and there was a stern look of determination in her eyes. Articus paused to look at her for a moment before heading down towards the crew quarters. Methalda followed his lead, pausing for a brief moment to take in a bit of Idrix's sour mood, before going on her way swiftly.

"What's her deal?" Methalda asked as they stepped into the crowded dining area. Sitting around the table, was Dorrin, Adam, Penny and Sillimon.

"She's waited her whole life to kill Gravi. Now that she has the weapon necessary, that goal is within reach. She doesn't want to waste any time," Adam explained.

"I wonder what she'll do with herself if she actually manages to kill Gravi," Sillimon inserted.

"Probably die," Dorrin said with a grin. Penny looked at him with disgust, then moved a little closer to Sillimon.

"She's old. That's what old people without a purpose do," Dorrin explained defensively.

"You know Dorrin," Sillimon paused. "If you weren't so blunt and strange, you might actually find yourself a woman."

All except Dorrin began to laugh, and that's when he stood up, holding up his index finger with a smug grin.

"The joke's on you. I'm not interested in women," he declared.

Adam looked at him aghast and jumped to his feet as well.

"Wait a minute," he halted. "Do you mean to tell me….that you're…."

Dorrin nodded with a proud smile, then quickly sat back down. Adam — on the other hand — remained standing, looking at his friend with a strange expression. Suddenly, he could hold his composure no more.

"It all makes sense," he laughed. He sloppily plopped down, his laughter sounding so infectious that the others couldn't help but join in.

"No wonder The Boss wasn't taking to you," Adam laughed.

The giggles continued for a few more minutes as the group pictured the doomed attempt at providing allure. Since Dorrin had joined The Decoyers, he had always projected a confidence with women. Now—it seemed—that was nothing but a ruse.

"So that's why she returned so soon," Methalda summarized. Dorrin nodded with a cheerful smile and winked awkwardly at Articus. He replied with an obstinate smile, then pushed his chair back.

"I'm going to go check on Dajreem," he said. And with that, he turned around and exited the room.

The forest had begun to give way, leaving the ruins of Rangmar visible. However, despite the furious quality of the petrified city, it was hardly as attention stealing as the tower of light glowing in the far distance.

"That's the place," Idrix said with a nod. "That's where we have to go."

"Doesn't this seem a bit risky?" Dajreem questioned. "We don't know what we are getting into. Plus we are not warriors."

Idrix looked at him sternly.

"This fight isn't yours. You need not worry about participating," she replied.

"But you're not a warrior either. Plus you're no youngster," he added.

She shook her head and turned around, making her way back to the stairs.

"It's not wise to speak to her like that," Jinn whispered. She looked down the stairs as Idrix vanished from sight.

"But you must agree with me. I mean what's the actual plan here?" Dajreem questioned.

"She won't be alone," Jinn responded.

Dajreem looked at her with confusion as the Maratan cleared the forest and entered the sandy plains of Rangmar. The air was chilly now since the sun had already set, leaving nothing but cold air in its wake.

"What do you mean she won't be alone? Who else is going to be crazy enough to fight a goddess with her?"

Jinn looked out towards a distant cloud of dust that was traveling a few hundred yards away. It was difficult to make anything out at this distance, but it appeared to be some kind of device that was plowing through the sands. She bowed her head in its direction and smiled briefly.

"What in the name of Undr is that?" Methalda questioned. All eyes turned, focusing on the distant cloud of sand and then looked towards Jinn.

"Is that?" Dajreem paused. "Are those Kajj?"

Jinn nodded *yes*, then turned towards the stairs. She gradually faded from sight, leaving the others standing around, scratching their heads as they tried to search for answers.

Chapter 39

There was a familiar bite in the air as Nikalas stepped outside Nasleigh Keep and looked up at the morning sky. There was still a light layer of mist that had yet to give way, offering his skin a bit of moisture, as he lingered in its chilly effects. He took a deep breath, taking notice of the lack of pleasant aromas he had once known the city for. Sighing with disappointment, he moved across the bridge and paused. The streets below looked bleak. The few citizens that wandered about looked as if they were weighed down with worry and fear. Despite getting rid of Agarvodis' shadow, the city still seemed very much under his effect.

"I've got to help these people," he whispered to himself. His first step down was slow, guilt and remorse filling him like a cracked tea cup. As he reached the bottom step, the townspeople began to bow, some even going so far as to get onto the blood-stained ground to show their respect.

"It's him," one of the townspeople whispered.

"The savior," called out another. Before he knew it, the streets had begun to fill, dozens of grateful citizens all pouring out of their homes, hoping to catch a glimpse. It was surreal, they looked at him like a god, and for a moment, he felt like one.

"Thank you," said an elderly woman. He stopped to look at the sad woman. Her eyes looked tired and her skin was rather loose, but despite all that had happened, she still looked hopeful.

"I'm just trying to help," Nikalas replied.

"You saved my sons. You brought them home to me," she explained. With a wide smile, she threw her arms around him, squeezing him firmly.

"Can I hug him mommy?"

The voice came from a child who stood idly at the far side of the crowd.

Nikalas looked at the child and gave him a thumbs-up. Suddenly, the child jumped with excitement, grabbing his mom's arm and pointing.

"Did you see that?" The young boy asked.

Nikalas smiled, then turned around, carefully making his way through the gathered crowd. *Let's give them a treat*, he thought to himself. He leapt into the air, prompting his wings to quickly emerge from the back of his robe. The crowd gasped as he soared in an upwards, twirling motion. His fluid, angelic-like quality was tantazling, even for those bearing loss and reeling from pain. All were mesmerized and motivated by what he represented. The true message which everyone needed — hope. All was not lost, and he was here to prove it. A wave of applause erupted through the crowd, bringing him a rush of satisfaction.

Once the excitement had begun to settle, he looked towards the barracks and quickly brought himself down among the crops. A few of the present soldiers nodded respectfully before returning to their work. It was anyone's guess why they still worked as farmers. They didn't need to, but Nikalas wasn't about to waste time trying to steer them away from providing for the city.

"Nikalas," Sabasio called out. He came, dressed in his uniform with a Beacon tossed on his back. As he came to a stop, he bowed, then returned to his position.

"Are we going to be ready?" Nikalas questioned. He looked around the filed towards the soldiers and noticed many of them didn't have Beacons.

"I believe the men will be ready to march by tomorrow," Sabasio replied.

"Why are there so few Beacons?" Nikalas asked.

"Agavordis took most of them," Sabasio sighed.

Nikalas took another look around; of the few hundred soldiers he saw, it seemed less than half of them had a Beacon.

Most were armed with traditional sword and shield. A form of weaponry he had serious doubts about.

"Do they know how to use those?" He inquired.

Sabasio laughed and approached a nearby sword carrying soldier.

"Show me what you can do, son," Sabasio ordered. The soldier nodded, and withdrew his blade. He quickly began to swing it back and forth, swinging at nothing but air, but with impressive speed nonetheless.

"We may have given them Beacons, but we always made sure they knew how to use the old weapons," Sabasio explained.

Nikalas looked at the young soldier and gave a foreign salute. The soldier looked at him with confusion, and then returned to his practices.

"We need to leave first thing in the morning," Nikalas explained. "This isn't negotiable. The men must be ready to fight by sundown tonight."

"They will be," Sabasio replied. Nikalas studied him for a moment, taking in as much as he could remember. He had seen him before, but only briefly. The last time he left, Thadeus Thundt was the general, but the war had seen an end to that.

"Very well," Nikalas whispered. He bowed briefly, then leapt into the air, letting his wings take him high in the sky.

"That's gonna get annoying boy," Nikalas whispered. Fawn quickly neighed as he dropped down next to him, flapping his wings enthusiastically.

"Yea," Nikalas halted. "I knew you were there. You're not as quiet as you think you are buddy." Fawn looked at him before taking off towards the sunrise.

"You wanna race huh?" Nikalas called out. His wings fluttered with more speed than ever before. He wasn't sure exactly how he was doing it, but he pressed on just the same. With his eyes locked ahead and tears forming at the corners, he rocketed forward. There was definitely something impressive about the speed he was able to summon, however, it was little match for Fawn. Displaying almost zero effort, Fawn propelled into the distance, sealing the deal on his victory in grandiose style.

"You win!" Nikalas called out. Fawn neighed once more, then disappeared into the clouds.

As he arrived back at Nasleigh Keep, he was greeted by the sight of his two mentors. They stood frozen, watching him with optimism as he carefully glided down towards them.

"What?" He asked, suddenly feeling y a tad insecure.

"Are the Vanguards going to be ready?" Didorumpus questioned.

"General Sabasio assured me they would be," he responded. He looked at them curiously, there was something strange about the way they were looking at him, but he couldn't put his finger on it.

"What?" He repeated. The two brothers shared a brief glimpse, then looked at him with awkward smirks.

"We saw the crowd down there," Kunklestick explained. There was sincerity in his eyes, something rarely glimpsed, but well worth the wait. Nikalas looked towards the ground with red cheeks.

"You're an idol to them Nikalas. You're giving them hope and a reason to fight," Kunklestick added.

"In times of death and despair, hope can be a powerful weapon," Didorumpus added.

"So what do I do with it?" Nikalas asked.

Kunklestick handed his staff to Didorumpus, then slowly meandered towards him. Nikalas moved back, unsure what to make of the strange expression masking his mentor's face. The elderly wizard opened his arms wide, and with a sloppy smile, embraced him in a hug.

"Thanks teach," Nikalas stammered. He lifted his arms, briefly patted his mentor and then brought his arms up, hoping to push him off.

"I'm proud of you Nikalas," Kunklestick murmured. The strange show of emotion lasted only a second or two. As Kunklestick pulled back, Nikalas took a deep breath, offering a smile as best he could, then took yet another step back.

The sun emerged from behind a cloud, bringing with it a radiant glow and some warmth. But an odor came with this warmth, and it was so foul that it threatened to bring tears to one's eyes. Nikalas looked around, then peered over the drawbridge at the sapphire blue liquid that flowed around the front of the castle. The sun beat down upon the Ricter, warming it up and allowing the fumes to manifest a bit stronger than without the effect of the sun.

"Let's move inside," Nikalas suggested. He brought his hand to his face, wiping some tears away.

"Excellent idea," Didorumpus replied. "As it turns out, I believe the staff has prepared a breakfast for us. Best not to let it go to waste."

The three of them nodded in agreement, and then proceeded through the doors. Once the sting of the acid-scented air left his nostrils, Nikalas wiped his forehead and eyes. Their journey to the dining hall was met with many spectators. Staff from all parts of the palace made their way towards them, nodding with appreciation as each of them walked by. Didorumpus tried his best to maintain a straight and professional composure, but the strangeness was hard to ignore. He, chuckled, but only for a moment.

They entered the dining room and were greeted by a feast of eggs, meats, sweet breads, and cheese. Kunklestick swiftly dashed towards the sweet breads, picking one up and hastily taking a bite.

"You and your sweet bread," Didorumpus remarked.

"Don't judge me for taking small bits of comfort wherever I can," Kunklestick replied with a full mouth.

Didorumpus looked at Nikalas and gestured for him to take a seat. He bowed in appreciation, then took the seat at the head of the table. As he pushed in his chair, he noticed Kunklestick looking at him with envy.

"What?" Nikalas demanded.

"I wanted that seat," his mentor replied bashfully.

"Well, it's too late. I'm already sitting here. Besides," he paused, looking at Didorumpus with satisfaction.

"I'm the savior remember?"

With that, he continued filling his plate, grabbing as many meats, eggs, and cheeses that he could. His crystal goblet was quickly filled with chilled red wine by an eager maid, as he took a sip, the sensation to his palate was most vindicating.

"Nikalas," Kunklestick said as he took a seat. "You've never been in a war. But Dido and I have. You may have power that he and I do not, but nevertheless, you must stick by our sides. This won't be like training because there will be no mercy to be found. Everything that moves out there will want to kill you."

"I know Kunklestick. I was the one who led the rescues remember? I know how to handle myself," Nikalas retorted.

"You do, you seem quite capable indeed. But your skills against dark magic have yet to be tested. Septus is quite powerful, I assure you. Even with your newfound skills, he is still a grave threat," Kunklestick explained.

"What my brother is trying to say is, don't attack Septus on your own," Didorumpus inserted. "We will need to use teamwork."

As the maids and servants began to clear the table, the three wizards stood and dismissed themselves. As they headed towards the foyer, they were greeted with bows and nods from yet another group of lined up, grateful individuals. Each wizard offered a similar gesture in return and continued on their way.

"What are you doing here?" Kunklestick called out. Standing in the middle of the foyer, was General Sabasio. He looked distressed, and his hands shook as he held a rolled-up parchment of paper towards the elder wizard. Kunklestick worriedly grabbed the document and quickly unrolled it.

"What is it?" Nikalas questioned. Kunklestick whispered the text to himself, then looked up at the general.

"When did you receive this?" He investigated.

"It only just arrived, sir," Sabasio responded.

Kunklestick nodded and gestured for the general to leave.

"Sir," Sabasio said with a bow. With that, he turned around and made his way back through the entrance. Didorumpus quickly snatched the parchment from his brother's hand, giving it a quick read.

"What's going on?" Nikalas demanded.

"It's from a hidden settlement of Delopar hiding in the ruins of Rangmar," Kunklestick replied. "It seems there were massive tremors recently."

"Tremors?" Nikalas questioned.

"Yes," Kunklestick replied.

"Well, what caused them? Quakes?"

Kunklestick glanced at Didorumpus and shook his head with concern.

"Gods," he replied.

Chapter 40

Vicham sat with his hands tied and leaned up against a pillar, as he looked at Gravi. She was back to normal size now; her fight with her brother had been undeniably hasty. Her years of preparation had paid off, it seemed. Next to him sat Wexel, who was even more restrained than he was. Her legs and arms were bound. If there was one thing to be said of Delopars, it's that they are quite cunning and hard to restrain. She sat with a twisted expression and a vengeful stare. Her eyes were intently narrowed on Gravi who was standing above the remains of Undr.

"You know, he always acted like he was the most powerful amongst us," Gravi explained. She reached down and lifted his arm. As she did, her arm returned to its natural state of pure energy. A sudden glow emerged, and before long, the energy in her arm began to pulsate.

"You can't deny the power of patience," she added. As she continued to absorb the energy, her eyes widened with excitement.

"So much power," she whispered.

"What did you actually accomplish?" Vicham asked aloud. Gravi turned towards him with a wide smile.

"Dominance," she replied. As the last of the energy was absorbed, Undr's body vanished, leaving nothing but a faint outline. She shuddered with excitement, then slowly approached her captives.

"Where I come from, this planet is nothing more than the size of a marble. Your whole galaxy is nothing more than a display, a toy for us to play with."

She stopped in front of Vicham with a confident smile.

"Killing you would be so simple. I need only touch you, and you'd be quickly reduced to nothing but dust. The same goes with your planet and your galaxy. You are all nothing but ants to me."

"So you need to hurt others to feel powerful?" Wexel questioned. Gravi looked at her with piercing eyes.

"Hey I get it," Wexel added. "I love killing. Makes you feel alive. But you're not really playing at our level are you?"

"Why would I?" Gravi questioned. "I make the game. I make the rules. I don't need to even acknowledge your level."

She turned around and began to head towards the center pool of misty red liquid.

"Everything about you is so insignificant that I can hardly comprehend any part of your species' logic."

She slowly climbed her way up the steps and came to a stop above the pool.

"Your protector is dead. The only one who had a chance of saving this pathetic place is gone, beaten by the very thing that gave him strength. Belief. Belief in right and wrong. Belief in justice and rules. We are gods. There are no rules."

She stepped into the pool, prompting her human form to vanish, revealing the mass of energy she truly was.

"So all this stuff with Septus, it was just part of some petty revenge?" Vicham questioned.

"Septus? You still don't get it, do you? Septus is an ant, just like you. He's a useful ant, but an ant nonetheless."

"So what do you plan to do with us?" Wexel asked. "I don't like being kept in suspense."

"Death will come to you all," Gravi replied. She floated out of the energy pool and began to reform her familiar appearance.

"I have my full powers back now. I will eradicate this galaxy, just like I tried to do all those years ago.

"Well that's disappointing," Wexel remarked. "You're going to give up your power over Furlasia so quickly?"

Gravi smirked as she knelt down in front of the young Delopar, grabbing her chin with a firm grip.

"You can't play mind games with me," she whispered. "I can't be manipulated into forgetting my goal."

Wexel sneered and shook her head free of the elderly woman's rough grip. Gravi stood back up, chuckling as she looked at the Delopar.

"My brother was very creative to have come up with such an interesting species. The Delopar truly are awe inspiring. Of that, even I can't deny."

She nodded towards some nearby slaves and motioned at them to approach her captives. As the mute slaves approached, Vicham began to squirm, trying his best to pry his hands free. The restraints were tight, far too tight. Gravi gleamed with satisfaction as he finally gave up his attempts.

"Take them to the pool," she ordered. Wexel's eyes widened and suddenly, she too began to relentlessly squirm. Vicham was first. In their typical mindless fashion, the slave reached down, breaking the restraints and lifting Vicham in a swift, effortless move.

"No!" Vicham called out. "Don't do this."

The slave continued towards the pool when suddenly, there was a loud crash. It came from the tower entrance by the sounds of it. Gravi looked towards the direction of the slaves, and then shed her humanoid appearance.

"Continue," she ordered, before speeding from the room in a flash of light.

The slave continued forward, ignoring Vicham's persistent pleas and kicks.

"What in the name of Undr is happening here?" A voice suddenly bellowed. The slave stopped, turning towards the side of the room and noticing there were a couple intruders standing with blades that seemed to be made of energy.

"Put him down, freak," Adam demanded. He lifted his sword in a threatening gesture, and looked at Dajreem.

"We can handle this, right?" he whispered.

The slave dropped Vicham to the ground, then began to approach them slowly.

"Is that thing naked?" Dajreem questioned. He too, lifted his blade, then looked at the two captives. Vicham jumped to his feet, and with a vengeful glare, charged towards the slave nearest to Wexel.

"Fuit!" Wexel called out as the slave crashed into the pillar that restrained her. Vicham stood satisfied, as the pillar cracked and the slave fell to the floor.

"Don't be so excited," Wexel remarked. "It's not dead. Get me out of these things."

In the distance, Adam and Dajreem had begun their attack on the slaves. The mysterious swords proved to be very useful. As tough as the creatures were, even they couldn't withstand searing hot metal.

"Watch out!" Adam warned. Dajreem turned, and with a gasp, quickly lifted his blade. The creature's arm crashed into it, severing it like a knife cutting through a melon.

"Thanks," Dajreem nodded. He turned forward, and suddenly, his enthusiastic mood seemed to fizzle out. Approaching them were close to a dozen more, all red-skinned and naked with blank eyes.

"Idrix better know what she's doing," he remarked. He looked onwards, towards the sight of doom, then planted his feet firmly in a fighting stance.

"Don't kill them!" Vicham called out.

"Umm. What?!" Adam questioned.

"They've been brainwashed," Vicham explained. Adam looked at the slaves and narrowed his eyes. There was a familiar shape to them, that much couldn't be denied. But besides the shape, they didn't look humanoid at all. They were sexless, and had unusual strength. Even if they used to be normal people of Furlasia, was there any reversing what had been done to them?

"Alright then," Dajreem replied. He reached for his belt and withdrew a small stone. With a quick toss, the stone landed in front of the creatures, and in an instant, multiple beams of jagged electricity emerged, grabbing the slaves and holding them still. Vicham watched with shock as the stone did its best to hold its captives.

"What is that thing?" He asked. Adam and Dajreem ran towards them, grabbing their arms and pulling them towards the entrance.

"Now's not a good time," Dajreem retorted.

The night sky was filled with lightning and clouds. Rain had begun to pour, splashing against the stone floor of the tower and making for a tricky exit. Adam looked at the large hole in the roof and shook his head.

"We are dealing with some next level nonsense," he huffed. The four of them kept moving, ignoring any slaves that approached them. After a couple winding turns, they emerged outside the tower. Beams of energy were flying all around in the distance and about two dozen Kajj floated in the air. Gravi stood in the middle of it all. Her size was huge, like it had been before, and in her hands, she held energy.

"What in the what?" Adam remarked.

Vicham looked at Wexel, and then stepped in front of their two rescuers.

"Who are you people?" Vicham questioned.

"We are The Decoyers. And we're here to kill that thing," Dajreem replied with a trembling index finger.

"You can't kill her," Vicham argued. "She's a goddess. The only thing that can kill her is the Arc Blade."

Dajreem smiled and pointed at a small faint light in the distance, which stood still on the battlefield.

"Is that it?" Vicham questioned. Dajreem silently nodded *yes*.

"So you're the thieves," Vicham said with realization.

"We had good reasons for taking it," Adam defended.

In the background, Gravi swiped her hands left to right, trying to hit the Kajj, but try as she might, each of her attacks simply passed through them.

"What are you things?" Gravi roared. The Kajj soldiers flew towards her in an organized swarm, and all at once, crashed into her chest. She stumbled back, shaking the ground with a massive earthquake.

"We've got company," Adam informed. The others turned around just in time to see a dozen more slaves marching through the doorway.

"Are you sure we can't kill them?" Dajreem questioned.

"Yes I'm sure. There are two people here who are friends. I can't risk them being killed," Vicham replied.

"Well, that's just great," Adam sneered. He lifted his hand, bringing it up and slapping one of the slaves across the face. The impact had no effect. Without uttering a single word, or letting out a slight whimper, the slave brought his hand out, grabbing Adam by the throat.

"No," Dajreem exclaimed. He reached to his belt and withdrew the sword.

"I'm sorry buddy. But these things have to die," Dajreem exclaimed. He lifted the blade, as he did, the energy returned back into the metal. With a quick motion, he swung, cutting one of the slaves in half with ease.

"I told you no," Vicham bellowed. He nodded at Wexel, as though she read his mind, she grabbed Dajreem, tossing him back, and causing him to drop the sword and fall into the dirt. She snickered with satisfaction, and jumped into the air, landing on the slave who held Adam.

Her claws dug into the back of the slave's neck, deep enough to puncture the muscles, but not enough to cause serious damage. Once her claws found the precise spot, the slave released its grip, dropping Adam to the ground with a firm thud.

Vicham quickly dropped down, grabbing Adam, and pulled him away from the chaos. Wexel leapt into the air, in typical Delopar fashion, and landed next to them.

"Thanks," Adam coughed.

As Dajreem caught his breath, he reached for the sword, climbing to his feet and looking at them angrily.

"I'm trying to save our lives," he declared with a firm stare.

Behind them, the roar of the Maratan could be heard. Vicham leaned, looking past Dajreem and towards the strange vehicle. He stared with wonderment as the Maratan traversed the hectic battlefield, firing beams at Gravi all the while.

"What is that thing?" He questioned.

"That's the Maratan," Adam replied.

"Where did you guys get such strange technology?" Vicham questioned.

"From them," Adam said, pointing at the floating entities that surrounded Gravi. At that moment, the Kajj formed a chain, and began sending black energy soaring towards her.

"Fools," Gravi hollered. She lifted her hand and pushed it into the energy, but as she did, the skin on her hand began to melt away, leaving nothing but the energy beneath the surface.

"What?" She stammered with surprise. The dark energy connected with hers, as it did, it began to change the color of her energy to black. Gravi screeched as the sensation started traveling through her body, burning away her disguise and leaving her as nothing but a large mass of energy.

"I've got nothing," Adam whispered. Suddenly, the Maratan began to head towards them, jumping over rocks and knocking down the small scattered trees like they were nothing but toys on a track.

"Guys," Wexel called out. Vicham and the others turned, taking notice of the incoming slaves.

The loud clamor of the Maratan continued to get louder, and just as Wexel hunched down, preparing to pounce, the vehicle skidded and crashed into the slaves. They tumbled like dominos, falling perfectly into one another until the whole mob was looking up towards the sky.

"Anyone need a ride?" Dorrin asked as he threw the door open.

"What took you so long?" Dajreem demanded while he and the others headed towards the entrance. They quickly filed their way inside, and once the last of them was in, Dorrin slammed the door shut, pounding his fist against the metal. The tires began to screech, the engine roared and the Maratan was once again, headed into battle.

"Who's driving?" Adam investigated.

"Ehh..Articus wanted to try it out," Dorrin replied with a grin. The vehicle continued to crawl along the rocky surface, making for a bumpy, yet appreciated ride. Vicham and Wexel followed Dorrin back to the crew quarters, studying the strange interior with curiosity. It was like nothing they had ever seen, but then again, so was everything else they had recently observed.

Adam turned to the right, and pulled open a jarringly squeaky door. Sitting inside was, Methalda, Penny and Sillimon and Kadeen. Each of them was dressed for combat. From their armor, down to their strange swords, they looked primed for a fight.

"We picked up some strays," Adam said with a gesture. Penny stood with excitement and held out her hand.

"I'm Penny. This is my fiancé, Sillimon and this bundle of joy is Methalda."

Methalda shot her a miffed stare, then returned her focus back down to her sword. She appeared to be whispering, praying perhaps, but whatever it was, she seemed quite focused.

"I'm Vicham of Terria and this is Wexel," he replied. A sudden bump shook the quarters, nearly causing him to fall over, but luckily, a cabinet to his near left prevented it.

"Get ready guys!" Dorrin called out. Vicham looked at Adam draped with concern.

"Ready for what?" he questioned.

"Part two," Dajreem replied. At that moment, a loud hum filled the clunky metal hall, and seconds later, the whole vehicle convulsed.

"Easy there," Penny warned as she reached out and grabbed Vicham who smiled appreciatively at her.

"What's part two?" He queried.

"The Kajj are gonna bring her down, giving Idrix a small window to puncture the source of her power. We're going to use these to help keep her down just a bit longer," Adam explained. He set a couple stones on the table. They were the very same stones he had seen him use not long ago. Their nature and mechanics still mystified him, but now was not the time for questions. With a glimmer of excitement, he reached below the table and grabbed a basket. It was cumbersome and weighty, but alas, he was able to lift it onto the table. It was filled with the stones. The others quickly began to reach inside, pulling out as many as they could carry.

"What do you think?" Vicham asked, looking at Wexel.

"This isn't what we bargained for. It's ok if you want to sit it out."

Wexel scoffed at the offer, then reached for the stones.

"Delopars don't sit things out," she huffed.

Vicham nodded with amusement, then he too, reached for the stones.

Chapter 41

It would've been completely understandable if one were to think that the war was over by looking at the streets of Morlay. It was high noon, and the city was back to its normal bustling self. What dread still remained, stayed hidden, as whispers on their breath, but not spoken aloud. The townsfolks did their best to keep the city moving. The shops had been opened, the schools were in session, even the chapels had returned to their normal demeanor.

As Emlin looked out the palace windows towards the city, she couldn't help but feel a bit nauseous. The appearance of normalcy almost seemed offensive. After all, the life of Septus was still very much in the balance. In her heart she knew, the chances of the wizards taking him down without killing him were slim, but that didn't stop her from hoping. Since the wizards had left, she had plenty of time to think. She knew what she hoped, and that was for Septus to have been under the influence of Drachen this whole time. If that were the case, then exile would be possible. But if he truly was the ugly person he seemed to be, then she would kill him herself.

Footsteps in the distance echoed against the walls, reminding her that today was the day. The day that the Tin Men would march once again. They would head to Cristol, home of the Arnouts and the first city to fall. It would be here that a new army will be built, here, where Furlasia would find hope.

"None of them seem ready," Dimitri informed. She turned, looking at the king's right-hand helper and shrugged.

"It doesn't matter. We are leaving today. I've spoken to Nikalas and the Vanguards have already begun their march," she replied. Dimitri stopped in front of her, folding his hands together and resting them near his groin. He was dressed rather strange today. He wore a long red robe with golden lace and brown fur on its neckline.

"How is Linuk?" She questioned.

"Some days he wakes up thinking he still has his eyesight. When that happens, the days are rough," Dimitri replied.

"Today is one of those days."

Emlin shook her head and looked towards the distant hall that led to the royal chambers.

"I should go visit him before I leave," she muttered. Her eyes continued to survey the foyer, taking notice of the cheerful servants and the eager guards. Everyone seemed to be acting as though everything was back to normal. But it wasn't.

"Is there something wrong with the water here?" She questioned.

"The servants all look happy, as though they forgot we are still at war."

Dimitri looked around, nodding as he noticed the cheerful poise many seemed to have. He studied the room, but where Emlin felt concern, he felt relief. He grinningly turned to her, offering a rarely seen smile. It was odd; even for him it felt odd. Joy wasn't a feeling he was used to. Envy, hate, sadness. Now those were feelings he had become good friends with. They welcomed him when the other feelings wouldn't.

"You too?" She sighed. "Furlasia is still in danger. You do understand that, right?"

"Of course, I do. They all do. But what's the point in walking around scared all the time? If you walk around petrified, then he wins," Dimitri replied. "We have to live. We have to live for those that died."

As she pursed her lips, she tried to consider his point. By all accounts it should've made sense, and perhaps it did. Perhaps, *she* was the one being foolish, weighed down by her own mental complications. Her thoughts of late seemed more puzzling than calculus, filled with unknowns and offering no finite solutions.

"Perhaps you're right," she moaned.

"What's really going on here Emlin? You look as though you are shouldering the entire war on your shoulders."

Her thoughts ran to Septus, to their past, and the unknown future. There was very little that could be done for someone who had split their mind as much as hers. Equal parts hate and love. Equal parts fear and courage. She felt a duty to Furlasia, to her father, to Inca and Broli, but no matter how hard she tried, she couldn't shake her other duty. Saving Septus.

"I don't want him to die," she exhaled. "We were friends. We were in love. He was nothing but genuine and filled with compassion. There was never any sign of darkness, never any sign of evil."

Dimitri took a few steps forward, put his arm around her and turned her around.

"Let me show you something," he replied.

With his arm firmly holding onto her, he slowly led them towards the exit. As they stepped outside, he began to lead her down the pathway, and then, came to a stop. Carefully removing his arm, he looked to her with a smile, then knelt down to the ground.

"Do you see this plant?"

He pointed at a small flower with an hourglass shape; the pedals, however, were closed tightly shut.

"What is that?" Emlin questioned.

"This is a honium. It's a unique flower that only grows here in Morlay. This flower isn't like other flowers. It doesn't care about happiness and sunshine. No, this flower only blooms during storms," he explained. As Emlin knelt down, she reached to touch it. Its green exterior felt silky, despite having a furry texture.

"You see," he paused. "Even in the gloomiest of times, there can still be beauty."

She smiled, looking at him with a bit of surprise.

"You keep impressing me, Dimitri," she grinned.

"That's a relief, because I'm generally unimpressive," he retorted. She let out a soft laugh, then rose to her feet.

"I know you're worried about Septus. But there are things that are beyond our control. Is he under some dark influence? We don't know. But what we do know is that he's killed a lot of people and he has to answer for that."

She opened her mouth preparing to protest, but he quickly lifted his hand.

"If he's possessed, then it's no different than being ill. We do what we can to treat them, but sometimes, despite our best intentions, it doesn't work out."

He stared at her firmly in the eye and grabbed her hands, lifting them up towards him.

"Terria needs you. You're fierce, you're wise, and you're honest. You need to prepare yourself for the possibility that Septus might not come out of this alive."

"For Terria," he whispered. With that, he turned around and headed back to the palace, leaving her alone with her thoughts. Who was this strange man? Who is Dimitri Slauters? *He surely must be wise, how else could he have been on the king's council?* As she watched him disappear, her mind drifted to Vicham. Her mentor, and guide in all things Terria. He had been an important role model all her life, and yet, ever since she became queen, she felt like she hardly knew him.

"Where are you?" She whispered to herself.

General Sinclair was a fierce man, if there was any humor in him, it was well-hidden. Morlay hadn't been up and running for long, but he had already gotten his favorite hair grease. As he watched the Tin Men get into their suits, he couldn't help but crack a smile. Leadership suited him, working under Killigan had always been a drag, but now, he was his own man.

The steam armor was a hassle to put on. It was a two-man job at many points, and as such, they had been split into pairs in order to get it done. The general demeanor seemed overall pretty optimistic. Despite having seen horrible things, the soldiers seemed well ready for another round. *This time, we'll win*, he thought to himself. *We have to.*

He nodded approvingly before turning around and making his way towards the main streets. He strolled past steam suits, swords, and Beacons, making notes of all he noticed. This was going to be the final push. Everything had to be in order. A sudden discomfort on his arm caused him to look down.

"Yuck," he proclaimed. He swatted at a small green winged slug that had attached to his elbow. The impact smashed it, causing a small amount of white blood to ooze from its body. He cringed as he flicked the remains onto the ground.

"You make that face for a bug but not for those who you slay in combat?" Emlin questioned with a smile. He bowed as he observed the Terrian queen approaching. She was donning a golden armor, and on her back, she carried her familiar bow and quiver.

"Should I start sneering with every kill I make?" He asked sternly. She stopped in front of him and folded her arms.

"No. But you should be aware that you are taking a life," she replied.

"Duly noted."

In the background, the Tin Men had begun to form lines, each of them standing tall and awaiting the next command. From the back of the barracks emerged a few steam carts, large ones, each capable of holding at least fifty men. They roared, blowing vulgar black smoke high into the air. Emlin watched with awe as the massive vehicles began to pour into the courtyard.

"We need those in Terria," she remarked with a smile.

"I'm sure that can be arranged," Sinclair replied. He turned around, walking with his legs spread wide towards the men. With each step he took, his armor rubbed against itself, causing scraping and bangs. It was far less majestic than

Terrian armor, but what really mattered was its protection, and from what she had seen, it was quite significant.

"I'm not gonna bother with a speech," he called out as he came to a stop in front of the assembled army.

"I'm not gonna bother reminding you all what is at stake here. We already know because we've seen it firsthand. All I'm going to say is, I'm holding each and every one of you personally responsible for killing no less than twenty Akordans."

He looked at Emlin, wondering if she had anything to add.

"Alright. Get on your assigned transports and let's get moving."

It took about an hour for the soldiers to all be loaded with their armor and weapons. The ride was cramped. With the shortage of transports, the occupancy had to be stretched a bit. It wouldn't be a pleasant ride, but the alternative was riding on horseback, which would take far longer.

At the front of the convoy sat a smaller cart that was enclosed on all sides and had a small window. It was here the general and Emlin would ride, separate from the men, and first onto the field. Emlin pulled the door open and looked inside. It was nothing glamorous. In fact, the horse drawn carriages of Terria were far more satisfactory to look at. Inside were two small metal benches that were bolted to the floor. The interior stank of burned coal, and from the position of the engine, it would likely be a noisy ride.

"Queen Emlin," Linuk called out. He was being led by a reluctant-looking Dimitri.

"Your highness," Emlin greeted. Her hand reached out, grabbing his and giving it a firm shake.

"I wish I could join you," Linuk sighed. "But I'm afraid I'd only serve to be a burden."

Emlin smiled, looking towards Dimitri and offering a wink.

"There are other ways you can help. Morlay needs to be beefed up a bit. Get the citizens back into their homes and keep the streets clear until you hear word from me or the wizards. If we fail, Septus will likely send troops here again. Make sure you're prepared," she explained.

Linuk nodded in understanding, and turned to Dimitri.

"I want you to take this," he said. Dimitri extended his arm and held out a carved diamond bow with a golden string.

Her eyes grew as she glanced at the meticulously-crafted weapon. It was like nothing she had ever seen.

"Where did you get this?" She asked.

"It was my great grandfather's," Linuk replied. "It was gifted to him by King Yorn for his service to the city."

"I can't take this."

She shook her head and held it back towards Dimitri.

"Yes, you can. That bow is one of the most powerful bows ever crafted and it's been sitting around collecting dust. I'm ordering that you use it," Linuk grinned.

"You can't order me. I'm a queen," she chuckled.

"Your highness," Sinclair said with a throat clear. "We must make haste."

She turned towards him, nodding with compliance and then slung the bow over her left shoulder. With a bow now hanging over both shoulders, she leaned in and gave Linuk a firm hug.

"The Blind King," she whispered. "He sure does see a lot, doesn't he?"

She pulled back and headed towards the cart. Once she was safely seated, Sinclair slammed the door shut, and gave a thump to the driver above.

"Be safe Emlin," Linuk called out. The air grew loud and filled with smoke as the convoy began to make its way forward. Emlin sat, looking towards the floor solemnly, her mind making a journey to one place, while her body was on a journey to another.

Chapter 42

Didorumpus and Kunklestick rode on the back of their steeds, following Nikalas as he led them and the Vanguards through Tordenth forest. The bugs were on the hunt today, attacking not just the soldiers, and wizards, but also the animals. Progress was slow, heavy rain from the day before had left the ground soft and full of puddles, some of them big enough to stop the horses. Still, they pushed forward, the end game was in sight, and the stakes were higher than ever. But this time around, there was a little more optimism among the men. Seeing Nikalas at the front of the line seemed an inspiration to all those that were initially reluctant about donning their armor once again.

The trees were filled with Okies and birds, even the occasional phoenix could be seen, but once spotted, they quickly took off. They rode in silence, thinking of nothing but the coming war, and the doom they faced. It wouldn't be an easy fight. Cristol was well-fortified, and with the Arnouts held as hostages and some of them even being turned, they faced an uphill battle. Despite all the reasons that this could go so very wrong, Nikalas felt a surprising amount of optimism. Morlay had been liberated, and as such, the Tin Men would be riding towards battle. And even though it was a shot in the dark, a messenger bird had been sent to Rangmar, bringing with it a call for an alliance and a promise to help rebuild the once great city. Kunklestick had expressed serious doubts about the generally hostile and standoffish felines joining the cause, but Nikalas felt different.

It had been a few hours since the convoy had departed Terria, and with the constant delays of flooded areas and downed trees, time had quickly flown by. Nikalas looked up towards the sky and sighed as he noticed a pink hue beginning to take form in the sky. It covered the horizon like an elegant, overpriced painting, whilst also signaling the end of their travels for the day.

"How far are we?" Nikalas questioned as he looked at Kunklestick.

Kunklestick looked around the forest, then reached into his robe and pulled out a small folded parchment from its innermost pocket. He released his hands, tightened his thighs and opened it.

"Hmm," he muttered. "I'd say we have good eight hours left."

"Jesus," Nikalas sighed. "Well, I want to get there by midday tomorrow. So I say we keep moving."

"It won't be long before the beasts of the night are lurking about," Didorumpus warned.

"Luckily for them, they have us," Nikalas retorted.

"We'll go a couple more hours, Nikalas, but then we need to make camp," Kunklestick replied.

He nodded in agreement and returned his focus forward.

Darkness had come, and the men and horses had grown restless. Concern spread among the convoy as the bugs infestation continued to grow. Kunklestick had summoned an energy barrier around as much of the convoy as he could, which made a great deal of difference, but unfortunately, it didn't cover enough of them. Too many soldiers were being devoured by bugs and mosquitos that were large enough to bring death to even certain smaller birds.

"Whoa," Nikalas called out to Wildfire as he pulled on her reins. The loyal horse happily came to a stop, as his mentors followed suit, the decision to make camp quickly became apparent. The convoy had stopped and the men had begun to dismount and unpack some of their gear.

"This spot seems sufficient," Kunklestick informed, pointing to a clearing in between a swarm of trees. He reached into his robe and pulled out his wand, and with a quick swipe, a large tent appeared, complete with torches and spots to secure the horses.

"What fricken spell is that?" Nikalas exclaimed. "Do you have any idea how useful that would've been to me when I went looking for the wall?"

Kunklestick secured Leddi to a post and then looked at Didorumpus with a grin.

"Getting to The Wall of Truth was part of your learning. Teaching you a spell that made survival even easier wouldn't have helped you learn to evolve."

"Alin asylus," he added with a smile.

Nikalas nodded in agreement and the three of them made their way inside the surprisingly elegant shelter. The ground inside was covered with a fine rug, there were three separate cots, and a table with food on it. As he stepped inside, Nikalas looked around with wonder and a bit of jealousy, then smiled at Didorumpus.

"This is pretty neat," he remarked.

"My brother always had a flair for decorating," Didorumpus jokingly replied. He looked towards his brother, then approached the cot that was directly in the middle of the room. In the distance, they could hear the arguments and the whispers of the Vanguards as they struggled to assemble their shelters.

"Why don't we help them?" Nikalas questioned.

"What good is it going to do to always bail people out of their challenging situations? If the Vanguards are to be an effective team, learning to assemble a camp seems like a good place to start."

Damnit, Nikalas thought. *He always manages to make sense.*

The night was harsh. In spite of being inside the warm shelter, the sounds of the creatures outside and the humidity of the forest made for difficult sleeping conditions. As Nikalas lay, looking up towards the darkness of the ceiling, he found himself fixating on the harsh breaths from his mentor. It wasn't like sleep apnea, his breaths weren't loud and pronounced, but there were many periods where it seemed like he had stopped breathing altogether. Nikalas wondered about his own nocturnal soundtrack; was it a soft, melodic breeze, or a rough storm?

Whenever he did manage to sleep from his oh-so-selfish mind, he was plagued with nightmares, dark visions of violence, pain, and suffering. Since his time in Cap Ti Mor, he couldn't help but let his mind wander to his parents, or at least his mother and the man he knew as his father. The elder gnome had warned that they were in danger and that they were, in fact, in Furlasia. He hadn't put much effort into locating them since returning, stopping Agavordis was a far more pressing matter, but he couldn't deny his mind's desire to see them again. And then there was the message from Vicham that warned of an ensuing conflict in the north. Whispers of gigantic beings filled his mind. Of all the oddities he had seen in Furlasia, this still seemed like a hard story to swallow.

He tossed and turned for what felt like another hour, then, by some bit of mercy, he fell asleep. The darkness of the night faded, giving way to a familiar room filled with light and not much else. In the middle of the pearl cavern, he stood, looking around and patiently awaiting the return of Lord Aldon.

"Nikalas," a stern voice whispered from behind. He happily turned and was greeted by a welcome sight, his father.

"Father," he smiled. "We are headed to war. I have released the enslaved Tin Men and Vanguards, and now we come for you."

Aldon looked at him with a prideful smirk, and then turned towards a white doorway that had no handle. As he stepped in front of it, the door flung open, revealing a dark night sky waiting on the other side.

"Come on," he instructed. He quickly stepped inside, disappearing as soon as his feet crossed the entrance. Nikalas shrugged and followed. His first step inside was greeted with a startling drop. He fell against a mound of sand, coughing as it splashed at his face. He wiped his face, spitting out the bits of sand that had managed to infiltrate his mouth, then suddenly, a loud thunderous clamor filled the air. He jumped to his feet, standing just in front of him with his back facing him, was Aldon. He stood calmly watching as two large beings fought each other in the dark night.

"What the hell?" Nikalas exclaimed. "So it's true?"

Aldon turned to him with a silent nod.

"Well this seems more important than dealing with Septus. At least he's not three hundred feet tall."

The large beings began to send energy towards each other, the beams crashing into the sand and sending a tremor along the ground.

"So that's him? That's Undr?" Nikalas asked.

"Yes. Undr and Gravi, the woman known in Furlasia as High Mother," Aldon turned towards him with a serious expression.

"Son, I know this seems serious. But this is not where your mind should be focusing," Aldon lectured.

"How can you say that? I mean just look!"

Nikalas pointed towards the battle of the titans with wide eyes and trembling hands.

"Even I can't handle something like this."

Gravi threw a right hook at Undr, knocking him to the ground. As he fell, the ground began to crack. She laughed maniacally and aimed her hands towards the sky, then moments later, a dozen beams of light came crashing down onto him.

"No!" Nikalas roared. "We've got to help him." He jumped into the air and began to flap his wings. He charged towards Gravi, letting himself become encompassed in energy, but then, suddenly, he found himself standing behind Aldon once again.

Gravi sent down her arm at Undr, letting it become pure energy and then pushed it into his chest with a forceful shove. His scream of pain was thunderous; the energy from within him began to flicker, sending out small sparks here and there.

"You were a fool to come here," Gravi laughed. "You fell for my spectacularly predictable trap like the imbecile I knew you were."

"You don't have to do this sister," Undr pleaded. "I can let you back in. Just please, end this."

"I don't need you brother. You've already let me in," she laughed. Her arm continued to glow, and then she quickly withdrew it from his chest.

"We have to stop her!" Nikalas called out. Aldon turned and pressed his hands to Nikalas' head.

"Don't you see son? There is no helping him," Aldon explained. "This has already happened."

As Nikalas looked forward, the chaos had ended, leaving nothing but a darkened sky stained by a blood red moon.

"The fight is over. Undr has been defeated. Gravi has what she needs to destroy everything," Aldon informed. Nikalas looked at him with hopelessness, then dropped onto the floor, placing his hands on his head with frustration.

"I can't win. No matter what, I'm always one step behind. I'm still getting beat by the bullies," he whispered.

"You still have a destiny son; an important destiny that is tied to the fate of Furlasia."

Nikalas lifted his head and shot him a look of skepticism.

"An elderly woman known as Idrix has a weapon that is crucial in ending Gravi, but she can't do it alone. She needs not just your help, but Septus' as well."

"What?!" Nikalas jumped up and stormed towards him.

"What the hell do you mean? I have to team up with the crazy guy who's been killing people left and right. I have spent months training to defeat him and now you're telling me I have to join him?"

"You have spent months training to fulfil your destiny, which is to save Furlasia. At no point was it decreed that you would have to kill Septus. On the contrary, you need him in order to fulfill your destiny."

The darkened sky of Sanlorus began to slowly fade away. Like a screensaver, it gave way, returning them back to the stark, white room they had previously been. Nikalas looked around and groaned at the realization that he was still in his dream.

"Septus will fight you," Aldon added. "He will try to destroy you, not because he doesn't like you, but because he doesn't understand you, and most importantly, doesn't understand himself."

Aldon summoned two chairs across from one another and beckoned Nikalas to have a seat. He did so with aggravation, letting himself sink into the remarkably uncomfortable metallic chair. One would think that in his own dreams, the furniture would at least be comfortable, but it seemed life wasn't in line with his thoughts no matter where he went.

"There is a power to the rings on his fingers, but there is also a burden. The power comes with baggage. Mental baggage. Your friend Emlin is right, he is under the influence of Drachen Crane, not entirely, some of his actions no doubt are his own, but he also hears the whispers of his father."

Nikalas looked dumbfounded as he was given the unfortunate news about him once again judging a situation wrongly.

"So," he paused. "I need to get the rings from him."
Aldon shook his head *no*.

"You will need Septus to have his power to fight Gravi," Aldon responded.

"But how do I stop him then?"

"There is a good man hidden underneath the confusion. Find him and you'll find your ally," Aldon replied. He looked up towards the ceiling, towards a bright light that had begun to form, sending glaring yellow rays down on them.

"It's time to wake up," he declared. The light continued to fill the room, becoming blindingly bright.

"Nikalas," Kunklestick called out. He stood with his robe partially opened and his staff in his hand. There was a faint red mark at the top of his chest that was mostly hidden by his curly, grey chest hair. Still, Nikalas couldn't help but focus on it, he had been around the unusual wizard for some time now and hadn't noticed the peculiar blemish. As he rubbed his eyes, he shrugged it off and climbed to his feet.

"Let's get going," he declared.

Once the three of them had finished gathering their things and their thoughts, they stepped outside and were greeted by the patient faces of the Vanguards and General Sabasio. Kunklestick turned around, waving his staff at the tent, and just as quickly as it had emerged, it vanished. Whispers erupted in the crowd, talks of miracles and wonders quietly filling the air. Nikalas cracked a coy grin as he looked at his mentor, then turned his focus to Wildfire.

"We should be at the city gates by midday," Kunklestick informed the convoy. With that, he and Didorumpus climbed atop their horses, giving them a light kick.

The journey went as promised. As the sun reached the peak of the sky, the shape of distant towers and the sparkle of elegant glass traveled to their eyes. The city looked dismal, the surrounding plains, which were normally covered with vibrant green grass, were instead covered in brown and yellow shells of a once beautiful landscape. The spider-cracked wall of glass looked as though it were ready to crumble. The large, wooden door that sealed the city was blackened by flames, leaving it its place a tall mess of delicate splinters. And then there were the ghouls, hundreds — nay —

thousands of them. Whatever was going on inside those walls, Agavordis seemed determined to keep it a secret.

Nikalas gave the reins of Wildfire a firm tug, beckoning the convoy to a halt. He then reached for his side and pulled out a small kaleidoscope. He squinted as he studied the harsh plains, taking notice of the ghouls and even a few giants. All things considered, it didn't really seem like too much to handle. He brought the scope down to his lap and smiled with satisfaction. In the distance, coming from their leftmost side, were the whines and hisses of the Tin army and their steam-powered convoy.

"Right on time," Didorumpus remarked. "Emlin did well to keep them on track."

Nikalas nodded in agreement, shooting his mentor a smile. Kunklestick nodded at the gesture and started coughing steadily.

"Dry air is no good for these old lungs it seems," he said as he patted his chest firmly.

At that moment, the skies of Cristol began to darken, as Nikalas looked onwards, he noticed the shadow over the plains was caused not by clouds, but by Arnouts. Hundreds of Arnouts, all floating in the sky, each of them holding swords in their hands.

"It seems he's bought himself a divine army," Didorumpus observed. Nikalas continued to study the new development, as a chilly breeze blew by, he gulped.

"Let's not act surprised," he said in shaky manner. A crash of thunder filled the sky, and with it, a barrage of lightning, each bolt landing just in front of the ghoulish army, bringing with it a wall of flames.

"He's here," Nikalas whispered.

Chapter 43

Emlin pushed the door to the cart open, and stepped outside. The air was brisk and the sky concealed by dark clouds. The plains had been set ablaze, making for a difficult trek forward, but that wouldn't stop her. General Sinclair stepped out behind her, looking up at the Arnouts and nodding his head as though to accept the challenge.

"Look there," Emlin pointed. "The Vanguards."

Sinclair followed her finger and sure enough, he could just make out the petite shapes of the Vanguard army. Emlin exhaled a sigh of relief at the realization that Nikalas and the other wizards were nearby. Despite the grim conditions, knowing they were here somehow brought comfort. The distant neigh of horses signaled the arrival of the remaining Tin Men. The army was now complete. Once each horse and cart came to a stop, the soldiers began to dismount, grabbing the swords and Beacons as they stepped onto the crusty grass.

"So what now?" Emlin questioned.

"We need to get the armies together and then you and I should discuss the plans with the wizards," Sinclair replied.

"Ok then," Emlin nodded. She turned and returned to the cart, opening the door hesitantly. She lifted her leg, preparing to climb inside when something caught her attention. A faint tremble beneath her feet. She turned around, looking at the General with confusion.

"Do you feel that?" She inquired. He scanned around, shaking his head with uncertainty, but then suddenly, he too felt the strange vibrations.

"What is that?" He whispered. He looked every which way as he frantically searched for the source, and just as he was about to give up, his eyes caught something in the distance.

"Well I'll be," he whispered. Emlin squinted with concern, then ran around the cart, holding her hand to her forehead as she attempted to block out the sun. As the bright flashes faded from her sight, she finally saw what had caused the tremor. There, approaching from the north like a herd of elephants, were the Delopars.

"By Undr," she whispered with joy. Excitedly, she turned and returned to the far side of the cart.

"It's the Delopar!" She exclaimed. "Do you think they're here to help?"

"Well," Sinclair paused and spit into the dirt. "I doubt they're just out for a stroll.

The stomping feet of the approaching Delopars continued to shake the ground with each passing moment. Eventually the battalion was close enough that facial features could be seen, as Emlin studied their expressions, she couldn't help but dwell on Inca. She was the first Delopar she had ever met, and since her death she hadn't seen another. Now here she was, faced with an entire army of them. Their arrival did come as a bit of a surprise. The Delopar were known to stick to themselves, not wanting to get involved in the affairs of others. Perhaps, the constant slaughter, and freely wandering Akordans finally pushed them over the limit.

The Delopar battalion came to a halt no more than one hundred feet away, as the soldiers took their places, a couple Delopars dressed in primitive metallic armor began to approach.

"Commissaries," Sinclair informed. Emlin shifted her weight, and quietly nodded. Looking towards the Vanguards, she could see three horses heading towards them as well.

"The wizards," she said with a pointed finger.

She excitedly waved at them and stood next to the General.

"Are you the leader of this army?" A tall, grey-furred Delopar asked sternly. His posture was perfect and he was easily the most well-built Delopar Emlin had ever laid eyes on.

"That's correct," Sinclair replied. "I am General Sinclair of the Tin Men and this is Queen Emlin of Terria."

"Terria?" The Delopar asked. "What is she doing all the way here in Morlay?"

Sinclair rolled his eyes and lifted his arm towards the flames in front of Cristol.

"My name is Rothor, and this is Rashik," the Delopar bowed.

The smaller Delopar approached and held out a hand.

"Nice to meet you," Rashik greeted softly. "Don't worry. I don't bite my allies."

Emlin gripped the Delopar's soft paws and gave it a firm squeeze. As she stepped back, Sinclair moved forward to accept the greetings.

"Now that we got that out of the way, let's get down to business," Rashik grinned.

"Oh look. More help," she suddenly exclaimed. Emlin turned and smiled as the wizards came to a stop.

"The Delopar?" Nikalas questioned with a smirk. He looked at Kunklestick and then jumped from his horse.

"So you're the savior I keep hearing about," Rashik observed. Nikalas nodded confidently then held out his hand.

"The name's Nikalas, and these two unfortunate chums are Kunklestick and his brother, Didorumpus."

"Oh, these two need no introductions," Rashik retorted. She eagerly held out her hand to the two approaching wizards.

"It's an honor to meet the legendary Kunklestick."

Kunklestick happily extended his hand and accepted the gesture.

"See that, Nikalas," he coyly grinned. "I'm legendary."

Nikalas rolled his eyes and approached Emlin, giving her a slight nudge with his elbow as he neared her side. She smiled and hugged him. It had been so long since he last felt her warm embrace, and even though her eyes still seemed set on Septus, it was a welcome hug indeed.

"On to business," Sinclair promptly declared. Rashik exchanged glances with the wizards, then nodded in agreement.

It hardly took ten minutes to come up with a battle plan. They would approach the city in order of skill set. The flames around Cristol would be an arduous challenge for anyone not well-armored, so it would be the Tin Men first, followed by the Delopar, and then the Vanguards. It took some back and forth banter for Kunklestick to accept the Vanguards falling behind, but once Rashik started laying out her plans for infiltrating the city, he finally agreed. With everyone now on the same page, Kunklestick, Didorumpus, Nikalas and Emlin rode ahead. There were only three horses, but Nikalas had offered her a ride and she happily accepted.

The ride to Cristol was silent, tense and filled with anxiety. Despite all the war movies and battle scenes Nikalas had seen, it simply couldn't compare to the real thing. As Wildfire slowly carried him forward, he found himself reflecting on all that had happened so far. There was a part of him that was grateful for those bullies in the park — after all — if they hadn't chased him, he wouldn't be here.

He grinned as he thought of it, and for a moment, he felt at ease. He was, after all, the *savior*. He laughed to himself as images of Spider-Man and Jesus crept into his head. Was he truly on the same level as those awesome dudes?

"What is so funny?" Didorumpus questioned. Nikalas shook himself free of his thoughts and looked at him, returning his face to its former serious expression.

"Oh nothing," he replied.

"You can't just burst into laughter on the back of a horse as you head towards an army of dead ghouls, and then say *nothing*," Didorumpus retorted. "It's against the wizarding code."

"He's not lying," Kunklestick chimed in. He looked them both over and then shrugged.

"Ok, fine. I was just thinking about how everyone calls me a savior. It seems pretty stupid to be honest."

"It is pretty stupid," Kunklestick replied. With that, he gave his horse a kick and took off into the distance. Nikalas sat dumbfounded as he watched his mentor ride ahead of the pack.

"Why would he say that?" He stammered.

"You said it first," Didorumpus pointed out, then he also took off.

"Can you believe those two?" Nikalas said, turning his head towards Emlin as best as he could. Suddenly, he started to fidget.

"Here," he said. "Take the reins. I'm gonna catch up with those jerks."

Without waiting for a reply, he jumped off the horse and took off into the air. Emlin startlingly gripped the reins, just in time, narrowly avoiding falling to the ground. As she gained control, she looked to the sky and sighed.

"Savior," she whispered to herself. "We shall see."

Nikalas quickly caught up to his mentors, shooting them each a dissatisfying glare whilst aiming his wings at the city.

"Why did you say that?" Nikalas demanded.

Kunklestick laughed as he kept his eyes ahead.

"Nikalas, you are too easy," he replied. "But yes, it is stupid to call you the savior. That's not how I intended it to be interpreted."

"Well what did you have in mind then?" Nikalas countered.

"I was thinking people could just call you Nikalas."

Nikalas nodded as he pondered on his mentor's response.

"Labels like savior feed vanity. If you are doing this for pride and attention, then you are no savior."

Nikalas smiled and turned around. With a quick flap of his wings, he pushed forward, and landed softly onto the ground moments later. The wall of flames blocked his sight of the ghouls, but that didn't matter. Their moaning and growls made them stand out like a sore thumb.

"Let's take care of this," he whispered. Reaching into his robe, he withdrew his wand, pulling it to the form of a staff and holding it straight out in front of him.

"Aguafenta," he whispered. At that moment, a large wave erupted from the ground, splashing into the flames and leaving nothing but a faint steam that floated gently towards the sky.

"Whoa," Kunklestick called to Leddi. The horses came to a sudden stop, prompting their hooves to dig into the muddy mess and nearly causing them to topple.

"I'm not a savior," Nikalas grinningly said as he turned towards them.

Suddenly, Didorumpus lifted his finger and pointed. "Nikalas look out!"

Standing in the middle of the steam, among the ghouls, was Agavordis; his face was shrouded by a hood, but his identity was clear as day. As he slowly looked up, the red light in his eyes was revealed, suddenly, his hands began to glow green.

"You are quite right. You are no savior," Agavordis remarked.

"Septus," Nikalas paused. "It doesn't have to be this way. We can help you. You can set things right."

As Emlin finally arrived, Agavordis looked at her. Suddenly, the red in his eyes faded away.

"This is who you've chosen?" Agavordis pointed. "Someone who will put you in harm's way?"

"I came here on my own," Emlin replied. She jumped down from her horse and landed in the mud.

"I came here to help end this corruption you've brought to our home."

Agavordis rolled his eyes as he studied her form. The bow on her back caught his eyes. For a moment, he was taken back to their times in the forest, when he had first taught her how to use one.

"You're not well Septus. Your father is controlling you. Give us the rings and we can help you break free," she pleaded.

Agavordis looked at her with a furrowed brow and slowly his eyes began to return to red.

"You're not getting my rings," he declared. As he clenched his jaw, he lifted his hand, summoning his energy and aiming it towards her.

"Stupid girl. Soon you will realize that you were better off at my side."

With that, he fired a beam straight at her. Kunklestick quickly summoned a shield, bringing it in front of her and blocking the beam.

"That wasn't cool," Nikalas remarked. He lifted his staff, summoning a ball of energy at its end and then swung it towards Agavordis. It crashed into a darkened cloud, sending a ripple across it but not much else. Agavordis began to laugh and move backwards, towards the ghouls. Their eyes now glowed red and their focus was locked intently on them.

"You should've stayed in Cap Ti Mor," Agavordis laughed. Suddenly, he floated into the air, looking at them with his haunting, red eyes.

"You take care of him," Didorumpus ordered. "We can handle these things."

Nikalas looked at him with worry, and opened his mouth to protest.

"Now, son!" Kunklestick sternly commanded.

Nikalas sighed and looked at Emlin.

"Be careful," he advised. With a wink and a smile, he leapt into the air, letting his wings carry him towards Agavordis.

"You've learned a new trick," Agavordis observed. "Well, I've learned some too."

Suddenly, the ground began to tremble. As Nikalas looked with concern, something most troubling caught his eyes; a massive army of Akordans, all with glowing eyes. He turned to Agavordis, disgusted and perplexed.

"You killed all those Akordans?" He pushed his staff into a wand and tucked it into his robe.

"They serve so much better when their minds belong to me."

"You're psychotic!" Nikalas roared. He dashed forward, sending an energy jab towards Agavordis. The impact crashed through the darkened globe, hitting him square in the chest with searing pain.

"Ahh!" Agavordis screeched. In an instant, he vanished, leaving nothing but a bit of black smoke.

"Coward," Nikalas whispered to himself. He looked down to the ground and saw that the armies had started fighting. Beams of energy filled the field, both from the wizards and from the Beacons. He had just thought to descend and assist, when a firm grip suddenly grabbed his neck, wrapping around him like a mighty python.

"You don't get to save Furlasia," Agavordis sneered. His grip grew tighter, prompting the world around to blur. Nikalas coughed as the bony arm against his throat continued to tighten.

"They are a vile people and they all deserve to perish!"

"And you're such a peach?" Nikalas questioned with a roar. He brought his hands up, gripping Agavordis' arm and began to pull.

"Is that the best you can do?" Agavordis laughed, tightening his grip.

"Nah," Nikalas choked. "I'm just trying not to kill you."

Pushing his cautious desire aside, he summoned his internal energy. An intense warmth began to appear as a blue glow spread its way across his skin. Agavordis eagerly released his grip, floating back with concern.

"It's time to end this Septus," Nikalas demanded. He turned towards him with a menacing stare as blue flames began to surround him.

"I'll never stop!" Agavordis yelled. He lifted his hands rapidly and began to fire at Nikalas. His green energy met with the blue flames surrounding Nikalas, creating a remarkable display.

"Destroy him," the voice from the sky suddenly roared. "He's trying to take Emlin from you."

Agavordis peered at Nikalas with contempt, and brought his hands up, summoning a sword.

"You'll never take her," Agavordis declared. He lurched forward, bringing the sword down against the ball of flames.

The two of them began to trade back and forth hits, soaring in the air like two comets shooting through space. From the ground, they appeared as nothing but faint colors dancing in the skies.

Their power was remarkable; both had skills the other didn't know about. For every beam that one of them fired, another would summon a shield. For every punch that one of them threw, another would offer a block. They were equals, incapable of topping one another while fighting in the traditional sense. This wasn't going to be a contest of power — no — it was going to be a contest of will.

Things seemed perilous on the ground. The Tin Men, Vanguards, and Delopars all did their best to remove the ghouls from the equation, but the subjected Arnouts proved to be a strong hindrance. Their skills were not unlike the wizards, and with only two wizards left to fight, they were feeling dreadfully outnumbered.

"Aim for the Arnouts," Sabasio called out to a few nearby soldiers. He wiped a bit of sweat from his forehead and aimed his Beacon upwards.

"Fire!" He cried. Tiny beams of yellow light filled the air, streamlining straight towards the aggressive Arnouts. Those that were hit, fell, those that were not, returned the favor with a similar attack.

Didorumpus and Kunklestick stood in the middle of a crowd of Akordans, aiming their wands and waving them around like crazed, sword wielding ninjas. Their attempts took out many, but with each soldier that was slain, the opposing army grew a bit stronger.

"Cyliamo Sensio," Didorumpus called out. As his staff crashed down to the mud, a wave of energy burst forward, knocking down a handful of ghouls. To his left, he noticed a few Delopar soldiers. They leapt in the air, slicing the throat of a ghoul, then leaping and doing the same to the next. As they employed their acrobatic fighting skills, it became quite apparent, they were a useful ally indeed.

Emlin stood with her back to a Tin Man, aiming her bow into the sky at the Arnouts. As she prepared to release the string, her eyes noticed two faint colors, spinning over the field like two mating flies. *Please stop this,* she wished to herself. In her heart, she wanted nothing more than for Septus to snap out of it. She was sure that it was mental sabotage. The question was, did Nikalas believe her, and did he even care? She released the arrow, but just as it neared its target, it was stopped. Using telepathy, a nearby Arnout turned the point around, sending it swiftly back towards her.

With the speed off a bullet it careened, until it finally crashed into an energized shield. Emlin turned, and nodded gratefully towards Kunklestick.

Chapter 44

Vicham and Wexel quickly jumped out of the Maratan, looking at Idrix and then tossing a few of the enchanted stones to the ground. From each one, a beam of jagged energy emerged, flying towards Gravi and wrapping around her. The others followed suit, and before long Gravi was completely strained by the energy of the stones.

"Now she's cranky," Adam called out. He looked up at the colossal goddess and gulped nervously. Surrounding Gravi in the skies above, were the Kajj. After being called upon by Jinn, they happily joined, bringing their many unique tricks and gadgets.

As Gravi roared, the Kajj soldiers continued to fire at her. Streams of dark mist emerged from their hands, blowing against her body like a leaf-blower on leaves. Her balance began to weaken and her arms began to waver.

"She's gonna fall!" Sillimon called out. Penny and Idrix stood in awe next to him, as they looked up at the unstable behemoth. Sure enough, the force from the Kajj proved enough. Gravi collapsed against the ground with such a strong force that a crack began to form.

"Now!" Jinn hollered. She nodded at Idrix. From the skies above arrived a Grimwort that quickly swooped down and offered Idrix a ride. She climbed aboard as quickly as she could, holding the Arc Blade in her hand all the while.

"Be careful," Jinn advised. Idrix nodded and gave the Grimwort a kick. Into the air they flew, giving her a perfect view of the others as they surrounded Gravi, tossing the energy stones to the ground as quickly as they could. With each new stone, came a new string of energy that added to the hold on the vengeful Goddess.

"You are all fools!" Gravi bellowed. "Insects that don't even realize how close they are to being squashed.

The Grimwort hovered above the contained Gravi, giving Idrix a downward view. In the center of Gravi's form was a distinctive pocket of orange energy.

"That's the spot," Idrix whispered to herself. She slung her right leg to the same side as the left and looked down with a gulp. She donned rubber pants that had been carefully designed to resist the energy Gravi expelled. Today, she would find out if her hard work and designs would truly hold up.

"For Solarian," she whispered. Without another moment's pause, she jumped, aiming the blade down. As she landed, the blade plunged inwards, burning a large hole in the energy mass, prompting a loud cry from Gravi. Idrix kept her eyes trained on the orange cloud within, pushing the blade down as best she could. The heat from the energy continued to increase.

"I will not fail," Idrix yelled. She pushed the blade down a bit harder, bringing the tip even closer to the orange. The longer she stayed atop the energy, however, the warmer it became and within seconds, the rubber pants were starting to melt.

"Ahh!" Idrix screamed. The skin of her legs had begun to blister and burn. As quick as she could, she pulled the blade back, and looked up to the sky.

"Help," she called out. The Grimwort dashed down towards her as quickly as she could, but suddenly, Idrix erupted into flames.

"No!" Jinn roared. She quickly jumped into the air and swooped towards the flaming Idrix. Her arms caught her and quickly carried her towards a distant tree line. Laying her on the ground, Jinn stood above and held out her hands, summoning a bit of dark mist and blowing out the flames. The smoke cleared to reveal a badly burned Idrix. "My friend," Jinn whispered, kneeling at her side. Idrix looked at her with bloodshot eyes and shallow breaths, her hands still gripping the Arc Blade.

Articus and Methalda tossed a couple stones towards Gravi, then charged over towards the wounded Idrix, stopping a few feet shy. Next came Penny, Sillimon, Adam and Dorrin. Each of them came to a halt, forming a line and gripping each other's hands with remorse.

"Is she dead?" Penny tearfully asked. Sillimon put his arm around her shoulder and pulled her close.

"You have to finish it," Idrix moaned.

Jinn mutely nodded and brought her right hand up to her eye, gently wiping away a tear that had begun to form.

Idrix smiled one last smile, then went still.

"Goodbye my friend. In all my years, I've never known a nobler person," Jinn whispered.

"No!" Penny cried out, running towards Idrix as fast as she could. She slid to the ground, gripping her charred hands and prying the Arc Blade free. She tossed it aside and gave the hand a firm squeeze.

"You're not going anywhere," Penny demanded. As the tears continued to pour down her face, Jinn climbed to her feet, turning towards the others and offering a subtle nod. In the distance, Gravi continued to struggle, working her way free of some of the energy ropes that contained her.

Alas, the restraints had been destroyed and she climbed back up. Her familiar appearance returned, hiding the orange energy cloud. Vicham looked at her and gulped as the goliath stood upright, looking at them with vengeful eyes. Looking at Wexel, he nodded at the Maratan, then began to dash towards it.

"Pitiful insects," Gravi taunted. She swiped her hand upwards, summoned a tear in the ground beneath the Maratan and swallowed it in a most unceremonious way.

"Whoa," Wexel exclaimed, stopping next to Vicham and grabbing his shoulder. The ground beneath them continued to shake, sending the crack towards them.

"What a way to go," Wexel grinned. "Fighting a giant goddess."

Vicham turned to her with concerned eyes, then shook his head *no*.

"Come on," he yelled, gripping her hand and giving her a pull. "She's not getting us that easily."

They charged across the fields, dodging rocks, jumping over cracks and pushing their way past any impasse Gravi had to offer. With his eyes locked on The Decoyers, he aimed forward , disregarding what little safety remained. As he reached the huddle, he noticed they were all staring intently at the ground ahead. His eyes quickly found the source of their focus; Idrix, badly burned, and vacant of life. As he studied the remains he sighed. Hopelessness had finally found him. They were in over their heads, that much was obvious.

"Irritating little pests," Gravi yelled, slapping her hands at the surrounding Kajj. No matter how hard she tried, she couldn't land an attack. The mist properties made them impossible to hit.

"Ahh!" Gravi roared. She brought her hands out and began summoning energy. The beams quickly found their targets, taking out the Kajj with ease. As their corpses fell to the ground, Jinn jumped up, looking remorsefully at her falling brethren.

"No," she whispered. Adam looked at her and placed a hand on her shoulder.

"Don't do it lad," he cautioned. "You'll only find the same fate."

"The Arc Blade is here," Articus exclaimed. "Surely we can finish the job."

He knelt down and picked it up. He eyed it with admiration as the blue glow danced across his skin.

"We've come too far to just surrender and accept death." He looked at Gravi, who had begun to march towards them, shaking the ground with each step.

"We can't win this," Jinn retorted. "We must flee if we are to survive."

With that, she looked up to the sky and whistled, summoning the attention of the surrounding Grimworts. There were five in total that came dashing towards the ground. As they landed, everyone quickly began to embark.

"Leaving so soon?" Gravi bellowed. Her hand let out a white streak of energy that crashed into the ground just behind them.

"Now!" Jinn hollared. The Grimworts leapt into the air and began heading south.

"You're not going anywhere," Gravi threatened. Her beams of energy filled the air, narrowly missing each time.

"Her aim isn't impressive, is it?" Dorrin joked. The Grimworts continued moving, heading swiftly towards Furlasia, which, at the moment, did not look friendly. The skyline was filled with dark clouds and dim flashes of light lingered within.

"I said," Gravi yelled. "You're not going anywhere!"

Suddenly her form began to change. What once resembled a person now looked like a beast. A tough-skinned beast with wings, red eyes and long sharp teeth.

"Well she can fly now," Adam pointed out. The others turned to look, instantly displaying looks of horror. The beast was hot on their tail. Her wings were so massive, that each flap sent a hurricane force wind to the ground below.

"We're doomed," Vicham whispered to Wexel. Her eyes studied the otherworldly creature that pursued them through the skies. *He's right*, she thought to herself.

Chapter 45

Nikalas continued to throw attacks at Agavordis, crashing into his energy shield each time. Beneath them, the war continued to rage on. Energy beams soared from the wizards towards the ghouls and Beacons filled the air with whines and hisses. The rotted giants provided the most challenge, taking out soldiers left and right, but as Kunklestick and Didorumpus continued their maneuvers, they were eventually toppled.

Chaos, misery and pain filled the air. What was music to Agavordis' ears, was torture to Nikalas. His forehead was draped in sweat and his hands shook like that of an elderly man. He tried his best to keep his wits about him, bringing a firm jab across Agavordis' chest.

"Ugh," Agavordis yelped as his shield crumbled. Nikalas quickly brought another fist towards him, striking him in the chin and sending a wave of heat through his skin.

"Ahh!" He cried out, gripping Nikalas' arm and sending a beam of his own. Nikalas quickly flipped upwards, dodging the attack apart from the very tip of his left wing. There was a definite sting, but it wasn't as bad as it could've been. Standing behind Agavordis, he threw his arms around him, using all the strength he had.

"You need to stop this," Nikalas pleaded. "You're not well. Your father is influencing you. He's controlling you through the rings."

"You're wrong!" Agavordis screeched. In an instant, he vanished, leaving Nikalas hovering alone in the sky.

"Hmm," he whispered to himself. There was a sudden stillness to the air around him. For a moment, he felt peace and calm. He was alone, high in the skies in the one place no one could hurt him. Up here, there was no grief, no rejection, and no depression. He hovered above the negativity, feeling almost like a god. He looked towards the ground, taking notice of a green streak of energy that decorated the battlefield.

"Septus," he sighed. He darted down towards the field like a fiery comet, keeping his eyes on Agavordis the whole time.

"We've got company," Epard warned. He looked up at Nikalas and nimbly summoned a black hole.

"Shit!" Nikalas bellowed. He crashed into it, vanishing just as fast as he had arrived.

"Good job," Agavordis complimented.

"Open another," he ordered. Epard nodded, and did as requested.

"I'm going after him," Agavordis informed. He enthusiastically jumped inside, vanishing just as Nikalas had done. Epard looked ahead with a grin. He felt rather proud of his young student. In a short amount of time, he had already surpassed the skills of his father. Septus was indeed the ultimate apprentice.

"Epard the wise," Kunklestick blurted out. His spell formed a blue sphere that formed around the dark gnome, trapping him in place.

"It's time to take you for a spin." Holding his staff in front of him, Kunklestick began to rotate it, bringing a centrifugal force to the sphere.

"You wizards are finished!" Epard roared. "Septus is going to finish what his father started and there's nothing you can do to stop it."

"I can do this," Kunklestick retorted. He quickly brought the sphere down to the ground, causing it to shatter. He promptly lifted Epard by the throat and looked him in the eyes.

"What are you gonna do? Kill me?" Epard taunted. "The great Kunklestick! Holy in his ways until he's truly tested."

"I don't have to kill you," Kunklestick replied. "I just need to restrain you."

One firm squeeze later, the gnome dropped to the ground unconscious.

"Now what?" Didorumpus questioned. Kunklestick turned with a grin.

"I think he'd make an excellent maid at the wizard hall," he replied. He gave the gnome a spiteful kick, then turned towards a group of soldiers.

"Soldier," he called out. A Vanguard quickly approached with a firm stance and a proper salute.

"Take this urchin outside the battlefield and restrain him."

"Yes sir," the soldier responded. He quickly bent down, picked up Epard and disappeared into the crowd.

"Where is Nikalas?" Didorumpus queried.

***

Nikalas scanned the area with curiosity. It was mostly dark, the ground felt like gravel and the air was musty. His breathing had only just begun to slow down. As his eyes adjusted to the dark, he noticed he was in a cavern. A familiar cavern with an unmistakable odor and unmissable whispers. He was in the quarry. The very one that once held Didorumpus captive for all those years.

"Hmm," Nikalas gawked. Suddenly, a beam of green light appeared, crashing into the ceiling above him and bringing rocks down around him.

"It is here my father doomed the wizard Didorumpus. And it is here I shall doom you," Agavordis laughed. He lifted both hands, sending more green beams forward.

"I don't think so," Nikalas replied. He lifted his wand, willing the rubble around him to lift, and then sent it soaring towards Agavordis. The beam of green energy crashed into them, turning them into a fine dust, which then continued forward, covering Agavordis and distorting his vision.

"Gripius," Nikalas called out. From the tip of his wand, emerged a fist. It shot forward, grabbing Agavordis and holding him firm.

"Your father is controlling you, Septus. He's infected you like a virus, poisoning your mind and driving Emlin away from you," Nikalas explained. He moved the fist over the pool of dark water, then lowered Agavordis into its depths.

"You've got to break free. For Emlin. For your love," Nikalas called out. He kept Agavordis submerged, counting under his breath as he did. The ground suddenly began to shake, suddenly, he was slammed into the coarse stone wall. His head hit with a thump, his vision muddled and his wand fell to the ground. A pair of red eyes emerged from the water and drifted ominously towards him. "Do not speak her name," Agavordis demanded. He lifted Nikalas to his feet, and then slammed a wall of green energy into him.

"You know nothing of our history. You know nothing of our love."

He summoned the rocks of the wall to liquify, and before long Nikalas was being held in place, unable to move anything besides his arms.

"You're right," Nikalas replied. "I don't. All I know is what she's told me. It's *Emlin* that told me you're not in your right mind. It's *she* who begged me not to kill you."

"As if you could kill me," Agavordis laughed. He slowly meandered to Nikalas and brought his fist across his face.

"Prophecy?" Agavordis sneered. "Kunklestick's failure. That is all you are."

He brought his fist up again, this time striking Nikalas in the gut with a glowing, energized fist.

"Ahh!" Nikalas bellowed.

"You're not well Septus. Emlin believes it, and I do too," Nikalas moaned. He closed his eyes and began to focus. Agavordis laughed, then suddenly, stepped back, grabbing his head in agony.

"No! Get out," he demanded. His legs began to weaken and before long, he dropped to the ground.

"Those are not for you."

"Everything is for me," Nikalas replied. His mind continued to search through the cavernous castle of Septus' mind. If Emlin was right, there would be a prison. A cell that held the real Septus hostage. The castle was insidious. Nightmareish creatures stood at every corner, screeching as he wandered past. They looked quite similar to gargoyles. Their skin — grey, their eyes dark and baggy and their teeth were far rotted.

"No!" Agavordis bellowed. "Get out!"

Nikalas kept his mind focused on his mental travels, paying no mind at all to the protests of Agavordis. As he continued to scan the halls, he came to a door. A strange door that didn't look like any of the others in this malevolent place. Its hinges were rusted, its handle was missing and its wood was burned. Grabbing the hole where the handle should've been, he pulled the door open and grinned. Dungeon. Dozens of cells lined the damp room, providing plenty of places to find the trapped soul.

Agavordis looked at Nikalas. His vision was blurred, his head was throbbing, but he had to try. He lifted his hand, summoning a dozen stone arms from the cavern wall. They obediently reached for Nikalas, but upon touching his shoulders, they began to crumble.

"How?" Agavordis yelled. He reached to his head as the pain began to intensify once again.

Nikalas walked the dim hall, peering into each cell until finally, he found one that was occupied. Sitting in the dark, naked and shaking was Septus. His hair hung down to his midback and his body looked frail.

"Septus," Nikalas whispered. The shadowy figure turned, looking at him with dark circles around his eyes, then slowly climbed to his feet.

"Nikalas?" He asked.

"Yea, it's me. I'm here to get you out of here," Nikalas replied. Septus began to shake his head nervously.

"You can't," he warned. "He'll find you. He'll lock you up in here too."

Nikalas looked around perplexed.

"Who?" He asked.

"My father," Septus replied. "He's very angry. He won't let me out anymore."

Nikalas reached into his pocket and withdrew his wand.

"Step back," he instructed. Septus quickly did as told, and once he was at a safe distance, Nikalas blew the cell door open.

"You shouldn't have done that," Septus warned as he ran through the cell.

"There are a lot of things I shouldn't have done that I did anyways," Nikalas replied.

He turned and looked towards the door he had come through.

"We gotta go, there are serious things taking place out there."

He began to run towards the door with Septus in tow. As they pushed through, he looked around. Everything had changed. The grim halls were now gone and instead he saw a properly lit hall, with wood floors, hanging lights and portraits hung all about.

"I know this place," he whispered. He began to make his way forward, pausing in front of a familiar family photo.

"How does he know this place," Nikalas softly questioned.

"I know all," a stern, ghastly voice called out. Nikalas turned and gulped. Standing behind Septus, was a tall, shadowy figure with familiar red eyes.

"Drachen I take it," Nikalas queried. "I recognize that glow of desperation you carry on you."

Drachen began to chuckle, then quickly raised his palm, striking Nikalas in the chest. The impact sent him careening back and tumbling through a wall like a feeble doll.

"Father, stop," Septus pleaded.

"Silence, boy," Drachen roared. He brought his hand across Septus' face, and pushed him to the floor like a playground bully.

"Your weakness is what led him here."

"No," Nikalas said as he pushed himself up. "His strength is what brought me here."

He pointed his staff forward, and sent a spinning ball of energy heading towards Drachen. His spell was quickly met by another, as the necromancer's spell connected, it changed the orb black.

Drachen laughed manically as the orb crept towards Nikalas. With each passing second of existence, spurts and bubbles of energy emerged, hitting the floors and walls with a sizzle. Soon, flames had begun to climb from the dilapidated floorboards. Nikalas coughed, covering his mouth, as his eyes began to water. Things were starting to look bleak, when a sudden thought came to him. *Wait a minute*, he thought to himself. *None of this is real.* He peered at Drachen and focused. His thoughts were unwavering. Nothing could shake him of his goal. Slowly, the orb began to change blue, and before long, crashed into Drachen. The dark figure shattered into a million pieces and quickly dissolved into the flames.

"Wow," Nikalas sighed, placing his hand to his knees. "He's a pretty crummy man. You don't need him."

Septus slowly rose to his feet, pressing his hand against his cheek as the pain continued to throb.

"He's very convincing," Septus explained. "Once he sinks his teeth in, there's no getting away."

Nikalas looked towards the ground, pointing confidently at the pile of dust.

"Well, now he's a pile of dust."

Septus nodded with appreciation, but then, something caught his eyes. The wall behind Nikalas had begun to liquify, causing the pictures to fall, and in their place, appeared two large eyes.

"Ummm," he shakenly said with a point. He quickly snatched the wand from Nikalas' hand and aimed it forward.

"Can't take the scumbag out of the ginger huh?" Nikalas declared.

"Inginimo," Septus proclaimed. A beam of green energy soared into the melted wall, striking Drachen and causing the whole house to shake.

"No!" Drachen called out. Nikalas turned, feeling suddenly enlightened as he noticed the flame covered wall.

"Oh," he muttered. With the flames now spreading over the whole wall and onto the ceiling, the eyes faded. Drachen was finally eliminated.

"Let's get out of here," Nikalas declared. He turned towards Septus, looking at the wand and then calmly holding out his hand.

"I've done a lot of bad," he whispered. "I killed them."

Nikalas grabbed the wand and took a desperate step forward.

"Yea. You've been an asshole. But now's not the time. We need to get back."

Septus stepped back with tear-filled eyes. Once again, they were back in the dark of the cavern from whence he had brought them. Septus paused as he looked at the grim surroundings.

"I can't let

"I can't let her see me," Septus whispered. "I killed Inca. She hates me."

Nikalas stomped forward and brought his hand firmly across Septus' face.

"You made a huge mess. I'm not sure how much of that was your father and how much was you. But it's time to start redeeming yourself. Emlin still believes in you. Are you gonna show her she was right? Or live out your days known as a monster?"

Septus stood in silence, lifting his hand and looking at the rings. They began to glow, the green hue illuminating his freckled face and exposing his anguish.

"Alright," he sighed. "Let's go."

He looked at their left and tossed a yellow portal. Looking at Nikalas once more, he sighed, and motioned for him to step inside.

"See you on the other side," Nikalas grinned. Lifting his wand, he jumped inside.

"Nikalas," Emlin exclaimed. "Where have you been?"

Laying on the ground in front of her, were dozens of ghouls. Her skin was clammy, her hair was tattered and a cut on her forehead oozed a bit of blood. She looked at him with frustration, and then fired an arrow over his shoulder. A faint thud signaled another demise. Nikalas smirked as he stepped towards her.

"Are you sure you even need my help?" He questioned. She huffed and wiped her forehead. Her eyes met with his, and for the briefest of moments, time stood still. The moment was short lived, however, and suddenly, her eyes widened with concern.

"Nikalas!" She called out.

Standing just to the left of Nikalas was the man she had once loved and learned to fear. He stood with a soft expression and a trembling lip. His eyes, for the first time in so long, looked normal.

"Emlin," Septus whispered.

She looked him over with hesitation, setting her bow slowly to the ground. As she continued to study him, she glanced at Nikalas, who offered her a modest nod of permission. She took the cue and guardedly approached.

"Are you normal now?" She questioned. Septus looked her in the eyes and shook his head with guilt. He glanced around, taking notice of Kunklestick and Didorumpus as they fought off a giant.

"I didn't mean for it to get like this," he explained. "My father, his presence in the rings was more powerful than I could've ever imagined."

He turned to Nikalas and nodded with appreciation.

"Nikalas saved me," Septus explained. "Freed me from the prison my father had made for me."

"Do you still have your powers?" She questioned. He nodded and nervously reached for her cheek.

"Uh ah," she declared as she stepped back. She reached to the ground and lifted her bow. With cold eyes, she drew back the string and took aim at him.

"Shut this down," she demanded. "Shut all of these creatures down."

Septus paused as he considered the notion that she would actually threaten to kill him. It made sense. He had more than earned it, but still, it felt like the ultimate gut punch. Exasperated, he closed his eyes and brought his focus to the surrounding army. A green aura slowly began to envelop him, and within, time seemed to slow. There were so many souls to locate, so many dead that needed to be stopped, it seemed impossible.

"What's taking so long?" Emlin queried. "Shut it down now!"

"I'm trying," Septus replied. "There's a lot of input to sort through. So many creatures."

Nikalas looked at Emlin, then quickly turned around, sending a beam of energy towards the giant. It crashed into the creature's chest, creating a fire and prompting it to collapse to its knees. Quickly, he cancelled it, sending another straight into the giant's head. To his dismay, it was of little effect. With a thunderous moan, the giant stood, looking at Nikalas and expelling a horrific growl.

"Uhh," Nikalas halted. He shot a dumbfounded look to his mentor, then jumped into the air.

"Inginimo," he called out.

"Hurry up," Emlin demanded. Septus gulped. Her persistent words of anger offered far more negatives than positives. The longer he tried to focus, the more pain he discovered, and soon, it felt as though his head were being crushed.

"Ahh!" He cried out.

"Septus?" Emlin questioned. His eyes remained shut and his focus remained unwavering. Through the ultimate migraine, he continued to focus, summoning more and more power from the rings.

"He can't do it," Nikalas muttered as he looked at the twisted face Septus was making. He hurriedly dropped to the ground and marched towards the pain-stricken necromancer. Emlin looked at him with a tearful gaze and nodded.

"I hope this works," he whispered. Lifting his wand, he fired a quick beam of energy into the aura that surrounded Septus. Suddenly, the aura began to spark, sending out violent streaks of energy in every direction. As the spell continued to strengthen, the aura began to spin, slow at first, and then faster and faster.

"Ahh!" Septus yelled. The spinning persisted, creating startling winds, and then suddenly, stopped. Around them, the creatures began to topple. Their skin turned black and soon, there was nothing but ash.

Septus released the spell, falling to the ground with weakened knees.

"Septus," Emlin called out. She hurriedly ran to his side and lifted his head and pressed her lips to his forehead.

"I knew you weren't really a monster," she whispered. At that moment, there were whispers from the crowd, and before long, hundreds of Beacons were aimed at them.

"Step away your highness," Sinclair ordered. He squinted one eye as he took aim, putting Septus right in his crosshairs. Emlin turned towards him, aghast at the threatening display.

"General?"

A loud screech suddenly filled the air, seizing all attention. Flying in the air, and emerging from a patch of dark clouds, was a creature unlike any that had ever been seen.

"By Undr," Emlin whispered. As she studied the situation, she noticed it appeared to be in pursuit of a few Grimworts.

"Just when I thought I'd seen everything," Nikalas murmured.

Chapter 46

As the beastly Gravi approached Cristol, the air began to dry and the sky began to darken. Her gaze was terrifying, her growl even more so, and her retched appearance even more than both. She was a deformity. An abomination unlike anything that had ever been seen. Wings of a dragon, the body of a serpent, legs and arms of a bear, and the face of a woman — a mutated woman with cat-like eyes and crusty skin.

With each flap of her wings, a powerful gale force wind would pummel the ground, knocking people over and kicking up a terrible mess of dust and dirt. Nikalas looked upwards with shock, struggling to find words for his thoughts. In front of the beast, were a few Grimworts that swiftly dove down as they got close.

"It's Gravi," Kunklestick anxiously informed. He and Didorumpus came to a stop next to Nikalas, Septus and Emlin, looking up and taking in the doom.

Behind them, the Vanguards and Tin Men had begun to line up, holding their weapons to the air with trembling fingers. Sabasio and Sinclair stood next to one another, looking at each other and then at the wizards.

The Grimworts landed, bringing with them at least one familiar face — Vicham. Nikalas charged to him with excitement, embracing him in a hug. They hadn't known each other terribly long before parting ways, but their time together was memorable. After all, it was Vicham that talked Hervott into freeing him from the dungeon.

"My friend," Nikalas greeted. He pulled back, allowing the seriousness of the situation to change his tone.

"What have you brought with you?"

Vicham looked up to the sky and pointed.

"Allow me to introduce High Mother, better known as Gravi," Vicham informed.

"High Mother?" Septus questioned. His skin went quickly pale as he approached. As Vicham took notice, he reached to his side, pulling out his sword.

"He's on our side now," Nikalas informed. He turned and looked to Septus. "Right?"

Septus nodded and glanced up towards the incoming beast.

"That's High Mother?" He questioned. "Fernalda?"

Vicham nodded, and turned towards Articus, who held in his hand an intriguing glowing blue sword.

"This is the Arc Blade. It's the only weapon that can kill her," Articus explained. Nikalas looked the weapon over and reached for its handle—as he gripped it—he looked at Septus.

"You have to help me," he disclosed. Septus looked around, at the field of death, at the piles of dust, at the trembling soldiers, and finally at Emlin, at the worry in her eyes.

"Ok," he whispered. "I'll help you."

Gravi let out a mighty roar, then landed in the middle of the field.

"Fire!" Sabasio called out. Quickly, the soldiers—both Vanguards and Tin Men—began to open fire towards the gigantic beast. The attacks had little effect.

"Let's show you what power really looks like," she sneered. With a malignant smirk, she charged towards them, waving her paw towards the army and sending a wave of energy forward. The spell was potent, treacherous and downright deadly. It took all of five seconds to erase over a hundred men from existence.

"Now!" Nikalas ordered. He tossed the Arc Blade to Septus, then leapt into the air.

"Inginimo imphis!" He declared. Three separate beams emerged from the tip of his wand, each of them crashing into her chest and causing her to stumble. From the ground, Kunklestick and Didorumpus did the same, casting the exact same spell towards the exact same spot.

"You think your pitiful little spells can hurt a goddess?" Gravi laughed. She lifted her paw again, aiming it *this* time towards the gates of Cristol.

"Watch your world crumble," she hissed. With a backwards swipe of her paw, another wall of energy emerged, crashing into the city gates and shattering it with ease.

Nikalas fired another round of beams, striking her in the back, but just as before, it did little damage.

"Need something better," he muttered to himself. He tucked his wand back into his robe, summoned an orb of energy around himself, and then dashed forward. He flew through her torso and emerged at the other side. His eyes now faced Cristol — or — what was left of it.

"Ahh!" Gravi exclaimed. "Now that's more like it."

She quickly reached forward, grabbed Nikalas and then closed her palm.

"You may be able to sting but you're still nothing but a bee trying to fight a giant," she said. She had just begun to apply pressure, hoping to squeeze Nikalas like a bug, when a sudden beam of energy crashed into her from the posterior. The intense energy began to surge through her, weakening her position and forcing her to return to her natural form.

Now free of her grip, Nikalas flew forward, once again pushing through her energy cloud and emerging on the other side.

"You idiot," she exclaimed. Maneuvering around, she noticed Septus hovering next to Nikalas with the Arc Blade held firmly in his hands.

"After all I've done to help you?" Gravi questioned. "You dare attack me?"

Septus looked at her, squinting with determination, and then lifted the sword.

"You were never trying to help me," he replied. "You were trying to help yourself."

He fervently dashed forward, plunging the sword into the center of the orange tinted energy. With the blade nestled securely in place, it began to heat up, growing brighter and brighter until suddenly, she began to shrink, returning to her human form. Septus pulled back, flying towards Nikalas with excitement.

"I think we did it," He grinned. Nikalas shook his head and pointed.

"I don't think so," he replied. At that moment, he soared to the ground, finding a spot next to his mentors.

"I don't understand," Jinn whispered to Articus. "The blade was meant to kill her."

"You actually thought steel could kill me?" Gravi taunted. She shook her head in annoyance and reached to the top of her dress.

"Your pitiful swords cannot kill a goddess."

With a firm pull, she ripped the top strap, pulling it off and revealing a body devoid of all gender identification.

"What in the heck?" Kunklestick cringed. As Gravi looked at them, her skin began to turn red, and in her hands, emerged two very large blades that glowed red.

"Insolent little scourges," she sneered. "You will all die."

Nikalas looked up as Septus began to descend towards him. As he touched down, he wandered towards them, followed quickly by Jinn. In her hands, she held a blade made of swirling shadows.

"You're an outcast, Gravi," Kunklestick informed.

"Unwanted and unimportant," Didorumpus added.

"And in the name of Undr," Jinn chimed in.

"Your time has come to an end," Septus sternly elucidated.

She lifted her blades up, releasing a robust roar, then charged forward. Her blade clashed against Septus', sending out a wave of energy that threatened to topple all in the area.

From the right side, Jinn moved in, swinging her blade, which was quickly met by Gravi's and countered with a firm push. As Jinn fell back, three more beams of energy darted past, crashing into Gravi's blade. She looked at the wizards in annoyance and harshly pushed the blade forward, sending the energy back to them and knocking them to the ground in a painful fashion.

"Enough of this, Fernalda," Septus demanded. He brought his sword forward with a stabbing motion that was unfortunately, quickly opposed. As she repelled his blade, she aimed her other blade, summoning a beam of energy from its tip.

"Septus!" Emlin cried out as he *too*, joined the pile of toppled wizards. She peered at Gravi with disgust, firing an arrow and then ran to his side.

"You were never meant to walk this land," Jinn declared. She soared forward, phasing through Gravi and then quickly bringing her blade into the goddess' back.

"Ahh!" Gravi growled, turning around and bringing both blades swinging towards Jinn. Each blade — however — passed right through her, landing in the dirt and getting wedged.

"Our creator created the Kajj to destroy you, and destroy you I shall," Jinn wailed. She brought her blade forward and swung it into Gravi, slicing her arm clean off and leaving an arm made of energy instead.

Gravi rapidly brought the arm forward, gripping Jinn and giving her a full jolt of her power.

"Inginimo," Nikalas called out. Together, he and the wizards fired energy. At the same time, Vicham, Articus and Methalda tossed some of the energy stones to the ground, which held her firmly in place.

Septus seized the opportunity, dashing forward with the Arc Blade raised and ready. He had just reached her, when suddenly, she turned around. Her arm gripped his throat with terrible strength and a burst of energy.

"Ohh, ahh!" He bellowed. As his skin began to blister, he lifted the blade, surprisingly pushing it into her chest. It began to glow, and suddenly, she could hold on no more. She relinquished her grip and pushed him firmly before falling to her knees. Her hands began to shake and the wound began to fester. At that moment, the blade fell to the ground and a blue streak of energy began to pour out from within.

"Hmmm," Didorumpus whispered with awe. The energy continued to pour out, landing on the ground and forming a familiar human shape.

"Undr?" Vicham whispered. "But how?"

"Sister," Undr shunned. He brought up his fist, bringing it across her jaw and dropping her to the ground.

"Get up," he demanded. She wiped her face, slowly coming to her feet and peered at him with humiliation.

In a quick instant, she dashed forward, crashing into him. The feud was on once again. This time — however — he wasn't on his own. Things were much too dire to sit around and hope, it seemed even divinity had met its match. The others all began firing their attacks, trying their best to steer their efforts towards her; a difficult task with all the constant movement taking place. Through the fields of Cristol the battle raged on, splitting the ground, and eradicating its contents.

Gravi's spiteful waves of energy disintegrated all it touched, and unfortunately, that was many. With each passing moment of the conflict, more and more innocents perished, a side effect that brought tears to Emlin's eyes. No matter how hard they attempted to limit the extent of her wrath, the collateral damage continued to pile up.

Gravi was terribly outnumbered, and yet, she still proved to be formidable. Despite being weakened and stripped of some of her powers, she still seemed to be the most powerful being on the battlefield. For his part, Undr did provide a lot of assistance, giving her a jolt whenever she turned her back to face the others. But the attacks did little to deter her, and with each failed attempt, hopelessness became more and more prevalent.

The field was a light show, a spectacular web of sizzling multicolored lights that created a dangerous environment for anyone not properly armored. Luckily, most of the soldiers had managed to get to safety, flooding inside the ruined Cristol and taking shelter with the Delopar.

Jinn and Septus continued their attempts at besting her with their blades, cutting off limbs here and there, but with each wound, the energy within would kick in, restoring the limb to its former glory. She seemed truly immortal, even against the god killer known as the Arc Blade.

"What are we missing?" Jinn hollered at Septus as she swung her sword forward.

"Hope," Gravi declared. "And a chance."

At that moment, a sudden wave of energy pushed past, pushing all three of them to the ground.

"Ugh," Septus moaned as he looked up in time to see Undr pounding on Gravi's face.

"It's over, sister," Undr roared. Over and over he brought his fist upon her face, each time creating a bright flash of light.

Nikalas looked at Kunklestick, nodded and then leapt into the air. As he looked the battlefield over, he couldn't help but feel aggravated. There was so much opposition, and yet somehow, she was prevailing. He continued to ponder, when suddenly he took notice of something he found to be interesting. She never engaged more than one or two at a time. Whenever it seemed the tide was turning, she could create an obstacle to split the group up.

"She can't take on all of us at once," he whispered to himself.

He looked down, located Septus and began to think. The Arc Blade had so far been quite capable at doing damage, but had yet to prove deadly. It had stolen her height, released Undr, and slowed her down, but it had not destroyed her. And yet, this was the weapon said to be capable of killing a god.

"Why isn't it working?" Nikalas questioned. His eyes continued to study the fight below. As Undr, Kunklestick and Didorumpus brought their attacks from the front, Jinn and Septus would bring theirs from the back. Her speed was impressive, blocking each attack just as fast as it was issued. It was almost as though she could be in two places at once.

"Father," he called out. "What do we do?"

He closed his eyes and tried to search his mind for any traces of Aldon, but there was nothing to be seen, nothing except a bright light.

"You said I would need Septus," Nikalas muttered. "What can he do that I can't?"

At that moment, a light went off in his head and he quickly dove to the ground, encompassing himself in flames and crashing into Gravi. She toppled over and crashed into a pile of rubble that fell on top of her. He quickly seized the moment and returned to the group.

"As a necromancer you can give life. Can you also take it?" He asked of Septus.

"Anyone can take a life, Nikalas," Kunklestick chimed in. "You don't need to be a necromancer to do that."

"Yes but not everyone can access the Sea of Souls. Only a necromancer can do that. Only a necromancer can pull a soul from this place of serenity. My question is, can he send a soul there?"

"You're speaking of a Zoimancer," Jinn chimed.

"So it is a thing?" Nikalas questioned.

"Yes, but it's nearly impossible to achieve," Jinn replied.

A groan in the distance signaled trouble once again. Gravi stood, pushing the rubble aside and looking towards them. There was hatred in her eyes, and with her eyes still focused on them, she aimed her blades towards a crowd of stagnant soldiers. The effect was instantaneous, hundreds of soldiers reduced to nothing but ash in the blink of an eye. With a menacing cackle, she turned around, looking at a wave of Delopars that were retreating towards Cristol. As before, she aimed at them, limiting them to ash in spectacular fashion.

"You choose to fight the helpless rather than those that can stand up to you?" Undr bellowed. He aimed his hands to the ground, summoning the ground beneath her to liquify.

She slowly began to sink into the murky substance, as he released his spell, she found herself securely wedged.

"You embarrass our father," he accused. His hands gripped her throat as they glowed with a fiery heat.

"You idiot," she wailed. "I don't need air like your pitiful creatures."

Undr continued to look at her with a blank, chilled expression. As the energy pulsated in his hand, her skin began to softly blink. He was siphoning her energy, taking it and adding it to his own.

"Noo!" She roared. With her power beginning to dwindle, she released from her chest, an outwards blast. Undr dropped, falling back with a hint of dismay masking his face.

"You're such a disappointment," she scoffed. Lifting her blades, she swung them towards him.

"Balathan," Didorumpus called out. A spiral ring of energy promptly soared towards her, severing her limbs and sending them in various directions.

Undr hastily jumped up. Looking at the scattered limbs, and fired energy towards them.

"What does it take?" Nikalas questioned of Jinn. She looked at Septus, shaking her head doubtfully.

"He needs to will his power into the blade. Once he does, the weapon can be used to strip her soul from her," Jinn explained.

Septus looked at the Arc Blade and nodded his head in understanding.

"Seems easy enough," he replied.

"You'll be giving up your powers," Jinn added. "Moving them into the blade and leaving yourself as just a mere mortal."

This statement made Septus pause, suddenly, he looked less interested. He shook his head in denial, then looked at Nikalas.

"There's got to be another way," he argued.

"I'm sorry, but there isn't," Jinn informed. "If your powers were all of your own, you could do this and retain your abilities, but that's not the case. Your powers come from the rings, therefore, you cannot transfer the power without losing them."

"Then no," Septus replied. "I won't do that. We can figure out something else."

At that moment, the sky darkened and a swirling red cloud began to form above Cristol. Flashes of light filled the sky, accompanied by rumbles of thunder and a bit of rain. Screams were heard from within the city, and it became quickly evident that the rain was no ordinary rain, it was Ricter. Drops of acid continued to fall, eroding the buildings and burning any caught under its effects. As if that wasn't enough, the swirling red cloud crashed down, bringing with it a massive twister comprised of scorching flames.

"Cyliamo Sensio," Kunklestick bellowed. Together, he and Didorumpus sent their spells cruising to Gravi, who had reformed and knocked Undr to the ground. As the spell neared, it hit something, bouncing back towards them with startling speed.

"Look out," Didorumpus warned, shoving his brother to the ground. Kunklestick hit the ground with a thud, unscathed by the repelled wall of energy. Didorumpus on the other hand, was not so lucky. He dropped to the ground with blistered skin, torrid pain radiating through his body.

"Brother!" Kunklestick called out.

Emlin marched in front of Septus, grabbing his hands and holding them firm.

"You have a chance here to save Furlasia — no — the entire planet," she lectured. "You have to do this."

Septus looked at the tears forming in her eyes, letting her pain wash over him. He hated it, hated seeing her so tormented. Hated what he had already done. There was an opportunity for redemption and he had to take it.

"How do I do it?" He asked, looking at Jinn with uncertainty.

"It'll be just as though you are casting a spell, you'll cast it into the blade, as you do, the rings will weaken and the sword will become empowered," she replied.

He looked at Nikalas, who nodded urgently. *Do it*, he thought to himself. He closed his eyes, placing the sword to the ground and then knelt before it. The glow of the blade felt warm as he placed his hand on it. *Focus*. In the distance, the tornado continued to consume Cristol, and soon, it was nothing but a pile of rubble.

"Come on," Septus whispered to himself. His focus remained unchanged and slowly but surely, the blade began to glow brighter, phasing through multiple colors. After a few more moments, the feeling of inner power had faded and he knew he had succeeded. He sighed with disappointment, then looked up at the incoming twister.

"Your time is over," Gravi laughed, grabbing Undr and launching him into the air, towards the twister.

Septus quickly rose, picking up the blade and looking towards Gravi. Filled with a swell of determination, he began to move forward, when suddenly, a hand grabbed him, causing him to cease.

"You can't," Emlin pleaded. "Your powers are gone now. If you approach her you'll die."

"Emlin," he paused. "You mean more to me than anything. More to me than my own life. I have to do this. I have to redeem myself."

"No," Emlin replied. "Killing yourself will not redeem what your father has done."

"You're right. But saving Furlasia will," he retorted. He shook himself free of her grip and charged forward. Emlin had just begun to chase him, when a beam of energy wrapped around her, pulling her back.

"Let me go," she wailed.

"I can't," Nikalas replied.

Chapter 47

Septus charged forward, holding the Arc Blade firmly in his grip and looking towards the woman he had once considered as his mother figure. With each step forward, he could feel the heat of her shield growing hotter. He gulped, taking a few more steps forward and pausing just in front of her.

"Haven't you seen already?" Gravi questioned. "Your blade cannot defeat me."

Septus studied her, looking at her red skin and genderless body. She looked demonic, not like any god or goddess he had ever heard of. No—she resembled a demon, an abomination unworthy of life. He lifted the blade and took a step closer to her shield.

"Don't be a fool, Septus," Gravi warned.

He ignored the words of caution and stepped inside the shield. To his dismay, he could no longer feel the swell of heat. With a quick motion, he thrust the blade forward, bringing it straight to where her heart would be.

"I told you," she laughed. "Your weapon cannot harm me."

At that moment, she began to tremble, and her eyes began to sink inwards.

"What?" She hollered. The twister quickly faded and the darkness of the clouds began to dissolve in the sky.

"How?" She pondered, dropping to the ground and beginning to wrinkle.

"Its over Gravi," Septus whispered. "I order you to spend the rest of your days trapped in the Sea of Souls."

She began to scream as her body continued to wither. As the moments passed, the blade continued to pulse.

"Noo!" She screeched. Septus nodded appreciatively, and took a step back. Her shell continued to shrivel and suddenly, a red light emerged from the blade, soaring into the sky before heading north.

"Goodbye Fernalda," Septus whispered. Her body fell over, looking quite similar to a raisin, and then slowly began to turn to dust.

"Septus," Emlin yelled, running towards him with excitement. As she neared, a faint blue light that had encompassed him began to fade. *A shield?* She turned towards Kunklestick, who was grinning with his staff firmly planted against the ground.

She threw her arms around Septus, embracing him in a firm hug and then pulled back with a pause.

"You did it!" She excitedly grinned. "She's gone."

Nikalas let out a deep sigh as he looked at Jinn. The Decoyers, Vicham and Wexel stood to his left. He turned, shooting Vicham a subtle nod and then began to saunter towards Kunklestick and Didorumpus.

"It's barely a rash," Kunklestick explained as he knelt next to his brother. Didorumpus shook his head in disbelief and looked at Nikalas.

"Be honest, Nikalas," he paused. "How bad do I look?"

"Oh, it's disgusting," Nikalas replied. Didorumpus sighed with hopelessness, giving his brother a frustrating stare.

"I saved your ass, ya know," he remined.

"I would've been fine," Kunklestick replied.

Nikalas grinned at the banter, and knelt down next to Didorumpus. Holding his hand above him, he began to summon a bit of his power. Before long, the wounds were gone and all had returned to normal.

"That's better," Nikalas confidently smiled. "I mean you're still ugly, but at least you're not burned."

He rose to his feet and began to survey the land. Cristol was in ruins, a crumbled mess of glass and bricks, and buried among all of it were the dead innocents that had fled.

Thousands had perished in the battle; there was no concealing that fact, no bringing back the dead or erasing what had happened. Furlasia was safe, but its population had been significantly cut down.

"Nikalas," Vicham called out. He sauntered towards him and paused with a solemn look in his eyes.

"I found your parents," he informed. "They were taken by Gravi and transformed into her slaves."

"What?" Nikalas concernedly asked. "Where are they?"

Vicham looked to the north and pointed.

"In Sanlorus, it's to the north of here," he replied.

Without a moment's hesitation, Nikalas leapt into the air, flying hastily towards the unknown land.

The wind blew through his hair, and behind him, he could hear the familiar neigh of Fawn. He didn't look back though—no—he had to see what Gravi had done. He traveled with determination as he passed over Rangmar. A bit further ahead, and he crossed into an area with unseen beauty, which had fields of vibrant green grass, lakes of shimmering water, and in the distance a tower. He landed in front of the tower and stood nervously, looking at the door.

"Come on," Nikalas coached to himself.

At that moment, the door to the tower flung open, and from within, emerged dozens of people from all walks of life; Delopars, Terrians, Arnouts and men. He studied them with surprise. There was nothing strange about them at all. They didn't look as though Gravi had turned them.

"Nikalas?" A voice called out. He peered forward with trembling hands and butterflies in his stomach. His parents emerged from deep within the crowd. He looked at them with an outlandish smile. It was as though time had stopped for them. He had expected them to look quite different, but oddly enough, they looked the same. The exact same. He excitedly charged forward, throwing his arms around his mother and giving her a firm squeeze.

"You have wings?" She questioned, pulling herself back and looking at him with dismay.

He nodded and looked at his father.

"I'm sure you have quite the story to tell," Stephen grinned. He stepped closer, offering Nikalas a hug.

"You have no idea," Nikalas replied.

The End

Epilogue

King Linuk sat on the throne, facing an audience that was truly unique. Directly in front of him stood Undr, the god who made their very existence possible. Then there was Kunklestick, Didorumpus, Emlin, Nikalas and Septus. Each of them was dressed in their usual attire, apart from Septus, who was currently sporting some nice shackles. Dozens of the city's citizens stood behind his audience of VIP; all of them were anxious, while some of them were angry.

"Septus Crane, you have been found guilty of war crimes and murder," Linuk informed. Emlin quietly nodded her head in acceptance and looked at Nikalas with approval.

"However, your part in the defeat of the heretic Gravi cannot be denied. It was your sacrifice that allowed her to be sealed away. Therefore, it is my decision, based on the input of this noble few, that you shall be drafted into a new peacekeeper assembly known as The Restorers. Together, with this new allegiance, you shall help rebuild Furlasia back to its former glory, starting in Cristol, the city ruined by the goddess Gravi."

"Hang him!" Someone yelled from within the crowd.

"He's a murderer!" Yelled another.

"Silence," Undr demanded, turning to face the crowd with disapproval.

"It is I, Undr, creator of everything you see around you. This decision did not come lightly. But like it or not, Septus helped save Furlasia. And apart from this, which is already considerable, we have learned his mind was not all of his own. This decision is final."

"And never forget, I am always watching what happens on this planet," he added.

Linuk nodded and rose from his seat.

"This matter has been concluded. Now go, return to your homes and let's bring Morlay back to its former greatness — scratch that — let's make it better," he declared.

With solemn faces, the crowd of citizens turned, making their way out of the palace and back into the streets. With the foyer now to themselves, Kunklestick turned, looking at Undr with wonder in his eyes.

"What troubles you my friend?" Undr questioned.

"There's some things I need to know," Kunklestick replied. He looked to Didorumpus for input, but received none. Shrugging, he turned his focus back to Undr.

"Why were you not able to defeat Gravi on your own? Why was she here in the first place?"

Undr grinned and sauntered towards him.

"The almighty father — my father — has placed special protections among all of the galaxies that limit our powers when we enter. This is to ensure that a corrupt god, like Gravi, cannot do maximum damage. As for why she was here, well, the answer to that is simple. She had sought to destroy the galaxies I was in charge of protecting. She resented me and my position with the almighty father. Therefore, as a punishment, I trapped her here, to live among the chaos she had caused," Undr explained.

"And why did you not come to our aid sooner?" Didorumpus asked. "There are a lot of lives that could be alive right now if you had."

"As part of my trapping her on this planet, I also hindered myself — accidentally of course. I built a doorway, a backdoor way for me to enter, but it came with certain conditions. It could not be opened unless things got too dire."

"Agavordis' first war was pretty dire," Didorumpus inputted.

Undr nodded in agreement, and sighed.

"Yes, it was. I'm sorry, my children. My seal on the door became too strong. I'm not sure how, but I have a hunch it was my father," Undr replied.

"Why would he do that?" Nikalas queried.

"One can never comprehend the actions of the almighty father. He is so far beyond us, that even *I* cannot comprehend his choices. But whatever his reason, I'm sure it was just."

As the sun's light began to make its way into the foyer, Undr turned, looking towards it with satisfaction.

"If any of my creations make me proud, it's that," he said with a pointed finger. "Its simple beauty."

He turned back to the others and bowed.

"It's time for me to go. This isn't the only galaxy that Gravi infected. There have been interesting things happening on another planet of mine. Her attempt to spread fear and hate has been quite successful. So successful, that there is an entire land ruled by it. Dark days are coming. I need to keep a watchful eye on it."

With that, he shed his familiar form, and returned to that of pure energy. The light from within was intense, filling the foyer with near blinding light. The elegant hue painted the foyer for a moment, then quickly vanished.

An hour later, Nikalas, Kunklestick and Didorumpus found themselves sitting across from one another, enjoying a tall glass of wine with soft music in the background.

"So what will you do now?" Didorumpus asked to Nikalas. "Are you going back to Earth?"

Nikalas shrugged with uncertainty.

"It's up to my parents. I'll go wherever they decide," he replied.

"That's very sweet of you, son," Stephen said, setting his cup down next to Nikalas.

"You should do what you want," Tricia added as she *too*, took a seat.

"What are you guys doing here?" Nikalas quizzed.

"Having a drink with our underage son," Stephen grinned. "The laws are different here than on Earth."

"How so?" Kunklestick questioned.

"Well, on Earth, you cannot engage in the consumption of spirits until you have reached the age of twenty-one," Tricia explained.

"That's ludicrous," Kunklestick retorted, lifting his glass and taking a tall swig.

"Absolutely ridiculous."

Nikalas chuckled and took a drink from his cup as well.

"In all seriousness though," Tricia added. "If you want to go back to Earth, then that's what we will do."

Nikalas pondered the idea, then shrugged, pointing towards his wings.

"Kinda hard to imagine people taking lightly to these," he explained.

"Who cares what others think, son," Stephen inserted. "You should do what you feel will bring you the most joy and satisfaction."

Kunklestick glanced at Nikalas with hopeful eyes, scratching his chest as he looked at his greatest pupil.

"Honestly, it doesn't feel like there is anything for me there," Nikalas replied. "My family is here; my friends are here."

"I want to stay," he finally surmised.

Tricia and Stephen shared a grateful glance between the two of them, then looked at Kunklestick with a smile. Tricia continued to watch the elderly wizard, finding interest in his constant scratching — then — as his robe pulled apart, she noticed a rather large red rash.

"Kunklestick," she pointed. "You need to visit the High Leech."

Didorumpus looked over, catching a peek of what she referred to and began to ponder its cause.

"Looks like a bug bite of some kind," he remarked.

"I'll go as soon as I finish this drink," Kunklestick retorted.

The conversations and laughs continued for another hour or so, and afterwards, just as promised, Kunklestick climbed to his feet.

"I've got to see a man about a rash," he slurred. He offered a quick bow, then turned to leave. He was followed shortly by Didorumpus. Music filled the air, music and the laughter of the usual patrons enjoying their normal dinner of booze and grub. Nikalas sat silently, looking at his parents with satisfaction.

"I'm so glad you guys are alive," he explained. "Things were really rough after you disappeared."

"I'm so sorry, son. We should never have come back here. We were homesick, but in hindsight, home is where your family is, and you were back on Earth. That's where we should've stayed," Tricia replied.

"Does dad know?" Nikalas questioned as he looked at Stephen with worry.

"About who I really am?"

"Well, I know you didn't inherit those wings or powers from your mother and I," Stephen laughed.

"And you're ok with the truth?"

"Nikalas," Stephen paused. "What good could possibly come out of being upset? You are my son. I may not have brought you to life, but I have cared for and raised you since you were born."

He leaned over, placing his hand carefully atop Tricia's.

"What happened with Aldon was a strange freak accident. Something no one could have seen coming. I'm not mad at him, I'm not mad at your mom. I'm grateful to them both."

"You are a miracle," Stephen added. He climbed to his feet and wandered over to Nikalas. With a firm grip, he embraced him, holding him tight and smiling all the while. After a brief hug that ended just before it got awkward, he pulled back.

"So how does he compare to the man in the stories I used to read you?"

Nikalas grinned, shaking his head with laughter.

Kunklestick sat quietly on the table in the High Leech's office. It was late, the unusually timed visit was a courtesy, a minor intrusion but certainly still an honor. As the young woman studied his rash, she would pull back, jotting down notes and muttering to herself. She was pretty in a certain way. Her hair was pulled back in a ponytail, her glasses were thin framed, and her nose — while pointy — was still cute.

"Can't say I've ever seen a High Leech as lovely as you, madam," Kunklestick said with a wink.

She blushed as she carried over an ointment.

"Anyone can do this," she replied. "Just takes some determination and willingness to learn."

Her hands carefully dabbed a bit of the ointment atop the rash, then looked at him approvingly.

"This stuff should fix the rash," she informed. "Now, the cause of the rash is a small bite. You are going to need to take —

At that moment, a loud scream filled the air, summoning his attention. Kunklestick quickly turned around, dashing out the door without listening to the rest of her instructions. Standing in the middle of the street trembling, was an elderly woman with white hair, and an interesting cane that featured the head of a dragon at its handle.

"What is it?" Kunklestick shakenly asked.

"I saw a man," she replied. "A small man. It was awful. He was the ugliest thing I've ever seen."

A far-off siren in the distance confirmed his thoughts. It came from the dungeons.

"Epard," he whispered to himself. "That clever little turd."

He looked at the elderly woman and gave her a soft pat on the shoulder.

"Don't worry. You're safe now. Go to your home," he instructed.

Didorumpus emerged from the shadows of a nearby alley. He rode atop a Wildfire while holding onto the reins for Leddi in his free hand.

"What did the High Leech say?" He questioned.

"It's all fine," Kunklestick replied. "She gave me some ointment."

Didorumpus cautiously nodded, then handed over the reins.

"What was she screaming about?"

"Epard escaped his cell," Kunklestick said.

"Should we get Nikalas?" Didorumpus pondered. Kunklestick turned, giving him a sneer and then shook his head.

"We can handle Epard. He's only a gnome."

He climbed atop Leddi and looked to his brother with confidence.

"Let's getting moving," he said with a cough. He gazed forward, looking towards the bright moon that was beginning to light the streets. With an oddly eager smile, he gave Leddi a faint kick.

"Haa."

Glossary

Akordans: Akordans are a race of aggressive yet intelligent reptilian type creatures that are reminiscent of Alligators. They are strong warriors and ill tempered, making them quite dangerous.

Delopar: Delopars are a race of feline type creatures reminiscent of leopards. They are cunning and wise and very calculated when it comes to battle. They are also one of Furlasia's oldest species.

Arnouts: Arnouts are a species that migrated to Furlasia within the past hundred years. They are gifted with wings, which allows them to fly at will. They also have various magical abilities.

Terrian: Terrians are a form of elf that resides in the city known as Terria. They mostly keep to themselves when it comes to regional politics, but amongst each other they are nosey and mischievous.

The Echo: The Echo is a godly realm that exists between Furlasia and the realm of the gods. It is populated only by Grimworts and it contains an energy that can gift those capable of tapping into it with magic.

Ricter: Ricter is an acidic liquid that flows through various rivers throughout Furlasia, eventually emptying into a large body of water near the Hark Mountains. It is dangerous and deadly to all to come into contact with.

Shewglomous: A Shewglomous is yet another ancient device left behind by the god Undr. It is a gift designed to allow communications among great distances. A few select people have even been said to have seen visions of the future within its glass.

Beacon: A beacon is a rare type of weapon that uses focused light to produce a massive amount of concentrated heat. Its blast can either be short quick burst, or long focused burst that burn through almost any material within seconds.

Uborox: An Uborox is a vicious wolf type creature, usually with brown sharp fur. They are quite fast and large enough to ride, the Akordans once had them tamed to serve them but that time has passed. Now they wander the forest as one of Furlasia's many dangers.

Worthiar: A Worthiar is a bear type creature that engulfs itself in flames when it feels threatened. When that happens all nearby best be prepared for a fight to the death.

Oekie: A primitive ape type creature that has red skin and is furless, they are constantly navigating the tree tops searching for food and keeping an eye on travelers.

Grimwort: A Grimwort is a creature that originated within The Echo and was eventually brought into Furlasia as a way of providing access to The Echo and to identify those worthy of using magic. They live quite long and eventually become large enough to travel atop.

Diastonism: One of Furlasia's up and coming religions it mostly exists within Terria. Many have called it radical as its beliefs revolve around a worldwide cleansing being necessary.

Penecoth: The most widely accepted religion in Furlasia that preaches compassion and the importance of being one with nature as a way of getting closer to the gods.

Adrasian: A race of highly strong beings that dwell in the land known as Adrasia. This race makes a formidable foe because of their higher than normal strength and endurance.

Daulest: The home of all. This is the name of the planet in which the whole story takes place. It is a planet with lots of water and a variety of different land masses.

M.P. VanderLoon is an author that lives in Rockford, MI. He and his husband live in a quiet neighborhood surrounded by plenty of land and nature. When he is not busy writing books, he doubles as a school bus driver for the public school systems. More information on him can be found in various places on the web, including, his website mpvanderloon.com, twitter.com/mpvanderloon, and also his facebook page.